Praise for *Blindness*

"Saramago's surreal allegory explores the ability of the human spirit to prevail in even the most absurdly unjust of conditions, yet he reinvents this familiar struggle with the stylistic eccentricity of a master." —*The New Yorker*

"Extraordinarily nuanced and evocative . . . This year's most propulsive, and most profound, thriller." —*The Village Voice*

"The reader gets caught up in the sheer momentum of the narrative . . . and the subtlety and beauty of the language's architecture. Saramago is the most tender of writers . . . with a clear-eyed and compassionate acknowledgment of things as they are, and a quality that can only be termed wisdom. We should be grateful when it is handed to us in such generous measures."
—*The New York Times Book Review*

"*Blindness* is a shattering work by a literary master."
—*The Boston Globe*

"Like Jonathan Swift Saramago uses airily matter-of-fact detail to frame a bitter parable; unlike Swift he pierces the parable with a dart of steely tenderness . . . out of his leisurely prose, the ferocity and tenderness shoot suddenly: arrows set alight. . . . Enchanting, sinuous dialogue." —*Los Angeles Times*

"It is the voice of *Blindness* that gives it its charm. By turns ironic, humorous and frank, there is a kind of wink of humor between author and reader that is perfectly imbued with fury at the excesses of the current century. *Blindness* reminds me of Kafka roaring with laughter as he read his stories to his friends. . . . *Blindness*' impact carries the force of an author whose sensibility is significant." —*The Washington Post*

"*Blindness* lives in the spread of its particulars, and in the conviction of its allegory . . . recalling *The Inferno* as well as Greek tragedy and satire. Saramago is an attractive and sinuous writer."
—James Woods, *The New Republic*

"Saramago writes phantasmagoria—in the midst of the most astonishing fantasy he has a meticulous sense of detail. It's very eloquent stuff." —Harold Bloom, author of *The Western Canon*

"Ingenious . . . It's hard to think of another living writer who has amassed such a remarkable body of concentrated work (only Doris Lessing comes to mind) within our lifetime. . . . Don't be put off by the intimidating fact that Saramago's a Nobel Prize winner. This is a writer who belongs to all of us."
—Bruce Allen, *The Raleigh News and Observer*

"*Blindness* may be as revolutionary in its own way and time as were, say, *The Trial* and *The Plague* in theirs. Another masterpiece." —*Kirkus Reviews* (starred review)

"This may be the novel's greatest gift—that something so ordinary leaps from the realm of commodities and shimmers as a mystery, a miracle hidden in the blindness of the everyday. It is a crowning moment in a novel full of magnificent writing."
—*The San Diego Union-Tribune*

"Brilliant . . . A most sophisticated fiction that retains its peculiar power to move and persuade." —*Publishers Weekly*

"Dazzling . . . The events that Saramago recounts are appalling, but none of them is incredible within the landscape of the text. Saramago has the tremendous ability to predict a reader's objections and address them. . . . His prose is intricate and orderly, his dialogues are stunningly lucid." —*The Boston Phoenix*

"Told in an ironically clinical voice, this haunting, all-too-believable novel is laid out in an appropriately disconcerting way. Conversations and actions run together with the seamless and threatening peculiarity of a nightmare. . . . Soul-wrenching."

—*The Detroit Free Press*

"Beautifully written in a concise, haunting prose . . . this unsettling, highly original work is essential reading."

—*Library Journal*

"Saramago's *Blindness* is the best novel I've read since Gabriel García Márquez' *Love in the Time of Cholera*. It is a novel of enormous skill and authority. . . . Like all great books it is simultaneously contemporary and timeless, and ambitiously confronts the human condition without a false note struck anywhere. Saramago is one of the great writers of our time, and *Blindness,* ironically is the product of his extraordinary vision."

—David Guterson, author of *Snow Falling on Cedars*

Blindness

ALSO BY JOSÉ SARAMAGO

Fiction

The Manual of Painting and Calligraphy

Baltasar and Blimunda

The Year of the Death of Ricardo Reis

The Gospel According to Jesus Christ

The History of the Siege of Lisbon

All the Names

The Tale of the Unknown Island

The Stone Raft

The Cave

The Double

Seeing

Death with Interruptions

Nonfiction

Journey to Portugal

JOSÉ SARAMAGO

Blindness

Translated from the Portuguese
by Giovanni Pontiero

A Harvest Book • Harcourt, Inc.
Orlando Austin New York San Diego London

First published in English in Great Britain in 1997 by The Harvill Press.

This is a translation of *Ensaio sobre a Cegueira* and is published with the financial assistance of the Instituto Português do Livro e das Bibliotecas, Lisbon, which is gratefully acknowledged.

The Library of Congress has cataloged the hardcover edition as follows:
Saramago, José.
[Ensaio sobre a cegueira. English]
Blindness: a novel/José Saramago; translated from the
Portuguese by Giovanni Pontiero.—1st ed.
p. cm.
Originally published in English in Great Britain
in 1997 by The Harvill Press.
ISBN 978-0-15-100251-1
ISBN 978-0-15-603558-3 (pbk.)
I. Pontiero, Giovanni. II. Title.
PQ9281.A66E6813 1998
869.3′42—dc21 98-12009

Text set in Dante MT
Designed by Lori McThomas Buley
Printed in the United States of America
First Harvest edition 1999
A C E G I K J H F D B

For Pilar
For my daughter Violante

IN MEMORIAM

Giovanni Pontiero

If you can see, look.
If you can look, observe.

FROM THE *Book of Exhortations*

Blindness

The amber light came on. Two of the cars ahead accelerated before the red light appeared. At the pedestrian crossing the sign of a green man lit up. The people who were waiting began to cross the road, stepping on the white stripes painted on the black surface of the asphalt, there is nothing less like a zebra, however, that is what it is called. The motorists kept an impatient foot on the clutch, leaving their cars at the ready, advancing, retreating like nervous horses that can sense the whiplash about to be inflicted. The pedestrians have just finished crossing but the sign allowing the cars to go will be delayed for some seconds, some people maintain that this delay, while apparently so insignificant, has only to be multiplied by the thousands of traffic lights that exist in the city and by the successive changes of their three colours to produce one of the most serious causes of traffic jams or bottlenecks, to use the more current term.

The green light came on at last, the cars moved off briskly, but then it became clear that not all of them were equally quick off the mark. The car at the head of the middle lane has stopped, there must be some mechanical fault, a loose accelerator pedal, a gear lever that has stuck, problem with the suspension, jammed brakes, breakdown in the electric circuit, unless he has simply run out of gas, it would not be the first time such a thing has happened. The next group of pedestrians to gather at the crossing see the driver of the stationary car wave his arms behind the windshield, while the cars behind him frantically sound their horns. Some drivers have already got out of their cars, prepared to push the stranded vehicle to a spot where it will not hold up the traffic, they beat furiously on the closed windows, the man inside turns his head in their direction, first to one side then the other, he is clearly shouting something, to judge by the movements of his mouth he appears to be repeating some words, not one word but three, as turns out to be the case when someone finally manages to open the door, I am blind.

Who would have believed it. Seen merely at a glance, the man's eyes seem healthy, the iris looks bright, luminous, the sclera white, as compact as porcelain. The eyes wide open, the wrinkled skin of the face, his eyebrows suddenly screwed up, all this, as anyone can see, signifies that he is distraught with anguish. With a rapid movement, what was in sight has disappeared behind the man's clenched fists, as if he were still trying to retain inside his mind the final image captured, a round red light at the traffic lights. I am blind, I am blind, he repeated in despair as they helped him to get out of the car, and the tears welling up made those eyes which he claimed were dead, shine even more. These things happen, it will pass you'll see, sometimes it's nerves, said a woman. The lights had already changed again, some inquisitive passersby had gathered around the group, and the drivers further back who did not know what was going on, protested at what they thought was some common accident, a smashed headlight, a dented fender, nothing to justify this upheaval, Call the police, they shouted and get that old wreck out of the way. The blind man pleaded, Please, will someone take me home. The woman who had suggested a case of nerves was of the opinion that an ambulance should be summoned to transport the poor man to the hospital, but the blind man refused to hear of it, quite unnecessary, all he wanted was that someone might accompany him to the entrance of the building where he lived. It's close by and you could do me no greater favour. And what about the car, asked someone. Another voice replied, The key is in the ignition, drive the car on to the pavement. No need, intervened a third voice, I'll take charge of the car and accompany this man home. There were murmurs of approval. The blind man felt himself being taken by the arm, Come, come with me, the same voice was saying to him. They eased him into the front passenger seat, and secured the safety belt. I can't see, I can't see, he murmured, still weeping. Tell me where you live, the man asked him. Through the car windows voracious faces spied, avid for some news. The blind man raised his hands to his eyes and gestured, Nothing, it's as if I were caught in a mist or had fallen into a milky sea. But blindness isn't like that, said the other fellow, they say that blindness is black, Well I see everything white, That little woman was probably right, it could be a matter of nerves, nerves are the very devil, No need to talk to me about it, it's a disaster, yes a disaster, Tell me where you live please, and at the same time the engine started up. Faltering, as if his lack of sight had weakened his memory, the blind man gave his address, then he said, I have no words to thank you, and the other replied, Now then, don't give it another thought, today it's your turn, tomorrow it will be mine, we never know what might lie in store for us, You're right, who would have thought, when I left the house this morning, that something as dreadful as this was about to happen. He was puzzled that they should still be at a standstill, Why aren't we moving, he asked, The light is on red, replied the other. From now on he would no longer know when the light was red.

As the blind man had said, his home was nearby. But the

pavements were crammed with vehicles, they could not find a space to park and were obliged to look for a spot in one of the side streets. There, because of the narrowness of the pavement, the door on the passenger's side would have been little more than a hand's-breadth from the wall, so in order to avoid the discomfort of dragging himself from one seat to the other with the brake and steering wheel in the way, the blind man had to get out before the car was parked. Abandoned in the middle of the road, feeling the ground shifting under his feet, he tried to suppress the sense of panic that welled up inside him. He waved his hands in front of his face, nervously, as if he were swimming in what he had described as a milky sea, but his mouth was already opening to let out a cry for help when at the last minute he felt the other's hand gently touch him on the arm, Calm down, I've got you. They proceeded very slowly, afraid of falling, the blind man dragged his feet, but this caused him to stumble on the uneven pavement, Be patient, we're almost there, the other murmured, and a little further ahead, he asked, Is there anyone at home to look after you, and the blind man replied, I don't know, my wife won't be back from work yet, today it so happened that I left earlier only to have this hit me. You'll see, it isn't anything serious, I've never heard of anyone suddenly going blind, And to think I used to boast that I didn't even need glasses, Well it just goes to show. They had arrived at the entrance to the building, two women from the neighbourhood looked on inquisitively at the sight of their neighbour being led by the arm but neither of them thought of asking, Have you got something in your eye, it never occurred to them nor would he have been able to reply, Yes, a milky sea. Once inside the building, the blind man said, Many thanks, I'm sorry for all the trouble I've caused you, I can manage on my own now, No need to apologise, I'll come up with you, I wouldn't be easy in my mind if I were to leave you here. They got into the narrow elevator with some difficulty, What floor do you live on, On the third, you cannot imagine how grateful I am, Don't thank me, today it's you, Yes, you're right, tomorrow it might be you. The elevator came to a halt, they stepped out on to the landing, Would you like me to help you open the door, Thanks, that's something I think I can do for myself. He took from his pocket a small bunch of keys, felt them one by one along the serrated edge, and said, It must be this one, and feeling for the keyhole with the fingertips of his left hand, he tried to open the door. It isn't this one, Let me have a look, I'll help you. The door opened at the third attempt. Then the blind man called inside, Are you there, no one replied, and he remarked, Just as I was saying, she still hasn't come back. Stretching out his hands, he groped his way along the corridor, then he came back cautiously, turning his head in the direction where he calculated the other fellow would be, How can I thank you, he said, It was the least I could do, said the good Samaritan, no need to thank me, and added, Do you want me to help you to get settled and keep you company until your wife arrives. This zeal suddenly struck the blind man as being suspect, obviously he would not invite a complete stranger to come in who, after all, might well be plotting at that very moment how to overcome, tie up and gag the poor defenceless blind man, and then lay hands on anything of value. There's no need, please don't bother, he said, I'm fine, and as he slowly began closing the door, he repeated, There's no need, there's no need.

Hearing the sound of the elevator descending he gave a sigh of relief. With a mechanical gesture, forgetting the state in which he found himself, he drew back the lid of the peep-hole and looked outside. It was as if there were a white wall on the other side. He could feel the contact of the metallic frame on his eyebrow, his eyelashes brushed against the tiny lens, but he could not see out, an impenetrable whiteness covered everything. He knew he was in his own home, he recognised the smell, the atmosphere, the silence, he could make out the items of furniture and objects simply by touching them, lightly running his fingers over them, but at the same time it was as if all of this were already dissolving into a kind of strange dimension, without direction or reference points, with neither north nor south, below nor above. Like most people, he had often played as a child at pretending to be blind, and, after keeping his eyes closed for five minutes, he had reached the conclusion that blindness, undoubtedly a terrible affliction, might still be relatively bearable if the unfortunate victim had retained sufficient memory, not just of the colours, but also of forms and planes, surfaces and shapes, assuming of course, that this one was not born blind. He had even reached the point of thinking that the darkness in which the blind live was nothing other than the simple absence of light, that what we call blindness was something that simply covered the appearance of beings and things, leaving them intact behind their black veil. Now, on the contrary, here he was, plunged into a whiteness so luminous, so total, that it swallowed up rather than absorbed, not just the colours, but the very things and beings, thus making them twice as invisible.

As he moved in the direction of the sitting-room, despite the caution with which he advanced, running a hesitant hand along the wall and not anticipating any obstacles, he sent a vase of flowers crashing to the floor. He had forgotten about any such vase, or perhaps his wife had put it there when she left for work with the intention of later finding some more suitable place. He bent down to appraise the damage. The water had spread over the polished floor. He tried to gather up the flowers, never thinking of the broken glass, a long sharp splinter pricked his finger and, at the pain, childish tears of helplessness sprang to his eyes, blind with whiteness in the middle of his flat, which was turning dark as evening fell. Still clutching the flowers and feeling the blood running down, he twisted round to get the handkerchief from his pocket and wrapped it round his finger as best he could. Then, fumbling, stumbling, skirting the furniture, treading warily so as not to trip on the rugs, he reached the sofa where he and his wife watched television. He sat down, rested the flowers on his lap, and, with the utmost care, unrolled the handkerchief. The blood, sticky to the touch, worried him, he thought it must be because he could not see it, his blood had turned into a viscous substance without colour, into something rather alien which nevertheless belonged to him, but like a self-inflicted threat directed at himself. Very slowly, gently probing with his good hand, he tried to locate the splinter of glass, as sharp as a tiny dagger, and, by bringing the nails of his thumb and forefinger together, he managed to extract all of it. He wrapped the handkerchief round the injured finger once more, this time tightly to stop the bleeding, and, weak and exhausted, he leaned back on the sofa. A minute later, because of one of those all too common abdications of the body, that chooses to give up in certain moments of anguish or despair, when, if it were guided by logic alone, all its nerves should be alert and tense, a kind of weariness crept over him, more drowsiness than real fatigue, but just as heavy. He dreamt at once that he was pretending to be blind, he dreamt that he was forever closing and opening his eyes, and that, on each occasion, as if he were returning from a journey, he found waiting for him, firm and unaltered, all the forms and colours of the world as he knew it. Beneath this reassuring certainty, he perceived nevertheless, the dull nagging of uncertainty, perhaps it was a deceptive dream, a dream from which he would have to emerge sooner or later, without knowing at this moment what reality awaited him. Then, if such a word has any meaning when applied to a weariness that lasted for only a few seconds, and already in that semi-vigilant state that prepares one for awakening, he seriously considered that it was unwise to remain in this state of indecision, shall I wake up, shall I not wake up, shall I wake up, shall I not wake up, there always comes a moment when one has no option but to take a risk, What am I doing here with these flowers on my lap and my eyes closed as if I were afraid of opening them, What are you doing there, sleeping with those flowers on your lap, his wife was asking him.

She did not wait for a reply. Pointedly, she set about gathering up the fragments of the vase and drying the floor, muttering all the while with an irritation she made no attempt to disguise, You might have cleaned up this mess yourself, instead of settling down to sleep as if it were no concern of yours. He said nothing, protecting his eyes behind tightly closed lids, suddenly agitated by a thought, And if I were to open my eyes and see, he asked himself, gripped by anxious hope. The woman drew near, noticed the bloodstained handkerchief, her vexation gone in an instant, Poor man, how did this happen, she asked compassionately as she undid the improvised bandage. Then he wanted with all his strength to see his wife kneeling at his feet, right there, where he knew she was, and then, certain that he would not see her, he opened his eyes, So you've wakened up at last, my sleepyhead, she said smiling. There was silence, and he said, I'm blind, I can't see. The woman lost her patience, Stop playing silly games, there are certain things we must not joke about, How I wish it were a joke, the truth is that I really am blind, I can't see anything, Please, don't frighten me, look at me, here, I'm here, the light is on, I know you're there, I can hear you, touch you, I can imagine you've switched on the light, but I am blind. She began to weep, clung to him, It isn't true, tell me that it isn't true. The flowers had slipped onto the floor, onto the bloodstained handkerchief, the blood had started to trickle again from the injured finger, and he, as if wanting to say with other words, That's the least of my worries, murmured, I see everything white, and he gave a sad smile. The woman sat down beside him, embraced him tightly, kissed him gently on the forehead, on the face, softly on the eyes, You'll see that this will pass, you haven't been ill, no one goes blind from one minute to the next, Perhaps, Tell me how it happened, what did you feel, when, where, no, not yet, wait, the first thing we must do is to consult an eye specialist, can you think of one, I'm afraid not, neither of us wears glasses, And if I were to take you to the hospital, There isn't likely to be any emergency service for eyes that cannot see, You're right, better that we should go straight to a doctor, I'll look in the telephone directory and locate a doctor who practises nearby. She got up, still questioning him, Do you notice any difference, None, he replied, Pay attention, I'm going to switch off the light and you can tell me, now, Nothing, What do you mean nothing, Nothing, I always see the same white, it's as if there were no night.

He could hear his wife rapidly leaf through the pages of the telephone directory, sniffling to hold back her tears, sighing, and finally saying, This one will do, let's hope he can see us. She dialled a number, asked if that was the surgery, if the doctor was there, if she could speak to him, No, no the doctor doesn't know me, the matter is extremely urgent, yes, please, I understand, then I'll explain the situation to you, but I beg of you to pass on what I have to say to the doctor, the fact is that my husband has suddenly gone blind, yes, yes, all of a sudden, no, no he is not one of the doctor's patients, my husband does not wear glasses and never has, yes, he has excellent eyesight, just like me, I also see perfectly well, ah, many thanks, I'll wait, I'll wait, yes, doctor, all of a sudden, he says he sees everything white, I have no idea what happened, I haven't had time to ask him, I've just arrived home to find him in this state, would you like me to ask him, ah, I'm so grateful to you doctor, we'll come right away, right away. The blind man rose to his feet, Wait, his wife said, first let me attend to this finger, she disappeared for several moments, came back with a bottle of peroxide, another of iodine, cotton wool, a box of bandages. As she dressed the wound, she asked him, Where did you leave the car, and suddenly confronted him, But in your condition you couldn't have driven the car, or you were already at home when it happened, No, it was on the street when I was stationary at a red light, some person brought me home, the car was left in the next street, Fine, let's go down, wait at the door while I go to find it, where did you put the keys, I don't know, he never gave them back to me, Who's he, The man who brought me home, it was a man, He must have left them somewhere, I'll have a look round, It's pointless searching, he didn't enter the flat, But the keys have to be somewhere, Most likely he forgot, inadvertently took them with him, This was all we needed, Use your keys, then we'll sort it out, Right, let's go, take my hand. The blind man said, If I have to stay like this, I'd rather be dead, Please, don't talk nonsense, things are bad enough, I'm the one who's blind, not you, you cannot imagine what it's like, The doctor will come up with some remedy, you'll see, I shall see.

They left. Below, in the lobby, his wife switched on the light and whispered in his ear. Wait for me here, if any neighbours should appear speak to them naturally, say you're waiting for me, no one looking at you would ever suspect that you cannot see and besides we don't have to tell people all our business, Yes, but don't be long. His wife went rushing off. No neighbour entered or left. The blind man knew from experience that the stairway would only be lit so long as he could hear the mechanism of the automatic switch, therefore he went on pressing the button whenever there was silence. The light, this light, had been transformed into noise for him. He could not understand why his wife was taking so long to return, the street was nearby, some eighty or a hundred metres, If we delay any longer, the doctor will be gone, he thought to himself. He could not avoid a mechanical gesture, raising his left wrist and lowering his eyes to look at his watch. He pursed his lips as if in sudden pain, and felt deeply grateful that there were no neighbours around at that moment, for there and then, were anyone to have spoken to him, he would have burst into tears. A car stopped in the street, At last, he thought, but then realised that it was not the sound of his car engine, This is a diesel engine, it must be a taxi, he said, pressing once more on the button for the light. His wife came back, flustered and upset, that good Samaritan of yours, that good soul, has taken our car, It isn't possible, you can't have looked properly, Of course I looked properly, there's nothing wrong with my eyesight, these last words came out inadvertently, You told me the car was in the next street, she corrected herself, and it isn't, unless they've left it in some other street, No, no, I'm certain it was left in this street, Well then it has disappeared, In that case, what about the keys, He took advantage of your confusion and distress and robbed us, And to think I didn't want him in the flat for fear he might steal something yet if he had kept me company until you arrived home, he could not have stolen our car, Let's go, we have a taxi waiting, I swear to you that I'd give a year of my life to see this rogue go blind as well. Don't speak so loud, And that they rob him of everything he possesses, He might turn up, Ah, so you think he'll knock on the door tomorrow and say he took the car in a moment of distraction, that he is sorry and inquire if you're feeling better.

They remained silent until they reached the doctor's surgery. She tried not to think about the stolen car, squeezed her husband's hand affectionately, while he, his head lowered so that the driver would not see his eyes through the rear-view mirror, could not stop asking himself how it was possible that such a terrible tragedy should have befallen him, Why me. He could hear the noise of the traffic, the odd loud voice whenever the taxi stopped, it often happens, we are still asleep and external sounds are already penetrating the veil of unconsciousness in which we are still wrapped up, as in a white sheet. As in a white sheet. He shook his head, sighing, his wife gently stroked his cheek, her way of saying, Keep calm, I'm here, and he leaned his head on her shoulder, indifferent to what the driver might think, If you were in my situation and unable to drive any more, he thought childishly, and oblivious of the absurdity of that remark, he congratulated himself amidst his despair that he was still capable of formulating a rational thought. On leaving the taxi, discreetly assisted by his wife, he seemed calm, but on entering the surgery where he was about to learn his fate, he asked his wife in a tremulous whisper, What will I be like when I get out of this place, and he shook his head as if he had given up all hope.

His wife informed the receptionist, I'm the person who rang half an hour ago because of my husband, and the receptionist showed them into a small room where other patients were waiting. There was an old man with a black patch over one eye, a young lad who looked cross-eyed, accompanied by a woman who must be his mother, a girl with dark glasses, two other people without any apparent distinguishing features, but no one who was blind, blind people do not consult an ophthalmologist. The woman guided her husband to an empty chair, and since all the other chairs were occupied, she remained standing beside him, We'll have to wait, she whispered in his ear. He realised why, he had heard the voices of those who were in the waiting-room, now he was assailed by another worry, thinking that the longer the doctor took to examine him, the worse his blindness would become to the point of being incurable. He fidgeted in his chair, restless, he was about to confide his worries to his wife, but just then the door opened and the receptionist said, Will you both come this way, and turning to the other patients, Doctor's orders, this man is an urgent case. The mother of the cross-eyed boy protested that her right was her right, and that she was first and had been waiting for more than an hour. The other patients supported her in a low voice, but not one of them, nor the woman herself, thought it wise to carry on complaining, in case the doctor should take offence and repay their impertinence by making them wait even longer, as has occurred. The old man with the patch over one eye was magnanimous, Let the poor man go ahead, he's in a much worse state than we are. The blind man did not hear him, they were already going into the doctor's consulting room, and the wife was saying, Many thanks for being so kind, doctor, it's just that my husband, and that said, she paused, because frankly she did not know what had really happened, she only knew that her husband was blind and that their car had been stolen. The doctor said, Please, be seated, and he himself went to help the patient into the chair, and then, touching him on the hand, he spoke to him directly, Now then, tell me what is wrong. The blind man explained that he was in his car, waiting for the red light to change when suddenly he could no longer see, that several people had rushed to his assistance, that an elderly woman, judging from her voice, had said that it was probably a case of nerves, and then a man had accompanied him home because he could not manage on his own, I see everything white, doctor. He said nothing about the stolen car.

The doctor asked him, Has anything like this ever happened to you before, or something similar, No, doctor, I don't even use glasses. And you say it came on all of a sudden, Yes, doctor, Like a light going out, More like a light going on, During the last few days have you felt any difference in your eyesight, No, doctor, Is there, or has there ever been any case of blindness in your family, Among the relatives I've known or have heard discussed, no one, Do you suffer from diabetes, No, doctor, From syphilis, No, doctor. From hypertension of the arteries or the brain cells,

I'm not sure about the brain cells, but none of these other things, we have regular medical check-ups at work. Have you taken a sharp knock on the head, today or yesterday, No, doctor, How old are you, Thirty-eight, Fine, let's take a look at these eyes. The blind man opened them wide, as if to facilitate the examination, but the doctor took him by the arm and installed him behind a scanner which anyone with imagination might see as a new version of the confessional, eyes replacing words, and the confessor looking directly into the sinner's soul, Rest your chin here, he advised him, keep your eyes open, and don't move. The woman drew close to her husband, put her hand on his shoulder, and said, This will be sorted out, you'll see. The doctor raised and lowered the binocular system at his side, turned finely adjusted knobs, and began his examination. He could find nothing in the cornea, nothing in the sclera, nothing in the iris, nothing in the retina, nothing in the lens of the eye, nothing in the luteous macula, nothing in the optic nerve, nothing elsewhere. He pushed the apparatus aside, rubbed his eyes, then carried out a second examination from the start, without speaking, and when he had finished there was a puzzled expression on his face, I cannot find any lesion, your eyes are perfect. The woman joined her hands in a gesture of happiness and exclaimed, Didn't I tell you, didn't I tell you, this can be resolved. Ignoring her, the blind man asked, May I remove my chin, doctor, Of course, forgive me, If my eyes are perfect as you say, why am I blind, For the moment I cannot say, we shall have to carry out more detailed tests, analyses, an ecography, an encephalogram, Do you think it has anything to do with the brain, It's a possibility, but I doubt it. Yet you say you can find nothing wrong with my eyes, That's right, How strange, What I'm trying to say is that if, in fact, you are blind, your blindness at this moment defies explanation, Do you doubt that I am blind, Not at all, the problem is the unusual nature of your case, personally, in all my years in practice, I've never come across anything like it, and I daresay no such case has ever been known in the entire history of ophthalmology, Do you think there is a cure, In principle, since I cannot find lesions of any kind or any congenital malformations, my reply should be in the affirmative, But apparently it is not in the affirmative, Only out of caution, only because I do not want to build up hopes that may turn out to be unjustified, I understand, That's the situation, And is there any treatment I should follow, some remedy or other, For the moment I prefer not to prescribe anything, for it would be like prescribing in the dark. There's an apt expression, observed the blind man. The doctor pretended not to hear, got off the revolving stool on which he had been seated to carry out the examination, and, standing up, he wrote out on his prescription pad the tests and analyses he judged to be necessary. He handed the sheet of paper to the wife, Take this and come back with your husband once you have the results, meanwhile if there should be any change in his condition, telephone me, How much do we owe you, doctor, Pay in reception. He accompanied them to the door, murmured words of reassurance, Let's wait and see, let's wait and see, you mustn't despair, and once they had gone he went into the small bathroom adjoining the consulting room and stared at length into the mirror, What can this be, he murmured. Then he returned to the consulting room, called out to the receptionist, Send in the next patient.

That night the blind man dreamt that he was blind.

On offering to help the blind man, the man who then stole his car, had not, at that precise moment, had any evil intention, quite the contrary, what he did was nothing more than to obey those feelings of generosity and altruism which, as everyone knows, are the two best traits of human nature and to be found in much more hardened criminals than this one, a simple car-thief without any hope of advancing in his profession, exploited by the real owners of this enterprise, for it is they who take advantage of the needs of the poor. When all is said and done, there is not all that much difference between helping a blind man only to rob him afterwards and looking after some tottering and stammering old person with one eye on the inheritance. It was only when he got close to the blind man's home that the idea came to him quite naturally, precisely, one might say, as if he had decided to buy a lottery ticket on catching sight of a ticket-vendor, he had no hunch, he bought the ticket to see what might come of it, resigned in advance to whatever capricious fortune might bring, something or nothing, others would say that he acted according to a conditioned reflex of his personality. The sceptics, who are many and stubborn, claim that, when it comes to human nature, if it is true that the opportunity does not always make the thief, it is also true that it helps a lot. As for us, we should like to think that if the blind man had accepted the second offer of this false Samaritan, at that final moment generosity might still have prevailed, we refer to his offer to keep the blind man company until his wife should arrive, who knows whether the moral responsibility, resulting from the trust thus bestowed, might not have inhibited the criminal temptation and caused the victory of those shining and noble sentiments which it is always possible to find even in the most depraved souls. To finish on a plebeian note, as the old proverb never tires of teaching us, while trying to cross himself the blind man only succeeded in breaking his own nose.

The moral conscience that so many thoughtless people have offended against and many more have rejected, is something that exists and has always existed, it was not an invention of the philosophers of the Quaternary, when the soul was little more than a muddled proposition. With the passing of time, as well as the social evolution and genetic exchange, we ended up putting our conscience in the colour of blood and in the salt of tears, and, as if that were not enough, we made our eyes into a kind of mirror turned inwards, with the result that they often show without reserve what we are verbally trying to deny. Add to this general observation, the particular circumstance that in simple spirits, the remorse caused by committing some evil act often becomes confused with ancestral fears of every kind, and the result will be that the punishment of the prevaricator ends up being, without mercy or pity, twice what he deserved. In this case it is, therefore, impossible to unravel what proportion of fear and what proportion of the afflicted conscience began to harass the thief the moment he started up the engine of the car and drove off. No doubt he could never feel tranquil sitting in the place of someone who was holding this same steering wheel when he suddenly turned blind, who looked through this windshield and suddenly could no longer see, it does not take much imagination for such thoughts to rouse the foul and insidious monster of fear, there it is already raising its head. But it was also remorse, the aggrieved expression of one's conscience, as already stated, or, if we prefer to describe it in suggestive terms, a conscience with teeth to bite, that was about to put before his eyes the forlorn image of the blind man as he was closing the door, There's no need, there's no need, the poor fellow had said, and from then on he would not be capable of taking a step without assistance.

The thief concentrated twice as hard on the traffic to prevent such terrifying thoughts from fully occupying his mind, he knew full well that he could not permit himself the smallest error, the tiniest distraction. There were always police around and it would only need one of them to stop him, May I see your identity card and driving licence, back to prison, what a hard life. He was most careful to obey the traffic lights, under no circumstances to go when the light was red, to respect the amber light, to wait patiently for the green light to come on. At a certain point, he realised that he had started to look at the lights in a way that was becoming obsessive. He then started to regulate the speed of the car to ensure that he always had a green light before him, even if, in order to ensure this, he had to increase the speed or, on the contrary, to reduce it to the extent of irritating the drivers behind him. In the end, disoriented as he was, tense beyond endurance, he drove the car into a minor road where he knew there were no traffic lights, and parked almost without looking, he was such a good driver. He felt as if his nerves were about to explode, these were the very words that crossed his mind. My nerves are about to explode. It was stifling inside the car. He lowered the windows on either side, but the air outside, if it was moving, did nothing to freshen the atmosphere inside. What am I going to do, he asked himself. The shed where he had to take the car was far away, in a village outside the city, and in his present frame of mind, he would never get there. Either the police will arrest me or, worse still, I'll have an accident, he muttered. It then occurred to him that it would be best to get out of the car for a bit and try to clear his thoughts, Perhaps the fresh air will blow the cobwebs away, just because that poor wretch turned blind is no reason why the same should happen to me, this is not some cold one catches, I'll take a turn round the block and it will pass. He got out and did not bother to lock the car, he would be back in a minute, and walked off. He had gone no more than thirty paces when he went blind.

In the surgery, the last patient to be seen was the good-natured old man, the one who had spoken so kindly about the poor man who had suddenly turned blind. He was there just to arrange a date for an operation on a cataract that had appeared in his one remaining eye, the black patch was covering a void, and had nothing to do with the matter in hand, These are ailments that come with old age, the doctor had said some time ago, when it matures we shall remove it, then you won't recognise the place you've been living in. When the old man with the black eyepatch left and the nurse said there were no more patients in the waiting-room, the doctor took out the file of the man who had turned up blind, he read it once, twice, reflected for several minutes and finally rang a colleague with whom he held the following conversation: I must tell you, today I dealt with the strangest case, a man who totally lost his sight from one instant to the next, the examination revealed no perceptible lesion or signs of any malformation from birth, he says he sees everything white, a kind of thick, milky whiteness that clings to his eyes, I'm trying to explain as best I can how he described it, yes, of course it's subjective, no, the man is relatively young, thirty-eight years old, have you ever heard of such a case, or read about it, or heard it mentioned, I thought as much, for the moment I cannot think of any solution, to gain time I've recommended some tests, yes, we could examine him together one of these days, after dinner I shall check some books, take another look at the bibliography, perhaps I'll find some clue, yes, I'm familiar with agnosia, it could be psychic blindness, but then it would be the first case with these characteristics, because there is no doubt that the man is really blind, and as we know, agnosia is the inability to recognise familiar objects, because it also occurred to me that this might be a case of amaurosis, but remember what I started to tell you, this blindness is white, precisely the opposite of amaurosis which is total darkness unless there is some form of white amaurosis, a white darkness, as it were, yes, I know, something unheard of, agreed, I'll call him tomorrow, explain that we should like to examine him together. Having ended his conversation, the doctor leaned back in his chair, remained there for a few minutes, then rose to his feet, removed his white coat with slow, weary movements. He went to the bathroom to wash his hands, but this time he did not ask the mirror, metaphysically, What can this be, he had recovered his scientific outlook, the fact that agnosia and amaurosis are identified and defined with great precision in books and in practice, did not preclude the appearance of variations, mutations, if the word is appropriate, and that day seemed to have arrived. There are a thousand reasons why the brain should close up, just this, and nothing else, like a late visitor arriving to find his own door shut. The ophthalmologist was a man with a taste for literature and a flair for coming up with the right quotation.

That evening, after dinner, he told his wife, A strange case turned up at the surgery today, it might be a variant of psychic blindness or amaurosis, but there appears to be no evidence of any such symptoms ever having been established, What are these illnesses, amaurosis and that other thing, his wife asked him. The doctor gave an explanation within the grasp of a layman and capable of satisfying her curiosity, then he went to the bookcase where he kept his medical books, some dating back to his university years, others more recent and some just published which he still had not had time to study. He checked the indexes and methodically began reading everything he could find about agnosia and amaurosis, with the uncomfortable impression of being an intruder in a field beyond his competence, the mysterious terrain of neurosurgery, about which he only had the vaguest notion. Late that night, he laid aside the books he had been studying, rubbed his weary eyes and leaned back in his chair. At that moment the alternative presented itself as clear as could be. If it were a case of agnosia, the patient would now be seeing what he had always seen, that is to say, there would have been no diminution of his visual powers, his brain would simply have been incapable of recognising a chair wherever there happened to be a chair, in other words, he would continue to react correctly to the luminous stimuli leading to the optic nerve, but, to use simple terms within the grasp of the layman, he would have lost the capacity to know what he knew and, moreover, to express it. As for amaurosis, here there was no doubt. For this to be effectively the case, the patient would have to see everything black, if you'll excuse the use of the verb to see, when this was a case of total darkness. The blind man had categorically stated that he could see, if you'll excuse that verb again, a thick, uniform white colour as if he had plunged with open eyes into a milky sea. A white amaurosis, apart from being etymologically a contradiction, would also be a neurological impossibility, since the brain, which would be unable to perceive the images, forms and colours of reality, would likewise be incapable, in a manner of speaking, of being covered in white, a continuous white, like a white painting without tonalities, the colours, forms and images that reality itself might present to someone with normal vision, however difficult it may be to speak, with any accuracy, of normal vision. With the clear conscience of having fetched up in a dead end, the doctor shook his head despondently and looked around him. His wife had already gone off to bed, he vaguely remembered her coming up to him for a moment and kissing him on the head, I'm off to bed, she must have told him, the flat was now silent, books scattered on the table, What's this, he thought to himself, and suddenly he felt afraid, as if he himself were about to turn blind any minute now and he already knew it. He held his breath and waited. Nothing happened. It happened a minute later as he was gathering up the books to return them to the bookshelf. First he perceived that he could no longer see his hands, then he knew he was blind.

The ailment of the girl with dark glasses was not serious, she was suffering from a mild form of conjunctivitis which the drops prescribed by the doctor would clear up in no time, You know what to do, for the next few days you should remove your glasses only when you sleep, he had told her. He had been cracking the same joke for years, we might even assume that it had been handed down from one generation of ophthalmologists to another, but it never failed, the doctor was smiling as he spoke, the patient smiled as she listened, and on this occasion it was worthwhile, because the girl had nice teeth and knew how to show them. Out of natural misanthropy or because of too many disappointments in life, any ordinary sceptic, familiar with the details of this woman's life, would insinuate that the prettiness of her smile was no more than a trick of the trade, a wicked and gratuitous assertion, because she had the same smile even as a toddler, a word no longer much in use, when her future was a closed book and the curiosity of opening it had not yet been born. To put it simply, this woman could be classed as a prostitute, but the complexity in the web of social relationships, whether by day or night, vertical or horizontal, of the period here described cautions us to avoid a tendency to make hasty and definitive judgments, a mania which, owing to our exaggerated self-confidence, we shall perhaps never be rid of. Although it may be evident just how much cloud there is in Juno, it is not entirely licit, to insist on confusing with a Greek goddess what is no more than an ordinary concentration of drops of water hovering in the atmosphere. Without any doubt, this woman goes to bed with men in exchange for money, a fact that might allow us to classify her without further consideration as a prostitute, but, since it is also true that she goes with a man only when she feels like it and with whom she wants to, we cannot dismiss the possibility that such a factual difference, must as a precaution determine her exclusion from the club as a whole. She has, like ordinary people, a profession, and, also like ordinary people, she takes advantage of any free time to indulge her body and satisfy needs, both individual and general. Were we not trying to reduce her to some primary definition, we should finally say of her, in the broad sense, that she lives as she pleases and moreover gets all the pleasure she can from life.

It was already dark when she left the surgery. She did not remove her glasses, the street lighting disturbed her, especially the illuminated ads. She went into a chemist to buy the drops the doctor had prescribed, decided to pay no attention when the man who served her commented how unfair it was that certain eyes should be covered by dark glasses, an observation that besides being impertinent in itself, and coming from a pharmacist's assistant if you please, went against her belief that dark glasses gave her an air of alluring mystery, capable of arousing the interest of men who were passing, to which she might reciprocate, were it not for the fact that today she had someone waiting for her, an encounter she had every reason to expect would lead to something good, as much in terms of material as in terms of other satisfactions. The man she was about to meet was an old acquaintance, he did not mind when she warned him she could not remove her glasses, an order, moreover, the doctor had not as yet given, and the man even found it amusing, something different. On leaving the pharmacy the girl hailed a taxi, gave the name of a hotel. Reclining on the seat, she was already savouring, if the term is appropriate, the various and multiple sensations of sensuous pleasure, from that first, knowing contact of lips, from that first intimate caress, to the successive explosions of an orgasm that would leave her exhausted and happy, as if she were about to be crucified, heaven protect us, in a dazzling and vertiginous firework. So we have every reason to conclude that the girl with dark glasses, if her partner has known how to fulfill his obligation, in terms of perfect timing and technique, always pays in advance and twice as much as she later charges. Lost in these thoughts, no doubt because she had just paid for a consultation, she asked herself whether it would not be a good idea to raise, starting from today, what, with cheerful euphemism, she was wont to describe as her just level of compensation.

She ordered the taxi-driver to stop one block before her destination, mingled with the people who were following in the same direction, as if allowing herself to be carried along by them, anonymous and without any outward sign of guilt or shame. She entered the hotel with a natural air, crossed the vestibule in the direction of the bar. She had arrived a few minutes early, therefore she had to wait, the hour of their meeting had been arranged with precision. She asked for a soft drink, which she drank at her leisure, without looking at anyone for she did not wish to be mistaken for a common whore in pursuit of men. A little later, like a tourist going up to her room to rest after having spent the afternoon in the museums, she headed for the elevator. Virtue, should there be anyone who still ignores the fact, always finds pitfalls on the extremely difficult path of perfection, but sin and vice are so favoured by fortune that no sooner did she get there than the elevator door opened. Two guests got out, an elderly couple, she stepped inside, pressed the button for the third floor, three hundred and twelve was the number awaiting her, it is here, she discreetly knocked on the door, ten minutes later she was naked, fifteen minutes later she was moaning, eighteen minutes later she was whispering words of love that she no longer needed to feign, after twenty minutes she began to lose her head, after twenty-one minutes she felt that her body was being lacerated with pleasure, after twenty-two minutes she called out, Now, now, and when she regained consciousness she said, exhausted and happy, I can still see everything white.

A policeman took the car-thief home. It would never have occurred to the circumspect and compassionate agent of authority that he was leading a hardened delinquent by the arm, not to prevent him from escaping, as might have happened on another occasion, but simply so that the poor man should not stumble and fall. In recompense, we can easily imagine the fright it gave the thief's wife, when, on opening the door, she came face to face with a policeman in uniform who had in tow, or so it seemed, a forlorn prisoner, to whom, judging from his miserable expression, something more awful must have happened than simply to find himself under arrest. The woman's first thought was that her husband had been caught in the act of stealing and the policeman had come to search the house, this idea, on the other hand, and however paradoxical it may seem, was somewhat reassuring, considering that her husband only stole cars, goods which on account of their size cannot be hidden under the bed. She was not left in doubt for long, the policeman informed her, This man is blind, look after him, and the woman who should have been relieved because the officer, after all, had simply accompanied her husband to his home, perceived the seriousness of the disaster that was to blight their lives when her husband, weeping his heart out, fell into her arms and told her what we already know.

The girl with the dark glasses was also accompanied to her parents' house by a policeman, but the piquancy of the circumstances in which blindness had manifested itself in her case, a naked woman screaming in a hotel and alarming the other guests, while the man who was with her tried to escape, pulling on his trousers in haste, somehow mitigated the obvious drama of the situation. Overcome with embarrassment, a feeling entirely compatible, for all the mutterings of hypocritical prudes and the would-be virtuous, with the mercenary rituals of love to which she dedicated herself, after the piercing shrieks she let out on realising that her loss of vision was not some new and unforeseen consequence of pleasure, the blind girl hardly dared to weep and lament her fate when unceremoniously, without giving her time to dress properly, and almost by force, she was evicted from the hotel. In a tone of voice that would have been sarcastic had it not been simply ill-mannered, the policeman wanted to know, after asking her where she lived, if she had the money for the taxi, in these cases, the State doesn't pay, he warned her, a procedure which, let us note in passing, is not without a certain logic, insofar as these women belong to that considerable number who pay no taxes on their immoral earnings. She gave an affirmative nod, but, being blind, just imagine, she thought the policeman might not have noticed her gesture and she murmured, Yes, I have the money, and then under her breath, added, If only I didn't, words that might strike us as being odd, but which, if we consider the circumvolutions of the human mind, where no short or direct routes exist, these same words end up by being absolutely clear, what she meant to say was that she had been punished because of her disreputable conduct, for her immorality, and this was the outcome. She had told her mother she would not be home for dinner, and in the end she was home early, even before her father.

The ophthalmologist's situation was different, not only because he happened to be at home when he was struck by blindness, but because, being a doctor, he was not going to surrender helplessly to despair, like those who only take note of their body when it hurts them. Even in the anguish of a situation like this, with a night of anxiety ahead of him, he was still capable of remembering what Homer wrote in the *Iliad,* the greatest poem about death and suffering ever written, A doctor is worth several men, words we should not accept as a straightforward expression of quantity, but above all, of quality, as we shall soon see. He summoned the courage to go to bed without disturbing his wife, not even when, muttering and half asleep, she stirred in the bed and snuggled up to him. He lay awake for hours on end, the little sleep he managed to snatch was from pure exhaustion. He hoped the night would never end rather than have to announce, he whose profession was to cure ailments in the eyes of others, I'm blind, but, at the same time, he was anxiously waiting for the light of day, and these are the exact words that came into his mind, The light of day, knowing that he would not see it. In fact, a blind ophthalmologist is not much good to anyone, but it was up to him to inform the health authorities, to warn them of this situation which might turn into a national catastrophe, nothing more nor less, of a form of blindness hitherto unknown, with every appearance of being highly contagious, and which, to all appearances, manifested itself without the previous existence of earlier pathological symptoms of an inflammatory, infectious or degenerative nature, as he was able to verify in the blind man who had come to consult him in his surgery, or as had been confirmed in his own case, a touch of myopia, a slight astigmatism, all so mild that he had decided, in the meantime, not to use corrective lenses. Eyes that had stopped seeing, eyes that were totally blind, yet meanwhile were in perfect condition, without any lesions, recent or old, acquired or innate. He recalled the detailed examination he had carried out on the blind man, how the various parts of the eye accessible to the ophthalmoscope appeared to be perfectly healthy, without any trace of morbid changes, a most rare situation in a man who claimed to be thirty-eight years old, and even in anyone younger. That man could not be blind, he thought, momentarily forgetting that he himself was blind, it's extraordinary how selfless some people can be, and this is not something new, let us remember what Homer said, although in apparently different words.

He pretended to be asleep when his wife got up. He felt the kiss she placed on the forehead, so gentle, as if she did not wish to rouse him from what she imagined to be a deep sleep, perhaps she thought, Poor man, he came to bed late after sitting up to study the extraordinary case of that poor blind man. Alone, as if he were about to be slowly garrotted by a thick cloud weighing on his chest and entering his nostrils, blinding him inside, the doctor let out a brief moan, and allowed two tears, They're probably white, he thought, to well up in his eyes and run over his temples, on either side of his face, now he could understand the fears of his patients, when they told him, Doctor, I think I'm losing my sight. Small domestic noises reached the bedroom, his wife would appear any minute now to see if he was still sleeping, it was almost time for them to go to the hospital. He got up cautiously, fumbled for his dressing-gown and slipped it on, then he went into the bathroom to pee. He turned to where he knew a mirror was, and this time he did not wonder, What's going on, he did not say, There are a thousand reasons why the human brain should close down, he simply stretched out his hands to touch the glass, he knew that his image was there watching him, his image could see him, he could not see his image. He heard his wife enter the bedroom, Ah, you're up already, and he replied, I am. He felt her by his side, Good morning, my love, they still greeted each other with words of affection after all these years of marriage, and then he said, as if both of them were acting in a play and this was his cue, I doubt whether it will be all that good, there's something wrong with my sight. She only took in the last part of the sentence, Let me take a look, she asked, and examined his eyes attentively, I can't see anything, the sentence was obviously borrowed, it was not in her script, he was the one who should have spoken those words, but he simply said, I can't see, and added, I suppose I must have been infected by the patient I saw yesterday.

With time and intimacy, doctors' wives also end up knowing something about medicine, and this one, so close to her husband in everything, had learned enough to know that blindness does not spread through contagion like an epidemic, blindness isn't something that can be caught just by a blind man looking at someone who is not, blindness is a private matter between a person and the eyes with which he or she was born. In any case, a doctor has an obligation to know what he is saying, that is why he is professionally trained at medical school, and if this doctor here, apart from having declared himself blind, openly admits that he has been infected, who is his wife to doubt him, however much she may know about medicine. It is understandable, therefore, that the poor woman, confronted by this irrefutable evidence, should react like any ordinary spouse, two of them we know already, clinging to her husband and showing natural signs of distress, And what are we going to do now, she asked amid tears, Advise the health authorities, the Ministry, that's the first thing to do, if it should turn out to be an epidemic, measures must be taken, But no one has ever heard of an epidemic of blindness, his wife insisted, anxious to hold on to this last shred of hope, Nor has anyone ever come across a blind man without any apparent reasons for his condition, and at this very moment there are at least two of them. No sooner had he uttered this last word than his expression changed. He pushed his wife away almost violently, he himself drew back, Keep away, don't come near me, I might infect you, and then beating on his forehead with clenched fists, What a fool, what a fool, what an idiot of a doctor, why did I not think of it before, we've spent the entire night together, I should have slept in the study with the door shut, and even so, Please, don't say such things, what has to be will be, come, let me get you some breakfast, Leave me, leave me, No, I won't leave you, shouted his wife, what do you want, to go stumbling around bumping into the furniture, searching for the telephone without eyes to find the numbers you need in the telephone directory, while I calmly observe this spectacle, stuck inside a bell-jar to avoid contamination. She took him firmly by the arm and said, Come along, love.

It was still early when the doctor had, we can imagine with what pleasure, finished the cup of coffee and toast his wife had insisted on preparing for him, much too early to find the people whom he had to inform at their desks. Logic and efficacy demanded that his report about what was happening should be made directly and as soon as possible to someone in authority at the Ministry of Health, but he soon changed his mind when he realised that to present himself simply as a doctor who had some important and urgent information to communicate, was not enough to convince the less exalted civil servant to whom, after much pleading, the telephone operator had agreed to put him through. The man wanted to know more details before passing him on to his immediate superior, and it was clear that a doctor with any sense of responsibility was not going to declare the outbreak of an epidemic of blindness to the first minor functionary who appeared before him, it would cause immediate panic. The functionary at the other end of the line replied,

You tell me you're a doctor, if you want me to believe you, then, of course, I believe you, but I have my orders, unless you tell me what you want to discuss I can take this matter no further, It's confidential, Confidential matters are not dealt with over the telephone, you'd better come here in person. I cannot leave the house, Do you mean you're ill, Yes, I'm ill, the blind man said after a pause. In that case you ought to call a doctor, a real doctor, quipped the functionary, and, delighted with his own wit, he hung up.

The man's insolence was like a slap in the face. Only after some minutes had passed, had he regained enough composure to tell his wife how rudely he had been treated. Then, as if he had just discovered something that he should have known a long time ago, he murmured sadly, This is the stuff we're made of, half indifference and half malice. He was about to ask mistrustfully, What now, when he realised that he had been wasting his time, that the only way of getting the information to the right quarters by a safe route would be to speak to the medical director of his own hospital service, doctor to doctor, without any civil servants in the middle, let him assume responsibility for making the bureaucratic system do its work. His wife dialled the number, she knew the hospital number by heart. The doctor identified himself when they replied, then said rapidly, I'm fine, thank you, no doubt the receptionist had inquired, How are you, doctor, that is what we say when we do not wish to play the weakling, we say Fine, even though we may be dying, and this is commonly known as taking one's courage in both hands, a phenomenon that has only been observed in the human species. When the director came to the telephone, Now then, what's all this about, the doctor asked if he was alone, if there was anyone within earshot, no need to worry about the receptionist, she had better things to do than listen in to conversations about ophthalmology, besides she was only interested in gynaecology.

The doctor's account was brief but full, with no circumlocutions, no superfluous words, with no redundancies, and expressed with a clinical dryness which, taking into account the situation, caused the director some surprise, But are you really blind, he asked, Totally blind, In any case, it might be a coincidence, there might not really have been, in the strict sense of the word, any contagion whatsoever, Agreed there is no proof of contagion, but this was not just a case of his turning blind and my turning blind, each of us in our own home, without our having seen each other, the man turned up blind at the surgery and I went blind a few hours later, How can we trace this man, I have his name and address on file in the surgery, I'll send someone there immediately, A doctor, Yes, of course, a colleague, Don't you think we ought to inform the Ministry about what is happening, For the moment that would be premature, think of the public alarm news of this kind would provoke, good grief, blindness isn't catching, Death isn't catching either, yet nevertheless we all die, Well, you stay at home while I deal with the matter, then I'll send someone to fetch you, I want to examine you, Don't forget that the fact that I am now blind is because I examined a blind man, You can't be sure of that, At least there is every indication here of cause and effect, Undoubtedly, yet it is still too early to draw any conclusions, two isolated cases have no statistical relevance, Unless, at this point, there are more than two of us, I can understand your state of mind but we must avoid any gloomy speculations that might turn out to be groundless, Many thanks, You'll be hearing from me soon, Goodbye.

Half an hour later, after he had managed, rather awkwardly, to shave, with some assistance from his wife, the telephone rang. It was the director again, but this time his voice sounded different, We have a boy here who has also suddenly gone blind, he sees everything white, his mother tells me he visited your surgery yesterday, Am I correct in thinking that this child has a divergent squint in the left eye, Yes, Then there's no doubt, it's him, I'm starting to get worried, the situation is becoming really serious, What about informing the Ministry, Yes, of course, I'll get on to the hospital management right away. After about three hours, when the doctor and his wife were having their lunch in silence, he toying with the bits of meat she had cut up for him, the telephone rang again. His wife went to answer, came back at once, You'll have to take the call, it's from the Ministry. She helped him to his feet, guided him into the study and handed him the telephone. The conversation was brief. The Ministry wanted to know the identity of the patients who had been at his surgery the previous day, the doctor replied that the clinical files contained all the relevant details, name, age, marital status, profession, home address, and he ended up offering to accompany the person or persons entrusted with rounding them up. At the other end of the line, the tone was curt, That won't be necessary. The telephone was passed on to someone else, a different voice came through, Good afternoon, this is the Minister speaking, on behalf of the Government I wish to thank you for your zeal, I'm certain that thanks to your prompt action we shall be able to limit and control the situation, meanwhile would you please do us the favour of remaining indoors. The closing words were spoken with courteous formality, but left him in no doubt that he was being given an order. The doctor replied, Yes, Minister, but the person at the other end had already put the phone down.

A few minutes later, the telephone rang yet again. It was the medical director, nervous, jumbling his words, I've just been told that the police have been informed of two cases of sudden blindness, Are they policemen, No, a man and a woman, they found him in the street screaming that he was blind, and the woman was in a hotel when she became blind, it seems she was in bed with someone, We need to check if they, too, are patients of mine, do you know their names, No names were mentioned, They have rung me from the Ministry, they're going to the surgery to collect the files, What a complicated business, You're telling me. The doctor replaced the receiver, raised his hands to his eyes and kept them there as if trying to defend his eyes from anything worse happening, then he said faintly, I'm so tired, Try to get some sleep, I'll take you to your bed, his wife said, It's pointless, I wouldn't be able to sleep, besides the day isn't over yet, something could still happen.

It was almost six o'clock when the telephone rang for the last time. The doctor, who was sitting beside it, picked up the receiver, Yes, speaking, he said, listened attentively to what he was being told and merely nodded his head slightly before ringing off, Who was that, his wife asked, The Ministry, an ambulance is coming to fetch me within the next half hour, Is that what you expected to happen, Yes, more or less, Where are they taking you, I don't know, presumably to a hospital, I'll pack a suitcase, sort out some clothes, the usual things, I'm not going on a trip, We don't know what it is. She led him gently into the bedroom, made him sit on the bed, You sit here quietly, I'll deal with everything. He could hear her going back and forth, opening and closing drawers and cupboards, removing clothes and then packing them into the suitcase on the floor, but what he could not see was that in addition to his own clothes, she had packed a number of blouses and skirts, a pair of slacks, a dress, some shoes that could only belong to a woman. It vaguely crossed his mind that he would not need so many clothes, but said nothing for this was not the moment to be worrying about such trivialities. He heard the locks click, then his wife said, Done, we're ready for the ambulance now. She carried the suitcase to the door leading to the stairs, refusing her husband's help when he said, Let me help you, that's something I can do, after all, I'm not an invalid. Then they went to sit on the sofa in the sitting-room and waited. They were holding hands, and he said, Who knows how long we shall be separated, and she replied, Don't let it worry you.

They waited for almost an hour. When the door-bell rang, she got up and went to open the door, but there was no one on the landing. She tried the internal telephone, Very well, he'll be right down, she said. She turned to her husband and told him, They're waiting downstairs, they have strict orders not to come up to the flat, It would appear the Ministry is really alarmed. Let's go. They went down in the elevator, she helped her husband to negotiate the last few steps and to get into the ambulance, then went back to the steps to fetch the suitcase, she lifted it up on her own and pushed it inside. At last she climbed in and sat beside her husband. The driver of the ambulance turned round to protest, I can only take him, those are my orders, I must ask you to get down. The woman calmly replied, You'll have to take me as well, I've just gone blind this very minute.

The suggestion had come from the minister himself. It was, whichever way one looked at it, a fortunate not to say perfect idea, both from the point of view of the merely sanitary aspects of the case and from that of the social implications and their political consequences. Until the causes were established, or, to use the appropriate terms, the etiology of the white evil, as, thanks to the inspiration of an imaginative assessor, this unpleasant-sounding blindness came to be called, until such time as treatment and a cure might be found, and perhaps a vaccine that might prevent the appearance of any cases in the future, all the people who had turned blind, as well as those who had been in physical contact or in any way close to these patients, should be rounded up and isolated so as to avoid any further cases of contagion, which, once confirmed, would multiply more or less according to what is mathematically referred to as a compound ratio. Quod erat demonstrandum, concluded the Minister. According to the ancient practice, inherited from the time of cholera and yellow fever, when ships that were contaminated or suspected of carrying infection had to remain out at sea for forty days, and in words within the grasp of the general public, it was a matter of putting all these people into quarantine, until further notice. These very words, Until further notice, apparently deliberate, but, in fact, enigmatic since he could not think of any others, were pronounced by the Minister, who later clarified his thinking, I meant that this could as easily mean forty days as forty weeks, or forty months, or forty years, the important thing is that they should stay in quarantine. Now we have to decide where we are going to put them, Minister, said the President of the Commission of Logistics and Security set up rapidly for the purpose and responsible for the transportation, isolation and supervision of the patients, What immediate facilities are available, the Minister wanted to know, We have a mental hospital standing empty until we decide what to do with it, several military installations which are no longer being used because of the recent restructuring of the army, a building designed for a trade fair that is nearing completion, and there is even, although no one has been able to explain why, a supermarket about to go into liquidation, In your opinion, which of these buildings would best suit our purpose, The barracks offer the greatest security, Naturally, There is, however, one drawback, the size of the place is likely to make it both difficult and costly to keep an eye on those interned, Yes, I can see that, As for the supermarket, we would probably run up against various legal obstacles, legal matters that would have to be taken into account, And what about the building for the trade fair, That's the one site I think we should ignore, Minister, Why, Industry wouldn't like it, millions have been invested in the project, So that leaves the mental hospital, Yes, Minister, the mental hospital, Well then, let's opt for the mental hospital, Besides, to all appearances, it's the place that offers the best facilities because not only does it have a perimeter wall, it also has the advantage of having two separate wings, one to be used for those who are actually blind, the other for those suspected of having the disease, as well as a central area which will serve, as it were, as a no man's land, through which those who turn blind will pass to join those who are already blind, There might be a problem, What is that, Minister, We shall find ourselves obliged to put staff there to supervise the transfers, and I doubt whether we will be able to count on volunteers, I doubt whether that will be necessary, Minister, Why, Should anyone suspected of infection turn blind, as will naturally happen sooner or later, you may be sure, Minister, that the others who still have their sight, will turn him out at once, You're right, Just as they would not allow in any blind person who suddenly felt like changing places, Good thinking, Thank you, Minister, may I give orders to proceed, Yes, you have carte blanche.

The Commission acted with speed and efficiency. Before nightfall, everyone who was known to be blind had been rounded up, as well as a considerable number of people who were assumed to be affected, at least those whom it had been possible to identify and locate in a rapid search operation carried out above all in the domestic and professional circles of those stricken with loss of vision. The first to be taken to the empty mental hospital were the doctor and his wife. There were soldiers on guard. The main gate was opened just enough to allow them to pass through, and then closed at once. Serving as a handrail, a thick rope stretched from the entrance to the main door of the building, Move a little to the right, there you will find a rope, grab it with your hand and go straight on, straight on until you come to some steps, there are six steps in all, the sergeant warned them. Once inside, the rope divided into two, one strand going to the left, the other to the right, the sergeant shouted, Keep to the right. As she dragged the suitcase along, the woman guided her husband to the ward that was nearest to the entrance. It was a long room, like a ward in an old-fashioned hospital, with two rows of beds that had been painted grey, although the paint had been peeling off for quite some time. The covers, the sheets and the blankets were of the same colour. The woman guided her husband to the far end of the ward, made him sit on one of the beds, and told him, Stay here, I'm going to look around. There were more wards, long and narrow corridors, rooms that must have been the doctors' offices, dingy latrines, a kitchen that still reeked of bad cooking, a vast refectory with zinc-topped tables, three padded cells in which the bottom six feet of the walls had padding and the rest was lined with cork. Behind the building there was an abandoned yard, with neglected trees, their trunks looking as if they had been flayed. There was litter everywhere. The doctor's wife went back inside. In a half-open cupboard she found strait-jackets. When she rejoined her husband, she asked him, Can you imagine where they've brought us, No, she was about to add, To a mental asylum, but he anticipated her, You're not blind, I cannot allow you to stay here, Yes, you're right, I'm not blind, Then I'm going to ask them to take you home, to tell them that you told a lie in order to remain with me, There's no point, they cannot hear you through there, and even if they could, they would pay no attention, But you can see, For the moment, I shall almost certainly turn blind myself one of these days, or any minute now, Please, go home, Don't insist, besides, I'll bet the soldiers would not let me get as far as the stairs, I cannot force you, No, my love, you can't, I'm staying to help you and the others who may come here, but don't tell them I can see, What others, You surely don't think we shall be here on our own, This is madness, What did you expect, we're in a mental asylum.

The other blind people arrived together. One after another, they had been apprehended at home, first of all the man driving the car, then the man who had stolen it, the girl with dark glasses, the boy with the squint whom they traced to the hospital where his mother had taken him. His mother did not come with him, she lacked the ingenuity of the doctor's wife who declared herself blind when there was nothing wrong with her eyesight, she is a simple soul, incapable of lying, even when it is for her own good. They came stumbling into the ward, clutching at the air, here there was no rope to guide them, they would have to learn from painful experience, the boy was weeping, calling out for his mother, and it was the girl with dark glasses who tried to console him, She's coming, she's coming, she told him, and since she was wearing her dark glasses she could just as well have been blind as not, the others moved their eyes from one side to another, and could see nothing, while because the girl was wearing those glasses, and saying, She's coming, she's coming, it was as if she really could see the boy's desperate mother coming in through the door. The doctor's wife leaned over and whispered into her husband's ear, Four more have arrived, a woman, two men and a boy, What do the men look like, asked the doctor in a low voice, She described them, and he told her, The latter I don't know, the other, from your description, might well be the blind man who came to see me at the surgery. The child has a squint and the girl is wearing dark glasses, she seems attractive, Both of them came to the surgery. Because of the din they were making as they searched for a place where they might feel safe, the new arrivals did not hear this conversation, they must have thought that there was no one else like themselves there, and they had not been without their sight long enough for their sense of hearing to have become keener than normal. At last, as if they had reached the conclusion that it was not worth while exchanging certainty for doubt, each of them sat on the first bed they had stumbled upon, so to speak, the two men ending up beside each other, without their knowing. In a low voice, the girl continued to console the boy, Don't cry, you'll see that your mother won't be long. There was silence, then the doctor's wife said so that she could be heard all the way down the ward as far as the door, There are two of us here, how many are you. The unexpected voice startled the new arrivals, but the two men remained silent, and it was the girl who replied, I think there are four of us, myself and this little boy, Who else, why don't the others speak up, asked the doctor's wife, I'm here, murmured a man's voice, as if he could only pronounce the words with difficulty, And so am I, growled in turn another masculine voice with obvious displeasure. The doctor's wife thought to herself, They're behaving as if they were afraid of getting to know each other. She watched them twitching, tense, their necks craned as if they were sniffing at something, yet curiously, their expressions were all the same, threatening and at the same time afraid, but the fear of one was not the fear of the other, and this was no less true of the threats they offered. What could be going on between them, she wondered.

At that moment, a loud, gruff voice was raised, by someone whose tone suggested he was used to giving orders. It came from a loudspeaker fixed above the door by which they had entered. The word Attention was uttered three times, then the voice began, the Government regrets having been forced to exercise with all urgency what it considers to be its rightful duty, to protect the population by all possible means in this present crisis, when something with all the appearance of an epidemic of blindness has broken out, provisionally known as the white sickness, and we are relying on the public spirit and cooperation of all citizens to stem any further contagion, assuming that we are dealing with a contagious disease and that we are not simply witnessing a series of as yet inexplicable coincidences. The decision to gather together in one place all those infected, and, in adjacent but separate quarters all those who have had any kind of contact with them, was not taken without careful consideration. The Government is fully aware of its responsibilities and hopes that those to whom this message is directed will, as the upright citizens they doubtless are, also assume their responsibilities, bearing in mind that the isolation in which they now find themselves will represent, above any personal considerations, an act of solidarity with the rest of the nation's community. That said, we ask everyone to listen attentively to the following instructions, first, the lights will be kept on at all times, any attempt to tamper with the switches will be useless, they don't work, second, leaving the building without authorisation will mean instant death, third, in each ward there is a telephone that can be used only to requisition from outside fresh supplies for purposes of hygiene and cleanliness, fourth, the internees will be responsible for washing their own clothes by hand, fifth, it is recommended that ward representatives should be elected, this is a recommendation rather than an order, the internees must organise themselves as they see fit, provided they comply with the aforesaid rules and those we are about to announce, sixth, three times daily containers with food will be deposited at the main door, on the right and on the left, destined respectively for the patients and those suspected of being contaminated, seventh, all the left-overs must be burnt, and this includes not only any food, but also the containers, plates and cutlery which are all made of combustible material, eighth, the burning should be done in the inner courtyards of the building or in the exercise yard, ninth, the internees are responsible for any damage caused by these fires, tenth, in the event of a fire getting out of control, whether accidentally or on purpose, the firemen will not intervene, eleventh, equally, the internees cannot count on any outside intervention should there be any outbreaks of illnesses, nor in the event of any disorder or aggression, twelfth, in the case of death, whatever the cause, the internees will bury the corpse in the yard without any formalities, thirteenth, contact between the wing of the patients and that of the people suspected of being contagious must be made in the central hall of the building by which they entered, fourteenth, should those suspected of being infected suddenly go blind, they will be transferred immediately to the other wing, fifteenth, this communication will be relayed daily at the same time for the benefit of all new arrivals. The Government and Nation expect every man and woman to do their duty. Good night.

In the silence that followed, the boy's voice could be clearly heard, I want my mummy, but the words were articulated without expression, like some automatic and repeater mechanism that had previously left a phrase suspended and was blurting it out now, at the wrong time. The doctor said, The orders we have just been given leave no room for doubt, we're isolated, probably more isolated than anyone has ever been and without any hope of getting out of this place until a cure is found for this disease, I recognise your voice, said the girl with dark glasses, I'm a doctor, an ophthalmologist, You must be the doctor I consulted yesterday, I recognise your voice, Yes, and who are you, I've been suffering from conjunctivitis and I assume it hasn't cleared up, but now, since I'm completely blind, it's of no importance, And the child who's with you, He's not mine, I have no children, Yesterday I examined a boy with a squint, was that you, the doctor asked, Yes, that was me, the boy's reply came out with the resentful tone of someone who prefers people not to mention his physical defect, and with good reason, for such defects, these as much as any others, are no sooner mentioned than they pass from being barely perceptible to being all too obvious. Is there anyone else here I know, the doctor asked, could the man who came to see me at the surgery yesterday accompanied by his wife be here by any chance, the man who suddenly went blind when out driving his car, That's me, replied the first blind man, Is there anyone else, please speak up, we are obliged to live here together for who knows how long, therefore it is essential that we should get to know each other. The car-thief muttered between his teeth, Yes, yes, he thought this would be sufficient to confirm his presence, but the doctor insisted, The voice is that of someone who is relatively young, you're not the elderly patient with the cataract, No doctor, that's not me, How did you go blind, I was walking along the street, And what else, Nothing else, I was walking along the street and I suddenly went blind. The doctor was about to ask if his blindness was also white, but stopped himself in time, why bother, whatever his reply, no matter whether his blindness was white or black, they would not get out of this place. He stretched out a hesitant hand to his wife and met her hand on the way. She kissed him on the cheek, no one else could see that wrinkled forehead, that tight mouth, those dead eyes, like glass, terrifying because they appeared to see and did not see, My time will come too, she thought, perhaps even at this very instant, not allowing me to finish what I am saying, at any moment, just as happened to them, or perhaps I'll wake up blind, or go blind as I close my eyes to sleep, thinking I've just dozed off.

She looked at the four blind people, they were sitting on their beds, the little luggage they had been able to bring at their feet, the boy with his school satchel, the others with suitcases, small, as if they had packed for the weekend. The girl with dark glasses was conversing in a low voice with the boy, on the row opposite, close to each other, with only an empty bed between them, the first blind man and the car-thief were, without realising it, sitting face to face. The doctor said, We all heard the orders, whatever happens now, one thing we can be sure of, no one will come to our assistance, therefore we ought to start getting organised without delay, because it won't be long before this ward fills up with people, this one and the others, How do you know there are more wards here, asked the girl, We went around the place before deciding on this ward which is closer to the main entrance, explained the doctor's wife, as she squeezed her husband's arm as if warning him to be cautious. The girl said, it would be better, doctor, if you were to take charge of the ward, after all, you are a doctor. What good is a doctor without eyes or medicines, But you have some authority. The doctor's wife smiled, I think you should accept, if the others are in agreement, of course, I don't think it's such a good idea, Why not, For the moment there are only six of us here, but by tomorrow we shall certainly be more, people will start arriving every day, it would be too much to expect that they should be prepared to accept the authority of someone they have not chosen and who, moreover, would have nothing to offer them in exchange for their respect, always assuming they were willing to accept my authority and my rules, Then it's going to be difficult to live here, We'll be very fortunate if it turns out to be only difficult. The girl with dark glasses said, I meant well, but frankly, doctor, you are right, it will be a case of everyone for himself.

Either because he was moved by these words or because he could no longer contain his fury, one of the men got abruptly to his feet, This fellow is to blame for our misfortune, if I had my eyesight now, I'd do him in, he bellowed, while pointing in the direction where he thought the other man to be. He was not all that far off, but his dramatic gesture was comical because his jabbing, accusing finger was pointing at an innocent bedside table. Keep calm, said the doctor, no one's to blame in an epidemic, everyone's a victim, If I hadn't been the decent fellow I am, if I hadn't helped him to find his way home, I'd still have my precious eyes, Who are you, asked the doctor, but the complainant did not reply and now seemed annoyed that he had said anything. Then the other man spoke, He took me home, it's true, but then took advantage of my condition to steal my car, That's a lie, I didn't steal anything, You most certainly did, If anyone nicked your car, it wasn't me, my reward for carrying out a kind action was to lose my sight, besides, where are the witnesses, that's what I'd like to know. This argument won't solve anything, said the doctor's wife, the car is outside, the two of you are in here, better to make your peace, don't forget we are going to have to live here together, You can count me out, said the first blind man, I'm off to another ward, as far away as possible from this crook who was capable of robbing a blind man, he claims that he turned blind because of me, well let him stay blind, at least it shows there is still some justice in this world. He picked up his suitcase and, shuffling his feet so as not to trip and groping with his free hand, he went along the aisle separating the two rows of beds, Where are the other wards, he asked, but did not hear the reply if there was one, because suddenly he found himself beneath an onslaught of arms and legs, the car-thief was carrying out as best he could his threat to take his revenge on this man who had caused all his misfortunes. One minute on top, the next underneath, they rolled about in the confined space, colliding now and then with the legs of the beds, while, terrified once more, the boy with the squint started crying again and calling out for his mother. The doctor's wife took her husband by the arm, she knew that alone she would never be able to persuade them to stop quarrelling, she led him along the passageway to the spot where the enraged opponents were panting for breath as they struggled on the ground. She guided her husband's hands, she herself took charge of the blind man whom she found more manageable, and with much effort, they managed to separate them. You're behaving foolishly, said the doctor angrily, if your idea is to turn this place into a hell, then you're going about it in the right way, but remember we're on our own here, we can expect no outside help, do you hear, He stole my car, whimpered the first blind man who had come off worst in the exchange of blows, Forget it, what does it matter, said the doctor's wife, you were no longer in a condition to drive the car when it disappeared, That's all very well, but it was mine, and this villain took it and left it who knows where, Most likely, said the doctor, the car is to be found at the spot where this man turned blind, You're an astute fellow, doctor, yes sir, no doubt about that, piped up the thief. The first blind man made a gesture as if to escape from the hands holding him, but without really trying, as if aware that not even his sense of outrage, however justified, would bring back his car, nor would the car restore his sight. But the thief threatened, If you think you're going to get away with this, then you're very much mistaken, all right, I stole your car, but you stole my eyesight, so who's the bigger thief, That's enough, the doctor protested, we're all blind here and we're not accusing or pointing the finger at anyone, I'm not interested in other people's misfortunes, the thief replied contemptuously, If you want to go to another ward, said the doctor to the first blind man, my wife will guide you there, she knows her way around better than me, No thanks, I've changed my mind, I prefer to stay in this one. The thief mocked him, The little boy is afraid of being on his own in case a certain bogeyman gets him, That's enough, shouted the doctor, losing his patience, Now listen to me, doctor, snarled the thief, we're all equal here and you don't give me any orders, No one is giving orders, I'm simply asking you to leave this poor fellow in peace, Fine, fine, but watch your step when you're dealing with me, I'm not easy to handle when somebody gets up my nose, otherwise I'm as good a friend as you're likely to meet, but the worst enemy you could possibly have. With aggressive movements and gestures, the thief fumbled for the bed where he had been sitting, pushed his suitcase underneath, then announced, I'm going to get some sleep, as if warning them, You'd better look the other way, I'm going to take my clothes off. The girl with dark glasses said to the boy with the squint,

And you'd better get into bed as well, stay on this side and if you need anything during the night, call me, I want to do a wee-wee, the boy said. On hearing him, all of them felt a sudden and urgent desire to urinate, and their thoughts were more or less as follows, Now how are we going to cope with this problem, the first blind man groped under the bed to see if there was a chamber pot, yet at the same time hoping he would not find one for he would be embarrassed if he had to urinate in the presence of other people, not that they could see him, of course, but the noise of someone peeing is indiscreet, unmistakable, men at least can use a strategy denied women, in this they are more fortunate. The thief had sat down on the bed and was now saying, Shit, where do you have to go to piss in this place, Watch your language, there's a child here, protested the girl with dark glasses, Certainly, sweetheart, but unless you can find a lavatory, it won't be long before your little boy has pee running down his legs. The doctor's wife intervened, Perhaps I can locate the toilets, I can remember having smelt them, I'll come with you, said the girl with dark glasses, taking the boy by the hand, I think it best that we should all go, the doctor observed, then we shall know the way whenever we need to go, I know what's on your mind, the car-thief thought to himself without daring to say it aloud, what you don't want is that your little wife should have to take me to pee every time I feel the urge. The implication behind that thought gave him a small erection that surprised him, as if the fact of being blind should have as a consequence, the loss or diminution of sexual desire. Good, he thought, all is not lost, after all, among the dead and the wounded someone will escape, and, drifting away from the conversation, he began to daydream. He didn't get very far, the doctor was already saying, Let's form a line, my wife will lead the way, everyone put their hand on the shoulder of the person in front, then there will be no danger of our getting lost. The first blind man spoke up, I'm not going anywhere with him, obviously referring to the crook who had robbed him.

Whether to look for each other or to avoid each other, they could scarcely move in the narrow aisle, all the more so since the doctor's wife had to proceed as if she were blind. At last, they were all in line, the girl with dark glasses led the boy with the squint by the hand, then the thief in underpants and a vest, the doctor behind him, and last of all, safe for the moment from any physical attack, the first blind man. They advanced very slowly, as if mistrustful of the person guiding them, groping in vain with their free hand, searching for the support of something solid, a wall, a door-frame. Placed behind the girl with dark glasses, the thief, aroused by the perfume she exuded and by the memory of his recent erection, decided to put his hands to better use, the one caressing the nape of her neck beneath her hair, the other, openly and unceremoniously fondling her breast. She wriggled to shake him off, but he was grabbing her firmly. Then the girl gave a backward kick as hard as she could. The heel of her shoe, sharp as a stiletto, pierced the flesh of the thief's bare thigh causing him to give a cry of surprise and pain. What's going on, asked the doctor's wife, looking back, I tripped, the girl with dark glasses replied, I seem to have injured the person behind me. Blood was already seeping out between the thief's fingers who, moaning and cursing, was trying to ascertain the consequences of her aggression, I'm injured, this bitch doesn't look where she's putting her feet, And you don't look where you're putting your hands, the girl replied curtly. The doctor's wife understood what had happened, at first she smiled, but then she saw how nasty the wound looked, blood was trickling down the poor devil's leg, and they had no peroxide, no iodine, no plasters, no bandages, no disinfectant, nothing. The line was now in disarray, the doctor was asking, Where is the wound, Here, Here, where, On my leg, can't you see, this bitch stuck the heel of her shoe in me, I tripped, I couldn't help it, repeated the girl before blurting out in exasperation, The bastard was touching me up, what sort of woman does he think I am. The doctor's wife intervened, This wound should be washed and dressed at once, And where is there any water, asked the thief, In the kitchen, in the kitchen there is water, but we don't all have to go, my husband and I will take him there, you others wait here, we'll be back soon, I want to do weewee, said the boy, Hold it in a bit longer, we'll be right back. The doctor's wife knew that she had to turn once to the right, and once to the left, then follow a narrow corridor that formed a right angle, the kitchen was at the far end. After a few paces she pretended that she was mistaken, stopped, retraced her footsteps, then said, Ah, now I remember, and from there they headed straight for the kitchen, there was no more time to be lost, the wound was bleeding profusely. At first, the water from the tap was dirty, it took some time for it to become clear. It was lukewarm and stale, as if it had been putrefying inside the pipes, but the wounded man received it with a sigh of relief. The wound looked ugly. And now, how are we going to bandage his leg, asked the doctor's wife. Beneath a table there were some filthy rags which must have been used as floor cloths, but it would be most unwise to use them to make a bandage, There doesn't appear to be anything here, she said, while pretending to keep up the search, But I can't be left like this, doctor, the bleeding won't stop, please help me, and forgive me if I was rude to you a short time ago, moaned the thief, We are trying to help you, otherwise we wouldn't be here, said the doctor and then he ordered him, Take off your vest, there's no other option. The wounded man mumbled that he needed his vest, but took it off. The doctor's wife lost no time in improvising a bandage which she wrapped round his thigh, pulled tight and managed to use the shoulder straps and the tail of the vest to tie a rough knot.

These were not movements a blind person could easily execute, but she was in no mood to waste time with any more pretence, it was enough to have pretended that she was lost. The thief sensed that there was something unusual here, logically it was the doctor who, although no more than an ophthalmologist, should have bandaged the wound, but the consolation of knowing that something was being done outweighed the doubts, vague as they were, that had momentarily crossed his mind. With him limping along, they went back to rejoin the others, and once there, the doctor's wife spotted immediately that the boy with the squint had not been able to hold out any longer and had wet his trousers. Neither the first blind man nor the girl with glasses had realised what had happened. At the boy's feet spread a puddle of urine, the hem of his trousers still dripping wet. But as if nothing had happened, the doctor's wife said, Let's go and find these lavatories. The blind stretched out their arms, looking for each other, though not the girl with dark glasses who made it quite clear that she had no intention of walking in front of that shameless creature who had touched her up, at last the line was formed, the thief changing places with the first blind man, with the doctor between them. The thief's limp was getting worse and he was dragging his leg. The tight bandage was bothering him and the wound was throbbing so badly that it was as if his heart had changed position and was lying at the bottom of some hole. The girl with dark glasses was once again leading the boy by the hand, but he kept his distance as much as possible, afraid that someone might discover his accident, such as the doctor, who muttered, There's a smell of urine here, and his wife felt she should confirm his impression, Yes, there is a smell, she could not say that it was coming from the lavatories because they were still some distance away, and, being obliged to behave as if she were blind, she could not reveal that the stench was coming from the boy's wet trousers.

They were agreed, both men and women, when they arrived at the lavatories, that the boy should be the first to relieve himself, but the men ended up going in together, without any distinction of urgency or age, the urinal was communal, it would have to be in a place like this, even the toilets. The women remained at the door, they are said to have more resistance, but there's a limit to everything, and the doctor's wife was soon suggesting, Perhaps there are other lavatories, but the girl with dark glasses said, Speaking for myself, I can wait, So can I, said the other woman, then there was a silence, then they began to speak, How did you come to lose your sight, Like everyone else, suddenly I could no longer see, Were you at home, No, So it happened when you left my husband's surgery, More or less, What do you mean by more or less, That it didn't happen right away, Did you feel any pain, No, there was no pain but when I opened my eyes I was blind, With me it was different, What do you mean by different, My eyes weren't closed, I went blind the moment my husband got into the ambulance, Fortunate, For whom, Your husband, this way you can be together, In that case I was also fortunate, You were, Are you married, No, no I'm not, and I don't think there will be any more marriages now, But this blindness is so abnormal, so alien to scientific knowledge that it cannot last forever. And suppose we were to stay like this for the rest of our lives, Us, Everyone, That would be horrible, a world full of blind people, It doesn't bear thinking about.

The boy with the squint was the first to emerge from the lavatory, he didn't even need to have gone in there. He had rolled his trousers halfway up his legs and removed his socks. He said, I'm back, whereupon the girl with dark glasses moved in the direction of the voice, did not succeed the first or second time, but at a third attempt found the boy's vacillating hand. Shortly afterwards, the doctor appeared, then the first blind man, one of them asked, Where are the rest of you, the doctor's wife was already holding her husband's arm, his other arm was touched and grabbed by the girl with dark glasses. For several moments the first blind man had no one to protect him, then someone placed a hand on his shoulder. Are we all here, asked the doctor's wife, The fellow with the injured leg has stayed behind to satisfy another need, her husband replied. Then the girl with dark glasses said, Perhaps there are other toilets, I'm getting desperate, forgive me, Let's go and find out, said the doctor's wife, and they went off hand in hand. Within ten minutes they were back, they had found a consulting room which had its own toilet. The thief had already reappeared, complaining about the cold and the pain in his leg. They re-formed the line in the same order by which they had come and, with less effort than before and without incident, they returned to the ward. Adroitly, without appearing to do so, the doctor's wife helped each of them to reach the bed they had previously occupied. Before entering the ward, as if it were self-evident to everyone, she suggested that the easiest way for each of them to find their place was to count the beds from the entrance, Ours, she said, are the last ones on the right-hand side, beds nineteen and twenty. The first to proceed down the aisle was the thief. Almost naked, he was shivering from head to foot and anxious to alleviate the pain in his leg, reason enough for him to be given priority. He went from bed to bed, fumbling on the floor in search of his suitcase, and when he recognised it, he said aloud, It's here, then added, Fourteen, On which side, asked the doctor's wife, On the left, he replied, once again vaguely surprised, as if she ought to know it without having to ask. The first blind man went next. He knew his bed was next but one to the thief's and on the same side. He was no longer afraid of sleeping near him, his leg was in such a dreadful state, and judging from his groans and sighs, he would find it hard to move. On arriving there, he said, Sixteen, on the left, and lay down fully dressed.

Then the girl with dark glasses pleaded in a low voice, Can we stay close to you on the other side, we shall feel safer there. The four of them advanced together and lost no time in getting settled. After a few minutes, the boy with the squint said, I'm hungry, and the girl with dark glasses murmured, Tomorrow, tomorrow we'll find something to eat, now go to sleep. Then she opened her handbag, searched for the tiny bottle she had bought in the chemist's. She removed her glasses, threw back her head and, keeping her eyes wide open, guiding one hand with the other, she applied the eye-drops. Not all of the drops went into her eyes, but conjunctivitis, given such careful treatment, soon clears up.

I must open my eyes, thought the doctor's wife. Through closed eyelids, when she woke up at various times during the night, she had perceived the dim light of the lamps that barely illuminated the ward, but now she seemed to notice a difference, another luminous presence, it could be the effect of the first glimmer of dawn, it could be that milky sea already drowning her eyes. She told herself that she would count up to ten and then open her eyelids, she said it twice, counted twice, failed to open them twice. She could hear her husband breathing deeply in the next bed and someone snoring, I wonder how the wound on that fellow's leg is doing, she asked herself, but knew at that moment that she felt no real compassion, what she wanted was to pretend that she was worried about something else, what she wanted was not to have to open her eyes. She opened them the following instant, just like that, not because of any conscious decision. Through the windows that began halfway up the wall and ended up a mere hand's-breadth from the ceiling, entered the dull, bluish light of dawn. I'm not blind, she murmured, and suddenly panicking, she raised herself on the bed, the girl with dark glasses, who was occupying a bed opposite, might have heard her. She was asleep. On the next bed, the one up against the wall, the boy was also sleeping, She did the same as me, the doctor's wife thought, she gave him the safest place, what fragile walls we'd make, a mere stone in the middle of the road without any hope other than to see the enemy trip over it, enemy, what enemy, no one will attack us here, even if we'd stolen and killed outside, no one is likely to come here to arrest us, that man who stole the car has never been so sure of his freedom, we're so remote from the world that any day now, we shall no longer know who we are, or even remember our names, and besides, what use would names be to us, no dog recognises another dog or knows the others by the names they have been given, a dog is identified by its scent and that is how it identifies others, here we are like another breed of dogs, we know each other's bark or speech, as for the rest, features, colour of eyes or hair, they are of no importance, it is as if they did not exist, I can still see but for how long, The light changed a little, it could not be night coming back, it had to be the sky clouding over, delaying the morning. A groan came from the thief's bed, If the wound has become infected, thought the doctor's wife, we have nothing to treat it with, no remedy, in these conditions the tiniest accident can become a tragedy, perhaps that is what they are waiting for, that we perish here, one after the other, when the beast dies, the poison dies with it. The doctor's wife rose from her bed, leaned over her husband, was about to wake him, but did not have the courage to drag him from his sleep and know that he continued to be blind. Barefoot, one step at a time, she went to the thief's bed. His eyes were open and unmoving. How are you feeling, whispered the doctor's wife. The thief turned his head in the direction of the voice and said, Bad, my leg is very painful, she was about to say to him, Let me see, but held back just in time, such imprudence, it was he who did not remember that there were only blind people there, he acted without thinking, as he would have done several hours ago, there outside, if a doctor had said to him, Let's have a look at this wound, and he raised the blanket. Even in the half-light, anyone capable of seeing would have noticed the mattress soaked in blood, the black hole of the wound with its swollen edges. The bandage had come undone. The doctor's wife carefully lowered the blanket, then with a rapid, delicate gesture, passed her hand over the man's forehead. His skin felt dry and burning hot. The light changed again, the clouds were drifting away. The doctor's wife returned to her bed, but this time did not lie down. She was watching her husband who was murmuring in his sleep, the shadowy forms of the others beneath the grey blankets, the grimy walls, the empty beds waiting to be occupied, and she serenely wished that she, too, could turn blind, penetrate the visible skin of things and pass to their inner side, to their dazzling and irremediable blindness.

Suddenly, from outside the ward, probably from the hallway separating the two wings of the building, came the sound of angry voices, Out, out, Get out, away with you, You cannot stay here, Orders have to be obeyed. The din got louder, then quietened down, a door slammed shut, all that could be heard now was a distressed sobbing, the unmistakable clatter made by someone who had just fallen over. In the ward they were all awake. They turned their heads towards the entrance, they did not need to be able to see to know that these were blind people who were arriving. The doctor's wife got up, how she would have liked to help the new arrivals, to say a kind word, to guide them to their beds, inform them, Take note, this is bed seven on the left-hand side, this is number four on the right, you can't go wrong, yes, there are six of us here, we came yesterday, yes, we were the first, our names, what do names matter, I believe one of the men has stolen a car, then there is the man who was robbed, there's a mysterious girl with dark glasses who puts drops in for her conjunctivitis, how do I know, being blind, that she wears dark glasses, well as it happens, my husband is an ophthalmologist and she went to consult him at his surgery, yes, he's also here, blindness struck all of us, ah, of course, there's also the boy with the squint. She did not move, she simply said to her husband, They're arriving. The doctor got out of bed, his wife helped him into his trousers, it didn't matter, no one could see, just then the blind internees came into the ward, there were five of them, three men and two women. The doctor said, raising his voice, Keep calm, no need to rush, there are six of us here, how many are you, there's room for everyone. They did not know how many they were, true they had come into contact with each other, sometimes even bumped into each other, as they were pushed from the wing on the left to this one, but they did not know how many they were. And they were carrying no luggage. When they woke up in their ward and found they were blind and started bemoaning their fate, the others put them out without a moment's hesitation, without even giving them time to take their leave of any relatives or friends who might be with them. The doctor's wife remarked, It would be best if they could be counted and each person gave their name. Motionless, the blind internees hesitated, but someone had to make a start, two of the men spoke at once, it always happens, both then fell silent, and it was the third man who began, Number one, he paused, it seemed he was about to give his name, but what he said was, I'm a policeman, and the doctor's wife thought to herself, He didn't give his name, he too knows that names are of no importance here. Another man was introducing himself, Number two, and he followed the example of the first man, I'm a taxi-driver. The third man said, Number three, I'm a pharmacist's assistant. Then a woman spoke up, Number four, I'm a hotel maid, and the last one of all, Number five, I work in an office. That's my wife, my wife, where are you, tell me where you are, Here, I'm here, she said bursting into tears and walking unsteadily along the aisle with her eyes wide open, her hands struggling against the milky sea flooding into them. More confident, he advanced towards her, Where are you, where are you, he was now murmuring as if in prayer. One hand found another, the next moment they were embracing, a single body, kisses in search of kisses, at times lost in mid-air for they could not see each other's cheeks, eyes, lips. Sobbing, the doctor's wife clung to her husband, as if she, too, had just been reunited, but what she was saying was, This is terrible, a real disaster. Then the voice of the boy with the squint could be heard asking, Is my mummy here as well. Seated on his bed, the girl with dark glasses murmured, She'll come, don't worry, she'll come.

Here, each person's real home is the place where they sleep, therefore little wonder that the first concern of the new arrivals should be to choose a bed, just as they had done in the other ward, when they still had eyes to see. In the case of the wife of the first blind man there could be no doubt, her rightful and natural place was beside her husband, in bed seventeen, leaving number eighteen in the middle, like an empty space separating her from the girl with dark glasses. Nor is it surprising that they should try as far as possible to stay close together, there are many affinities here, some already known, others that are about to be revealed, for example, it was the pharmacist's assistant who sold eye-drops to the girl with dark glasses, this was the taxi-driver who took the first blind man to the doctor, this fellow who has identified himself as being a policeman found the blind thief weeping like a lost child, and as for the hotel maid, she was the first person to enter the room when the girl with dark glasses had a screaming fit. It is nevertheless certain that not all of these affinities will become explicit and known, either because of a lack of opportunity, or because no one so much as imagined that they could possibly exist, or because of a simple question of sensibility and tact. The hotel maid would never dream that the woman she saw naked is here, we know that the pharmacist's assistant served other customers wearing dark glasses who came to purchase eye-drops, no one would be imprudent enough to denounce to the policeman the presence of someone who stole a car, the taxi-driver would swear that during the last few days he had no blind man as a passenger. Naturally, the first blind man told his wife in a low voice that one of the internees is the scoundrel who went off with their car, What a coincidence, eh, but, since in the meantime, he knew that the poor devil was badly injured in one leg, he was generous enough to add, He's been punished enough. And she, because of her deep distress at being blind and her great joy on regaining her husband, joy and sorrow can go together, not like oil and water, she no longer remembered what she had said two days before, that she would give a year of her life if this rogue, her word, were to go blind. And if there was some last shadow of resentment still troubling her spirit, it certainly blew over when the wounded man moaned pitifully, Doctor, please help me. Allowing himself to be guided by his wife, the doctor gently probed the edges of his wound, he could do nothing more, nor was there any point in trying to bathe it, the infection might have been caused by the deep penetration of a shoe heel that had been in contact with the surface of the streets and the floors here in the building, or equally by pathogenic agents in all probability to be found in the contaminated almost stagnant water, coming from antiquated pipes in appalling condition. The girl with dark glasses who had got up on hearing his moan, began approaching slowly, counting the beds. She leaned forward, stretched out her hand, which brushed against the face of the doctor's wife, and then, having reached, who knows how, the wounded man's hand, which was burning hot, she said sadly, Please, forgive me, it was entirely my fault, there was no need for me to do what I did, Forget it, replied the man, these things happen in life, I shouldn't have done what I did either.

Almost covering these last words, the harsh voice from the loudspeaker came booming out, Attention, attention, your food has been left at the entrance as well as supplies for your hygiene and cleanliness, the blind should go first to collect their food, those in the wing for the contaminated will be informed when it's their turn, attention, attention, your food has been left at the entrance, the blind should make their way there first, the blind first. Dazed by fever, the wounded man did not grasp all the words, he thought they were being told to leave, that their detention was over, and he made as if to get up, but the doctor's wife held him back, Where are you going, Didn't you hear, he asked, they said the blind should leave, Yes, but only to go and collect our food. The wounded man gave a despondent sigh, and once more could feel the pain piercing through his flesh. The doctor said, Stay here, I'll go, I'm coming with you, said his wife. Just as they were about to leave the ward, a man who had come from the other wing, inquired, Who is this fellow, the reply came from the first blind man, He's a doctor, an eye-specialist, That's a good one, said the taxi-driver, just our luck to end up with the one doctor who can do nothing for us, We're also landed with a taxi-driver who can't take us anywhere, replied the girl with dark glasses sarcastically.

The container with the food was in the hallway. The doctor asked his wife, Guide me to the main door, Why, I'm going to tell them that there is someone here with a serious infection and that we have no medicines, Remember the warning, Yes, but perhaps when confronted with a concrete case, I doubt it, Me, too, but we ought to try. At the top of the steps leading to the forecourt, the daylight dazzled his wife, and not because it was too intense, there were dark clouds passing across the sky, and it looked as if it might rain, In such a short time I've become unused to bright light, she thought. Just at that moment, a soldier shouted from the gate, Stop, turn back, I have orders to shoot, and then, in the same tone of voice, pointing his gun, Sergeant, there are some people here trying to leave, We have no wish to leave, the doctor protested, In my opinion that is not what they want, said the sergeant as he approached, and, looking through the bars of the main gate, he asked, What's going on, A person who has injured his leg has an infected wound, we urgently need antibiotics and other medicines, My orders are crystal-clear, no one is to be allowed to leave, and the only thing we can allow in is food, If the infection should get worse which looks all too certain, it could soon prove fatal, That isn't my affair, Then contact your superiors, Look here, blind man, let me tell you something, either the two of you get back to where you came from, or you'll be shot, Let's go, said the wife, there's nothing to be done, they're not to blame, they're terrified and are only obeying orders, I can't believe that this is happening, it's against all the rules of humanity, You'd better believe it, because the truth couldn't be clearer, Are you two still there, I'm going to count up to three and if they're not out of my sight by then, they can be sure they won't get back, ooone, twooo, threee, that's it, he was as good as his word, and turning to the soldiers, Even if it were my own brother, he did not explain to whom he was referring, whether it was to the man who had come to request medicines or to the other fellow with the infected leg. Inside, the wounded man wanted to know if they were going to supply them with medicines, How do you know I went to ask for supplies, asked the doctor, I guessed as much, after all, you are a doctor, I'm very sorry, Does that mean there will be no medicines, Yes, So, that's that.

The food had been carefully calculated for five people. There were bottles of milk and biscuits, but whoever had prepared their rations had forgotten to provide any glasses, nor were there any plates, or cutlery, these would probably come with the lunch. The doctor's wife went to give the wounded man something to drink, but he vomited. The taxi-driver complained that he did not like milk, he asked if he could have coffee. Some, after having eaten, went back to bed, the first blind man took his wife to visit the various places, they were the only two to leave the ward. The pharmacist's assistant asked to be allowed to speak to the doctor, he wanted the doctor to tell him if he had formed any opinion about their illness, I don't believe this can strictly be called an illness, the doctor started to explain, and then with much simplification, he summed up what he had researched in his reference books before becoming blind. Several beds further on, the taxi-driver was listening attentively, and when the doctor had finished his report, he shouted down the ward, I'll bet what happened is that the channels that go from the eyes to the brain got congested, Stupid fool, growled the pharmacist's assistant with indignation, Who knows, the doctor could not resist a smile, in truth the eyes are nothing more than lenses, it is the brain that actually does the seeing, just as an image appears on the film, and if the channels did get blocked up, as that man suggested, it's the same as a carburetor, if the fuel can't reach it, the engine does not work and the car won't go, as simple as that, as you can see, the doctor told the pharmacist's assistant, And how much longer, doctor, do you think we're going to be kept here, asked the hotel maid, At least for as long as we are unable to see, And how long will that be, Frankly, I don't think anyone knows, it's either something that will pass or it might go on for ever, How I'd love to know. The maid sighed and after several moments, I'd also like to know what happened to that girl, What girl, asked the pharmacist's assistant, That girl from the hotel, what a shock she gave me, there in the middle of the room, as naked as the day she was born, wearing nothing but a pair of dark glasses, and screaming that she was blind, she's probably the one who infected me. The doctor's wife looked, saw the girl slowly remove her dark glasses, hiding her movements, then put them under her pillow, while asking the boy with the squint, Would you like another biscuit, For the first time since she had arrived there, the doctor's wife felt as if she were behind a microscope and observing the behaviour of a number of human beings who did not even suspect her presence, and this suddenly struck her as being contemptible and obscene. I have no right to look if the others cannot see me, she thought to herself. With a shaky hand, the girl applied a few eye-drops. This would always allow her to say that these were not tears running from her eyes.

Hours later, when the loudspeaker announced that they should come and collect their lunch, the first blind man and the taxi-driver offered to go on this mission for which eyes were not essential, it was enough to be able to touch. The containers were some distance from the door that connected the hallway to the corridors, to find them they had to go down on all fours, sweeping the floor ahead with one arm outstretched, while the other served as a third paw, and if they had no difficulty in returning to the ward, it was because the doctor's wife had come up with the idea, which she was at pains to justify from personal experience, of tearing a blanket into strips, and using these to make an improvised rope, one end of which would remain attached to the outside handle of the door of the ward, while the other end would be tied in turn to the ankle of whoever had to go to fetch their food. The two men went off, the plates and cutlery arrived, but the portions were still only for five, in all likelihood the sergeant in charge of the patrol was unaware that there were six more blind people there, since once outside the entrance, even when paying attention to what might be happening behind the main door, in the shadows of the hallway, it was only by chance that anyone could be seen passing from one wing to another. The taxi-driver offered to go and demand the missing portions of food, and he went alone, he had no wish to be accompanied, We're not five, there are eleven of us, he shouted at the soldiers, and the same sergeant replied from the other side, Save your breath, there are many more to come yet, he said it in a tone of voice that must have seemed derisive to the taxi-driver, if we take into account the words spoken by the latter when he returned to the ward, It was as if he were making fun of me. They shared out the food, five portions divided by ten, since the wounded man was still refusing to eat, all he asked for was some water, and he begged them to moisten his lips. His skin was burning hot. And since he could not bear the contact and weight of the blanket on the wound for very long, he uncovered his leg from time to time, but the cold air in the ward soon obliged him to cover up again, and this went on for hours. He would moan at regular intervals with what sounded like a stifled gasp, as if the constant and persistent pain had suddenly got worse before he could get it under control.

In the middle of the afternoon, three more blind people arrived, expelled from the other wing. One was an employee from the surgery, whom the doctor's wife recognised at once, and the others, as destiny had decreed, were the man who had been with the girl with dark glasses in the hotel and the ill-mannered policeman who had taken her home. No sooner had they reached their beds and seated themselves, than the employee from the surgery began weeping in despair, the two men said nothing, as if still unable to grasp what had happened to them. Suddenly, from the street, came the cries of people shouting, orders being given in a booming voice, a rebellious uproar. The blind internees all turned their heads in the direction of the door and waited. They could not see, but knew what was about to happen within the next few minutes. The doctor's wife, seated on the bed beside her husband, said in a low voice, It had to be, the promised hell is about to begin. He squeezed her hand and murmured, Don't move, from now on there is nothing you can do. The shouting had died down, now a confusion of sounds was coming from the hallway, these were the blind, driven like sheep, bumping into each other, crammed together in the doorways, some lost their sense of direction and ended up in other wards, but the majority, stumbling along, huddled into groups or dispersed one by one, desperately waving their hands in the air like people drowning, burst into the ward in a whirlwind, as if being pushed from the outside by a bulldozer. A number of them fell and were trampled underfoot. Confined in the narrow aisles, the new arrivals gradually began filling the spaces between the beds, and here, like a ship caught in a storm that has finally managed to reach port, they took possession of their berths, in this case their beds, insisting that there was no room for anyone else, and that latecomers should find themselves a place elsewhere. From the far end, the doctor shouted that there were other wards, but the few who remained without a bed were frightened of getting lost in the labyrinth of rooms, corridors, closed doors, stairways they might only discover at the last minute. Finally they realised they could not stay there and, struggling to find the door by which they had entered, they ventured forth into the unknown. As if searching for one last safe refuge, the five blind internees in the second group had managed to occupy the beds, which, between them and those in the first group, had remained empty. Only the wounded man remained isolated, without protection, on bed fourteen on the left-hand side.

A quarter of an hour later, apart from some weeping and wailing, the discreet sounds of people settling down, calm rather than peace of mind was restored in the ward. All the beds were now occupied. The evening was drawing in, the dim lamps seemed to gain strength. Then they heard the abrupt voice of the loudspeaker. As on the first day, instructions were repeated as to how the wards should be maintained and the rules the internees should obey, The Government regrets having to enforce to the letter what it considers its right and duty, to protect the population with all the means at its disposal during this present crisis, etc., etc. When the voice stopped, an indignant chorus of protests broke out, We're locked up here, We're all going to die in here, This isn't right, Where are the doctors we were promised, this was something new, the authorities had promised doctors, medical assistance, perhaps even a complete cure. The doctor did not say that if they were in need of a doctor he was there at their disposal. He would never say that again. His hands alone are not enough for a doctor, a doctor cures with medicines, drugs, chemical compounds and combinations of this and that, and here there is no trace of any such materials, nor any hope of getting them. He did not even have the sight of his eyes to notice any sickly pallor, to observe any reddening of the peripheric circulation, how often, without any need for closer examination, these external signs proved to be as useful as an entire clinical history, or the colouring of mucus and pigmentation, with every probability of coming up with the right diagnosis, You won't escape this one. Since the nearby beds were all occupied, his wife could no longer keep him informed of what was happening, but he sensed the tense, uneasy atmosphere, bordering on open conflict, that had been created with the arrival of the latest group of internees. The very air in the ward seemed to have become heavier, emitting strong lingering odours, with sudden wafts that were simply nauseating, What will this place be like within a week, he asked himself, and it horrified him to think that in a week's time, they would still be confined here, Assuming there won't be any problems with food supplies, and who can be sure there isn't already a shortage, I doubt, for example, whether those outside have any idea from one minute to the next, how many of us are interned here, the question is how they will solve the matter of hygiene, I'm not referring to how we shall keep ourselves clean, struck blind only a few days ago and without anyone to help us, or whether the showers will work and for how long, I'm referring to the rest, to all the other likely problems, for if the lavatories should get blocked, even one of them, this place would be transformed into a sewer. He rubbed his face with his hands, he could feel the roughness of his beard after three days without shaving, It's preferable like this, I hope they won't have the unfortunate idea of sending us razor blades and scissors. He had everything necessary for shaving in his suitcase, but was conscious of the fact that it would be a mistake to try, And where, where, not here in the ward, among all these people, true my wife could shave me, but it would not be long before the others got wind of it and expressed surprise that there should be someone here capable of offering these services, and there inside, in the showers, such confusion, dear God, how we miss having our sight, to be able to see, to see, even if they were only faint shadows, to stand before the mirror, see a dark diffused patch and be able to say, That's my face, anything that has light does not belong to me.

The complaints subsided little by little, someone from one of the other wards came to ask if there was any food left over and the taxi-driver was quick to reply, Not a crumb, and the pharmacist's assistant to show some good will, mitigated the peremptory refusal, There might be more to come. But nothing would come. Darkness fell. From outside came neither food nor words. Cries could be heard coming from the adjoining ward, then there was silence, if anyone was weeping they did so very quietly, the weeping did not penetrate the walls. The doctor's wife went to see how the injured man was faring, It's me, she said, carefully raising the blanket. His leg presented a terrifying sight, completely swollen from the thigh down, and the wound, a black circle with bloody purplish blotches, had got much larger, as if the flesh had been stretched from inside. It gave off a stench that was both fetid and slightly sweet. How are you feeling, the doctor's wife asked him, Thanks for coming, Tell me how you're feeling, Bad, Are you in pain, Yes and no, What do you mean, It hurts, but it's as if the leg were no longer mine, as if it were separated from my body, I can't explain, it's a strange feeling, as if I were lying here watching my leg hurt me, That's because you're feverish, Probably, Now try to get some sleep. The doctor's wife placed her hand on his forehead, then made to withdraw, but before she could even wish him good-night, the invalid grabbed her by the arm and drew her towards him obliging her to get close to his face, I know you can see, he said in a low voice. The doctor's wife trembled with surprise and murmured, You're wrong, whatever put such an idea into your head, I see as much as anybody here, Don't try to deceive me, I know very well that you can see, but don't worry, I won't breathe a word to anyone, Sleep, sleep, Don't you trust me, Of course, I do, Don't you trust the word of a thief, I said I trusted you. Then why don't you tell me the truth, We'll talk tomorrow, now go to sleep, Yes, tomorrow, if I get that far, We mustn't think the worst, I do, or perhaps it's the fever thinking for me. The doctor's wife rejoined her husband and whispered in his ear, the wound looks awful, could it be gangrene, It seems unlikely in such a short time, Whatever it is, he's in a bad way, And those of us who are cooped up here, said the doctor in a deliberately loud voice, as if being struck blind were not enough, we might just as well have our hands and feet tied. From bed fourteen, left-hand side, the invalid replied, No one is going to tie me up, doctor.

The hours passed, one by one, the blind internees had fallen asleep. Some had covered their heads with a blanket, as if anxious that a pitch-black darkness, a real one, might extinguish once and for all the dim suns that their eyes had become. The three lamps suspended from the high ceiling, out of arm's reach, cast a dull, yellowish light over the beds, a light incapable of even creating shadows. Forty persons were sleeping or desperately trying to get to sleep, some were sighing and murmuring in their dreams, perhaps in their dream they could see what they were dreaming, perhaps they were saying to themselves, If this is a dream, I don't want to wake up. All their watches had stopped, either they had forgotten to wind them or had decided it was pointless, only that of the doctor's wife was still working. It was after three in the morning. Further along, very slowly, resting on his elbows, the thief raised his body into a sitting position. He had no feeling in his leg, nothing except the pain, the rest had ceased to belong to him. His knee was quite stiff. He rolled his body over on to the side of his healthy leg, which he allowed to hang out of the bed, then with both hands under his thigh, he tried to move his injured leg in the same direction. Like a pack of wolves suddenly roused, the pain went through his entire body, before returning to the dark crater from which it came. Resting on his hands, he gradually dragged his body across the mattress in the direction of the aisle. When he reached the rail at the foot of the bed, he had to rest. He was gasping for breath as if he were suffering from asthma, his head swayed on his shoulders, he could barely keep it upright. After several minutes, his breathing became more regular and he got slowly to his feet, putting his weight on his good leg. He knew that the other one would be no good to him, that he would have to drag it behind him wherever he went. He suddenly felt dizzy, an irrepressible shiver went through his body, the cold and fever made his teeth chatter. Supporting himself on the metal frames of the beds, passing from one to the other as if along a chain, he slowly advanced between the sleeping bodies. He dragged his injured leg like a bag. No one noticed him, no one asked, Where are you going at this hour, had anyone done so, he knew what he would reply, I'm off for a pee, he would say, he didn't want the doctor's wife to call out to him, she was someone he could not deceive or lie to, he would have to tell her what was on his mind, I can't go on rotting away in this hole, I realise that your husband has done everything he could to help me, but when I had to steal a car I wouldn't go and ask someone else to steal it for me, this is much the same, I'm the one who has to go, when they see me in this state they'll recognise at once that I'm in a bad way, put me in an ambulance and take me to a hospital, there must be hospitals just for the blind, one more won't make any difference, they'll treat my wound, cure me, I've heard that's what they do to those condemned to death, if they've got appendicitis they operate first and execute them afterwards, so that they die healthy, as far as I'm concerned, if they want, they can bring me back here, I don't mind. He advanced further, clenching his teeth to suppress any moaning, but he could not resist an anguished sob when, on reaching the end of the row, he lost his balance. He had miscounted the beds, he thought there was one more and came up against a void. Lying on the floor, he did not stir until he was certain that no one had woken up with the din made by his fall. Then he realised that this position was perfect for a blind person, if he were to advance on all fours he would find the way more easily. He dragged himself along until he reached the hallway, there he paused to consider how he should proceed, whether it would be better to call from the door or go up to the gate, taking advantage of the rope that had served as a handrail and almost certainly was still there. He knew full well that if he were to call for help from there, they would immediately order him to go back, but the alternative of having only a swaying rope as his support, after what he had suffered, notwithstanding the solid support of the beds, made him somewhat hesitant. After some minutes, he thought he had found the solution. I'll go on all fours, he thought, keeping under the rope, and from time to time I'll raise my hand to see whether I'm on the right track, this is just like stealing a car, ways and means can always be found. Suddenly, taking him by surprise, his conscience awoke and censured him bitterly for having allowed himself to steal a car from an unfortunate blind man. The fact that I'm in this situation now, he reasoned, isn't because I stole his car, it's because I accompanied him home, that was my big mistake. His conscience was in no mood for casuistic discussions, his reasons were simple and clear, A blind man is sacred, you don't steal from a blind man. Technically speaking, I didn't rob him, he wasn't carrying the car in his pocket, nor did I hold a gun to his head, the accused protested in his defence, Forget the sophisms, muttered his conscience, and get on your way.

The cold dawn air cooled his face. How well one breathes out here, he thought to himself. He had the impression that his leg was much less painful, but this did not surprise him, sometime before, and more than once, the same thing had happened. He was now outside the main door, he would soon be at the steps, That's going to be the most awkward bit, he thought, going down the steps head first. He raised one arm to check that the rope was there, and continued on. Just as he had foreseen, it was not easy to get from one step to the next, especially because of his leg which was no help to him, and the proof was not long in coming, when, in the middle of the steps, one of his hands having slipped, his body lurched to one side and was dragged along by the dead weight of his wretched leg. The pain came back instantly, as if someone were sawing, drilling, and hammering the wound, and even he was at a loss to explain how he prevented himself from crying out. For several long minutes, he remained prostrate, face down on the ground. A rapid gust of wind at ground level, left him shivering. He was wearing nothing but a shirt and his underpants. The wound was pressed against the ground, and he thought, It might get infected, a foolish thought, he was forgetting that he had been dragging his leg along the ground all the way from the ward, Well, it doesn't matter, they'll treat it before it turns infectious, he thought afterwards, to put his mind at rest, and he turned sideways to reach the rope more easily. He did not find it right away. He forgot that he had ended up in a vertical position in relation to the rope when he had rolled down the steps, but instinct told him that he should stay put. Then his reasoning guided him as he moved into a sitting position and then slowly back until his haunches made contact with the first step, and with a triumphant sense of victory he clutched the rough cord in his raised hand. Probably it was this same feeling that led him to discover almost immediately, a way of moving without his wound rubbing on the ground, by turning his back towards the main gate and sitting up and using his arms like crutches, as cripples used to do, he eased his seated body along in tiny stages. Backwards, yes, because in this case as in others, pulling was much easier than pushing. In this way, his leg suffered less, besides which the gentle slope of the forecourt going down towards the gate was a great help. As for the rope, he was in no danger of losing it, he was almost touching it with his head. He wondered whether he would have much further to go before reaching the main gate, getting there on foot, better still on two feet was not the same as advancing backwards half a hand's-breadth inch by inch. Forgetting for an instant that he was blind, he turned his head as if to confirm how far he still had to go and found himself confronted by the same impenetrable whiteness. Could it be night, could it be day, he asked himself, well if it were day they would already have spotted me, besides, they had only delivered breakfast and that was many hours ago. He was surprised to discover the speed and accuracy of his reasoning and how logical he could be, he saw himself in a different light, a new man, and were it not for this damn leg he would swear he had never felt so well in his entire life. His lower back came up against the metal plate at the bottom of the main gate. He had arrived. Huddled inside the sentry box to protect himself from the cold, the guard on duty thought he had heard faint noises he could not identify, in any case he did not think they could have come from inside, it must have been a sudden rustling of the trees, a branch the wind had caused to brush against the railings. These were followed by another noise, but this time it was different, a bang, the sound of crashing to be more precise, which could not have been caused by the wind. Nervously the guard came out of his sentry box, his finger on the trigger of his automatic rifle, and looked towards the main gate. He could not see anything. The noise, however, was back, louder, as if someone were scratching their fingernails on a rough surface. The metal plate on the gate, he thought to himself. He was about to head for the field tent where the sergeant was sleeping, but held back at the thought that if he raised a false alarm he would be given an earful, sergeants do not like being disturbed when they are sleeping, even when there is some good reason. He looked back at the main gate and waited in a state of tension. Very slowly, between two vertical iron bars, like a ghost, a white face began to appear. The face of a blind man. Fear made the soldier's blood freeze, and fear drove him to aim his weapon and release a blast of gunfire at close range.

The noise of the blast immediately brought the soldiers, half dressed, from their tents. These were the soldiers from the detachment entrusted with guarding the mental asylum and its inmates. The sergeant was already on the scene, What the hell is going on, A blind man, a blind man, stuttered the soldier,

Where, He was there and he pointed at the main gate with the butt of his weapon, I can see nothing there, He was there, I saw him. The soldiers had finished getting into their gear and were waiting in line, their rifles at the ready. Switch on the floodlight, the sergeant ordered. One of the soldiers got up on to the platform of the vehicle. Seconds later the blinding rays lit up the main gate and the front of the building. There's no one there, you fool, said the sergeant, and he was just about to deliver a few more choice insults in the same vein when he saw spreading out from under the gate, in that dazzling glare, a black puddle. You've finished him off, he said. Then, remembering the strict orders they had been given, he yelled, Get back, this is infectious. The soldiers drew back, terrified, but continued to watch the pool of blood that was slowly spreading in the gaps between the small cobblestones in the path. Do you think the man's dead, asked the sergeant, He must be, the shot struck him right in the face, replied the soldier, now pleased with the obvious demonstration of the accuracy of his aim. At that moment, another soldier shouted nervously, Sergeant, sergeant, look over there. Standing at the top of the steps, lit up by the white light coming from the searchlight, a number of blind internees could be seen, more than ten of them, Stay where you are, bellowed the sergeant, if you take another step, I'll blast the lot of you. At the windows of the buildings opposite, several people, woken up by the noise of gunshots, were looking out in terror. Then the sergeant shouted, Four of you come and fetch the body. Because they could neither see nor count, six blind men came forward. I said four, the sergeant bawled hysterically. The blind internees touched each other, then touched again, and two of them stayed behind. Holding on to the rope, the others began moving forward.

We must see if there's a spade or shovel or whatever around, something that can be used to dig, said the doctor. It was morning, with much effort they had brought the corpse into the inner courtyard, placed it on the ground amongst the litter and the dead leaves from the trees. Now they had to bury it. Only the doctor's wife knew the hideous state of the dead man's body, the face and skull blown to smithereens by the gunshots, three holes where bullets had penetrated the neck and the region of the breastbone. She also knew that in the entire building there was nothing that could be used to dig a grave. She had searched the parts of the asylum to which they had been confined and had found nothing apart from an iron bar. It would help but was not enough. And through the closed windows of the corridor that ran the full length of the wing reserved for those suspected of being infected, lower down on this side of the wall, she had seen the terrified faces of the people awaiting their turn, that inevitable moment when they would have to say to the others, I've gone blind, or when, if they were to try to conceal what had happened, some clumsy gesture might betray them, a movement of their head in search of shade, an unjustified stumble into someone sighted. All this the doctor also knew, what he had said was part of the deception they had both concocted, so that now his wife could say, And suppose we were to ask the soldiers to throw a shovel over the wall. A good idea, let's try, and everyone was agreed, only the girl with dark glasses expressed no opinion about this question of finding a spade or shovel, the only sounds coming from her meanwhile were tears and wailing, It was my fault, she sobbed, and it was true, no one could deny it, but it is also true, if this brings her any consolation, that if, before every action, we were to begin by weighing up the consequences, thinking about them in earnest, first the immediate consequences, then the probable, then the possible, then the imaginable ones, we should never move beyond the point where our first thought brought us to a halt. The good and the evil resulting from our words and deeds go on apportioning themselves, one assumes in a reasonably uniform and balanced way, throughout all the days to follow, including those endless days, when we shall not be here to find out, to congratulate ourselves or ask for pardon, indeed there are those who claim that this is the much-talked-of immortality, Possibly, but this man is dead and must be buried. Therefore the doctor and his wife went off to parley, the disconsolate girl with dark glasses said she was coming with them. Pricked by her conscience. No sooner did they appear at the main entrance than a soldier shouted, Halt, and as if afraid that this verbal command, however vigorous, might not be heeded, he fired into the air. Terrified, they retreated into the shadows of the hallway, behind the thick wooden panels of the open door. Then the doctor's wife advanced alone, from where she was standing she could watch the soldier's movements and take refuge in time, if necessary. We have nothing with which to bury the dead man, she said, we need a spade. At the main gate, but on the other side from where the blind man had fallen, another soldier appeared. He was a sergeant, but not the same one as before, What do you want, he shouted, We need a shovel or spade. There is no such thing here, on your way. We must bury the corpse, Don't bother about any burial, leave it there to rot, If we simply leave it lying there, the air will be infected, Then let it be infected and much good may it do you, Air circulates and moves around as much here as there. The relevance of her argument forced the soldier to reflect. He had come to replace the other sergeant, who had gone blind and been taken without delay to the quarters where the sick belonging to the army were interned. Needless to say, the air force and navy also had their own installations, but less extensive or important, the personnel of both forces being less numerous. The woman is right, reflected the sergeant, in a situation like this there is no doubt that one cannot be careful enough. As a safety measure, two soldiers equipped with gas masks, had already poured two large bottles of ammonia over the pool of blood, and the lingering fumes still brought tears to the soldiers' eyes and a stinging sensation to their throats and nostrils. The sergeant finally declared. I'll see what can be done, And what about our food, asked the doctor's wife, taking advantage of this opportunity to remind him, The food still hasn't arrived, In our wing alone there are more than fifty people, we're hungry, what you're sending us simply isn't enough, Supplying food is not the army's responsibility, Someone ought to be dealing with this problem, the Government undertook to feed us, Get back inside, I don't want to see anyone at this door, What about the spade, the doctor's wife insisted, but the sergeant had already gone. It was mid-morning when a voice came over the loudspeaker in the ward, Attention, attention, the internees brightened up, they thought this was an announcement about their food, but no, it was about the spade, Someone should come and fetch it, but not in a group, one person only should come forward, I'll go, for I've already spoken to them, said the doctor's wife. The moment she went through the main entrance door, she saw the spade. From the position and distance to where it had landed, closer to the gate than the steps, it must have been thrown over the fence, I mustn't forget that I'm supposed to be blind, the doctor's wife thought, Where is it, she asked, Go down the stairs and I'll guide you, replied the sergeant, you're doing fine, now keep going in the same direction, like so, like so, stop, turn slightly to the right, no, to the left, less, less than that, now forward, so long as you keep going, you'll come right up against it, shit, I told you not to change direction, cold, cold, you're getting warmer again, warmer still, right, now take a half turn and I'll guide you from there, I don't want you going round and round in circles and ending up at the gate, Don't you worry, she thought, from here I'll make straight for the door, after all, what does it matter, even if you were to suspect that I'm not blind, what do I care, you won't be coming in here to take me away. She slung the spade over her shoulder like a gravedigger on his way to work, and walked in the direction of the door without faltering for a moment, Did you see that, sergeant, exclaimed one of the soldiers, you would think she could see. The blind learn quickly how to find their way around, the sergeant explained confidently.

It was hard work digging a grave. The soil was hard, trampled down, there were tree roots just below the surface. The taxi-driver, the two policemen and the first blind man took it in turns to dig. Confronted by death, what is expected of nature is that rancour should lose its force and poison, it is true that people say that past hatreds die hard, and of this there is ample proof in literature and life, but the feeling here, deep down, as it were, was not hatred and, in no sense old, for how does the theft of a car compare with the life of the man who stole it, and especially given the miserable state of his corpse, for one does not need eyes to know that this face has neither nose nor mouth. They were unable to dig any deeper than about three feet. Had the dead man been fat, his belly would have been sticking out above ground level, but the thief was skinny, a real bag of bones, even skinnier after the fasting of recent days, the grave was big enough for two corpses his size. There were no prayers for the dead. We could have put a cross there, the girl with dark glasses reminded them, she spoke from remorse, but as far as anyone there was aware while alive, the deceased had never given a thought to God or religion, best to say nothing, if any other attitude is justified in the face of death, besides, bear in mind that making a cross is much less easy than it may seem, not to mention the little time it would last with all these blind people around who cannot see where they are treading. They returned to the ward. In the busier places, so long as it is not completely open, like the yard, the blind no longer lose their way, with one arm held out in front and several fingers moving like the antennae of insects, they can find their way everywhere, it is even probable that in the more gifted of the blind there soon develops what is referred to as frontal vision. Take the doctor's wife, for example, it is quite extraordinary how she manages to get around and orient herself through this veritable maze of rooms, nooks and corridors, how she knows precisely where to turn the corner, how she can come to a halt before a door and open it without a moment's hesitation, how she has no need to count the beds before reaching her own. At this moment she is seated on her husband's bed, she is talking to him, as usual in a low voice, one can see these are educated people, and they always have something to say to each other, they are not like the other married couple, the first blind man and his wife, after those first emotional moments on being reunited, they have scarcely spoken, in all probability, their present unhappiness outweighs their past love, with time they will get used to this situation. The one person who is forever complaining of feeling hungry is the boy with the squint, despite the fact that the girl with the dark glasses has practically taken the food from her own mouth to give him. Many hours have passed since he last asked about his mummy, but no doubt he will start to miss her again after having eaten, when his body finds itself released from the brute selfishness that stems from the simple, but pressing need to sustain itself. Whether because of what happened early that morning, or for reasons beyond our ken, the sad truth is that no containers were delivered at breakfast time. It is nearly time for lunch, almost one o'clock on the watch the doctor's wife has just furtively consulted, therefore it is not surprising that the impatience of their gastric juices has driven some of the blind internees, both from this wing and from the other, to go and wait in the hallway for the food to arrive, and this for two excellent reasons, the public one, on the part of some, because in this way they would gain time, the private one, on the part of others, because, as everyone knows, first come first served. In all, there were about ten blind internees listening for the noise of the outer gate when it was opened, for the footsteps of the soldiers who would deliver those blessed containers. In their turn, fearful of suddenly being stricken by blindness if they were to come into close contact with the blind waiting in the hallway, the contaminated internees from the left wing dare not leave, but several of them are peering through a gap in the door, anxiously awaiting their turn. Time passed. Tired of waiting, some of the blind internees had sat down on the ground, later two or three of them returned to their wards. Shortly afterwards, the unmistakable metallic creaking of the gate could be heard. In their excitement, the blind internees, pushing each other, began moving in the direction where, judging from the sounds outside, they imagined the door to be, but suddenly, overcome by a vague sense of disquiet that they would not have time to define or explain, they came to a halt and retreated in confusion, while the footsteps of the soldiers bringing their food and those of the armed escort accompanying them could already be heard quite clearly.

Still suffering from the shock of the tragic episode of the previous night, the soldiers who delivered the containers had agreed that they would not leave them within reach of the doors leading to the wings, as they had more or less done before, they would just dump them in the hallway, and retreat. Let them sort it out for themselves. The dazzle of the strong light from outside and the abrupt transition into the shadows of the hallway prevented them at first from seeing the group of blind internees. But they soon spotted them. Howling in terror, they dropped the containers on the ground and fled like madmen straight out of the door. The two soldiers forming the escort, who were waiting outside, reacted admirably in the face of danger. Mastering, God alone knows how and why, their legitimate fear, they advanced to the threshold of the door and emptied their magazines. The blind internees fell one on top of the other, and, as they fell, their bodies were still being riddled with bullets which was a sheer waste of ammunition, it all happened so incredibly slowly, one body, then another, it seemed they would never stop falling, as you sometimes see in films and on television. If we are still in an age when a soldier has to account for the bullets fired, they will swear on the flag that they acted in legitimate defence, as well as in defence of their unarmed comrades who were on a humanitarian mission and suddenly found themselves threatened and outnumbered by a group of blind internees. In a mad rush they retreated to the gate, covered by the rifles which the soldiers on patrol were pointing unsteadily between the railings as if the blind internees who had survived, were about to make a retaliatory attack. His face drained of colour, one of the soldiers who had fired, said nervously, You won't get me going back in there at any price. From one moment to the next, on this same day, when evening was falling, at the hour of changing guard, he became one more blind man among the other blind men, what saved him was that he belonged to the army, otherwise he would have remained there along with the blind internees, the companions of those whom he had shot dead, and God knows what they might have done to him. The sergeant's only comment was, It would have been better to let them die of hunger, when the beast dies, the poison dies with it. As we know, others had often said and thought the same, happily, some precious remnant of concern for humanity prompted him to add, From now on, we shall leave the containers at the halfway point, let them come and fetch them, we'll keep them under surveillance, and at the slightest suspicious movement, we fire. He headed for the command post, switched on the microphone and, putting the words together as best he could, calling to mind words he remembered hearing on vaguely comparable occasions, he announced, The army regrets having been forced to repress with weapons a seditious movement responsible for creating a situation of imminent risk, for which the army was neither directly nor indirectly to blame, and you are advised that from now on the internees will collect their food outside the building, and will suffer the consequences should there be any attempt to repeat the disruption that took place now and last night. He paused, uncertain how he should finish, he had forgotten his own words, he certainly had them, but could only repeat, We were not to blame, we were not to blame.

Inside the building, the blast of gunfire deafeningly echoing in the confined space of the hallway, had caused the utmost panic. At first it was thought that the soldiers were about to burst into the wards and shoot everything in sight, that the Government had changed its tactics, had opted for the wholesale liquidation of the internees, some crawled under their beds, others, in sheer terror, did not move, some might have thought it was better so, better no health than too little, if a person has to go, let it be quick. The first to react were the contaminated internees. They had started to flee when the shooting broke out, but then the silence encouraged them to go back, and once again they headed for the door leading into the hallway. They saw the bodies lying in a heap, the blood wending its way sinuously on the tiled floor where it slowly spread, as if it were a living thing, and then the containers with food. Hunger drove them on, there stood that much desired sustenance, true it was intended for the blind, their own food was still on its way, in accordance with the regulations, but who cares about the regulations, no one can see us, the candle that lights the way burns brightest, as the ancients have continuously reminded us throughout the ages, and the ancients know about these things. Their hunger, however, had the strength only to take them three steps forward, reason intervened and warned them that for anybody imprudent enough to advance there was danger lurking in those lifeless bodies, above all, in that blood, who could tell what vapours, what emanations, what poisonous miasmas might not already be oozing forth from the open wounds of the corpses. They're dead, they can't do any harm, someone remarked, the intention was to reassure himself and others, but his words made matters worse, it was true that these blind internees were dead, that they could not move, see, could neither stir nor breathe, but who can say that this white blindness is not some spiritual malaise, and if we assume this to be the case, then the spirits of those blind casualties have never been as free as they are now, released from their bodies, and therefore free to do whatever they like, above all, to do evil, which, as everyone knows, has always been the easiest thing to do. But the containers of food, standing there exposed, immediately attracted their attention, such are the demands of the stomach, they heed nothing even when it is for their own good. From one of the containers leaked a white liquid which was slowly spreading towards the pool of blood, to all appearances it was milk, the colour unmistakable. More courageous, or simply more fatalistic, the distinction is not always easy to make, two of the contaminated internees stepped forward, and they were just about to lay their greedy hands on the first container when a group of blind internees appeared in the doorway leading to the other wing. The imagination can play such tricks, especially in morbid circumstances such as these, that for these two men who had gone on a foray, it was as if the dead had suddenly risen from the ground, as blind as before, no doubt, but much more dangerous, for almost certainly filled by a spirit of revenge. They prudently backed away in silence towards the entrance to their wing, perhaps the blind internees were beginning to take care of the corpses as charity and respect decreed, or, if not, they might leave behind without noticing one of the containers, however small, in fact there were not all that many contaminated internees there, perhaps the best solution would be to ask them, Please, take pity on us, at least leave a small container for us, after what has happened it is most likely that no more food will be delivered today. The blind moved as one would expect of the blind, groping their way, stumbling, dragging their feet, yet as if organised, they knew how to distribute tasks efficiently, some of them splashing about in the sticky blood and milk, began at once to withdraw and transport the corpses to the yard, others dealt with the eight containers, one by one, that had been dumped by the soldiers. Among the blind internees there was a woman who gave the impression of being everywhere at the same time, helping to load, acting as if she were guiding the men, something that was obviously impossible for a blind woman, and, whether by chance or intentionally, more than once she turned her head towards the wing where the contaminated were interned, as if she could see them or sense their presence. In a short time the hallway was empty, with no other traces than the huge bloodstain, and another small one alongside, white, from the milk that had spilled, apart from these only criss-crossing footprints in red or simply wet. Resigned, the contaminated internees closed the door and went in search of crumbs, they were so downhearted that one of them was on the point of saying, and this shows just how desperate they were, If we really have to end up blind, if that is our fate, we might as well move over into the other wing now, there at least we'll have something to eat, Perhaps the soldiers will still bring our rations, someone suggested, Have you ever been in the army, another asked him, No, Just as I thought.

Bearing in mind that the dead belonged to the one as much as the other, the occupants of the first and second wards gathered together in order to decide whether they should eat first and then bury the corpses, or the other way round. No one seemed interested in knowing who had died. Five of them had installed themselves in the second ward, difficult to say if they had already known each other, or if they did not, if they had the time and inclination to introduce themselves to each other and unburden their hearts. The doctor's wife could not remember having seen them when they arrived. The remaining four, yes, these she recognised, they had slept with her, in a manner of speaking, under the same roof, although this was all she knew about one of them, and how could she know more, a man with any self-respect does not go around discussing his private affairs with the first person he meets, such as having been in a hotel room where he made love to a girl with dark glasses, who, in her turn, if we mean her, has no idea that he has been interned here and that she is still so close to the man who was the cause of her seeing everything white. The taxi-driver and the two policemen were the other casualties, three robust fellows who could take care of themselves, whose professions meant, in different ways, looking after others, and in the end there they lie, cruelly mowed down in their prime and waiting for others to decide their fate. They will have to wait until those who survived have finished eating, not because of the usual egoism of the living, but because someone sensibly remembered that to bury nine corpses in that hard soil and with only one spade was a chore that would take until dinner-time at least. And since it would not be admissible that the volunteers endowed with good will should work while the others stuffed their bellies, it was decided to leave the corpses until later. The food arrived in individual portions, therefore easy to share out, that's yours, and yours, until there was no more. But the anxiety of some of the less fair-minded blind internees came to complicate what in normal circumstances would have been so straightforward, and although a serene and impartial judgment cautions us to admit that the excesses that took place had some justification, we need only remember, for example, that no one could know, at the outset, whether there would be enough food for everyone. In fact, it is fairly clear that it is not easy to count blind people or to distribute rations without eyes capable of seeing either the rations or the people. Moreover, some of the inmates from the second ward, with more than reprehensible dishonesty, tried to give the impression that there were more of them than there actually were. As always, this is where the presence of the doctor's wife proved to be useful. A few timely words have always managed to resolve problems that a verbose speech would only make worse. No less ill-intentioned and perverse were those who not only tried, but actually succeeded in receiving double rations. The doctor's wife was aware of this abuse, but thought it wise to say nothing. She could not even bear to think of the consequences that would ensue if it were to be discovered that she was not blind, at the very least she would find herself at the beck and call of everyone, at worst, she might become the slave of some of them. The idea, aired at the outset, that someone should assume responsibility for each ward, might have helped, who knows? to solve these difficulties and others, alas, more serious, on condition however, that the authority of the person in charge, undeniably fragile, undeniably precarious, undeniably called into question at every moment, should be clearly exercised for the benefit of all and as such be acknowledged by the majority. Unless we succeed in this, she thought, we shall end up murdering one another in here. She promised herself that she would discuss these delicate matters with her husband and went on sharing out the rations.

Some out of indolence, others because they had a delicate stomach, had no inclination to go and practise grave-digging just after they had eaten. Because of his profession, the doctor felt more responsible than the others, and when he said without much enthusiasm, Let's go and bury the corpses, there was not a single volunteer. Stretched out on their beds, the blind internees were interested only in being left in peace to digest their food, some fell asleep immediately, hardly surprising, after the frightening experience they had been through, the body, even though poorly nourished, abandoned itself to the slow workings of digestive chemistry. Later, as evening was drawing in, when, because of the progressive waning of natural light, the dim lamps appeared to gain some strength, showing at the same time, weak as they were, the little purpose they served, the doctor, accompanied by his wife, persuaded two men from his ward to accompany them to the compound, even if only to balance out the work that had to be done and separate the corpses that were already stiff, once it had been decided that each ward would bury its own dead. The advantage enjoyed by these blind men was what might be called the illusion of light. In fact, it made no difference to them whether it was day or night, the first light of dawn or the evening twilight, the silent hours of early morning or the bustling din of noon, these blind people were for ever surrounded by a resplendent whiteness, like the sun shining through mist. For the latter, blindness did not mean being plunged into banal darkness, but living inside a luminous halo. When the doctor let slip that they were going to separate the corpses, the first blind man, who was one of those who had agreed to help him, wanted to know how they would be able to recognise them, a logical question on the part of a blind man which left the doctor in some confusion. This time his wife thought it would be unwise to come to his assistance for fear of giving the game away. The doctor got out of the difficulty gracefully by the radical method of coming clean, that is to say, by acknowledging his mistake, People, he said, in the tone of voice of someone amused at his own expense, get so used to having eyes that they think they can use them when they no longer serve for anything, in fact, all we know is that there are four from our ward here, the taxi-driver, the two policemen, and one other who was with us, therefore the solution is to pick up four of these corpses at random, bury them with due respect, and in this way we fulfill our obligation. The first blind man agreed, his companion likewise, and once again, taking it in turn, they began digging graves. These helpers would never come to know, blind as they were, that, without exception, the corpses buried were precisely those of whom they had been speaking, nor need we mention the work done, seemingly at random, by the doctor, his hand guided by that of his wife, she would grab a leg or arm, and all he had to say was, This one. When they had already buried two corpses, there finally emerged from the ward, three men disposed to help, most likely they would have been less willing had someone told them that it was already the dead of night. Psychologically, even when a man is blind, we must acknowledge that there is a considerable difference between digging graves by the light of day and after the sun has gone down. The moment they were back in the ward, sweating, covered in earth, the sickly smell of decomposed flesh still in their nostrils, the voice over the loudspeaker repeated the usual instructions. There was no reference whatsoever to what had happened, no mention of gunfire or casualties shot at point-blank range. Warnings such as, To abandon the building without any authorisation will mean immediate death, or The internees will bury the corpses in the grounds without any formalities, now, thanks to the harsh experience of life, supreme mistress of all disciplines, these warnings took on real meaning, while the announcement that promised containers of food three times a day seemed grotesquely ironic or, worse, contemptuous. When the voice fell silent, the doctor, on his own, because he was getting to know every nook and cranny in the place, went to the door of the other ward to inform the inmates, We have buried our dead, Well, if you've buried some, you can bury the rest, replied a man's voice from within, The agreement was that each ward would bury its own dead, we counted four and buried them, That's fine, tomorrow we'll deal with those from here, said another masculine voice, and then in a different tone of voice, he asked, Has no more food turned up, No, replied the doctor, But the loudspeaker said three times a day, I doubt whether they are likely always to keep their promise, Then we'll have to ration the food that might arrive, said a woman's voice, That seems a good idea, if you like, we can talk about it tomorrow, Agreed, said the woman. The doctor was already on the point of leaving when the voice of the first man to speak could be heard, Who's giving the orders here, He paused, expecting to be given an answer, and it came from the same feminine voice, Unless we organise ourselves in earnest, hunger and fear will take over here, it is shameful that we didn't go with the others to bury the dead, Why don't you go and do the burying since you're so clever and sure of yourself, I cannot go alone but I'm prepared to help, There's no point in arguing, intervened another masculine voice, we'll settle this first thing in the morning. The doctor sighed, life together was going to be difficult. He was already heading back to his ward when he felt a pressing need to relieve himself. At the spot where he found himself, he was not sure that he would be able to find the lavatories, but he decided to take a chance. He was hoping that someone would at least have remembered to leave there the toilet paper which had been delivered with the containers of food. He got lost twice on the way and was in some distress because he was beginning to feel desperate and just when he could hold back no longer, he was finally able to take down his trousers and crouch over the open latrine. The stench choked him. He had the impression of having stepped on some soft pulp, the excrement of someone who had missed the hole of the latrine or who had decided to relieve himself without any consideration for others. He tried to imagine what the place must look like, for him it was all white, luminous, resplendent, he had no way of knowing whether the walls and ground were white and he came to the absurd conclusion that the light and whiteness there were giving off the awful stench. We shall go mad with horror, he thought. Then he tried to clean himself but there was no paper. He ran his hand over the wall behind him, where he expected to find the rolls of toilet paper or nails, where in the absence of anything better, any old scraps of paper had been stuck up. Nothing. He felt unhappy, disconsolate, more unfortunate than he could bear, crushed there, protecting his trousers which were brushing against that disgusting floor, blind, blind, blind, and, unable to control himself, he began to weep quietly. Fumbling, he took a few steps and bumped into the opposite wall. He stretched out one arm, then the other, and finally found a door. He could hear the shuffling footsteps of someone who must also have been looking for the lavatories, and who kept tripping, Where the hell are they? the person was muttering in a neutral voice, as if deep down, he was not all that interested in finding out. He passed close to the toilets without realising there was someone there, but no matter, the situation did not degenerate into indecency, if it could be called that, a man caught in an embarrassing situation, his clothes in disarray, at the last minute, moved by a disconcerting sense of shame, the doctor had pulled up his trousers. Then he lowered them, when he thought he was alone, but not in time, he knew he was dirty, dirtier than he could ever remember having been in his life. There are many ways of becoming an animal, he thought, this is just the first of them. However, he could not really complain, he still had someone who did not mind cleaning him.

Lying on their beds, the blind internees waited for sleep to take pity on their misery. Discreetly, as if there was some danger that others might see this distressing sight, the doctor's wife had helped her husband to clean himself as well as she could. There was now that sorrowful silence one finds in hospitals when the patients are asleep and suffer even as they sleep. Sitting up and alert, the doctor's wife looked at the beds, at the shadowy forms, the fixed pallor of a face, an arm that moved while dreaming. She wondered whether she would ever go blind like them, what inexplicable reasons had saved her from blindness so far. With a weary gesture, she raised her hands to draw back her hair, and thought, We're all going to stink to high heaven. At that moment sighs could be heard, moaning, tiny cries, muffled at first, sounds that seemed to be words, that ought to be words, but whose meaning got lost in the crescendo that transformed them into shouts and grunts and finally heavy, stertorous breathing. Someone protested at the far end of the ward. Pigs, they're like pigs. They were not pigs, only a blind man and a blind woman who probably knew nothing more about each other than this.

An empty belly wakes up early. Some of the blind internees opened their eyes when morning was still some way off, and in their case it was not so much because of hunger, but because their biological clock, or whatever you call it, was no longer working properly, they assumed it was daylight, then thought, I've overslept and soon realised that they were wrong, their fellow-inmates were snoring their heads off, there was no mistaking that. Now as we know from books, and even more so from personal experience, anyone who gets up early by inclination or has been forced to rise early out of necessity finds it intolerable that others should go on sleeping soundly, and with good reason in the case to which we are referring, for there is a marked difference between a blind person who is sleeping and a blind person who has opened his eyes to no purpose. These observations of a psychological nature, whose subtlety has no apparent relevance considering the extraordinary scale of the cataclysm which our narrative is struggling to relate, only serve to explain why all the blind internees were awake so early, some, as was said at the outset, were roused by the churning of their empty stomachs in need of food, others were dragged from their sleep by the nervous impatience of the early risers, who did not hesitate to make more noise than the inevitable and tolerable when people cohabit in barracks and wards. Here there are not only persons of discretion and good manners, but some real vulgarians who relieve themselves each morning by coughing up phlegm and passing wind without regard for anyone who might be present, and if truth be told, they behave just as badly for most of the day, making the atmosphere increasingly heavy, and there is nothing to be done, the only opening is the door, the windows cannot be reached they are so high.

Lying beside her husband, as close as possible given the narrowness of the bed, but also out of choice, how much it had cost them in the middle of the night to maintain some decorum, not to behave like those whom someone had referred to as pigs, the doctor's wife looked at her watch. It was twenty-three minutes past two. She took a closer look, saw that the second hand was not moving. She had forgotten to wind up the wretched watch, or wretched her, wretched me, for not even this simple task had she remembered to carry out after only three days of isolation. Unable to control herself, she burst into convulsive weeping, as if the worst of all disasters had suddenly befallen her. The doctor thought his wife had gone blind, that what he so greatly feared had finally happened, and, beside himself, was on the point of asking, Have you gone blind, when at the last minute he heard her whisper, No, no, it isn't that, it isn't that, and then in a drawn-out whisper, almost inaudible, both their heads under the blanket, How stupid of me, I forgot to wind my watch, and she went on sobbing, inconsolable. Getting up from her bed on the other side of the passageway, the girl with dark glasses moved in the direction of the sobbing with arms outstretched, You're upset, can I get you anything, she asked as she advanced, and touched the two bodies on the bed with her hands. Discretion demanded that she should withdraw immediately, and this certainly was the order that came from her brain, but her hands did not obey, they simply made more subtle contact, gently caressing the thick, warm blanket. Can I get you anything, the girl asked once more, and, by now she had removed her hands, raised them until they became lost in that sterile whiteness, helpless. Still sobbing, the doctor's wife got out of bed, embraced the girl and said, It's nothing, I just suddenly felt sad, If you who are so strong are becoming disheartened, then there really is no salvation for us, complained the girl. Calmer now, the doctor's wife thought, looking straight at her, The signs of conjunctivitis have almost gone, what a pity I cannot tell her, she would be pleased. Yes, in all probability she would be pleased, although any such satisfaction would be absurd, not so much because the girl was blind, but since all the others there were blind as well, what good would it do her to have beautiful bright eyes such as these if there is no one to see them. The doctor's wife said, We all have our moments of weakness, just as well that we are still capable of weeping, tears are often our salvation, there are times when we would die if we did not weep, There is no salvation for us, the girl with dark glasses repeated, Who can tell, this blindness is not like any other, it might disappear as suddenly as it came, It will come too late for those who have died, We all have to die, But not to be killed and I have killed someone, Don't blame yourself, it was a question of circumstances, here we are all guilty and innocent, much worse was the behaviour of the soldiers who are here to protect us, and even they can invoke the greatest of all excuses, fear, What if the wretched fellow did fondle me, he would be alive right now, and my body would be no different from what it is now, Think no more about it, rest, try to sleep. She accompanied the girl to her bed, Come now, get into bed, You're very kind, said the girl, then lowering her voice, I don't know what to do, it's almost time for my period and I haven't brought any sanitary napkins, Don't worry, I have some. The hands of the girl with dark glasses searched for somewhere to hold on to, but it was the doctor's wife who gently held them in her own hands, Rest, rest. The girl closed her eyes, remained like that for a minute, she might have fallen asleep were it not for the quarrel that suddenly erupted, someone had gone to the lavatory and on his return found his bed occupied, no harm was meant, the other fellow had got up for the same reason, they had passed each other on the way, and obviously it did not occur to either of them to say, Take care not to get into the wrong bed when you come back. Standing there, the doctor's wife watched the two blind men who were arguing, she noticed they made no gestures, that they barely moved their bodies, having quickly learned that only their voice and hearing now served any purpose, true, they had their arms, that they could fight, grapple, come to blows, as the saying goes, but a bed swapped by mistake was not worth so much fuss, if only all life's deceptions were like this one, and all they had to do was to come to some agreement, Number two is mine, yours is number three, let that be understood once and for all, Were it not for the fact that we're blind this mix-up would never have happened, You're right, our problem is that we're blind. The doctor's wife said to her husband, The whole world is right here.

Not quite all of it. The food, for example, was there on the outside and taking ages to arrive. From both wards, some men had gone to station themselves in the hallway, waiting for orders to come over the loudspeaker. They kept shuffling their feet, nervous and impatient. They knew that they would have to go out to the forecourt to fetch the containers which the soldiers, fulfilling their promise, would leave in the area between the main gate and the steps, and they feared that there might be some ploy or snare, How do we know that they won't start firing, After what they've done already, they're capable of anything, They are not to be trusted, You won't get me going out there, Nor me, Someone has to go if we want to eat, I don't know if it isn't better to die being shot than to die of hunger, I'm going, Me too, We don't all have to go, The soldiers might not like it, Or get worried and think we're trying to escape, that's probably why they shot the man with the injured leg, We've got to make up our minds, We can't be too careful, remember what happened yesterday, nine casualties no more no less, The soldiers were afraid of us, And I'm afraid of them, What I'd like to know is if they too go blind, Who's they, The soldiers, In my opinion they ought to be the first. They were all in agreement, yet without asking themselves why, and there was no one there to give them the one good reason, Because then they would not be able to aim their rifles. The time passed and passed, and the loudspeaker remained silent. Have you already tried to bury your dead, a blind man from the first ward asked for the want of something to say, Not yet, They're beginning to smell and infect everything around, Well let them infect everything and stink to high heaven, as far as I'm concerned, I've no intention of doing anything until I've eaten, as someone once said, first you eat then you wash the pan, That isn't the custom, your maxim is wrong, generally it is after burying their dead that the mourners eat and drink, With me it's the other way round. After a few minutes one of these blind men said, There's one thing that bothers me, What's that, How are we going to distribute the food, As we did before, we know how many we are, the rations are counted, everyone receives his share, it's the simplest and fairest way, But it didn't work, some internees were left without any food, And there were also those who got double rations, The distribution was badly organised, It will always be badly organised unless people show some respect and discipline, If only we had someone here who could see just a little, Well, he'd try coming up with some ruse in order to make sure he got the lion's share, As the saying goes, in the country of the blind, the one-eyed man is king, Forget about sayings, But this is not the same, Here not even the cross-eyed would be saved, As I see it, the best solution would be to share the food out in equal parts throughout the wards, then each internee can be self-sufficient, Who spoke, It was me, Who's me, Me, which ward are you from, From ward two, Who would have believed such cunning, since ward two has fewer patients such an arrangement would be to their advantage and they would get more to eat than us, since our ward is full, I was only trying to be helpful, the proverb also says that if the one who does the sharing out fails to get the better part, he's either a fool or a dullard, Shit, that's quite enough of proverbs, these sayings get on my nerves, What we should do is to take all the food to the refectory, each ward elects three of its inmates to do the sharing out, so that with six people counting there would be little danger of abuse and deception, And how are we to know that they are telling the truth when the others say how many there are in their ward, We're dealing with honest people, Is that a proverb too, No, that's me saying it, My dear fellow, I don't know about honest but we're certainly hungry.

As if it had been waiting all this time for the code word, some cue, an open sesame, the voice finally came over the loudspeaker, Attention, attention, the internees may come and collect their food, but be careful, if anyone gets too close to the gate they will receive a preliminary warning, and unless they turn back immediately, the second warning will be a bullet. The blind internees advanced slowly, some, more confident, towards the right where they thought they would find the door, the others, less sure of their ability to get their bearings, preferred to slide along the wall, in this way there was no possibility of mistaking the way, when they reached the corner all they had to do was to follow the wall at a right angle and there they would find the door. The hectoring voice over the loudspeaker impatiently repeated the summons. The change of tone, unmistakable even for those who had no reason to be suspicious, terrified the blind internees. One of them declared, I'm not budging from here, what they want to do is to catch us outside and then kill us all, I'm not moving either, said another, Nor me, chipped in a third. They were frozen to the spot, undecided, some wanted to go, but fear was getting the better of all of them. The voice came again, Unless within the next three minutes someone appears to collect the containers, we shall take them away. This threat failed to overcome their fear, only pushed it into the innermost caverns of their mind, like hunted animals that await an opportunity to attack. Each one trying to hide behind the other, the blind internees moved fearfully out on to the landing at the top of the steps. They could not see that the containers were not alongside the guide rope where they expected to find them, for they were not to know that the soldiers, out of fear of being contaminated, had refused to go anywhere near the rope which the blind internees were holding on to. The food containers were stacked up together, more or less at the spot where the doctor's wife had collected the spade. Come forward, come forward, ordered the sergeant. In some confusion, the blind internees tried to get into a line so as to advance in orderly fashion, but the sergeant bellowed at them, You won't find the containers there, let go of the rope, let go of it, move over to the right, *your* right, *your* right, fools, you don't need eyes to know which side you have your right hand. The warning was given just in time, some of the blind internees who were punctilious in these matters, had interpreted the order literally, if it was on the right, logically that would mean on the right of the person speaking, therefore they were trying to pass under the rope to go in search of the containers which were God knows where. In different circumstances, this grotesque spectacle would have caused the most restrained spectator to burst into howls of laughter, it was too funny for words, some of the blind internees advancing on all fours, their faces practically touching the ground as if they were pigs, one arm outstretched in mid-air, while others, perhaps afraid that the white space, without a roof to protect them, would swallow them up, clung desperately to the rope and listened attentively, expecting to hear at any minute that first exclamation of triumph once the containers were discovered. The soldiers would have liked to aim their weapons and, without compunction, shoot down those imbeciles moving before their eyes like lame crabs, waving their unsteady pincers in search of their missing leg. They knew what had been said in the barracks that morning by the regimental commander, that the problem of these blind internees could be resolved only by physically wiping out the lot of them, those already there and those still to come, without any phoney humanitarian considerations, his very words, just as one amputates a gangrenous limb in order to save the rest of the body, The rabies of a dead dog, he said, to illustrate the point, is cured by nature. For some of the soldiers, less sensitive to the beauties of figurative language, it was difficult to understand what a dog with rabies had to do with the blind, but the word of a regimental commander, once again figuratively speaking, is worth its weight in gold, no man rises to so high a rank in the army without being right in everything he thinks, says and does. A blind man had finally bumped into the containers and called out as he got hold of them, They're here, they're here, if this man were to recover his eyesight one day, he would certainly not announce the wonderful news with greater joy. Within seconds, the others had pounced on the containers, a confusion of arms and legs, each man pulling a container towards his side and claiming priority, I'll carry it, no, I will. Those who were still holding on to the rope began to feel nervous, they now had something else to fear, that they might be excluded on account of their idleness or cowardice, when the food was shared out, Ah, you men refused to get down on the ground with your arse in the air and risk the danger of being shot, so nothing to eat for you, remember the proverb, nothing ventured nothing gained. Persuaded by these sententious words, one of the blind men let go of the rope and went, with arms outstretched, in the direction of the uproar, They're not going to leave me out, but suddenly the voices fell silent and there was only the noise of people crawling on the ground, muffled interjections, a dispersed and confused mass of sounds coming from everywhere and nowhere. He paused, undecided, tried to go back to the security of the rope, but he had lost his sense of direction, there are no stars in his white sky, and what could now be heard was the sergeant's voice as it ordered those arguing over the containers to get back to the steps, for what he was saying could have been meant only for them, to arrive where you want to be, everything depends on where you are. There were no longer any blind internees holding on to the rope, all they had to do was to return the way they had come, and now they were waiting at the top of the steps for the others to arrive. The blind man who had lost his way did not dare to move from where he was. In a state of anguish, he let out a loud cry, Please, help me, unaware that the soldiers had their rifles trained on him as they waited for him to tread on that invisible line dividing life from death. Are you going to stay there all day, you blind bat, asked the sergeant, in a somewhat nervous voice, the truth being that he did not share the opinion of his commander, Who can guarantee that the same fate won't come knocking at the door tomorrow, as for the soldiers it is well known that they need only to be given an order and they kill, to be given another order and they die, You will shoot only when I say so, the sergeant shouted. These words made the blind man realise that his life was in danger. He fell to his knees and beseeched them, Please help me, tell me where I have to go, Keep on walking, blind man, keep on walking this way, a soldier called from beyond in a tone of false camaraderie, the blind man got up, took three paces, then suddenly came to another halt, the tense of the verb aroused his suspicion, keep on walking this way is not the same as keep going, keep on walking this way tells you that this way, this very way, in this direction, you will arrive where you are being summoned, only to come up against the bullet that will replace one form of blindness with another. This initiative, which we might well describe as criminal, was taken by a soldier of disreputable character, whom the sergeant immediately rebuked with two sharp commands given successively, Halt, Half turn, followed by a severe call to order directed at this disobedient fellow, who to all appearances belonged to that class of people who are not to be trusted with a rifle. Encouraged by the sergeant's kind intervention, the blind internees who had reached the top of the steps suddenly made a tremendous racket which served as a magnetic pole for the blind man who had lost his way. Now more sure of himself, he advanced in a straight line, Keep on shouting, keep on shouting, he beseeched them, while the other blind internees applauded as if they were watching someone complete a long, dynamic but exhausting sprint. He was given a rapturous welcome, the least they could do, in the face of adversity, whether proven or foreseeable, you know who your friends are.

This camaraderie did not last long. Taking advantage of the uproar, some of the blind internees had sneaked off with a number of containers, as many as they could carry, a patently disloyal way of forestalling any hypothetical injustices in the distribution. Those of good faith, who are always to be found no matter what people may say, protested with indignation, that they couldn't live like this, If we cannot trust each other, where are we going to end up? some asked rhetorically, although with full justification, What these rogues are asking for is a good hiding, threatened others, they had not asked for any such thing, but everyone understood what those words meant, an inaccurate expression that can be tolerated only because it is so very apt. Already gathered in the hallway, the blind internees came to an agreement, this being the most practical way of resolving the first part of the difficult situation in which they found themselves, that they would distribute the remaining containers equally between the two wards, fortunately an even number, and set up a committee, also on an equal basis, to carry out an investigation with a view to recovering the missing, that is to say, stolen containers. They wasted some time in debate, as was becoming their habit, the before and the after, that is to say, whether they should eat first and then investigate, or the other way round, the prevailing opinion being that, taking into account all the hours of enforced fasting they had spent, it would be more convenient to start by satisfying their stomachs and then proceeding with their inquiries, And don't forget that you have to bury your dead, said someone from the first ward, We haven't killed them yet and you want us to bury them, replied one witty fellow, amusing himself with this play on words. Everyone laughed. However they were soon to discover that the culprits were not to be found in the wards. At the doors of both wards, waiting for their food to arrive, the blind internees claimed to have heard passing along the corridors people who seemed to be in a great hurry, but no one had entered the wards, much less carrying containers of food, that they could swear to. Someone remembered that the safest way of identifying these fellows would be if they were all to return to their respective beds, obviously those that remained unoccupied must belong to the thieves, so all they had to do was to wait until they returned from wherever they had been hiding and licking their chops and then pounce on them, so that they might learn to respect the sacred principle of collective property. To proceed with this plan, however opportune and in keeping with a deep-seated sense of justice, had one serious disadvantage insofar as it would mean postponing, no one could foresee for how long, that much desired breakfast, already gone cold. Let's eat first, suggested one of the blind men, and the majority agreed that it was better that they should eat first. Alas, only the little that had remained after that infamous theft. At this hour, in some hiding place amongst these old and dilapidated buildings, the thieves must be gorging themselves on double and triple rations that unexpectedly seemed to have improved, consisting of coffee with milk, cold in fact, biscuits and bread with margarine, while decent folk had to content themselves with two or three times less, and not even that. Outside the loudspeaker could be heard summoning the contagious to fetch their food rations, the sound also reached some of the internees in the first wing, as they were sadly chewing on water biscuits. One of the blind men, undoubtedly influenced by the unwholesome atmosphere left by the theft of food, had an idea, If we were to wait in the hallway, they would get the fright of their lives just to see us there, they might even drop the odd container, but the doctor said he did not think this would be right, it would be an injustice to punish those without blame. When they had all finished eating, the doctor's wife and the girl with dark glasses carried the cardboard containers into the yard, the empty flasks of milk and coffee, the paper cups, in a word, everything that could not be eaten. We must burn the rubbish, the doctor's wife then suggested, and get rid of these horrible flies.

Seated on their respective beds, the blind internees settled down to wait for the pack of thieves to return, Thieving dogs, that's what they are, commented a rough voice, unaware that he was responding to a reminiscence of someone who is not to blame for not knowing how to say things in any other manner. But the scoundrels did not appear, they must have suspected something, suspicions no doubt raised by some astute fellow amongst them like the one here who suggested giving them a good hiding. The minutes went by, several of the blind men had stretched out, some were already asleep. For this, my friends, is what it means to eat and sleep. All things considered, things could be worse. So long as they go on supplying us with food, for we cannot live without it, this is like being in a hotel. By contrast, what a torment it would be for a blind man out there in the city, yes, a real torment. Stumbling through the streets, everyone fleeing at the very sight of him, his family in a panic, terrified of approaching him, a mother's love, a child's love, a myth, they would probably treat me just as I am treated in this place, lock me up in a room and, if I was very lucky, leave a plate outside the door. Looking at the situation objectively, without preconceptions or resentments which always cloud our reasoning, it had to be acknowledged that the authorities had shown great vision when they decided to unite the blind with the blind, each with his own, which is a wise rule for those who have to live together, like lepers, and there can be no doubt that the doctor there at the far end of the ward is right when he says that we must organise ourselves, the question, in fact, is one of organisation, first the food, then the organisation, both are indispensable for life, to choose a number of reliable men and women and put them in charge, to establish approved rules for our co-existence here in the ward, simple things, like sweeping the floor, tidying up and washing, we've nothing to complain about there, they have even provided us with soap and detergent, making sure our beds are always made, the important thing is not to lose our self-respect, to avoid any conflict with the soldiers who are only doing their duty by keeping us under guard, we do not want any more casualties, asking around if there is anyone willing to entertain us in the evening with stories, fables, anecdotes, whatever, just think how fortunate we would be if someone knew the Bible by heart, we could repeat everything since the creation of the world, the important thing is that we should listen to one another, pity we haven't a radio, music has always been a great distraction, and we could follow the news bulletins, for example, if a cure were to be discovered for our illness, how we should rejoice.

Then the inevitable happened. They heard shots being fired in the street, They're coming to kill us, someone shouted, Calm down, said the doctor, we must be logical, if they wanted to kill us, they would come here to shoot us, not outside. The doctor was right, it was the sergeant who had given the order to shoot in the air, not some soldier who had suddenly been struck blind when his finger was on the trigger, clearly there was no other way of controlling and intimidating the new internees as they stumbled from the vans, the Ministry of Health had informed the Ministry of Defence, We're despatching four van-loads, And how many does that make, About two hundred internees, Where are all these people going to be accommodated, the wards reserved for the blind internees are the three in the wing on the right, according to the information we've been given, the total capacity is one hundred and twenty, and there are already some sixty to seventy internees inside, minus a dozen or so whom we were obliged to kill, There is one solution, open up all the wards, That would mean the contaminated coming into direct contact with those who are blind, In all probability, sooner or later, the former will also go blind, besides, the situation being as it is, I suppose we'll all be contaminated, there cannot be a single person who has not been within sight of a blind man, If a blind man cannot see, I ask myself, how can he transmit this disease through his sight, General, this must be the most logical illness in the world, the eye that is blind transmits the blindness to the eye that sees, what could be simpler, We have a colonel here who believes the solution would be to shoot the blind as soon as they appear, Corpses instead of blind men would scarcely improve the situation, To be blind is not the same as being dead, Yes, but to be dead is to be blind, So there are going to be about two hundred of them, Yes, And what shall we do with the taxi-drivers, Put them inside as well. That same day, in the late afternoon, the Ministry of Defence contacted the Ministry of Health, Would you like to hear the latest news, that colonel we mentioned earlier has gone blind, It'll be interesting to see what he thinks of that bright idea of his now, He already thought, he shot himself in the head, Now that's what I call a consistent attitude, The army is always ready to set an example.

The gate had been opened wide. In keeping with barracks routine, the sergeant ordered that a column should be formed five deep, but the blind internees were unable to get the numbers right, sometimes they were more than five, at other times less, and they all ended up by crowding around the entrance, like the civilians they were, without any sense of order, they did not even remember to send the women and children ahead, as in other shipwrecks. It has to be said before we forget, that not all of the gunshots had been fired in the air, one of the van-drivers had refused to go with the blind internees, he protested that he could see perfectly well, the outcome, three seconds later, was to prove the point made by the Ministry of Health when it decreed that to be dead is to be blind. The sergeant gave the aforementioned orders, Keep going, there's a stairway with six steps, when you get there, go slowly up the steps, if anyone trips, who knows what will happen, the only recommendation overlooked was that they should follow the rope, but clearly if they had used it they would have taken forever to enter, Listen, cautioned the sergeant, his mind at rest because all of them were already inside the gate, there are three wards on the right and three on the left, each ward has forty beds, families should stay together, avoid crowding, wait at the entrance and ask those who are already interned for assistance, everything is going to be all right, settle in and keep calm, keep calm, your food will be delivered later.

It would not be right to imagine that these blind people, in such great numbers, proceed like lambs to the slaughter, bleating as is their wont, somewhat crowded, it is true, yet that is how they had always existed, cheek by jowl, mingling breaths and smells, There are some here who cannot stop crying, others who are shouting in fear or rage, others who are cursing, someone uttered a terrible, futile threat, If I get my hands on you, presumably he was referring to the soldiers, I'll gouge your eyes out. Inevitably, the first internees to reach the stairway had to probe with one foot, the height and depth of the steps, the pressure of those coming from behind knocked two or three of those in front to the ground, fortunately nothing more serious occurred, nothing except a few grazed shins, the sergeant's advice had proved to be a blessing. A number of the new arrivals had already entered the hallway, but two hundred persons cannot be expected to sort themselves out all that easily, moreover blind and without a guide, this painful situation being made even worse by the fact that we are in an old building and badly designed at that, it is not enough for a sergeant who knows only about military affairs to say, there are three wards on each side, you have to know what it's like inside, doorways so narrow that they look more like bottlenecks, corridors as crazy as the other inmates of the asylum, opening for no clear reason and closing who knows where, and no one is ever likely to find out. Instinctively, the vanguard of blind internees had divided into two columns, moving on both sides along the walls in search of a door they might enter, a safe method, undoubtedly, assuming there are no items of furniture blocking the way. Sooner or later, with know-how and patience, the new inmates will settle in, but not before the latest battle has been won between the first lines of the column on the left and the contaminated confined to that side. It was only to be expected. There was an agreement, there was even a regulation drawn up by the Ministry of Health, that this wing would be reserved for the contaminated, and if it was true that it could be foreseen that in all likelihood, every one of them would end up blind, it was also true, in terms of pure logic, that until they became blind there was no guarantee that they were fated to blindness. There is then a person sitting peacefully at home, confident that at least in his case all will turn out well, when suddenly he sees coming directly towards him a howling mob of the people he most fears. At first, the contaminated thought this was a group of inmates like themselves, only more numerous, but the deception was short-lived, these people were blind all right, You can't come in here, this wing is ours, it isn't for the blind, you belong to the wing on the other side, shouted those on guard at the door. Some of the blind internees tried to do a turnaround and find another entrance, they didn't care if they went left or right, but the mass of those who continued to flock in from outside, jostled them relentlessly. The contaminated defended the door with punches and kicks, the blind retaliated as best they could, they could not see their adversaries, but knew where the blows were coming from. Two hundred people could not get into the hallway, or anything like that number, so it was not long before the door leading to the courtyard, despite being fairly wide, was completely blocked, as if obstructed by a plug, they could go neither backwards nor forwards, those who were inside, crushed and flattened, tried to protect themselves by kicking and elbowing their neighbours, who were suffocating, cries could be heard, blind children were sobbing, blind mothers were fainting, while the vast crowd that had been unable to enter pushed even harder, terrified by the bellowing of the soldiers, who could not understand why those idiots had not gone through. There was one terrible moment of violent backsurge as people struggled to extricate themselves from the confusion, from the imminent danger of being crushed, let us put ourselves in the place of the soldiers, suddenly they see a considerable number of those who had entered come hurtling out, they immediately thought the worst, that the new arrivals were about to turn back, let us remember the precedents, there might well have been a massacre. Fortunately, the sergeant was once more equal to the crisis, he himself fired into the air, simply to attract attention, and shouted over the loudspeaker, Calm down, those on the steps should draw back a little, clear the way, stop pushing and try to help each other. That was asking too much, the struggle inside continued, but the hallway gradually emptied thanks to a much greater number of blind internees moving to the door of the right wing, there they were received by blind inmates who were happy to direct them to the third ward, so far free, or to the beds in the second ward which were still unoccupied. For one moment it looked as if the battle would be resolved in favour of the contaminated, not because they were stronger and had more sight, but because the blind internees, having perceived that the entrance on the other side was less encumbered, broke off all contacts, as the sergeant would say in his discussions about strategy and basic military tactics. However, the triumph of the defenders was of short duration. From the door of the right wing came voices announcing that there was no more room, that all the wards were full, there were even some blind internees still being pushed into the hallway, precisely at that moment when, once the human stopper up until then blocking the main entrance dispersed, once the considerable number of blind internees who were outside, were able to advance and take shelter under the roof where, safe from the threats of the soldiers, they would live. The result of these two displacements, practically simultaneous, was to rekindle the struggle at the entrance of the wing on the left-hand side, once again blows were exchanged, once more there were shouts, and, as if this were not enough, in their confusion some of the bewildered blind internees, who had found and forced open the hallway door leading directly into the inner courtyard, cried out that there were corpses out there. Imagine their horror. They withdrew as best they could, There are corpses out there, they repeated, as if they would be the next to die, and, within a second, the hallway was once more the raging whirlpool it had been at its worst, then, in a sudden and desperate impulse, the human mass swerved towards the wing on the left, carrying all before it, the resistance of the contaminated broken, many of them no longer merely contaminated, others, running like madmen, were still trying to escape their black destiny. They ran in vain. One after the other they were stricken with blindness, their eyes suddenly drowned in that hideous white tide inundating the corridors, the wards, the entire space. Out there in the hallway, in the yard, the blind internees, helpless, some badly bruised from the blows, others from being trampled, dragged themselves along, most of them were elderly, many women and children, beings with few or no defences, and it was nothing short of a miracle that there were not more corpses in need of burial. Scattered on the ground, apart from some shoes that had lost their feet, lie bags, suitcases, baskets, each individual's bit of wealth, lost for ever, anyone coming across these objects will insist that what he is carrying is his.

An old man with a black patch over one eye, came in from the yard. He, too, had either lost his luggage or had not brought any. He had been the first to stumble over the corpses, but he did not cry out. He remained beside them and waited for peace and silence to be restored. He waited for an hour. Now it is his turn to seek shelter. Slowly, with his arms outstretched, he searched for the way. He found the door of the first ward on the right-hand side, heard voices coming from within, then asked, Any chance of a bed here.

The arrival of so many blind people appeared to have brought at least one advantage, or, rather, two advantages, the first of these being of a psychological nature, as it were, for there is a vast difference between waiting for new inmates to turn up at any minute, and realising that the building is completely full at last, that from now on it will be possible to establish and maintain stable and lasting relations with one's neighbours, without the disturbances there have been up until now, because of the constant interruptions and interventions by the new arrivals which obliged us to be for ever reconstituting the channels of communication. The second advantage, of a practical, direct and substantial nature, was that the authorities outside, both civilian and military, had understood that it was one thing to provide food for two or three dozen people, more or less tolerant, more or less prepared, because of their small number, to resign themselves to occasional mistakes or delays in the delivery of food, and quite another to be faced with the sudden and complex responsibility of feeding two hundred and forty human beings of every type, background and temperament. Two hundred and forty, take note, and that is just a manner of speaking, for there are at least twenty blind internees who have not managed to find a bed and are sleeping on the floor. In any case, it has to be recognised that thirty persons being fed on rations meant for ten is not the same as sharing out to two hundred and sixty, food intended for two hundred and forty. The difference is almost imperceptible. Now then, it was the conscious assumption of this increased responsibility, and perhaps, a hypothesis not to be disregarded, the fear that further disturbances might break out, that determined a change of procedure on the part of the authorities, in the sense of giving orders that the food should be delivered on time and in the right quantity. Obviously, after the struggle, in every respect lamentable, that we had to witness, accommodating so many blind internees was not going to be easy or free of conflict, we need only remember those poor contaminated creatures who before could still see and now see nothing, of the separated couples and their lost children, of the discomfort of those who had been trampled and knocked down, some of them twice or three times, of those who are going around in search of their cherished possessions without finding them, one would have to be completely insensitive to forget, as if it were nothing, the misfortunes of these poor people. However, it cannot be denied that the announcement that lunch was about to be delivered was like a consoling balm for everyone. And if it is undeniable that, given the lack of adequate organisation for this operation or of any authority capable of imposing the necessary discipline, the collection of such large quantities of food and its distribution to feed so many mouths led to further misunderstandings, we must concede that the atmosphere changed considerably for the better, when throughout that ancient asylum there was nothing to be heard except the noise of two hundred and sixty mouths masticating. Who is going to clean up this mess afterwards is a question so far unanswered, only in the late afternoon will the voice on the loudspeaker repeat the rules of orderly conduct that must be observed for the good of all, and then it will become clear with what degree of respect the new arrivals treat these rules. It is no small thing that the inmates of the second ward in the right wing have decided, at long last, to bury their dead, at least we shall be rid of that particular stench, the smell of the living, however fetid, will be easier to get used to.

As for the first ward, perhaps because it was the oldest and therefore most established in the process and pursuit of adaptation to the state of blindness, a quarter of an hour after its inmates had finished eating, there was not so much as a scrap of dirty paper on the floor, a forgotten plate or dripping receptacle. Everything had been gathered up, the smaller objects placed inside the larger ones, the dirtiest of them placed inside those that were less dirty, as any rationalised regulation of hygiene would demand, as attentive to the greatest efficiency possible in gathering up leftovers and litter, as to the economy of effort needed to carry out this task. The state of mind which perforce will have to determine social conduct of this nature cannot be improvised nor does it come about spontaneously. In the case under scrutiny, the pedagogical approach of the blind woman at the far end of the ward seems to have had a decisive influence, that woman married to the ophthalmologist, who has never tired of telling us, If we cannot live entirely like human beings, at least let us do everything in our power not to live entirely like animals, words she repeated so often that the rest of the ward ended up by transforming her advice into a maxim, a dictum, into a doctrine, a rule of life, words which deep down were so simple and elementary, probably it was just that state of mind, propitious to any understanding of needs and circumstances, that contributed, even if only in a minor way to the warm welcome the old man with the black eyepatch found there when he peered through the door and asked those inside, Any chance of a bed here. By a happy coincidence, clearly indicative of future consequences, there was a bed, the only one, and it is anyone's guess how it survived, as it were, the invasion, in that bed the car-thief had suffered unspeakable pain, perhaps that is why it had retained an aura of suffering that kept people at a distance. These are the workings of destiny, arcane mysteries, and this coincidence was not the first, far from it, we need only observe that all the eye-patients who happened to be in the surgery when the first blind man appeared there have ended up in this ward, and even then it was thought that the situation would go no further, In a low voice, as always, so that no one would suspect the secret of her presence there, the doctor's wife whispered into her husband's ear, Perhaps he was also one of your patients, he is an elderly man, bald, with white hair, and he has a black patch over one eye, I remember you telling me about him, Which eye, The left, It must be him. The doctor advanced to the passageway and said, slightly raising his voice, I'd like to touch the person who has just joined us, I would ask him to make his way in this direction and I shall make my way towards him. They bumped into each other midway, fingers touching fingers, like two ants that recognise each other from the manoeuvring of their antennae, but this won't be the case here, the doctor asked his permission, ran his hands over the old man's face, and quickly found the patch. There is no doubt, here is the one person who was missing here, the patient with the black patch, he exclaimed, What do you mean, who are you, asked the old man, I am, or rather I was your ophthalmologist, do you remember, we were agreeing on a date for your cataract operation, How did you recognise me, Above all, by your voice, the voice is the sight of the person who cannot see, Yes, the voice, I'm also beginning to recognise yours, who would have thought it, doctor, now there's no need for an operation, If there is a cure for this, we will both need it, I remember you telling me, doctor, that after my operation I would no longer recognise the world in which I was living, we now know how right you were,

When did you turn blind, Last night, And they've brought you here already, The panic out there is such that it won't be long before they start killing people off the moment they know they have gone blind, Here they have already eliminated ten, said a man's voice, I found them, the old man with the black eyepatch simply said, They were from the other ward, we buried our dead at once, added the same voice, as if concluding a report. The girl with dark glasses had approached, Do you remember me, I was wearing dark glasses, I remember you well, despite my cataract, I remember that you were very pretty, the girl smiled, Thank you, she said, and went back to her place. From there, she called out, The little boy is here too, I want my mummy, the boy's voice could be heard saying, as if worn out from some remote and useless weeping. And I was the first to go blind, said the first blind man, and I'm here with my wife, And I'm the girl from the surgery, said the girl from the surgery. The doctor's wife said, It only remains for me to introduce myself, and she said who she was. Then the old man, as if to repay the welcome, announced, I have a radio, A radio, exclaimed the girl with dark glasses as she clapped her hands, music, how nice, Yes, but it's a small radio, with batteries, and batteries do not last forever, the old man reminded her, Don't tell me we shall be cooped up here forever, said the first blind man, Forever, no, forever is always far too long a time, We'll be able to listen to the news, the doctor observed, And a little music, insisted the girl with dark glasses, Not everyone likes the same music, but we're all certainly interested in knowing what things are like outside, it would be better to save the radio for that, I agree, said the old man with the black eyepatch. He took the tiny radio from his jacket pocket and switched it on. He began searching for the different stations, but his hand was still too unsteady to tune into one wavelength, and to begin with all that could be heard were intermittent noises, fragments of music and words, at last his hand grew steadier, the music became recognisable, Leave it there for a bit, pleaded the girl with dark glasses, the words got clearer, That isn't the news, said the doctor's wife, and then, as if an idea had suddenly struck her, What time is it, she asked, but she knew that no one there could tell her. The tuning knob continued to extract noises from the tiny box, then it settled down, it was a song, a song of no significance, but the blind internees slowly began gathering round, without pushing, they stopped the moment they felt a presence before them and there they remained, listening, their eyes wide open tuned in the direction of the voice that was singing, some were crying, as probably only the blind can cry, the tears simply flowing as from a fountain. The song came to an end, the announcer said, At the third stroke it will be four o'clock. One of the blind women asked, laughing, Four in the afternoon or four in the morning, and it was as if her laughter hurt her. Furtively, the doctor's wife adjusted her watch and wound it up, it was four in the afternoon, although, to tell the truth, a watch is unconcerned, it goes from one to twelve, the rest are just ideas in the human mind. What's that faint sound, asked the girl with dark glasses, it sounded like, It was me, I heard them say on the radio that it was four o'clock and I wound up my watch, it was one of those automatic movements we so often make, anticipated the doctor's wife. Then she thought that it had not been worth putting herself at risk like that, all she had to do was to glance at the wrist-watches of the blind who had arrived that day, one of them must have a watch in working order. The old man with the black eyepatch had one, as she noticed just that moment, and the time on his watch was correct. Then the doctor asked, Tell us what the situation is like out there. The old man with the black eyepatch said, Of course, but I'd better sit, I'm dead on my feet. Three or four to a bed, keeping each other company on this occasion, the blind internees settled down as best they could, they fell silent, and then the old man with the black eyepatch told them what he knew, what he had seen with his own eyes when he could still see, what he had overheard during the few days that elapsed between the start of the epidemic and his own blindness.

In the first twenty-four hours, he said, if the rumour going round was true, there were hundreds of cases, all alike, all showing the same symptoms, all instantaneous, the disconcerting absence of lesions, the resplendent whiteness of their field of vision, no pain either before or after. On the second day there was talk of some reduction in the number of new cases, it went from hundreds to dozens and this led the Government to announce at once that it was reasonable to suppose that the situation would soon be under control. From this point onwards, apart from a few inevitable comments, the story of the old man with the black eyepatch will no longer be followed to the letter, being replaced by a reorganised version of his discourse, re-evaluated in the light of a correct and more appropriate vocabulary. The reason for this previously unforeseen change is the rather formal controlled language, used by the narrator, which almost disqualifies him as a complementary reporter, however important he may be, because without him we would have no way of knowing what happened in the outside world, as a complementary reporter, as we were saying, of these extraordinary events, when as we know the description of any facts can only gain with the rigour and suitability of the terms used. Returning to the matter in hand, the Government therefore ruled out the originally formulated hypothesis that the country was being swept by an epidemic without precedent, provoked by some morbid as yet unidentified agent that took effect instantaneously and was marked by a complete absence of any previous signs of incubation or latency. Instead, they said, that in accordance with the latest scientific opinion and the consequent and updated administrative interpretation, they were dealing with an accidental and unfortunate temporary concurrence of circumstances, also as yet unverified, in whose pathogenic development it was possible, the Government's communiqué emphasised, starting from the analysis of the available data, to detect the proximity of a clear curve of resolution and signs that it was on the wane. A television commentator came up with an apt metaphor when he compared the epidemic, or whatever it might be, to an arrow shot into the air, which upon reaching its highest point, pauses for a moment as if suspended, and then begins to trace its obligatory descending curve, which, God willing, and with this invocation the commentator returned to the triviality of human discourse and to the so-called epidemic, gravity tending to increase the speed of it, until this terrible nightmare tormenting us finally disappears, these were words that appeared constantly in the media, and always concluded by formulating the pious wish that the unfortunate people who had become blind might soon recover their sight, promising them meanwhile, the solidarity of society as a whole, both official and private. In some remote past, similar arguments and metaphors had been translated by the intrepid optimism of the common people into sayings such as, Nothing lasts forever, be it good or bad, the excellent maxims of one who has had time to learn from the ups and downs of life and fortune, and which, transported into the land of the blind, should be read as follows, Yesterday we could see, today we can't, tomorrow we shall see again, with a slight interrogatory note on the third and final line of the phrase, as if prudence, at the last moment, had decided, just in case, to add a touch of a doubt to the hopeful conclusion.

Sadly, the futility of such hopes soon became manifest, the

Government's expectations and the predictions of the scientific community simply sank without trace. Blindness was spreading, not like a sudden tide flooding everything and carrying all before it, but like an insidious infiltration of a thousand and one turbulent rivulets which, having slowly drenched the earth, suddenly submerge it completely. Faced with this social catastrophe, already on the point of taking the bit between their teeth, the authorities hastily organised medical conferences, especially those bringing together ophthalmologists and neurologists. Because of the time it would inevitably take to organise, a congress that some had called for was never convened, but in compensation there were colloquia, seminars, round-table discussions, some open to the public, others held behind closed doors. The overall effect of the patent futility of the debates and the occurrence of certain cases of sudden blindness during the sessions, with the speaker calling out, I'm blind, I'm blind, prompted almost all the newspapers, the radio and television, to lose interest in such initiatives, apart from the discreet and, in every sense, laudable behaviour of certain organs of communication which, living off sensational stories of every kind, off the fortunes and misfortunes of others, were not prepared to miss an opportunity to report live, with all the drama the situation warranted, the sudden blindness, for example, of a professor of ophthalmology.

The proof of the progressive deterioration of morale in general was provided by the Government itself, its strategy changing twice within the space of some six days. To begin with, the Government was confident that it was possible to circumscribe the disease by confining the blind and the contaminated within specific areas, such as the asylum in which we find ourselves. Then the inexorable rise in the number of cases of blindness led some influential members of the Government, fearful that the official initiative would not suffice for the task in hand, and that it might result in heavy political costs, to defend the idea that it was up to families to keep their blind indoors, never allowing them to go out on the street, so as not to worsen the already difficult traffic situation or to offend the sensibility of persons who still had their eyesight and who, indifferent to more or less reassuring opinions, believed that the white disease was spreading by visual contact, like the evil eye. Indeed, it was not appropriate to expect any other reaction from someone who, preoccupied with his thoughts, be they sad, indifferent, or happy, if such thoughts still exist, suddenly saw the change in expression of a person heading in his direction, his face revealing all the signs of total horror, and then that inevitable cry, I'm blind, I'm blind. No one's nerves could withstand it. The worst thing is that whole families, especially the smaller ones, rapidly became families of blind people, leaving no one who could guide and look after them, nor protect sighted neighbours from them, and it was clear that these blind people, however caring a father, mother or child they might be, could not take care of each other, otherwise they would meet the same fate as the blind people in the painting, walking together, falling together and dying together.

Faced with this situation, the Government had no alternative but to go rapidly into reverse gear, broadening the criteria it had established about the places and spaces that could be requisitioned, resulting in the immediate and improvised utilisation of abandoned factories, disused churches, sports pavilions and empty warehouses. For the last two days there has been talk of setting up army tents, added the old man with the black eyepatch. At the beginning, the very beginning, several charitable organisations were still offering volunteers to assist the blind, to make their beds, clean out the lavatories, wash their clothes, prepare their food, the minimum of care without which life soon becomes unbearable, even for those who can see. These dear people went blind immediately but at least the generosity of their gesture would go down in history. Did any of them come here, asked the old man with the black eyepatch, No, replied the doctor's wife, no one has come, Perhaps it was a rumour, And what about the city and the traffic, asked the first blind man, remembering his own car and that of the taxi-driver who had driven him to the surgery and had helped him to dig the grave, Traffic is in a state of chaos, replied the old man with the black eyepatch, and gave details of specific cases and accidents. When, for the first time, a bus-driver was suddenly struck by blindness as he was driving his vehicle on a public road, despite the casualties and injuries resulting from the disaster, people did not pay much attention for the same reason, that is to say, out of force of habit, and the director of public relations of the transport company felt able to declare, without further ado, that the disaster had been caused by human error, regrettable no doubt, but, all things considered, as unforeseeable as a heart attack in the case of someone who had never suffered from a heart complaint. Our employees, explained the director, as well as the mechanical and electrical parts of our buses, are periodically subjected to rigorous checks, as can be seen, showing a direct and clear relation of cause and effect, in the extremely low percentage of accidents in which, generally speaking, our company's vehicles have been involved. This laboured explanation appeared in the newspapers, but people had more on their minds than worrying about a simple bus accident, after all, it would have been no worse if its brakes had failed. Moreover, two days later, this was precisely the cause of another accident, but the world being what it is, where the truth often has to masquerade as falsehood to achieve its ends, the rumour went round that the driver had gone blind. There was no way of convincing the public of what had in fact happened, and the outcome was soon evident, from one moment to the next people stopped using buses, they said they would rather go blind themselves than die because others had gone blind. A third accident, soon afterwards and for the same reason, involving a vehicle that was carrying no passengers, gave rise to comment such as the following, couched in a knowingly popular tone, That could have been me. Nor could they imagine, those who spoke like this, how right they were. When two pilots both went blind at once a commercial plane crashed and burst into flames the moment it hit the ground, killing all the passengers and crew, notwithstanding that in this case, the mechanical and electrical equipment were in perfect working order, as the black box, the only survivor, would later reveal. A tragedy of these dimensions was not the same as an ordinary bus accident, the result being that those who still had any illusions soon lost them, from then on engine noises were no longer heard and no wheel, large or small, fast or slow, was ever to turn again. Those people who were previously in the habit of complaining about the ever-increasing traffic problems, pedestrians who, at first sight, appeared not to know where they were going because the cars, stationary or moving, were constantly impeding their progress, drivers who having gone round the block countless times before finally finding a place to park their car, became pedestrians and started protesting for the same reasons, after having first voiced their own complaints, all of them must now be content, except for the obvious fact that, since there was no one left who dared to drive a vehicle, not even to get from A to B, the cars, trucks, motor-bikes, even the bicycles, were scattered chaotically throughout the entire city, abandoned wherever fear had gained the upper hand over any sense of propriety, as evidenced by the grotesque sight of a tow-away vehicle with a car suspended from the front axle, probably the first man to turn blind had been the truck-driver. The situation was bad for everyone, but for those stricken with blindness it was catastrophic, since, according to the current expression, they could not see where they were putting their feet. It was pitiful to watch them bumping into the abandoned cars, one after the other, bruising their shins, some fell, pleading, Is there anyone who can help me to my feet, but there were also those who, naturally brutish or made so by despair, cursed and fought off any helping hand that came to their assistance, Leave me alone, your turn will come soon enough, then the compassionate person would take fright and make a quick escape, disappear into that dense white mist, suddenly conscious of the risk to which their kindness had exposed them, perhaps to go blind only a few steps further on.

That's how things are out there, the old man with the black eyepatch concluded his account, and I don't know everything, I can only speak of what I was able to see with my own eyes, here he broke off, paused and corrected himself, Not with my eyes, because I only had one, now not even that, well, I still have it but it's no use to me, I've never asked you why you didn't have a glass eye instead of wearing that patch, And why should I have wanted to, tell me that, asked the old man with the black eyepatch, It's normal because it looks better, besides it's much more hygienic, it can be removed, washed and replaced like dentures, Yes sir, but tell me what it would be like today if all those who now find themselves blind had lost, I say physically lost, both their eyes, what good would it do them now to be walking around with two glass eyes, You're right, no good at all, With all of us ending up blind, as appears to be happening, who's interested in aesthetics, and as for hygiene, tell me, doctor, what kind of hygiene could you hope for in this place, Perhaps only in a world of the blind will things be what they truly are, said the doctor, And what about people, asked the girl with dark glasses, People, too, no one will be there to see them, An idea has just occurred to me, said the old man with the black eye-patch, let's play a game to pass the time, How can we play a game if we cannot see what we are playing, asked the wife of the first blind man, Well, not a game exactly, each of us must say what we saw at the moment we went blind, That could be embarrassing, someone pointed out, Those who do not wish to take part in the game can remain silent, the important thing is that no one should try to invent anything, Give us an example, said the doctor, Certainly, replied the old man with the black eye-patch, I went blind when I was looking at my blind eye, What do you mean, It's very simple, I felt as if the inside of the empty orbit were inflamed and I removed the patch to satisfy my curiosity and just at that moment I went blind, It sounds like an allegory, said an unknown voice, the eye that refuses to acknowledge its own absence, As for me, said the doctor, I was at home consulting some reference books on ophthalmology, precisely because of what is happening, the last thing I saw were my hands resting on a book, My final image was different, said the doctor's wife, the inside of an ambulance as I was helping my husband to get in, I've already explained to the doctor what happened to me, said the first blind man, I had stopped at the lights, the signal was red, there were people crossing the street from one side to the other, at that very moment I turned blind, then that fellow who died the other day took me home, obviously I couldn't see his face, As for me, said the wife of the first blind man, the last thing I can remember seeing was my handkerchief, I was sitting at home and crying my heart out, I raised the handkerchief to my eyes and went blind that very moment, In my case, said the girl from the surgery, I had just gotten into the elevator, I stretched out my hand to press the button and suddenly stopped seeing, you can imagine my distress, trapped in there and all alone, I didn't know whether I would go up or down, and I couldn't find the button to open the door, My situation, said the pharmacist's assistant, was simpler, I heard that people were going blind, then I began to wonder what it would be like if I too were to go blind, I closed my eyes to try it and when I opened them I was blind, Sounds like another allegory, interrupted the unknown voice, if you want to be blind, then blind you will be. They remained silent. The other blind internees had gone back to their beds, no easy task, for while it is true that they knew their respective numbers, only by starting to count from one end of the ward, from one upwards or from twenty downwards, could they be certain of arriving where they wanted to be. When the murmur of their counting, as monotonous as a litany, died away, the girl with dark glasses related what had happened to her, I was in a hotel room with a man lying on top of me, at that point she fell silent, she felt too ashamed to say what she was doing there, that she had seen everything white, but the old man with the black eyepatch asked, And you saw everything white, Yes, she replied, Perhaps your blindness is different from ours, said the old man with the black eyepatch. The only person still to speak was the chambermaid, I was making a bed, a certain person had gone blind there, I held up the white sheet up before me and spread it out, tucked it in at the sides as one does, and as I was smoothing it out with both hands, suddenly I could no longer see, I remember how I was smoothing the sheet out, very slowly, it was the bottom sheet, she added, as if this had some special significance. Has everyone told their story about the last time they could see, asked the old man with the black eyepatch, I'll tell you mine, if there's no one else, said the unknown voice, If there is, he can speak after you, so fire away, The last thing I saw was a painting, A painting, repeated the old man with the black eyepatch, and where was this painting, I had gone to the museum, it was a picture of a cornfield with crows and cypress trees and a sun that gave the impression of having been made up of the fragments of other suns, Sounds like a

Dutch painter, I think it was, but there was a drowning dog in it, already half submerged, poor creature, In that case it must be by a Spanish painter, before him no one had ever painted a dog in that situation, after him no other painter had the courage to try. Probably, and there was a cart laden with hay, drawn by horses and crossing a stream, Was there a house on the left, Yes, Then it was by an English painter, Could be, but I don't think so, because there was a woman as well with a child in her arms, Mothers and children are all too common in paintings, True, I've noticed, What I don't understand is how in one painting there should be so many pictures and by such different painters, And there were some men eating, There have been so many lunches, afternoon snacks and suppers in the history of art, that this detail in itself is not enough to tell us who was eating, There were thirteen men altogether, Ah, then it's easy, go on, There was also a naked woman with fair hair, inside a conch that was floating on the sea, and masses of flowers around her, Obviously Italian, And there was a battle, As in those paintings depicting banquets and mothers with children in their arms, these details are not enough to reveal who painted the picture, There were corpses and wounded men, It's only natural, sooner or later, all children die, and soldiers too, And a horse stricken with terror, With its eyes about to pop out of their sockets, Exactly, Horses are like that, and what other pictures were there in your painting, Alas, I never managed to find out, I went blind just as I was looking at the horse. Fear can cause blindness, said the girl with dark glasses, Never a truer word, that could not be truer, we were already blind the moment we turned blind, fear struck us blind, fear will keep us blind, Who is speaking, asked the doctor, A blind man, replied a voice, just a blind man, for that is all we have here. Then the old man with the black eyepatch asked, How many blind persons are needed to make a blindness, No one could provide the answer. The girl with dark glasses asked him to switch on the radio, there might be some news. They gave the news later, meanwhile they listened to a little music. At a certain point some blind internees appeared in the doorway of the ward, one of them said, What a pity no one thought of bringing a guitar. The news was not very encouraging, a rumour was going round that the formation of a government of unity and national salvation was imminent.

When, at the beginning, the blind internees in this ward could still be counted on ten fingers, when an exchange of two or three words was enough to convert strangers into companions in misfortune, and with another three or four words they could forgive each other all their faults, some of them really quite serious, and if a complete pardon was not forthcoming, it was simply a question of being patient and waiting for a few days, then it became all too clear how many absurd afflictions the poor wretches had to suffer, each time their bodies demanded to be urgently relieved or as we say, to satisfy their needs. Despite this, and although knowing that perfect manners are somewhat rare and that even the most discreet and modest natures have their weak points, it has to be conceded that the first blind people to be brought here under quarantine, were capable, more or less conscientiously, of bearing with dignity the cross imposed by the eminently scatological nature of the human species. Now, with all the beds occupied, all two hundred and forty, not counting the blind inmates who have to sleep on the floor, no imagination, however fertile and creative in making comparisons, images and metaphors, could aptly describe the filth here. It is not just the state to which the lavatories were soon reduced, fetid caverns such as the gutters in hell full of condemned souls must be, but also the lack of respect shown by some of the inmates or the sudden urgency of others that turned the corridors and other passageways into latrines, at first only occasionally but now as a matter of habit. The careless or impatient thought, It doesn't matter, no one can see me, and they went no further. When it became impossible in any sense, to reach the lavatories, the blind internees began using the yard as a place to relieve themselves and clear their bowels. Those who were delicate by nature or upbringing spent the whole day restraining themselves, they put up with it as best they could until nightfall, they presumed it would be night when most people were asleep in the wards, then off they would go, clutching their stomachs or squeezing their legs together, in search of a foot or two of clean ground, if there was any amidst that endless carpet of trampled excrement, and, to make matters worse, in danger of getting lost in the infinite space of the yard, where there were no guiding signs other than the few trees whose trunks had managed to survive the mania for exploration of the former inmates, and also the slight mounds, now almost flattened, that barely covered the dead. Once a day, always in the late afternoon, like an alarm clock set to go off at the same hour, the voice over the loudspeaker would repeat the familiar instructions and prohibitions, insist on the advantages of making regular use of cleansing products, remind the inmates that there was a telephone in each ward in order to request the necessary supplies whenever they ran out, but what was really needed there was a powerful jet from a hose to wash away all that shit, then an army of plumbers to repair the cisterns and get them working again, then water, lots of water, to wash the waste down the pipes where it belongs, then, we beseech you, eyes, a pair of eyes, a hand capable of leading and guiding us, a voice that will say to me, This way. These blind internees, unless we come to their assistance, will soon turn into animals, worse still, into blind animals. This was not spoken by the unknown voice that talked of the paintings and images of this world, the person saying it, though in other words, late at night, is the doctor's wife lying beside her husband, their heads under the same blanket, A solution has to be found for this awful mess, I can't stand it and I can't go on pretending that I can't see, Think of the consequences, they will almost certainly try to turn you into their slave, a general dogsbody, you will be at the beck and call of everyone, they will expect you to feed them, wash them, put them to bed and get them up in the morning and have you take them from here to there, blow their noses and dry their tears, they will call out for you when you are asleep, insult you if you keep them waiting, How can you of all people expect me to go on looking at these miseries, to have them permanently before my eyes, and not lift a finger to help, You're already doing more than enough, What use am I, when my main concern is that no one should find out that I can see, Some will hate you for seeing, don't think that blindness has made us better people, It hasn't made us any worse, We're on our way though, just look at what happens when it's time to share out the food, Precisely, someone who can see could supervise the distribution of food to all those who are here, share it out with impartiality, with common sense, there would be no more complaints, these constant arguments that are driving me mad would cease, you have no idea what it is like to watch two blind people fighting, Fighting has always been, more or less, a form of blindness, This is different, Do what you think best, but don't forget what we are here, blind, simply blind, blind people with no fine speeches or commiserations, the charitable, picturesque world of the little blind orphans is finished, we are now in the harsh, cruel, implacable kingdom of the blind, If only you could see what I am obliged to see, you would want to be blind, I believe you, but there's no need, because I'm already blind, Forgive me, my love, if you only knew, I know, I know, I've spent my life looking into people's eyes, it is the only part of the body where a soul might still exist and if those eyes are lost, Tomorrow I'm going to tell them I can see, Let's hope you won't live to regret it, Tomorrow I'll tell them, she paused then added, Unless by then I, too, have finally entered their world.

But it was not to be just yet. When she woke up next morning, very early as usual, her eyes could see as clearly as before. All the blind internees in the ward were asleep. She wondered how she should tell them, whether she should gather them all together and announce the news, perhaps it might be preferable to do it in a discreet manner, without ostentation, to say, for example, as if not wishing to treat the matter too seriously, Just imagine, who would have thought that I would keep my sight amongst so many who have turned blind, or whether, perhaps more wisely, pretend that she really had been blind and had suddenly regained her sight, it might even be a way of giving the others some hope. If she can see again, they would say to each other, perhaps we will, too, on the other hand, they might tell her, If that's the case, then get out, be off with you, whereupon she would reply that she could not leave the place without her husband, and since the army would not release any blind person from quarantine, there was nothing for it but to allow her to stay. Some of the blind internees were stirring in their beds and, as every morning, they were relieving themselves of wind, but this did not make the atmosphere any more nauseating, saturation point must already have been reached. It was not just the fetid smell that came from the lavatories in gusts that made you want to throw up, it was also the accumulated body odour of two hundred and fifty people, whose bodies were steeped in their own sweat, who were neither able nor knew how to wash themselves, who wore clothes that got filthier by the day, who slept in beds where they had frequently defecated. What use would soaps, bleach, detergents be, abandoned somewhere around the place, if many of the showers were blocked or had become detached from the pipes, if the drains overflowed with the dirty water that spread outside the wash-rooms, soaking the floorboards in the corridors, infiltrating the cracks in the flag-stones. What madness is this to think of interfering, the doctor's wife began to reflect, even if they were not to demand that I should be at their service, and nothing is less certain, I myself would not be able to stand it without setting about washing and cleaning for as long as I had the strength, this is not a job for one person. Her courage which before had seemed so resolute, began to crumble, to gradually desert her when confronted with the abject reality that invaded her nostrils and offended her eyes, now that the moment had come to pass from words to actions. I'm a coward, she murmured in exasperation, it would have been better to be blind than go around like some faint-hearted missionary. Three blind internees had got up, one of them was the pharmacist's assistant, they were about to take up their positions in the hallway to collect the allocation of food intended for the first ward. It could not be claimed, given their lack of eyesight, that the distribution was made by eye, one container more, one container less, on the contrary, it was pitiful to see how they got muddled over the counting and had to start all over again, someone with a more suspicious nature wanted to know exactly what the others were carrying, arguments always broke out in the end, the odd shove, a slap for the blind women, as was inevitable. In the ward everyone was now awake, ready to receive their ration, with experience they had devised a fairly easy system of distribution, they began by carrying all the food to the far end of the ward, where the doctor and his wife had their beds as well as the girl with dark glasses and the boy who was calling for his mummy, and that is where the inmates went to fetch their food, two at a time, starting from the beds nearest the entrance, number one on the right, number one on the left, number two on the right, number two on the left, and so on and so forth, without any ill-tempered exchanges or jostling, it took longer, it is true, but keeping the peace made the waiting worthwhile. The first, that is to say, those who had the food right there within arm's reach, were the last to serve themselves, except for the boy with the squint, of course, who always finished eating before the girl with dark glasses received her portion, so that part of what should have been hers invariably finished up in the boy's stomach. All the blind internees had their heads turned towards the door, hoping to hear the footsteps of their fellow-inmates, the faltering, unmistakable sound of someone carrying something, but this was not the noise that could suddenly be heard but rather that of people running swiftly, were such a feat possible for people who could not see where they were putting their feet. Yet how else could you describe it when they appeared panting for breath at the door. What could have happened out there to send them running in here, and there were the three of them trying to get through the door at the same time to give the unexpected news, They wouldn't allow us to bring the food, said one of them, and the other two repeated his words, They wouldn't allow us, Who, the soldiers, asked some voice or other, No, the blind internees, What blind internees, we're all blind here, We don't know who they are, said the pharmacist's assistant, but I think they must belong to the group that all arrived together, the last group to arrive, And what's this about not allowing you to bring the food, asked the doctor, so far there has never been any problem, They say all that's over, from now on anyone who wants to eat will have to pay. Protests came from all sides of the ward, It cannot be, They've taken away our food, The thieves, A disgrace, the blind against the blind, I never thought I'd live to see anything like this, Let's go and complain to the sergeant. Someone more resolute proposed that they should all go together to demand what was rightfully theirs, It won't be easy, said the pharmacist's assistant, there are lots of them, I had the clear impression they form a large group, and the worst is that they are armed, What do you mean by armed, At the very least they have cudgels, this arm of mine still hurts from the blow I received, said one of the others, Let's try and settle this peacefully, said the doctor, I'll go with you to speak to these people, there must be some misunderstanding, Of course, doctor, you have my support, said the pharmacist's assistant, but from the way they're behaving, I very much doubt that you will be able to persuade them, Be that as it may, we have to go there, we cannot leave things like this, I'm coming with you, said the doctor's wife. The tiny group left the ward except for the one who was complaining about his arm, he felt that he had done his duty and stayed behind to relate to the others his hazardous adventure, their food rations two paces away, and a human wall to defend them, With cudgels, he insisted.

Advancing together, like a platoon, they forced their way through the blind inmates from the other wards. When they reached the hallway, the doctor's wife realised at once that no diplomatic conversation would be possible, and probably never likely to be. In the middle of the hallway, surrounding the containers of food, a circle of blind inmates armed with sticks and metal rods from the beds, pointing outwards like bayonets or lances, confronted the desperation of the blind inmates who were surrounding them and making awkward attempts to force their way through the line of defence, some with the hope of finding an opening, a gap someone had been careless enough not to close properly, they warded off the blows with raised arms, others crawled along on all fours until they bumped into the legs of their adversaries who repelled them with a blow to their backs or a vigorous kick. Hitting out blindly, as the saying goes. These scenes were accompanied by indignant protests, furious cries, We demand our food, We have a right to eat, Rogues, This is outrageous, Incredible though it may seem, there was one ingenuous or distracted soul who said, Call the police, perhaps there were some policemen amongst them, blindness, as everyone knows, has no regard for professions or occupations, but a policeman struck blind is not the same as a blind policeman, and as for the two we knew, they are dead and, after a great deal of effort, buried. Driven by the foolish hope that some authority would restore to the mental asylum its former tranquillity, impose justice, bring back some peace of mind, a blind woman made her way as best she could to the main entrance and called out for all to hear, Help us, these rogues are trying to steal our food. The soldiers pretended not to hear, the orders the sergeant had received from a captain who had passed through on an official visit could not have been clearer, If they end up killing each other, so much the better, there will be fewer of them. The blind woman ranted and raved as mad women did in bygone days, she herself almost demented, but from sheer desperation. In the end, realising that her pleas were futile, she fell silent, went back inside to sob her heart out and, oblivious of where she was going, she received a blow on the head that sent her to the floor. The doctor's wife wanted to run and help her up, but there was such confusion that she could not move as much as two paces. The blind internees who had come to demand their food were already beginning to withdraw in disarray, their sense of direction completely lost, they tripped over one another, fell, got up, fell again, some did not even make any attempt, gave up, remained lying prostrate on the ground, exhausted, miserable, racked with pain, their faces pressed against the tiled floor. Then the doctor's wife, terrified, saw one of the blind hoodlums take a gun from his pocket and raise it brusquely into the air. The blast caused a large piece of stucco to come crashing down from the ceiling on to their unprotected heads, increasing the panic. The hoodlum shouted, Be quiet everyone and keep your mouths shut, if anyone dares to raise their voice, I'll shoot straight out, no matter who gets hit, then there will be no more complaints. The blind internees did not move. The fellow with the gun continued, Let it be known and there is no turning back, that from today onwards we shall take charge of the food, you've all been warned, and let no one take it into their head to go out there to look for it, we shall put guards at the entrance, and anyone who tries to go against these orders will suffer the consequences, the food will now be sold, anyone who wants to eat must pay. How are we to pay, asked the doctor's wife, I said no one was to speak, bellowed the armed hoodlum, waving his weapon before him. Someone has to speak, we must know how we're to proceed, where are we going to fetch the food, do we all go together, or one at a time, This woman is up to something, commented one of the group, if you were to shoot her, there would be one mouth less to feed, If I could see her, she'd already have a bullet in her belly. Then addressing everyone, Go back to your wards immediately, this very minute, once we've carried the food inside, we'll decide what is to be done, And what about payment, rejoined the doctor's wife, how much shall we be expected to pay for a coffee with milk and a biscuit, She's really asking for it, that one, said the same voice, Leave her to me, said the other fellow, and changing tone, Each ward will nominate two people to be in charge of collecting people's valuables, all their valuables of whatever kind, money, jewels, rings, bracelets, earrings, watches, everything they possess, and they will take the lot to the third ward on the left, where we are accommodated, and if you want some friendly advice, don't get any ideas about trying to cheat us, we know that there are those amongst you who will hide some of your valuables, but I warn you to think again, unless we feel that you have handed in enough, you will simply not get any food and be left to chew your banknotes and munch on your diamonds. A blind man from the second ward on the right asked, And what are we to do, do we hand over everything at once, or do we pay according to what we eat, It would seem I haven't explained things clearly enough, said the fellow with the gun, laughing, first you pay, then you eat and, as for the rest, to pay according to what you've eaten would make keeping accounts extremely complicated, best to hand over everything at one go and then we shall see how much food you deserve, but let me warn you again, don't try to conceal anything for it will cost you dear, and lest anyone accuses us of not proceeding honestly, note that after handing over whatever you possess we shall carry out an inspection, woe betide you if we find so much as a penny, and now I want everybody out of here as quickly as possible. He raised his arm and fired another shot. Some more stucco crashed to the ground. And as for you, said the hoodlum with the gun, I won't forget your voice, Nor I your face, replied the doctor's wife.

No one appeared to notice the absurdity of a blind woman saying that she won't forget a face she could not see. The blind internees had already withdrawn as quickly as they could, in search of the doors, and those from the first ward were soon informing their fellow-inmates of the situation, From what we've heard, I don't believe that for the moment we can do anything other than obey, said the doctor, there must be quite a number of them, and worst of all, they have weapons. We can arm ourselves too, said the pharmacist's assistant, Yes, some sticks cut from the trees if there are any branches left within arm's reach, some metal rods removed from our beds that we shall scarcely have the strength to wield, while they have at least one firearm at their disposal, I refuse to hand over my belongings to these sons of a blind bitch, someone remarked, Nor I, joined in another, That's it, either we all hand over everything, or nobody gives anything, said the doctor, We have no alternative, said his wife, besides, the régime in here, must be the same as the one they imposed outside, anyone who doesn't want to pay can suit himself, that's his privilege, but he'll get nothing to eat and he cannot expect to be fed at the expense of the rest of us, We shall all give up what we've got and hand over everything, said the doctor, And what about those who have nothing to give, asked the pharmacist's assistant, They will eat whatever the others decide to give them, as the saying rightly goes, from each according to his abilities, to each according to his needs. There was a pause, and the old man with the black eyepatch asked, Well then, who are we going to ask to be in charge, I suggest the doctor, said the girl with the dark glasses. It was not necessary to proceed to a vote, the entire ward was in agreement. There have to be two of us, the doctor reminded them, is anyone willing to offer, he asked, I'm willing, if no one else comes forward, said the first blind man, Very well, let us start collecting, we need a sack, a bag, a small suitcase, any of these things will do, I can get rid of this, said the doctor's wife, and began at once to empty a bag in which she had gathered cosmetics and other odds and ends at a time when she could never have imagined the conditions in which she was now obliged to live. Amongst the bottles, boxes and tubes from another world, there was a pair of long, finely pointed scissors. She could not remember having put them there, but there they were. The doctor's wife raised her head. The blind internees were waiting, her husband had gone up to the bed of the first blind man, he was talking to him, the girl with the dark glasses was saying to the boy with the squint that the food would be arriving soon, on the floor, tucked behind the bedside table, was a bloodstained sanitary napkin, as if the girl with dark glasses were anxious, with maidenly and pointless modesty, to hide it from the eyes of those who could not see. The doctor's wife looked at the scissors, she tried to think why she should be staring at them in this way, in what way, like this, but she could think of no reason, frankly what reason could she hope to find in a simple pair of long scissors, lying in her open hands, with its two nickel-plated blades, the tips sharp and gleaming, Do you have it there, her husband asked her, Yes, here it is, she replied, and held out the arm holding the empty bag while she put the other arm behind her back to conceal the scissors, What's the matter, asked the doctor, Nothing, replied his wife, who could just as easily have answered, Nothing you can see, my voice must have sounded strange, that's all, nothing else. Accompanied by the first blind man, the doctor moved towards her, took the bag in his hesitant hands and said, Start getting your things ready, we're about to begin collecting. His wife unclasped her watch, did the same for her husband, removed her earrings, a tiny ring set with rubies, the gold chain she wore round her neck, her wedding ring, that of her husband, both of them easy to remove, Our fingers have got thinner, she thought, she began putting everything into the bag, then the money they had brought from home, a fair amount of notes varying in value, some coins, That's everything, she said, Are you sure, said the doctor, take a careful look, That's everything we have of any value. The girl with dark glasses had already gathered together her belongings, they were not so very different, she had two bracelets instead of one, but no wedding ring. The doctor's wife waited until her husband and the first blind man had turned their backs and for the girl with dark glasses to bend down to the boy with the squint, Think of me as your mummy, she was saying, I'll pay for us both, and then she withdrew to the wall at the far end. There, as all along the other walls, there were large nails sticking out that must have been used by the mad to hang treasures and other baubles. She chose the highest nail she could reach, and hung the scissors there. Then she sat down on her bed. Slowly, her husband and the first blind man were heading in the direction of the door, they would stop to collect possessions on both sides from those who had something to offer, some protested that they were being robbed shamefully, and that was the honest truth, others divested themselves of their possessions with a kind of indifference, as if thinking that, all things considered, there is nothing in this world that belongs to us in an absolute sense, another all too transparent truth. When they reached the door of the ward, having finished their collection, the doctor asked, Have we handed over everything, a number of resigned voices answered yes, some chose to say nothing and in the fullness of time we shall know whether this was in order to avoid telling a lie. The doctor's wife looked up at the scissors. She was surprised to find them so far up, hanging from one of the nails, as if she herself had not put them there, then she reflected that it had been an excellent idea to bring them, now she could trim her husband's beard, make him look more presentable, since, as we know, living in these conditions, it is impossible for a man to shave as normal. When she looked again in the direction of the door, the two men had already disappeared into the shadows of the corridor and were making their way to the third ward on the left, where they had been instructed to go and pay for their food. Today's food, tomorrow's as well, and perhaps for the rest of the week, And then, the question had no answer, everything we possessed will have gone in payment.

Surprisingly enough, the corridors were not congested as usual, because normally as the internees left their wards they inevitably tripped, collided and fell, those assaulted swore, hurled obscenities, their assailants retaliated with further insults, but no one paid any attention, a person has to give vent to his feelings somehow, especially if he is blind. Ahead there was the sound of footsteps and voices, they must be the emissaries from the other wards who were complying with the same orders, What a situation we're in, doctor, said the first blind man, as if our blindness were not enough, we've fallen into the clutches of blind thieves, that seems to be my fate, first there was the car-thief, now this rabble who are stealing our food at gunpoint, That's the difference, they're armed, But cartridges don't last for ever, Nothing lasts for ever, but in this case it might be preferable if it did, Why, If the cartridges were to run out, then that would mean that someone had used them up, and we already have too many corpses, We're in an impossible situation, It has been impossible ever since we came into this place, yet we go on putting up with it, You're an optimist, doctor, No, I'm not an optimist, but I cannot imagine anything worse than our present existence, Well, I'm not entirely convinced that there are limits to misfortune and evil, You may be right, said the doctor, and then, as if he were talking to himself, Something has to happen here, a conclusion that contains a certain contradiction, either there is something worse than this, after all, or, from now on, things are going to get better, although all the indications suggest otherwise. Having steadily made their way and having turned several corners, they were approaching the third ward. Neither the doctor nor the first blind man had ever ventured here, but the construction of the two wings, logically enough, had strictly adhered to a symmetrical pattern, anyone familiar with the wing on the right would have no difficulty in getting their bearings in the wing on the left, and vice-versa, you had only to turn to the left on the one side while on the other you had to turn right. They could hear voices, they must be of those ahead of them, We'll have to wait, said the doctor in a low voice, Why, Those inside will want to know precisely what these inmates are carrying, for them it is not all that important, since they have already eaten they're in no hurry, It must be almost time for lunch, Even if they could see, it would do this group no good to know it, they no longer even have watches. A quarter of an hour later, give or take a minute, the barter was over. Two men passed in front of the doctor and the first blind man, from their conversation it was apparent that they were carrying food, Careful, don't drop anything, said one of them, and the other was muttering, What I don't know is whether there will be enough for everyone. We'll have to tighten our belts. Sliding his hand along the wall, with the first blind man right behind him, the doctor advanced until his hands came into contact with the door jamb, We're from the first ward on the right, he shouted. He made as if to take a step forward, but his leg came up against an obstacle. He realised it was a bed standing crosswise, placed there to serve as a trading counter, They're organised, he thought to himself, this has not suddenly been improvised, he heard voices, footsteps, How many of them are there, his wife had mentioned ten, but it was not inconceivable that there might be many more, certainly not all of them were there when they went to get the food. The fellow with the gun was their leader, it was his jeering voice that was saying, Now, let's see what riches the first ward on the right has brought us, and then, in a much lower tone, addressing someone who must have been standing nearby, Take note. The doctor remained puzzled, what could this mean, the fellow had said, Take note, so there must be someone here who can write, someone who is not blind, so that makes two, We must be careful, he thought, tomorrow this rascal might be standing right next to us and we wouldn't even know it, this thought of the doctor's was scarcely any different from what the first blind man was thinking, With a gun and a spy, we're sunk, we shall never be able to raise our heads again. The blind man inside, the leader of the thieves, had already opened the bag, with practised hands he was lifting out, stroking and identifying the objects and money, clearly he could make out by touch what was gold and what was not, by touch he could also tell the value of the notes and coins, easy when one is experienced, it was only after some minutes that the doctor began to hear the unmistakable sound of punching paper, which he immediately identified, there nearby was someone writing in the braille alphabet, also known as anaglyptography, the sound could be heard, at once quiet and clear, of the pointer as it punched the thick paper and hit the metallic plate underneath. So there was a normal blind person amongst these blind delinquents, a blind person just like all those people who were once referred to as being blind, the poor fellow had obviously been roped in with all the rest, but this was not the moment to pry and start asking, are you one of the recent blind men or have you been blind for some years, tell us how you came to lose your sight. They were certainly lucky, not only had they won a clerk in the raffle, they could also use him as a guide, a blind person with experience as a blind person is something else, he's worth his weight in gold. The inventory went on, now and then the thug with the gun consulted the accountant, What do you think of this, and he would interrupt his bookkeeping to give an opinion, A cheap imitation, he would say, in which case the fellow with the gun would comment, If there is a lot of this, they won't get any food, or Good stuff, and then the commentary would be, There's nothing like dealing with honest people. In the end, three containers of food were lifted on to the bed, Take this, said the armed leader. The doctor counted them, Three are not enough, we used to receive four when the food was only for us, at that same moment he felt the cold barrel of the gun against his neck, for a blind man his aim was not bad, I'll have a container removed every time you complain, now beat it, take these and thank the Lord that you've still got something to eat. The doctor murmured, Very well, grabbed two of the containers while the first blind man took charge of the third one and, much slower now, because they were laden, they retraced the route that had brought them to the ward. When they arrived in the hallway, where there did not appear to be anyone around, the doctor said, I'll never again have such an opportunity, What do you mean, asked the first blind man, He put his gun to my neck, I could have grabbed it from him, That would be risky, Not as risky as it seems, I knew where the gun was resting, he had no way of knowing where my hands were, even so, at that moment I'm convinced that he was the blinder of the two of us, what a pity I didn't think of it, or did think of it but lacked the courage, And then what, asked the first blind man, What do you mean, Let's assume you had managed to grab his weapon, I don't believe you would have been capable of using it, If I were certain it would resolve the situation, yes I would, But you're not certain, No, in fact I'm not, Then better that they should keep their arms, at least so long as they do not use them against us. To threaten someone with a gun is the same as attacking them, If you had taken his gun, the real war would have started, and in all likelihood we would never have got out of that place alive, You're right, said the doctor, I'll pretend I had thought all that through, You mustn't forget, doctor, what you told me a little while ago, What did I say, That something has to happen, It has happened and I didn't make the most of it, It has to be something else, not that.

When they entered the ward and had to present the meagre amount of food they had brought to put on the table, some thought they were to blame for not having protested and demanded more, that's why they had been nominated as the representatives of the group. Then the doctor explained what had happened, he told them about the blind clerk, about the insulting behaviour of the blind man with the gun, also about the gun itself. The malcontents lowered their voices, ended up by agreeing that undoubtedly the ward's interests were in the right hands. The food was finally distributed, there were those who could not resist reminding the impatient that little is better than nothing, besides, by now it must be almost time for lunch, The worst thing would be if we got to be like that famous horse that died when it had already got out of the habit of eating, someone remarked. The others gave a wan smile and one said, It wouldn't be so bad if it's true that when the horse dies, it doesn't know it's going to die.

The old man with the black eyepatch had understood that the portable radio, as much for the fragility of its structure as for the information known about the length of its useful life, was to be excluded from the list of valuables they had to hand over in payment for their food, in consideration of the fact that the usefulness of the set depended in the first place on whether there were or were not batteries inside and, in the second place, on how long they would last. Judging by the rather husky voices still coming from the tiny box, it was obvious that little more could be expected of it. Therefore the old man with the black eyepatch decided not to have any more general broadcasts, additionally because the blind internees in the third ward on the left might turn up and take a different view, not owing to the material value of the set, which is virtually negligible in the short term, as we have seen, but owing to its immediate utility, which is undoubtedly considerable, not to mention the feasible hypothesis that where there is at least one gun there might also be batteries. So the old man with the black eyepatch said that, from now on, he would listen to the news under the blanket, with his head completely covered, and that if there were any interesting news-item, he would alert the others at once. The girl with dark glasses asked him to allow her to listen to a little music from time to time, So as not to forget, she argued, but he was inflexible, insisted that the important thing was to know what was going on outside, anyone who wanted music could listen to it in their own head, after all our memory ought to be put to some good use. The old man with the black eyepatch was right, the music on the radio was already as grating as only a painful memory can be, so for this reason he kept the volume as low as possible, waiting for the news to come on. Then he turned the sound up a little and listened attentively so as not to lose a single syllable. Then he summarised the news-items in his own words, and transmitted them to his immediate neighbours. And so from bed to bed, the news slowly circulated round the ward, increasingly distorted as it was passed on from one inmate to the next, in this way diminishing or exaggerating the details, according to the personal optimism or pessimism of those relaying the information. Until that moment when the words dried up and the old man with the black eyepatch found he had nothing more to say. And it was not because the radio had broken down or the batteries were used up, experience of life and lives has convincingly shown that no one can govern time, it was unlikely that this tiny set would last long, but finally someone fell silent before it went dead. Throughout this first day spent in the clutches of those blind thugs, the old man with the black eyepatch had been listening to the radio and passing on the news, rejecting the patent falseness of the optimistic prophecies being officially communicated and now, well into the night, with his head out of the blanket at last, he was listening carefully to the wheeze into which the waning power of the radio had transformed the announcer's voice, when suddenly he heard him call out, I'm blind, then the noise of something striking the microphone, a hasty sequence of confused sounds, exclamations, then sudden silence. The only radio station he had been able to get on the set had gone silent. For some time to come, the old man with the black eyepatch kept his ear to the box that was now inert, as if waiting for the announcer's voice to return and for the news to continue. However, he sensed, or rather knew, that it would return no more. The white sickness had not only blinded the announcer. Like a line of gunpowder, it had quickly and successively reached all those who happened to be in the studio. Then the old man with the black eyepatch dropped the radio on the floor. The blind thugs, if they were to come sniffing out hidden jewels, would find justification, had such a thought crossed their mind, for the omission of portable radios from their list of valuables. The old man with the black eyepatch pulled the blanket up over his head so that he could weep freely.

Little by little, under the murky yellowish light of the dim lamps, the ward descended into a deep slumber, bodies comforted by the three meals consumed that day, as had rarely happened before. If things continue like this, we'll end up once more reaching the conclusion that even in the worst misfortunes it is possible to find enough good to be able to bear the aforesaid misfortunes with patience, which, applied to the present situation, means that contrary to the first disquieting predictions, the concentration of food supplies into a single entity for apportioning and distribution, had its positive aspects, after all, however much certain idealists might protest that they would have preferred to go on struggling for life by their own means, even if their stubbornness meant going hungry. Unconcerned about tomorrow, forgetful that he who pays in advance always ends up being badly served, the majority of the blind internees, in all the wards, slept soundly. The others, tired of searching in vain for an honourable way out of the vexations suffered, also fell asleep one by one, dreaming of better days than these, days of greater freedom if not of greater abundance. In the first ward on the right, only the doctor's wife was still awake. Lying on her bed, she was thinking about what her husband had told her, when for a moment he suspected that amongst the blind thieves there was someone who could see, someone whom they might use as a spy. It was curious that they had not touched on the subject again, as if it had not occurred to the doctor, accustomed as he was to the fact, that his own wife could still see. It crossed her mind, but she said nothing, she had no desire to utter the obvious words, What he is unable to do after all, I can do. What is that, the doctor would ask, pretending not to understand. Now, with her eyes fixed on the scissors hanging on the wall, the doctor's wife was asking herself, What use is my eyesight, It had exposed her to greater horror than she could ever have imagined, it had convinced her that she would rather be blind, nothing else. Moving cautiously, she sat up in bed. Opposite her, the girl with the dark glasses and the boy with the squint were asleep. She noticed that the two beds were very close together, the girl had pushed hers over, almost certainly to be closer to the boy should he need to be comforted or have someone to dry his tears in the absence of his mother. Why did I not think of it before, I could have pushed our beds together and we could have slept together, without this constant worry that he might fall out of bed. She looked at her husband, who was fast asleep, in a deep sleep from sheer exhaustion. She had not got round to telling him that she had brought the scissors, that one of these days she would have to trim his beard, a task that even a blind man is capable of carrying out so long as he does not bring the blades too close to his skin. She has found a good excuse for not mentioning the scissors, Afterwards all the men here would be pestering me and I'd find myself doing nothing except trimming beards. She swung her body outwards, rested her feet on the floor and searched for her shoes. As she was about to slip them on, she held back, stared at them closely, then shook her head and, without making a noise, put them back. She passed along the aisle between the beds and slowly made her way towards the door of the ward. Her bare feet came into contact with the slimy excrement on the floor, but she knew that out there in the corridors it would be much worse. She kept looking from one side to the other, to see if any of the blind internees were awake, although whether several of them might be keeping vigil, or the entire ward, was of no importance so long as she did not make a noise, and even if she did, we know how pressing our bodily needs can be, they do not choose their hour, in a word, what she did not want was that her husband should wake up and sense her absence in time to ask her, Where are you going, which is probably the question husbands most frequently put to their wives, the other being Where have you been, One of the blind women was sitting up in bed, her shoulders resting against the low head-rest, her empty gaze fixed on the wall opposite, but she could not see it. The doctor's wife paused for a moment, as if not sure whether to touch that invisible thread that hovered in the air, as if the slightest contact would irrevocably destroy it. The blind woman raised her arm, she must have perceived some gentle vibration in the atmosphere, then she let it drop, no longer interested, it was enough not to be able to sleep because of her neighbours' snoring. The doctor's wife continued walking in ever greater haste as she approached the door. Before heading for the hallway, she looked along the corridor that led to the other wards on this side, further ahead, to the lavatories, and ultimately to the kitchen and refectory. There were blind inmates lying up against the walls, those who on arrival had been unsuccessful in finding a bed, either because in the assault they had lagged behind, or because they lacked the strength to contest a bed and win their battle. Ten metres away, a blind man was lying on top of a blind woman, the man caught between her legs, they were being as discreet as they could, they were the discreet kind, but you would not have needed very sharp hearing to know what they were up to, especially when first one and then the other could no longer repress their sighs and groans, some inarticulate word, which are the signs that all that is about to end. The doctor's wife stopped in her tracks to watch them, not out of envy, she had her husband and the satisfaction he gave her, but because of an impression of another order, for which she could find no name, perhaps a feeling of sympathy, as if she were thinking of saying to them, Don't mind my being here, I also know what this means, continue, perhaps a feeling of compassion, Even if this instant of supreme pleasure should last you a lifetime, you will never become united as one. The blind man and the blind woman were now resting, apart, the one lying beside the other, but they were still holding hands, they were young, perhaps even lovers who had gone to the cinema and turned blind there, or perhaps some miraculous coincidence brought them together in this place, and, this being the case, how did they recognise each other, good heavens, by their voices, of course, it is not only the voice of blood that needs no eyes, love, which people say is blind, also has a voice of its own. In all probability, though, they were taken at the same time, in which case those clasped hands are not something recent, they have been clasped since the beginning.

The doctor's wife sighed, raised her hands to her eyes, she had to because she could barely see, but she was not alarmed, she knew they were only tears. Then she continued on her way. On reaching the hallway, she went up to the door leading to the courtyard. She looked outside. Behind the gate there was a light which outlined the black silhouette of a soldier. On the other side of the street, the buildings were all in darkness. She went out on to the top of the steps. There was no danger. Even if the soldier were to become aware of her shadow, he would only shoot if she, having descended the stairs, were to get nearer, after being warned, from that other invisible line which represented for him the frontier of his safety. Accustomed now to the constant noises in the ward, the doctor's wife found the silence strange, a silence that seemed to occupy the space of an absence, as if humanity, the whole of humanity, had disappeared, leaving only a light and a soldier keeping watch over it. She sat on the ground, her back resting against the door jamb, in the same position in which she had seen the blind woman in the ward, and stared ahead like her. The night was cold, the wind blew along the front of the building, it seemed impossible that there should still be wind in this world, that the night should be black, she wasn't thinking of herself, she was thinking of the blind for whom the day was endless. Above the light, another silhouette appeared, it was probably the guard's relief, Nothing to report, the soldier would be saying before going off to his tent to get some sleep, neither of them had any idea what was happening behind that door, probably the noise of the shots had not even been heard out here, an ordinary gun does not make much noise. A pair of scissors even less, thought the doctor's wife. She did not waste time asking herself where such a thought had come from, she was only surprised at its slowness, at how the first word had been so slow in appearing, the slowness of those to follow, and how she found that the thought was already there before, somewhere or other, and only the words were missing, like a body searching in the bed for the hollow that had been prepared for it by the mere idea of lying down. The soldier approached the gate, although he is standing against the light, it is clear that he is looking in this direction, he must have noticed the motionless shadow, although, for the moment, there is not enough light to see that it is only a woman seated on the ground, her arms cradling her legs and her chin resting on her knees, the soldier points the beam of a torch at her, now there can be no doubt, it is a woman who is about to get up with a movement as slow as her previous thought had been, but the soldier is not to know this, all he knows is that he is afraid of that figure of a woman who seems to be taking ages to get to her feet, in a flash he asks himself whether he should raise the alarm, the next moment he decides against it, after all, it is only a woman and she is some way away, in any case, as a precaution he points his weapon in her direction, but this means putting the torch aside and, with that movement, the luminous beam shone directly into his eyes, like a sudden burning, an impression of being dazzled remained in his retina. When he recovered his vision, the woman had disappeared, now this guard will be unable to say to the person who comes to relieve him, Nothing to report.

The doctor's wife is already in the left wing, in the corridor that will take her to the third ward. Here too there are blind inmates sleeping on the floor, more of them than in the right wing. She walks noiselessly, slowly, she can feel the slime on the ground sticking to her feet. She looks inside the first two wards, and sees what she expected to see, bodies lying under blankets, there is a blind man who is also unable to sleep and says so in a desperate voice, she can hear the staccato snoring of almost everyone else. As for the smell that all this gives off, it does not surprise her, there is no other smell in the entire building, it is the smell of her own body, of the clothes she is wearing. On turning the corner into the corridor giving access to the third ward, she came to a halt. There is a man at the door, another guard. He has a stick in his hand, he is wielding it in slow motion, to one side then the next, as if blocking the passage of anyone who might try to approach. Here there are no blind inmates sleeping on the ground and the corridor is clear. The blind man at the door continues his uniform toing-and-froing, he seems never to tire, but it is not so, after several minutes he takes his staff in the other hand and starts all over again. The doctor's wife advanced keeping close to the wall on the other side, taking care not to rub against it. The curve made by the stick does not even reach halfway across the wide corridor, one is tempted to say that this guard is on duty with an unloaded weapon. The doctor's wife is now directly opposite the blind man, she can see the ward behind him. Not all the beds are occupied. How many are there, she wondered. She advanced a little further, almost to the point where his stick could reach, and there she came to a halt, the blind man had turned his head to the side where she was standing, as if he had sensed something unusual, a sigh, a tremor in the air. He was a tall man, with large hands. First he stretched out before him the hand holding the stick and with rapid gestures swept the emptiness before him, then took a short step, for one second, the doctor's wife feared that he might be able to see her, that he was only looking for the best place to attack her, Those eyes are not blind, she thought with alarm. Yes, of course they were blind, as blind as those of all the inmates living under this roof, between these walls, all of them, all of them except her. In a low voice, almost in a whisper, the man asked, Who's there, he did not shout like a real guard, Who goes there, friend or foe, the appropriate reply would be, Friend, whereupon he would say, Pass, but keep your distance, however, things did not turn out this way, he merely shook his head as if he were saying to himself, What nonsense, how could anyone be there, at this hour everyone is asleep. Fumbling with his free hand, he retreated back towards the door, and, calmed by his own words, he let his arms hang. He felt sleepy, he had been waiting for ages for one of his comrades to come and relieve him, but for this to happen it was necessary that the other, on hearing the inner voice of duty, should wake up by himself, for there were no alarm clocks around nor any means of using them. Cautiously, the doctor's wife reached the other side of the door and looked inside. The ward was not full. She made a rapid calculation, decided there must be some nineteen or twenty occupants. At the far end, she saw a number of food containers piled up, others were lying on the empty beds. As was only to be expected, they don't distribute all the food they receive, she thought. The blind man seemed to be getting worried again, but made no attempt to investigate. The minutes passed. The sound of someone coughing loudly, obviously a heavy smoker, could be heard coming from inside. The blind man turned his head apprehensively, at last he would get some sleep. None of those lying in bed got up. Then the blind man, slowly, as if afraid that they might surprise him in the act of abandoning his post or infringing at one go all the rules guards are obliged to observe, sat down on the edge of the bed blocking the entrance. For a few moments, he nodded, then he succumbed to the river of sleep, and in all certainty as he went under he must have thought, It doesn't matter, no one can see me. The doctor's wife counted once more those who were asleep inside, Including him there are twenty of them, at least she had gathered some real information, her nocturnal excursion had not been in vain, But was this my only reason for coming here, she asked herself, and she preferred not to pursue the answer. The blind man was sleeping, his head resting against the doorjamb, his stick had slipped silently to the floor, there was a defenceless blind man and with no columns to bring crashing down around him. The doctor's wife consciously wanted to think that this man had stolen the food, had stolen what rightfully belonged to others, that he took food from the mouths of children, but despite these thoughts, she did not feel any contempt, not even the slightest irritation, nothing other than a strange compassion for that drooping body before her, the head lolling backwards, the long neck covered in swollen veins. For the first time since she had left the ward she felt a cold shiver run through her, it was as if the flagstones were turning her feet to ice, as if they were being scorched. Let's hope it isn't fever, she thought. It couldn't be, more likely some infinite weariness, a longing to curl up inside herself, her eyes, especially her eyes, turned inwards, more, more, more, until they could reach and observe inside her own brain, there where the difference between seeing and not seeing is invisible to the naked eye. Slowly, ever more slowly, dragging her body, she retraced her footsteps to the place where she belonged, she passed by blind internees who seemed like sleepwalkers, as she must have seemed to them, she did not even have to pretend that she was blind. The blind lovers were no longer holding hands, they were asleep and lying huddled beside each other, she in the curve made by his body to keep warm, and taking a closer look, they were holding hands, after all, his arm over her body, their fingers clasped. There inside the ward, the blind woman who had been unable to sleep was still sitting up in bed, waiting until she became so tired that her body would finally overcome the obstinate resistance of her mind. All the others appeared to be sleeping, some with their heads covered, as if they were still searching for some impossible darkness. On the bedside table of the girl with dark glasses stood the bottle of eye-drops. Her eyes were already better, but she was not to know.

If, because of a sudden illumination that might quell his suspicions, the blind man entrusted with keeping an account of the ill-gotten gains of the miscreants had decided to come over to this side with his writing board, his thick paper and puncher, he would now almost certainly be occupied in drafting the instructive and lamentable chronicle of the inadequate diet and the many other privations of these new fellow-inmates who have been well and truly fleeced. He would begin by saying that from where he had come, the usurpers had not only expelled the respectable blind inmates from the ward in order to take possession of the entire space, but, furthermore, had forbidden the inmates of the other two wards on the left-hand side any access or use of the respective sanitary installations, as they are called. He would remark that the immediate outcome of this infamous tyranny was that all those poor people would flock to the lavatories on this side, with consequences easy to imagine for anyone who still remembers the earlier state of the place. He would point out that it is impossible to walk through the inner courtyard without tripping over blind inmates getting rid of their diarrhoea or in contortions from ineffectual straining that had promised much and in the end resolved nothing, and, being an observant soul, he would not fail, deliberately, to register the patent contradiction between the small amount the inmates consumed and the vast quantity they excreted, perhaps thus showing that the famous relationship between cause and effect, so often cited, is not, at least from a quantitative point of view, always to be trusted. He would also say that while at this hour the ward of this thieving rabble must be crammed with containers of food, here it will not be long before the poor wretches are reduced to gathering up crumbs from the filthy floors. Nor would the blind accountant forget to condemn, in his dual role as participant in the process and its chronicler, the criminal conduct of these blind oppressors, who prefer to allow the food to go bad rather than give it to those who are in such great need, for while it is true that some of this foodstuff can last for weeks without going off, the rest, especially the cooked food, unless eaten immediately, soon turns sour or becomes covered in mould, and is therefore no longer fit for human consumption, if this sorry lot can still be thought of as human beings. Changing the subject but not the theme, the chronicler would write, with much sorrow in his heart, that the illnesses here are not solely those of the digestive tract, whether from lack of food or because of poor digestion of what was eaten, most of the people arriving here, though blind, were not only healthy, but some to all appearances were positively bursting with health, now they are like the others, unable to raise themselves from their miserable beds, stricken by influenza that spread who knows how. And not a single aspirin is there to be found anywhere in these five wards to lower their temperatures and relieve the pain of their headaches, what little was left was soon gone, after one had rummaged even through the lining of the women's handbags. Out of discretion, the chronicler would abandon any idea of making a detailed report of all the other ills that are afflicting most of the nearly three hundred inmates being kept in this inhumane quarantine, but he could not fail to mention at least two cases of fairly advanced cancer, for the authorities had no humanitarian scruples when rounding up the blind and confining them here, they even stated that the law once made is the same for everyone and that democracy is incompatible with preferential treatment. As cruel fate would have it, amongst all these inmates there is only one doctor, and an ophthalmologist at that, the last thing we needed. Arriving at this point, the blind accountant, tired of describing so much misery and sorrow, would let his metal punch fall to the table, he would search with a trembling hand for the piece of stale bread he had put to one side while he fulfilled his obligations as chronicler of the end of time, but he would not find it, because another blind man, whose sense of smell had become very keen out of dire necessity, had filched it. Then, renouncing his fraternal gesture, the altruistic impulse that had brought him rushing to this side, the blind accountant would decide that the best course of action, if he was still in time, was to return to the third ward on the left, there, at least, however much the injustices of those hoodlums stirred up in him feelings of honest indignation, he would not go hungry.

This is really the crux of the matter. Each time those sent to fetch the food return to their ward with the meagre rations they have been given there is an outburst of angry protest. There is always someone who proposes collective action, a mass demonstration, using the forceful argument about the cumulative strength of their numbers, confirmed time and time again and sublimated in the dialectic affirmation that determined wills, in general merely capable of being added one to the other, are also very capable in certain circumstances of multiplying among themselves ad infinitum. However, it was not long before the inmates calmed down, it was enough that someone more prudent, with the simple and objective intention of pondering the advantages and risks of the action proposed, should remind the enthusiasts of the fatal effects handguns tend to have, Those who went ahead, they would say, would know what awaits them there, and as for those behind, best not to think of what might happen in the likely event that we should take fright at the first shot, more of us would be crushed to death than shot down. As an intermediate decision, it was decided in one of the wards, and word of this decision was passed on to the others, that, for the collection of food, they would not send the usual emissaries who had been subjected to derision but a sizable group, some ten or twelve persons to be more precise, who would try to express as one voice, the general discontent. Volunteers were asked to come forward, but, perhaps because of the aforementioned warnings of the more cautious, few came forward for this mission in any of the wards. Fortunately, this patent show of moral weakness ceased to have any importance, and even to be a cause for shame, when, proving prudence to be the correct response, the outcome of the expedition organised by the ward that had thought up the idea became known. The eight courageous souls who had been so bold were immediately chased away with cudgels, and while it is true that only one bullet was fired, it is also true that it was not aimed as high as the first shots, the proof being that the protesters claimed they had heard it whistle right past their heads. Whether there had been any intent to kill we shall perhaps discover later, for the present we shall give the marksman the benefit of the doubt, that is to say, either that the shot was no more than a warning, although a more serious one, or the leader of these rogues underestimated the height of the demonstrators whom he imagined to be shorter, or, a disconcerting thought, his mistake was to imagine them taller than they really were, in which case an intent to kill would inevitably have to be considered. Leaving aside these trifling questions for the moment and turning to issues of general concern, which are those that matter, it was truly providential, even if merely a coincidence, that the protesters should have declared themselves the representatives of such and such a ward. In this way, only that ward had to fast for three days as a punishment, and fortunately for them, for they could have had their provisions cut off for ever, as is only just when someone dares to bite the hand that feeds him. So, during these three days, there was no other solution for those from the rebellious ward than to go from door to door and beg a crust of bread, for pity's sake, if possible with a bit of meat or cheese, they did not die of hunger, to be sure, but they had to take an earful, With ideas like that, what do you expect, If we had listened to you, where would we be now, but worst of all was to be told, Be patient, be patient, there are no crueller words, better to be insulted. And when the three days of punishment were over and it was thought that a new day was about to dawn, it became clear that the punishment of that unhappy ward where the forty rebellious inmates were quartered, was not yet over after all, for the rations which up until now had barely been enough for twenty, were now reduced to the point where they would not satisfy the hunger of ten. You can imagine, therefore, their outrage and indignation, and also, let it hurt whom it may, facts are facts, the fear of the remaining wards, who already saw themselves being besieged by the needy, their reactions divided between the classic duties of human solidarity and the observance of the ancient and no less time-honoured precept that charity begins at home.

Things were at this stage when an order came from the hoodlums that more money and valuables should be handed over inasmuch as they considered that the food supplies had exceeded the value of the initial payment, which moreover, according to them, had generously been calculated to be on the high side. The wards replied in despair that not so much as a coin was left in their pockets, that all the valuables collected had been scrupulously handed in, and that, a truly shameful argument, no decision could be altogether equitable if it were to ignore the difference in value of the various contributions, that is to say, in simple language, it was not fair that the upright man should pay for the sinner, and therefore that they should not cut off the provisions from someone, who in all probability, still had a balance to their credit. Obviously, none of the wards knew the value of what had been handed over by the others, but each ward thought it had every right to go on eating when the rest had already used up their credit. Fortunately, thanks to the fact that these latent conflicts were nipped in the bud, the hoodlums were adamant, their order had to be obeyed by everyone, if there had been any differences in the evaluation these were known only to the blind accountant. In the wards the exchanges were heated and bitter, sometimes becoming violent. Some suspected that certain selfish and dishonest inmates had withheld some of their valuables when the collection took place, and therefore had been given food at the expense of those who had given away everything to benefit the community. Others alleged, adopting what up until that moment had been a collective argument, that what they had handed over, should in itself be enough for them to go on being fed for many days to come, instead of being forced to feed parasites. The threat made by the blind thugs at the outset, that they would carry out an inspection of the wards and punish those who had disobeyed their orders, ended up by being carried out inside each of the wards, the honest at loggerheads with the dishonest, and even the malicious. No great fortunes were discovered, but some watches and rings came to light, mostly belonging to men rather than women. As for the punishments exacted by internal justice, these were nothing more than a few random slaps, a few half-hearted and badly aimed punches, most of the exchanges were verbal insults, some accusing expression culled from the rhetoric of the past, for example, You'd steal from your own mother, just imagine, as if a similar ignominy, and others of even greater consideration would only be committed the day that everyone went blind, and, having lost the light of their eyes, even lost the guiding spirit of respect. The blind thugs received the payment with threats of harsh reprisals, which fortunately they did not carry out, the assumption being that they had forgotten, when the truth is that they already had another idea, as would soon be revealed. If they were to carry out their threats and further injustices, they would aggravate the situation, perhaps with immediate dramatic consequences, insofar as two of the wards, in order to conceal their crime of holding back valuables, presented themselves in the name of others, burdening the innocent wards with transgressions they had not committed, one of them so honest, in fact, that it had handed over everything on the first day. Fortunately, in order to spare himself more work, the blind accountant had decided to keep note of the various contributions that had just been made on a single and separate sheet of paper, and this was to everyone's advantage, both the innocent and the guilty, for the fiscal irregularity would almost certainly have caught his attention if he had entered them against the respective accounts.

After a week, the blind hoodlums sent a message saying that they wanted women. Just like that, Bring us women. This unexpected demand, although not altogether unusual, caused an outcry as one might have expected, the bewildered emissaries who had come with the order returned at once to communicate that the wards, the three on the right and the two on the left, not excepting the blind men and women who were sleeping on the floor, had decided unanimously to ignore this degrading imposition, arguing that human dignity, in this instance feminine, could not be debased to this extent, and that if the third ward on the left-hand side had no women, the responsibility, if any, could not be laid at their door. The reply was curt and intransigent, Unless you bring us women, you don't eat. Humiliated, the emissaries returned to the wards with this order, Either you go there or they will give us nothing to eat. The women on their own, those without any partner, or at least any fixed partner, protested at once, they were not prepared to pay for the food for other women's menfolk with what they had between their legs, one of them was even so bold as to say, forgetting the respect she owed her own sex, I'll go there if I want to, but whatever I may earn is for me, and if I so please, I'll move in with them, then I'll have a bed and my keep assured. These were the unequivocal words she uttered, but she did not put them into action, she remembered in time the horrors she would experience if she had to cope on her own with the erotic frenzy of twenty desperate men whose urgency gave the impression they were blinded by lust. However, this declaration made so lightly in the second ward on the right-hand side, did not fall on stony ground, one of the emissaries, with a particular sense of occasion, supported her by proposing that women volunteers should come forward for this service, taking into account that what one does on one's own initiative is generally less arduous than if one has to do something under duress. Only one last scruple, one last reminder of the need for caution, prevented him from ending his appeal by quoting the well-known proverb, When the spirit is willing, your feet are light. Even so, no sooner had he stopped speaking than the protests erupted, anger broke out on all sides, without pity or compassion, the men were morally defeated, they were accused of being yobs, pimps, parasites, vampires, exploiters, panderers, according to the culture, social background and personal disposition of the women who were rightly indignant. Some of them declared their remorse at having given in, out of sheer generosity and compassion, to the sexual overtures of their companions in misfortune who were now showing their ingratitude by trying to push them into the worst of fates. The men tried to justify themselves, that it was not quite like that, that they should not dramatise, what the hell, by talking things over, people can come to some understanding, it was only because custom demands that volunteers should be asked to come forward in difficult and dangerous situations, as this one undoubtedly is, We are all at risk of dying of hunger, both you and us. Some of the women calmed down by this reasoning, but one of the others, suddenly inspired, threw another log on the fire when she asked ironically, And what would you do if these rascals instead of asking for women had asked for men, what would you do then, speak up so that everyone can hear. The women were jubilant, Tell us, tell us, they chorused, delighted at having backed the men up against the wall, caught in the snares of their own reasoning from which there was no escape, now they wanted to see how far that much lauded masculine logic would go, There are no pansies here, one man dared to protest, And no whores either, retorted the woman who had asked the provocative question, and even if there were, they might not be prepared to prostitute themselves for you. Put out, the men shrugged their shoulders, aware that there was only one answer capable of satisfying these vindictive women. If they were to ask for men, we would go, but not one of them had the courage to utter these brief, explicit and uninhibited words, and they were so dismayed that they forgot that there was no great harm in saying this, since those sons of bitches were not interested in relieving themselves with men but with women.

Now what did not occur to any of the men appeared to have occurred to the women, there could be no other explanation for the silence that gradually descended on the ward where these confrontations took place, as if they had understood that for them, victory in a verbal battle of wits was no different from the defeat that would inevitably follow, perhaps in the other wards the debate had been much the same, since we know that human reason and unreason are the same everywhere. Here, the person who passed the final judgment was a woman already in her fifties who had her old mother with her and no other means of providing her with food, I'll go, she said, without knowing that these words echoed those spoken by the doctor's wife in the first ward on the right-hand side, I'll go, there are few women in this ward, perhaps for that reason the protests were fewer or less vehement, there was the girl with dark glasses, there was the wife of the first blind man, there was the girl from the surgery, there was the chambermaid, there was one woman nobody knew anything about, there was the woman who could not sleep, but she was so unhappy and wretched that it would be best to leave her in peace, for there was no reason why only the men should benefit from the women's solidarity. The first blind man had begun by declaring that his wife would not be subjected to the shame of giving her body to strangers in exchange for whatever, she had no desire to do so nor would he permit it, for dignity has no price, that when someone starts making small concessions, in the end life loses all meaning. The doctor then asked him what meaning he saw in the situation in which all of them there found themselves, starving, covered in filth up to their ears, ridden with lice, eaten by bedbugs, bitten by fleas, I, too, would prefer my wife not to go, but what I want serves no purpose, she has said she is prepared to go, that was her decision, I know that my manly pride, this thing we call male pride, if after so many humiliations we still preserve something worthy of that name, I know that it will suffer, it already is, I cannot avoid it, but it is probably the only solution, if we want to live, Each person proceeds according to whatever morals they have, that's how I see it and I have no intention of changing my ideas, the first blind man retorted aggressively. Then the girl with dark glasses said, The others don't know how many women are here, therefore you can keep yours for your exclusive use, we shall feed both you and her, I'd be interested to see how you feel then about your dignity, how the bread we bring you will taste, That's not the point, the first blind man started to reply, the point is, but his words tailed off, were left hanging in the air, in reality he did not know what the point was, everything he had said earlier had been no more than certain vague opinions, nothing more than opinions belonging to another world, not to this one, what he ought to do, no doubt about it, was to raise his hands to heaven thanking fortune that his shame might remain, as it were, at home, rather than bear the vexation of knowing that he was being kept alive by the wives of others. By the doctor's wife, to be absolutely precise, because as for the rest, apart from the girl with dark glasses, unmarried and free, about whose dissipated life-style we have more than enough information, if they had husbands they were not to be seen. The silence that followed the interrupted phrase seemed to be waiting for someone to clarify the situation once and for all, for this reason it was not long before the person who had to speak spoke up, this was the wife of the first blind man, who said without so much as a tremor in her voice, I'm no different from the others, I'll do whatever they do, You'll do as I say, interrupted her husband, Stop giving orders, they won't do much good here, you're as blind as I am, It's indecent, It's up to you not to be indecent, from now on you don't eat, this was her cruel reply, unexpected in someone who until today had been so docile and respectful towards her husband. There was a short burst of laughter, it came from the hotel maid, Ah, eat, eat, what is he to do, poor fellow, suddenly her laughter turned to weeping, her words changed, What are we to do, she said, it was almost a question, an almost resigned question to which there was no answer, like a despondent shaking of the head, so much so that the girl from the surgery did nothing but repeat, What are we to do. The doctor's wife looked up at the scissors hanging on the wall, from the expression in her eyes you would say she was asking herself the same question, unless what she was looking for was an answer to the question she threw back at them, What do you want from me.

However, to everything its proper season, just because you rise early does not mean that you will die sooner. The blind inmates in the third ward on the left-hand side are well organised, they had already decided that they would begin with those closest, with the women from the wards in their wing. The application of this method of rotation, a more than apt expression, has all the advantages and no drawbacks, in the first place, because it will allow them to know, at any given moment, what has been done and what remains to be done, like looking at a clock and saying of the day that is passing, I've lived from here to here, I've so much or so little left, in the second place, because when the round of the wards has been completed, the return to the beginning will bring with it an undeniable air of renovation, especially for those with a very short sensory memory. So let the women in the wards in the right wing enjoy themselves, I can cope with the misfortunes of my neighbours, words that none of the women spoke but which they all thought, in truth, the human being to lack that second skin we call egoism has not yet been born, it lasts much longer than the other one, that bleeds so readily. It also has to be said that these women are enjoying themselves on two counts, such are the mysteries of the human soul, for the inescapable impending threat of the humiliation to which they are to be subjected, aroused and exacerbated in each ward sensual appetites that increasing familiarity had jaded, it was as if the men were desperately putting their mark on the women before they were taken off, it was as if the women wanted to fill their memory with sensations experienced voluntarily in order to be able better to defend themselves from the aggression of those sensations which, if they could, they would reject. It is inevitable that we should ask, taking as an example the first ward on the right-hand side, how the question of the difference between the number of men and women was resolved, even discounting the impotent of the males in the group, as in the case of the old man with the black eyepatch as well as others, unidentified, both old and young, who for one reason or another, neither said nor did anything worth bringing into our narrative. As has already been mentioned, there are seven women in this ward, including the blind woman who suffers from insomnia and whom nobody knows, and the so-called normal couples, are no more than two, which would leave an unbalanced number of men, because the boy with the squint does not yet count. Perhaps in the other wards there are more women than men, but an unwritten law, that soon gained acceptance here and subsequently became statutory decrees that all matters have to be resolved in the wards in which they have surfaced in accordance with the precepts of the ancients, whose wisdom we shall never tire of praising, if you would be well served, serve yourself. Therefore the women from the first ward on the right-hand side will give relief to the men who live under the same roof, with the exception of the doctor's wife, who, for some reason or other, no one dared to solicit either with words or an extended hand. Already the wife of the first blind man, after having made the first move with that abrupt reply she had given her husband, did, albeit discreetly, what the other women had done, as she herself had announced. There are, however, certain resistances against which neither reason nor sentiment can do anything, such as is the case of the girl with dark glasses, whom the pharmacist's assistant, however many arguments he offered, however many pleas he made, was unable to win over, thus paying for his lack of respect at the outset. This same girl, there's no understanding women, who is the prettiest of all the women here, the one with the shapeliest figure, the most attractive, the one whom all the men craved when the word about her exceptional looks got around, finally got into bed one night of her own free will with the old man with the black eyepatch, who received her like summer rain and satisfied her as best he could, pretty well given his age, thus proving once more, that appearances are deceptive, that it is not from someone's face and the litheness of their body that we can judge their strength of heart. Everyone in the ward thought that it was nothing more than an act of charity that the girl with dark glasses should have offered herself to the old man with the black eyepatch, but there were men there, sensitive and dreamers, who having already enjoyed her favours, began to allow their thoughts to wander, to think there could be no greater prize in this world than for a man to find himself stretched out on his bed, all alone, thinking the impossible, only to realise that a woman is gently lifting the covers and slipping under them, slowly rubbing her body against his body, and then lying still, waiting for the heat of their blood to calm the sudden tremor of their startled skin. And all this for no good reason, just because she wanted to. These are fortunes that do not go to waste, sometimes a man has to be old and wear a black eyepatch covering an eye-socket that is definitively blind. And then there are certain things that are best left unexplained, it's best just to say what happened, not to probe people's inner thoughts and feelings, as on that occasion when the doctor's wife had got out of bed to go and cover up the boy with the squint whose blanket had slipped off. She did not go back to bed at once. Leaning against the wall at the far end of the ward, in the narrow space between the two rows of beds, she was looking in desperation at the door at the other end, that door through which they had entered on a day that seemed so remote and that now led nowhere. She was standing there when she saw her husband get up, and, staring straight ahead as if he were sleepwalking, make his way to the bed of the girl with dark glasses. She made no attempt to stop him. Standing motionless, she saw him lift the covers and then lie down, whereupon the girl woke up and received him without protest, she saw how those two mouths searched until they found each other, and then the inevitable happened, the pleasure of the one, the pleasure of the other, the pleasure of both of them, the muffled cries, she said, Oh, doctor, and these words could have sounded so ridiculous but did not, he said, Forgive me, I don't know what came over me, in fact, we were right, how could we, who hardly see, know what even he does not know, Lying on the narrow bed, they could not have imagined that they were being watched, the doctor certainly could not, he was suddenly worried, would his wife be asleep, he asked himself, or was she wandering the corridors as she did every night, he made to go back to his own bed, but a voice said, Don't get up, and a hand rested on his chest with the lightness of a bird, he was about to speak, perhaps about to repeat that he did not know what had got into him, but the voice said, If you say nothing it will be easier for me to understand. The girl with dark glasses began to weep, What an unhappy lot we are, she murmured, and then, I wanted it too, I wanted it too, you are not to blame, Be quiet the doctor's wife said gently, let's all keep quiet, there are times when words serve no purpose, if only I, too, could weep, say everything with tears, not have to speak in order to be understood. She sat on the edge of the bed, stretched her arm over the two bodies, as if gathering them in the same embrace, and, bending over the girl with dark glasses, she whispered in her ear, I can see. The girl remained still, serene, simply puzzled that she should feel no surprise, it was as if she had known from the very first day but had not wanted to say so aloud since this was a secret that did not belong to her. She turned her head ever so slightly and responded by whispering into the ear of the doctor's wife, I knew, at least, I'm not entirely sure, but I think I knew, It's a secret, you mustn't tell a soul, don't worry, I trust you, And so you should, I'd rather die than betray you, You must call me "tu," Oh, no, I couldn't, I simply couldn't do it. They went on whispering to each other, first one, then the other, touching each other's hair, the lobe of the ear, with their lips, it was an insignificant dialogue, it was a profoundly serious dialogue, if this contradiction can be reconciled, a brief conspiratorial conversation that appeared to ignore the man lying between the two of them, but involved him in a logic outside the world of commonplace ideas and realities. Then the doctor's wife said to her husband, Lie there for a little longer, if you wish, No, I'm going back to our bed, Then I'll help you. She sat up to give him greater freedom of movement, contemplated for an instant the two blind heads resting side by side on the soiled pillow, their faces dirty, their hair tangled, only their eyes shining to no purpose. He got up slowly, looking for support, then remained motionless at the side of the bed, undecided, as if he had suddenly lost all notion of the place where he found himself, then she, as she had always done, took him by one arm, but the gesture now had another meaning, never had he so badly needed someone to guide him as at this moment, although he would never know to what extent, only the two women really knew, when the doctor's wife stroked the girl's cheek with her other hand and the girl impulsively took it and raised it to her lips. The doctor thought he could hear sobbing, an almost inaudible sound that could have come only from tears trickling slowly down to the corners of the mouth where they disappear to recommence the eternal cycle of inexplicable human joys and sorrows. The girl with dark glasses was about to remain alone, she was the one who ought to be consoled, for this reason the doctor's wife was slow to remove her hand.

Next day, at dinner-time, if a few miserable pieces of stale bread and mouldy meat deserved such a name, there appeared in the doorway of the ward three blind men from the other side. How many women have you got in here, one of them asked, Six, replied the doctor's wife, with the good intention of leaving out the blind woman who suffered from insomnia, but she corrected her in a subdued voice, There are seven of us. The blind thugs laughed, Too bad, said one of them, you'll just have to work all the harder tonight, and another suggested, Perhaps we'd better go and look for reinforcements in the next ward, It isn't worth it, said the third blind man who knew his sums, it works out at three men for each woman, they can stand it. This brought another burst of laughter, and the fellow who had asked how many women there were, gave the order, When you've finished, come over to us, and added, That's if you want to eat tomorrow and suckle your menfolk. They said these words in all the wards, and still laughed at the joke with as much gusto as on the day they had invented it. They doubled up with laughter, stamped their feet, beat their thick cudgels on the ground, until one of them suddenly cautioned, Listen here, if any of you has got the curse, we don't want you, we'll leave it until the next time, No one's got the curse, the doctor's wife calmly informed him, Then prepare yourselves and don't be long, we're waiting for you. They turned and disappeared. The ward remained in silence. A minute later, the wife of the first blind man said, I cannot eat any more, she had precious little in her hand, and she could not bear to eat it. Nor me, said the blind woman who suffered from insomnia, Nor me, said the woman whom nobody seems to know, I've already finished, said the hotel maid, Me too, said the girl from the surgery, I'll throw up in the face of the first man who comes near me, said the girl with dark glasses. They were all on their feet, shaking and resolute. Then the doctor's wife said, I'll go in front. The first blind man covered his head with the blanket as if this might serve some purpose, since he was already blind, the doctor drew his wife towards him and, without saying anything, gave her a quick kiss on the forehead, what more could he do, it wouldn't make much difference to the other men, they had neither the rights nor the obligations of a husband as far as any of these women were concerned, therefore no one could come up to them and say, A consenting cuckold is a cuckold twice over. The girl with dark glasses got in behind the doctor's wife, then came the hotel maid, the girl from the surgery, the wife of the first blind man, the woman no one knows and, finally, the blind woman suffering from insomnia, a grotesque line-up of foul-smelling women, their clothes filthy and in tatters, it seems impossible that the animal drive for sex should be so powerful, to the point of blinding a man's sense of smell, the most delicate of the senses, there are even some theologians who affirm, although not in these exact words, that the worst thing about trying to live a reasonable life in hell is getting used to the dreadful stench down there. Slowly, guided by the doctor's wife, each of them with her hand on the shoulder of the one in front, the women started walking. They were all barefoot because they did not want to lose their shoes amidst the trials and tribulations they were about to endure. When they arrived in the hallway of the main entrance, the doctor's wife headed for the outer door, no doubt anxious to know if the world still existed. When she felt the fresh air, the hotel maid remembered, frightened, We can't go out, the soldiers are out there, and the blind woman suffering from insomnia said, All the better for us, in less than a minute we'd be dead, that is how we ought to be, all dead, You mean us, asked the girl from the surgery, No, all of us, all the women in here, at least then we'd have the best of reasons for being blind. She had never had so much to say for herself since she'd been brought here. The doctor's wife said, Let's go, only those who have to die will die, death doesn't give any warning when it singles you out. They passed through the door that gave access to the left wing, they made their way down the long corridors, the women from the first two wards could, if they had wished, tell them what awaited them, but they were curled up in their beds like animals that had been given a good thrashing, the men did not dare to touch them, nor did they make any attempt to get close, because the women immediately started screaming.

In the last corridor, at the far end, the doctor's wife saw a blind man who was keeping a lookout, as usual. He must have heard their shuffling footsteps, and informed the others, They're coming, they're coming. From within came cries, whinnying, guffaws of laughter. Four blind men lost no time in removing the bed that was blocking the entrance, Quickly, girls, come in, come in, we're all here like studs in heat, you're going to get your bellies filled, said one of them. The blind thugs surrounded them, tried to fondle them, but fell back in disarray, when their leader, the one who had the gun, shouted, The first choice is mine as you well know. The eyes of all those men anxiously sought out the women, some extended avid hands, if in passing they happened to touch one of them they finally knew where to look. In the middle of the aisle, between the beds, the women stood like soldiers on parade waiting to be inspected. The leader of the blind hoodlums, gun in hand, came up to them, as agile and frisky as if he were able to see them. He placed his free hand on the woman suffering from insomnia, who was first in line, fondled her back and front, her hips, her breasts, between her legs. The blind woman began to scream and he pushed her away, You're a worthless whore. He passed on to the next one, who happened to be the woman that no one knew, now he was fondling her with both hands, having put his gun into his trouser pocket, I say, this one isn't at all bad, and then he moved on to the wife of the first blind man, then the employee from the surgery, then the hotel maid, and exclaimed, Listen, men, these fillies are pretty good. The blind hoodlums whinnied, stamped their feet on the ground, Let's get on with it, it's getting late, some yelled, Take it easy, said the thug with the gun, let me first take a look at the others. He fondled the girl with dark glasses and gave a whistle, Now then, here's a stroke of luck, no filly quite like this one has turned up before. Excited, as he went on fondling the girl, he passed on to the doctor's wife, gave another whistle, This one is on the mature side, but could turn out to be quite a woman. He drew the two women towards him, and almost drooled as he said, I'll keep these two, when I've finished with them, I'll pass them on to the rest of you. He dragged them to the end of the ward, where the containers of food, packets, tins had been piled up, enough supplies to feed a regiment. The women, all of them, were already screaming their heads off, blows, slaps, orders could be heard, Shut up, you whores, these bitches are all the same, they always have to start yelling, Give it to her good and hard and she'll soon be quiet, Just wait until it's my turn and you'll see how they'll be asking for more, Hurry up there, I can't wait another minute. The blind woman suffering from insomnia wailed in desperation beneath an enormous fellow, the other four were surrounded by men with their trousers down who were jostling each other like hyenas around a carcass. The doctor's wife found herself beside the bed where she had been taken, she was standing, her trembling hands gripping the railings of the bed, she watched how the blind leader with the gun tugged and tore the skirt of the girl with dark glasses, how he took down his trousers and, guiding himself with his fingers, pointed his member at the girl's sex, how he pushed and forced, she could hear the grunts, the obscenities, the girl with dark glasses said nothing, she only opened her mouth to vomit, her head to one side, her eyes turned towards the other woman, he did not even notice what was happening, the smell of vomit is only noticed when the atmosphere and all the rest does not smell the same, at last the man shuddered from head to foot, gave three violent jolts as if he were riveting three girders, panted like a suffocating pig, he had finished. The girl with dark glasses wept in silence. The blind man with the gun withdrew his penis, still dripping and said in a hesitant voice, as he stretched out his arm to the doctor's wife, Don't get jealous, I'll be dealing with you next, and then raising his voice, I say, boys, you can come and get this one, but treat her nicely for I may need her again. Half a dozen blind men advanced unsteadily along the passageway, grabbed the girl with dark glasses and almost dragged her away. I'm first, I'm first, said all of them. The blind man with the gun had sat down on the bed, his flaccid penis was resting on the edge of the mattress, his trousers rolled down round his ankles. Kneel down here between my legs, he said. The doctor's wife got on to her knees. Suck me, he said, No, she replied, Either you suck me, or I'll give you a good thrashing, and you won't get any food, he told her, Aren't you afraid I might bite off your penis, she asked him, You can try, I have my hands on your neck, I'd strangle you first if you tried to draw blood, he replied menacingly. Then he said, I seem to recognise your voice, And I recognise your face, You're blind and cannot see me, No, I cannot see you, Then why do you say that you recognise my face, Because that voice can have only one face, Suck me, and forget the chitchat, No, Either you suck me, or your ward won't see another crumb of bread, go back there and tell them that if they have nothing to eat it's because you refused to suck me, and then come back to tell me what happened. The doctor's wife leaned forward, with the tips of two fingers on her right hand she held and raised the man's sticky penis, her left hand resting on the floor, touched his trousers, groped, felt the cold metallic hardness of the gun, I can kill him, she thought. She could not. With his trousers round his ankles, it was impossible to reach the pocket where he had put his weapon. I cannot kill him now, she thought. She moved her head forward, opened her mouth, closed it, closed her eyes in order not to see and began sucking.

Day was breaking when the blind hoodlums allowed the women to go. The blind woman suffering from insomnia had to be carried away in the arms of her companions, who could scarcely drag themselves along. For hours they had passed from one man to another, from humiliation to humiliation, from outrage to outrage, exposed to everything that can be done to a woman while leaving her still alive. As you know, payment is in kind, tell those pathetic men of yours that they have to come and fetch the grub, the blind man with the gun said mockingly as they left. And he added derisively, See you again, girls, so prepare yourselves for the next session. The other blind hoodlums repeated more or less in chorus, See you again, some called them fillies, others whores, but their waning libido was obvious from the lack of conviction in their voices. Deaf, blind, silent, tottering on their feet, with barely enough will-power not to let go of the hand of the woman in front, the hand, not the shoulder, as when they had come, certainly not one of them would have known what to reply if they had been asked, Why are you holding hands as you go, it simply came about, there are gestures for which we cannot always find an easy explanation, sometimes not even a difficult one can be found. As they crossed the hallway, the doctor's wife looked outside, the soldiers were there as well as a truck that was almost certainly being used to distribute the food to those in quarantine. Just at that moment, the blind woman suffering from insomnia lost the power of her legs, literally, as if they had been cut off with a single blow, her heart also gave up, it did not even finish the rhythmic contraction it had started, at last we know why this blind woman could not sleep, now she will sleep, let us not wake her. She's dead, said the doctor's wife, and her voice was expressionless, if it were possible for such a voice, as dead as the word it had spoken, to have come from a living mouth. She raised the suddenly dislocated body, the legs covered in blood, her abdomen bruised, her poor breasts uncovered, brutally scarred, teeth marks on her shoulder where she had been bitten. This is the image of my body, she thought, the image of the body of all the women here, between these outrages and our sorrows there is only one difference, we, for the present, are still alive. Where shall we take her, asked the girl with dark glasses, For the moment to the ward, later we shall bury her, said the doctor's wife.

The men were waiting at the door, only the first blind man was missing, he had covered his head with his blanket once more when he realised the women were coming back, and the boy with the squint, who was asleep. Without hesitation, without having to count the beds, the doctor's wife laid the blind woman who suffered from insomnia on the bed she had occupied. She was unconcerned that the others might find it strange, after all, everyone there knew that she was the blind woman who was most familiar with every nook and cranny in the place. She's dead, she repeated, What happened, asked the doctor, but his wife made no attempt to answer him, his question might be simply what it appeared to mean, How did she die, but it could also imply What did they do to you in there, now, neither for the one nor for the other of these questions could there be an answer, she simply died, from what scarcely matters, it is foolish for anyone to ask what someone died from, in time the cause will be forgotten, only two words remain, She died, and we are no longer the same women as when we left here, the words they would have spoken we can no longer speak, and as for the others, the unnameable exists, that is its name, nothing else. Go and fetch the food, said the doctor's wife. Chance, fate, fortune, destiny, or whatever is the precise term for that which has so many names, is made of pure irony, how else could we understand why it was precisely the husbands of two of the women who were chosen to represent the ward and collect their food, when no one could imagine that the price would be what had just been paid. It could have been other men, unmarried, free, with no conjugal honour to defend, but then it had to be these two, who certainly will not now wish to bear the shame of extending a hand to beg from these degenerate rogues who have violated their wives. The first blind man said it, with all the emphasis of a firm decision, Whoever wishes can go, but I'm not going, I'll go, said the doctor, I'll go with you, said the old man with the black eyepatch. There won't be much food, but I warn you it's quite a weight, I still have the strength to carry the bread I eat, What always weighs more is the bread of the others, I have no right to complain, the weight carried by the others will buy me my food. Let us try to imagine, not the dialogue for that is over and done with, but the men who took part in it, they are there, face to face, as if they could see each other, which in this case is impossible, it is enough that the memory of each of them should bring out from the dazzling whiteness of the world the mouth that is articulating the words, and then, like a slow irradiation coming from this centre, the rest of the faces will start to appear, one an old man, the other not so old, and anyone who can still see in this way cannot really be called blind. When they moved off to go and collect the wages of shame, as the first blind man protested with rhetorical indignation, the doctor's wife said to the other women, Stay here, I'll be right back. She knew what she wanted, she did not know if she would find it. She needed a bucket or something that would serve the purpose, she wanted to fill it with water, even if fetid, even if polluted, she wanted to wash the corpse of the woman who had suffered from insomnia, to wipe away her own blood and the sperm of others, to deliver her purified to the earth, if it still makes sense to speak of the purity of the body in this asylum where we are living, for purity of the soul, as we know, is beyond everyone's reach.

Blind men lay stretched out on the long tables in the refectory. From a dripping tap over a sink full of garbage, trickled a thread of water. The doctor's wife looked around her in search of a bucket or basin but could see nothing that might serve her purpose. One of the blind men was disturbed by this presence and asked, Who's there, She did not reply, she knew that she would not be welcome, that no one would say, You need water, then take it, and if it's to wash the corpse of a dead woman, take all the water you want. Scattered on the floor were plastic bags, those used for the food, some of them large. She thought they must be torn, then reflected that by using two or three, one inside the other, not much water would be lost. She acted quickly, the blind men were already getting down from the tables and asking, Who's there, even more alarmed when they heard the sound of running water, they headed in that direction, the doctor's wife got out of the way and pushed a table across their path so that they could not come near, she then retrieved her bag, the water was running slowly, in desperation she forced the tap, then, as if it had been released from some prison, the water spurted out, splashed all over the place and soaked her from head to foot. The blind men took fright and drew back, they thought a pipe must have burst, and they had all the more reason to think so when the flood reached their feet, they were not to know that it had been spilled by the stranger who had entered, as it happened the woman had realised that she would not be able to carry so much weight. She tied a knot in the bag, threw it over her shoulder, and, as best she could, fled.

When the doctor and the old man with the black eyepatch entered the ward with the food, they did not see, could not see, seven naked women and the corpse of the woman who suffered from insomnia stretched out on her bed, cleaner than she had ever been in all her life, while another woman was washing her companions, one by one, and then herself.

On the fourth day, the thugs reappeared. They had come to exact payment from the women in the second ward, but they paused for a moment at the door of the first ward to ask if the women there had yet recovered from the sexual orgy of the other night, A great night, yes sir, exclaimed one of them licking his chops and another confirmed, Those seven were worth fourteen, it's true that one of them was no great shakes, but in the middle of all that uproar who noticed, their men are lucky sods, if they're man enough for them. It would be better if they weren't, then they'd be more eager. From the far end of the ward, the doctor's wife said, There are no longer seven of us, Has one of you vamoosed, someone in the group asked, laughing, She didn't vamoose, she died, Oh, hell, then you lot will have to work all the harder next time, It wasn't much of a loss, she was no great shakes, said the doctor's wife. Disconcerted, the messengers did not know how to respond, what they had just heard struck them as indecent, some of them even came round to thinking that when all is said and done all women are bitches, such a lack of respect, to refer to a woman like that, just because her tits weren't in the right place and she had no arse to speak of. The doctor's wife was looking at them, as they hovered there in the doorway, undecided, moving their bodies like mechanical dolls. She recognised them, she had been raped by all three of them. At last, one of them tapped his stick on the ground, Let's go, he said. Their tapping and their warning cries, Keep back, keep back, it's us, died away as they made their way along the corridor, then there was silence, vague sounds, the women from the second ward were receiving the order to present themselves after dinner. Once more the tapping of sticks could be heard, Keep back, keep back, the shadows of the three blind men passed through the doorway and they were gone.

The doctor's wife who had been telling the boy with the squint a story, raised her arm and, without a sound, took the scissors from the nail. She said to the boy, Later I'll tell you the rest of the story. No one in the ward had asked her why she had spoken with such disdain of the blind woman who had suffered from insomnia. After a while, she removed her shoes and went to reassure her husband, I won't be long, I'm coming straight back. She headed for the door. There she paused and remained waiting. Ten minutes later the women from the second ward appeared in the corridor. There were fifteen of them. Some were crying. They were not in line, but in groups, tied to each other with strips of cloth that had clearly been torn from their bedclothes. When they had passed, the doctor's wife followed them. Not one of them perceived that they had company. They knew what awaited them, the news of the abuses they would suffer was no secret, nor were these abuses anything really new, for in all certainty this is how the world began. What terrified them was not so much the rape, but the orgy, the shame, the anticipation of the terrible night ahead, fifteen women sprawled on the beds and on the floor, the men going from one to the other, snorting like pigs, The worst thing of all is that I might feel some pleasure, one of the women thought to herself. When they entered the corridor giving access to the ward they were heading for, the blind man on the lookout alerted the others, I can hear them, they'll be here any minute. The bed being used as a gate was quickly removed, one by one the women entered, Wow, so many of them, exclaimed the blind accountant, as he counted them enthusiastically, Eleven, twelve, thirteen, fourteen, fifteen, fifteen, there are fifteen of them. He went after the last one, put his eager hands up her skirt, This one is game, she's mine, he was saying. They had finished sizing up the women and making a preliminary assessment of their physical attributes. In fact, if all of them were condemned to endure the same fate, there was no point in wasting time and cooling their desire as they made their choice according to height and the measurement of busts and hips. They were soon taking them off to bed, already stripping them by force, and it was not long before the usual weeping and pleas for mercy could be heard, but the replies when they came, were always the same, If you want to eat, open your legs. And they opened their legs, some were ordered to use their mouth like the one who was crouched down between the knees of the leader of these ruffians and this one was saying nothing. The doctor's wife entered the ward, slipped slowly between the beds, but she need not even have taken these precautions, no one would have heard her had she been wearing clogs, and if, in the middle of the fracas, some blind man were to touch her and become aware that it was a woman, the worst that could happen to her would be having to join the others, not that anyone would notice, in a situation like this it is not easy to tell the difference between fifteen and sixteen.

The leader of these hoodlums still had his bed at the far end of the ward where the containers of food were stacked. The beds near his had been removed, the fellow liked to move at will without having to keep bumping into his neighbours. Killing him was going to be simple. As she slowly advanced along the narrow aisle, the doctor's wife studied the movements of the man she was about to kill, how he threw his head back as he took his pleasure, as if he were offering her his neck. Slowly, the doctor's wife approached, circled the bed and positioned herself behind him. The blind woman went on doing what was expected of her. The doctor's wife slowly raised the scissors, the blades slightly apart so that they might penetrate like two daggers. Just then, at the last minute, the blind man seemed to be aware of someone's presence, but his orgasm had transported him from the world of normal sensations, had deprived him of any reflexes, You won't have time to come, the doctor's wife reflected as she brought her arm down with tremendous force. The scissors dug deep into the blind man's throat, turning on themselves they struggled with the cartilage and the membraneous tissues, then furiously went deeper until they came up against the cervical vertebrae. His cry was barely audible, it might have been the grunting of an animal about to ejaculate, as was happening to some of the other men, and perhaps it was, and at the same time as a spurt of blood splashed on to her face, the blind woman received the discharge of semen in her mouth. It was her cry that startled the blind men, they were more than used to hearing cries, but this was quite unlike the others. The blind woman was screaming, where had this blood come from, probably, without knowing how, she had done what it had crossed her mind to do and bitten off his penis. The blind men left the women, approached groping their way, What's going on, what's all this screaming, they asked, but the blind woman now had a hand over her mouth, someone had whispered in her ear, Be quiet, and then gently pulled her back, Say nothing, it was a woman's voice, and this calmed her, if that is possible in such distressing circumstances. The blind accountant arrived ahead of the others, he was the first to touch the body which had toppled across the bed, the first to run his hands over it, He's dead, he exclaimed almost immediately. The head was hanging down on the other side of the bed, the blood was still spurting out, They've killed him, he said. The blind men stopped in their tracks, they could not believe their ears, How could they have killed him, who killed him, They've made an enormous slit in his throat, it must have been that whore who was with him, we've got to get her. The blind men stirred once more, more slowly this time, as if they were afraid of coming up against the blade that had killed their leader. They could not see that the blind accountant was hastily rummaging through the dead man's pockets, that he was removing his gun and a small plastic bag with about ten cartridges. Everyone was suddenly distracted by an outcry from the women, already on their feet, in panic, anxious to get away from that place, but some had lost any notion of where the ward door was located, they went in the wrong direction and ran into the blind men who thought the women were about to attack them, whereupon the confusion of bodies reached new heights of delirium. At the far end of the ward, the doctor's wife quietly awaited the right moment to make her escape. She had a firm grip on the blind woman, in her other hand she held the scissors ready to land the first blow if any man should come near her. For the moment, the free space was in her favour, but she knew that she could not linger there. A number of women had finally found the door, others were struggling to free themselves from the hands holding them back, there was even the odd one still trying to throttle the enemy and deliver another corpse. The blind accountant called out with authority to his men, Keep calm, don't lose your nerve, we'll get to the bottom of this matter, and anxious to make his order all the more convincing he fired a shot into the air. The outcome was exactly the opposite of what he expected. Surprised to discover that the gun was already in other hands and that they were about to have a new leader, the blind hoodlums stopped struggling with the women, gave up trying to dominate them, one of the men having given up the struggle altogether because he had been strangled. It was at this point that the doctor's wife decided to move. Striking blows left and right, she opened a path. Now it was the blind thugs who were calling out, who were being knocked over and climbing all over each other, anyone there with eyes to see, would perceive that, compared with this, the previous upheaval had been a joke. The doctor's wife had no desire to kill, all she wanted was to get out as quickly as possible and, above all, not to leave a single blind woman behind. This one probably won't survive, she thought as she dug the scissors into a man's chest. Another shot was heard, Let's go, let's go, said the doctor's wife, pushing any blind women whom she encountered ahead of her. She helped them to their feet, repeated, Quickly, quickly, and now it was the blind accountant who was shouting from the far end of the ward, Grab them, don't let them escape, but it was too late, the women were already out in the corridor, they fled, stumbling as they went, half dressed, holding on to their rags as best they could. Standing still at the entrance to the ward, the doctor's wife called out in a rage, Remember what I said the other day, that I'd never forget his face, and from now on think about what I am telling you, for I won't forget your faces either, You'll pay dearly for this outrage, threatened the blind accountant, you and your companions and those so-called men of yours, You neither know who I am nor where I've come from, You're from the first ward on the other side, volunteered one of the men who had gone to summon the women, and the blind accountant added, Your voice is unmistakable, you need only utter one word in my presence and you're dead, The other fellow said the same thing and now he's a corpse, But I'm not a blind man like him or you, when you lot turned blind, I already knew everything about this world, You know nothing about my blindness. You're not blind, you can't fool me, Perhaps I'm the blindest of all, I've already killed and I'll kill again if I have to, You'll die first of hunger, from today onwards there will be no more food, even if you were all to come offering on a tray the three holes you were born with. For each day that we're deprived of food because of you, one of the men here will die the moment he steps outside this door, You won't get away with this, Oh, yes we will, from now on we shall be collecting the food, and you can eat what you've hoarded there, Bitch, Bitches are neither men nor women, they're bitches, and you know now what they're worth. Enraged, the blind accountant fired in the direction of the door. The bullet whizzed past the heads of the blind men without hitting anyone and lodged itself in the corridor wall. You didn't get me, said the doctor's wife, and take care, if your ammunition runs out, there are others here who would like to be leader too.

She moved away, took a few steps, still firm, then advanced along the wall of the corridor, almost fainting, suddenly her legs gave way, and she fell to the ground. Her eyes clouded over, I'm going blind, she thought, but then realised it would not be just yet, these were only tears blurring her vision, tears such as she had never shed in all her life, I've killed a man, she said in a low voice, I wanted to kill him and I have. She turned her head in the direction of the ward door, if the blind men were to come now, she would be unable to defend herself. The corridor was deserted. The woman had disappeared, the blind men, still startled by the gunfire and even more by the corpses of their own men, did not dare come out. Little by little she regained her strength. Her tears continued to flow, slower and more serene, as if confronted by something irremediable. She struggled to her feet. She had blood on her hands and clothes, and suddenly her exhausted body told her that she was old, Old and a murderess, she thought, but she knew that if it were necessary, she would kill again, And when is it necessary to kill, she asked herself as she headed in the direction of the hallway, and she herself answered the question, When what is still alive is already dead. She shook her head and thought, And what does that mean, words, nothing but words. She walked on alone. She approached the door leading to the forecourt. Between the railings of the gate she could just make out the shadow of a soldier who was keeping guard. There are still people out there, people who can see. The sound of footsteps behind her caused her to tremble, It's them, she thought and turned round rapidly with her scissors at the ready. It was her husband. As they went past, the women from the second ward had been shouting out what had happened on the other side, that a woman had stabbed and killed the leader of the thugs, that there had been shooting, the doctor did not ask them to identify the woman, it could only be his wife, she had told the boy with the squint that she would tell him the rest of the story later, and what would have become of her now, probably dead as well, I'm here, she said; and went up to him and embraced him, not noticing that she was smearing him with blood, or noticing but unconcerned, for until now they had shared everything. What happened, the doctor asked, they said a man was killed, Yes, I killed him, Why, Someone had to do it, and there was no one else, And now, Now we're free, they know what awaits them if they ever try to abuse us again, There's likely to be a battle, a war, The blind are always at war, always have been at war, Will you kill again, If I have to, I shall never be free from this blindness, And what about the food, We shall fetch it, I doubt whether they'll dare to come here, at least for the next few days they'll be afraid the same might happen to them, that a pair of scissors will slit their throat, We failed to put up resistance as we should have done when they first came making demands, Of course, we were afraid and fear isn't always a wise counsellor, let's get back, for our greater safety we ought to barricade the door of the wards by putting beds on top of beds, as they do, if some of us have to sleep on the floor, too bad, better that than to die of hunger.

In the days that followed, they asked themselves if that was not what was about to happen to them. At first they were not surprised, from the outset they had become used to it, there had always been delays in the delivery of food, the blind thugs were right when they said the soldiers were sometimes late, but then they perverted this reasoning when, in a playful tone of voice, they affirmed that for this reason they had no choice but to impose rationing, these are the painful obligations of those who have to govern. On the third day when there was no longer as much as a rind or crumb, the doctor's wife with some companions, went out into the forecourt and asked, Hey, why the delay, whatever happened to our food, we haven't eaten for the last two days. Another sergeant, not the one from the time before, came up to the railing to declare that the army was not responsible, that no one there was trying to take the bread from their mouths, that military honour would never allow it, if there was no food it was because there was no food, and all of you stay where you are, the first one to advance knows the fate that waits for him, the orders have not changed. This warning was enough to send them back inside, and they conferred amongst themselves, And now what do we do if they won't bring us any food, They might bring some tomorrow, Or the day after tomorrow, Or when we no longer have the strength to move, We ought to go out, We wouldn't even get as far as the gate, If only we had our sight, If we had our sight we wouldn't have landed in this hell, I wonder what life is like out there, Perhaps those bastards might give us something to eat if we went there to ask, after all if there's a shortage for us, they must be running short too, That's why they're unlikely to give us anything they've got, And before their food runs out we will have died of starvation, What are we to do then, They were seated on the floor, under the yellowish light of the only lamp in the hallway, more or less in a circle, the doctor and the doctor's wife, the old man with the black eyepatch, amongst the other men and women, one or two from each ward, from the wing on the left as well as from the one on the right, and then, this world of the blind being what it is, there occurred what always occurs, one of the men said, All I know is that we would never have found ourselves in this situation if their leader hadn't been killed, what did it matter if the women had to go there twice a month to give these men what nature gave them to give, I ask myself. Some found this amusing, some forced a smile, those inclined to protest were deterred by an empty stomach, and the same man insisted, What I'd like to know is who did the stabbing, The women who were there at the time swear it was none of them, What we ought to do is to take the law into our own hands and bring the culprit to justice, If we knew who was responsible, we'd say this is the person you're looking for, now give us the food, If we knew who was responsible. The doctor's wife lowered her head and thought, He's right, if anyone here should die of hunger it will be my fault, but then, giving voice to the rage she could feel welling up inside her contradicting any acceptance of responsibility, But let these men be the first to die so that my guilt may pay for their guilt. Then she thought, raising her eyes, And if I were now to tell them that it was I who killed him, they would hand me over, knowing that they would be delivering me to certain death. Whether it was the effect of hunger or because the thought suddenly seduced her like some abyss, her head spun as if she were in a daze, her body moved despite herself, her mouth opened to speak, but just at that moment someone grabbed and squeezed her arm, she looked, it was the old man with the black eyepatch, who said, Anyone who gave himself up, I'd kill him with my own hands, Why, people in the circle asked, Because if shame still has any meaning in this hell where we're expected to live and which we've turned into the hell of hells, it is thanks to that person who had the courage to go and kill the hyena in its lair, Agreed, but shame won't fill our plates, Whoever you may be, you're right in what you say, there have always been those who have filled their bellies because they had no sense of shame, but we, who have nothing, apart from this last shred of undeserved dignity, let us at least show that we are still capable of fighting for what is rightfully ours, What are you trying to say, That having started off by sending in the women and eaten at their expense like low-life pimps, the time has now come for sending in the men, if there are any, Explain yourself, but first tell us where you are from, I'm from the first ward on the right-hand side, Go on then, It's very simple, let's go and collect the food with our own hands, Those men are armed, As far as we know, they have only one gun and the ammunition will run out sooner or later, They have enough to make sure that some of us will die, Others have died for less, I'm not prepared to lose my life so that the rest can enjoy themselves. Would you also be prepared to starve, if someone should lose his life so that you might have food, the old man with the black eyepatch asked sarcastically, and the other man gave no reply.

In the entrance of the door leading to the wards in the right-hand wing, appeared a woman who had been listening out of sight. She was the one who had received the spurt of blood in her face, the one into whose mouth the dead man had ejaculated, the one in whose ear the doctor's wife had whispered, Be quiet, and now the doctor's wife is thinking, From here where I'm sitting in the midst of others, I cannot tell you to be quiet, don't give me away, but no doubt you recognise my voice, it's impossible that you could have forgotten it, my hand covered your mouth, your body against mine, and I said, Be quiet, and the moment has come to know whom I really saved, to know who you are, that is why I am about to speak, that is why I am about to say in a loud, clear voice so that you might accuse me, if this is your destiny and mine, I am now saying, Not only the men will go, but also the women, we shall return to that place where they humiliated us so that none of that humiliation may remain, so that we might rid ourselves of it in the same way that we spat out what they ejaculated into our mouths. She uttered these words and waited, until the woman replied, Wherever you go, I shall go, that was what she said. The old man with the black eyepatch smiled, it seemed a happy smile, and perhaps it was, this is not the moment to ask him, it is much more interesting to observe the expression of surprise on the faces of the other blind men, as if something had passed over their heads, a bird, a cloud, a first hesitant glimmer of light. The doctor took his wife's hand, then asked, Are there still people here intent on discovering who killed that fellow, or are we agreed that the hand that stabbed him was the hand of all of us, or to be more precise, the hand of each one of us. No one replied. The doctor's wife said, Let's give them a little longer, if, by tomorrow, the soldiers have not brought our food, then we advance. They got up, went their separate ways, some to the right, others to the left, imprudently they had not reflected that some blind man from the ward of the thugs might have been listening, fortunately the devil is not always behind the door, a saying that could not have been more appropriate. Somewhat less appropriate was the blast that came from the loudspeaker, recently it had spoken on certain days, on others not at all, but always at the same time, as had been promised, clearly there was a timer in the transmitter which at the precise moment started up the recorded tape, the reason why it should have broken down from time to time we are never likely to know, these are matters for the outside world, it is in any case serious enough, insofar as it muddled up the calendar, the so-called counting of the days, which some blind men, natural obsessives, or lovers of order, which is a moderate form of obsession, had tried scrupulously to follow by making little knots in a piece of string, this was done by those who did not trust their memory, as if they were writing a diary. Now it was the time that was out of phase, the mechanism must have broken down, a twisted relay, some loose soldering, let's hope the recording will not keep going back for ever to the beginning, that was all we needed as well as being blind and mad. Along the corridors, through the wards, like some final and futile warning, boomed an authoritarian voice, the Government regrets having been forced to exercise with all urgency what it considers to be its rightful duty, to protect the population by all possible means in this present crisis, when something with all the appearance of an epidemic of blindness has broken out, provisionally known as the white sickness, and we are relying on the civic spirit and cooperation of all citizens to stem any further contagious, assuming that we are dealing with a contagious disease and that we are not simply witnessing a series of as yet inexplicable coincidences. The decision to gather together in one place all those infected, and, in adjacent but separate quarters all those who have had any kind of contact with them, was not taken without careful consideration. The Government is fully aware of its responsibilities and hopes that those to whom this message is directed will, as the upright citizens they doubtless are, also assume their responsibilities, bearing in mind that the isolation in which they now find themselves will represent, above any personal considerations, an act of solidarity with the rest of the nation's community. That said, we ask everyone to listen attentively to the following instructions, first, the lights will be kept on at all times, any attempt to tamper with the switches will be useless, they don't work, second, leaving the building without authorisation will mean instant death, third, in each ward there is a telephone that can be used only to requisition from outside fresh supplies for purposes of hygiene and cleanliness, fourth, the internees will be responsible for washing their own clothes by hand, fifth, it is recommended that ward representatives should be elected, this is a recommendation rather than an order, the internees must organise themselves as they see fit, provided they comply with the aforesaid rules and those we are about to announce, sixth, three times daily containers with food will be deposited at the main door, on the right and on the left, destined respectively for the patients and those suspected of being contaminated, seventh, all the left-overs must be burnt, and this includes not only any food, but also the containers, plates and cutlery which are all made of combustible material, eighth, the burning should be done in the inner courtyards of the building or in the exercise yard, ninth, the internees are responsible for any damage caused by these fires, tenth, in the event of a fire getting out of control, whether accidentally or on purpose, the firemen will not intervene, eleventh, equally, the internees cannot count on any outside intervention should there be any outbreaks of illnesses, nor in the event of any disorder or aggression, twelfth, in the case of death, whatever the cause, the internees will bury the corpse in the yard without any formalities, thirteenth, contact between the wing of the patients and that of the people suspected of being contagious must be made in the central hall of the building by which they entered, fourteenth, should those suspected of being infected suddenly go blind, they will be transferred immediately to the other wing, fifteenth, this communication will be relayed daily at the same time for the benefit of all new arrivals. The Government, but at that very moment the lights went out and the loudspeaker fell silent. Unconcerned, a blind man tied a knot in the piece of string he was holding in his hands, then he tried to count them, the knots, the days, but he gave up, there were knots overlapping, blind knots in a manner of speaking. The doctor's wife said to her husband, The lights have gone out, Some lamp that had fused, and little wonder when they have been switched on for all this time, They've all gone out, the problem must have been outside, Now you're as blind as the rest of us, I'll wait until the sun comes up. She went out of the ward, crossed the hallway, looked outside. This part of the city was in darkness, the army's searchlight was not working, it must have been connected to the general network, and now, to all appearances, the power was off.

The following day, some earlier, others later, because the sun does not rise at the same time for all those who are blind, it often depends on the keenness of hearing of each of them, men and women from the various wards began gathering on the outer steps of the building with the exception, needless to say, of the ward occupied by the hoodlums, who at this hour must be having their breakfast. They were waiting for the thud of the gate being opened, the loud screeching of hinges that needed to be greased, the sounds that announced the arrival of their food, then the voice of the sergeant on duty, Don't move from where you are, let no one approach, the dragging of soldiers' feet, the dull sound of the containers being dumped on the ground, the hasty retreat, once more the creaking of the gate, and finally the authorisation, Now you can come out. They waited until it was almost midday and midday became the afternoon. No one, not even the doctor's wife, wanted to ask about the food. So long as they did not ask the question they would not hear the dreaded no, and so long as it was not spoken they would go on hoping to hear words like these, It's coming, it's coming, be patient, put up with your hunger for just a little longer. Some, however much they wanted, could not stand it any longer, they fainted there and then as if they had suddenly fallen asleep, fortunately the doctor's wife was there to come to the rescue, it was incredible how this woman managed to notice everything that was happening, she must be endowed with a sixth sense, some sort of a vision without eyes, thanks to which those miserable wretches did not remain there to broil in the sun, they were carried indoors at once, and with time, water and gentle slaps on the face, all of them eventually came round. But there was no point in counting on the latter for the war, they would not even be able to grab a she-cat by the tail, an old-fashioned expression which never explained for what extraordinary reason a she-cat should be easier to deal with than a tom-cat. Finally the old man with the black eyepatch said, The food hasn't come, the food won't come, let's go and get our food. They got up, God knows how, and went to assemble in the ward furthest away from the stronghold of the hoodlums, rather than have any repetition of the imprudence of the other day. From there they sent spies to the other wing, blind inmates who lived there and were more familiar with the surroundings, At the first suspicious movement, come and warn us. The doctor's wife went with them and came back with some disheartening information, They have barricaded the entrance with four beds stacked one on top of the other, How did you know there were four, someone asked, That wasn't difficult, I felt them, Did no one realise you were there, I don't think so, What are we going to do, Let's go, the old man with the black eyepatch suggested once more, let's stick to what was decided, it's either that or we're condemned to a slow death. Some will die sooner if we go there, said the first blind man, Anyone who is going to die is already dead and does not know it, That we're going to die is something we know from the moment we are born, That's why, in some ways, it's as if we were born dead, That's enough of your foolish talk, said the girl with the dark glasses, I cannot go there alone, but if we are now going to go back on what was agreed, then I'm simply going to lie on my bed and allow myself to die, Only those whose days are numbered will die, no one else, said the doctor, and raising his voice, he asked, Those who are determined to go, raise their hand, this is what happens to those who do not think twice before opening their mouth to speak, what was the point in asking them to raise their hands if there was no one there to count them, or so it was generally believed, and then say, Thirteen, in which case a new discussion would almost certainly start up to establish what, in the light of logic, would be more correct, whether to ask for another volunteer to avoid that unlucky number, or to avoid it by default, drawing lots to decide who should drop out. Some had raised their hand with little conviction, with a gesture that betrayed hesitation and doubt, whether because aware of the danger to which they were about to expose themselves, or because they realised the absurdity of the order. The doctor laughed, How ridiculous, to ask you to put up your hands, let's proceed in another manner, let those who cannot or do not wish to go withdraw, the rest stay behind to agree upon the action to be taken. There were stirrings, footsteps, murmurs, sighs, little by little, the weak and nervous dropped out, the doctor's idea had been as excellent as it was generous, in this way it will be less easy to know who had remained and who was no longer there. The doctor's wife counted those who had remained, they were seventeen, counting herself and her husband. From the first ward on the right hand side, there was the old man with the black eyepatch, the pharmacist's assistant, the girl with dark glasses, and all the volunteers from the other wards were men with the exception of that woman who had said, Wherever you go, I shall go, she is here too. They lined up along the passageway, the doctor counted them, Seventeen, we're seventeen, That's not very many, remarked the pharmacist's assistant, we'll never manage. The front line of attack, if I may use a rather military term, will have to be a narrow one, said the old man with the black eyepatch, we have to be able to fit through a door, I'm convinced it would only complicate matters if there were more of us, They'd shoot the lot of us, agreed another, and everyone seemed pleased that in the end they were few.

Their arms we are already familiar with, bars taken from the beds, which might serve just as well as a crowbar or a lance, according to whether the sappers or assault troops were going into battle. The old man with the black eyepatch, who had clearly learned something about tactics in his youth, suggested that everyone should stay together, facing in the same direction, since this was the only way to avoid attacking each other, and that they should advance in absolute silence, so that the attack might benefit from the element of surprise, Let's take off our shoes, he suggested. Then it's going to be difficult for each of us to find our own shoes, someone said, and another commented, Any shoes left over will truly be dead men's shoes, with the difference that in this case, at least, there will always be someone to step into them, What is all this talk about dead men's shoes, It's a saying, to wait for dead men's shoes means to wait for nothing at all, Why, Because the shoes the dead were buried in were made of cardboard, they served their purpose, souls have no feet, as far as we know, And there's another point, interrupted the old man with the black eyepatch, when we get there, six of us, the six who are feeling bravest, will shove the beds inside as hard as they can, so that all of us may enter, In that case, we'll have to lay down our arms, I don't think that will be necessary, they might even help, if used upright. He paused, then said, with a sombre note in his voice, Above all, we must not split up, if we do we're as good as dead, And what about the women, said the girl with dark glasses, don't forget the women, Are you going as well, asked the old man with the black eyepatch, I'd rather you didn't, And why not, I'd like to know, You're very young, In this place, age is of no account, nor sex, therefore don't forget the women,

No, I won't forget, the voice in which the old man with the black eyepatch spoke these words appeared to come from another dialogue, those that follow were already in their place, On the contrary, if only one of you women could see what we cannot see, take us along the right path, with the tip of our metal bars at the throats of these ruffians, as accurately as that other woman did, That would be asking too much, we can't easily repeat what we've done once already, besides, who's to say that she didn't die there and then, there has been no news of her, the doctor's wife reminded them, Women are born again in one another, the respectable are reborn as whores, whores are reborn as respectable women, said the girl with dark glasses. This was followed by a long silence, for the women everything had been said, the men would have to find the words, and they knew already that they would be incapable of doing so.

They filed out, the six braver ones in front as had been agreed, amongst them was the doctor and the pharmacist's assistant, then came the others, each armed with a metal rod from his bed, a brigade of squalid, ragged lancers, as they crossed the hallway one of them dropped his weapon, which made a deafening sound on the tiled floor like a blast of gunfire, if the hoodlums were to hear the noise and get wind of what we're up to, then we're lost. Without telling anyone, not even her husband, the doctor's wife ran ahead, looked along the corridor, then very slowly, keeping close to the wall, she gradually drew nearer to the entrance of the ward, there she listened attentively, the voices within did not sound alarmed. She brought back this information without delay and the advance recommenced. Apart from the slowness and the silence with which the army moved, the occupants of the two wards that were located before the stronghold of the hoodlums, aware of what was about to happen, gathered at the doors so as not to miss the imminent clamour of battle, and some of those more on edge, excited by the smell of gunpowder about to be lit, decided at the last minute to accompany the group, a few went back to arm themselves, they were no longer seventeen, they had at least doubled in number, the reinforcements would certainly displease the old man with the black eyepatch, but he was never to know that he was commanding two regiments instead of one. Through the few windows that looked on to the inner courtyard entered the last glimmer of light, grey, moribund, as it rapidly faded, already slipping away into the deep black well of the night ahead. Apart from the inconsolable sadness caused by the blindness from which they inexplicably continued to suffer, the blind internees, this at least was in their favour, were spared any fits of depression produced by these and other similar atmospheric changes, proven to be the cause of innumerable acts of despair in the remote past when people had eyes to see. When they reached the door of that cursed ward, it was already so dark that the doctor's wife failed to notice that there were not four but eight beds forming a barrier, doubled in number in the meantime like the assailants, however with more serious immediate consequences for the latter, as will soon be confirmed. The voice of the old man with the black eyepatch let out a cry, it was the order, he did not remember the usual expression, Charge, or perhaps he did, but it would have struck him as ridiculous to treat with such military consideration, a barrier of filthy beds, full of fleas and bugs, their mattresses rotted from sweat and urine, the blankets like rags, no longer grey, but all the colours that disgust might wear, this the doctor's wife already knew, not that she could see it now, since she had not even noticed the reinforced barricade. The blind inmates advanced like archangels surrounded by their own splendour, they thudded into the obstacle with their weapons upright as they had been instructed, but the beds did not move, no doubt the strength of this brave vanguard was not much greater than that of the weaklings who came behind and by now could scarcely hold their lances, like someone who carried a cross on his back and now has to wait to be raised up on it. The silence had disappeared, those outside were shouting, those inside started shouting, probably no one has noticed to this day how absolutely terrible are the cries of the blind, they appear to be shouting for no good reason, we want to tell them to be quiet and then end up shouting ourselves, all that's wanting is for us to be blind too, but that day will come. This then was the situation, some shouting as they attacked, others shouting as they defended themselves, while those on the outside, desperate at not having been able to move the beds, flung down their weapons willy-nilly and, all of them at once, at least those who managed to squeeze into the space in the doorway, and those who couldn't fit in pressed behind those in front, they started pushing and pushing and it looked as if they might succeed, the beds had even moved a little, when suddenly, without prior warning or threat, three shots rang out, it was the blind accountant aiming low. Two of the assailants fell, wounded, the others quickly retreated in disarray, they tripped on the metal rods and fell, as if demented the walls of the corridor multiplied their shouts, shouting was coming from the other wards too. It was now almost pitch-black, it was impossible to know who had been hit by the bullets, obviously one could ask from afar, Who are you, but it did not seem appropriate, the wounded must be treated with respect and consideration, we must approach them gently, place our hand on their forehead, unless that is where the bullet unfortunately happened to strike, then we must ask them in a low voice how they are feeling, assure them it is not serious, the stretcher-bearers are already on the way, and finally give them some water, but only if they are not wounded in the stomach, as is expressly recommended in the first-aid handbook. What shall we do now, asked the doctor's wife, there are two casualties lying there on the ground. No one asked her how she knew there were two of them, after all, there had been three shots, without reckoning with the effect of the ricochets, if there had been any. We must go and look for them, said the doctor, The risk is great, observed the old man with the black eyepatch despondently, who had seen that his assault tactics had resulted in disaster, if they suspect there are people here they'll start firing again, he paused and added sighing, But we must go there, speaking for myself, I'm ready, I'm going too, said the doctor's wife, there will be less danger if we crawl, the important thing is to find them quickly, before those inside there have time to react, I'm going too, said the woman who had declared the other day, Wherever you go, I go, of the many that were there no one thought to say that it was very easy to check who was wounded, correction, wounded or dead, for the moment no one yet knows, it was enough that they should all start saying, I'm going, I'm not going, those who remained silent were the latter.

And so the four volunteers began crawling, the two women in the middle, a man on either side as it happened, they were not acting out of male courtesy or some gentlemanly instinct so that the women should be protected, the truth is that everything will depend on the angle of the shot, if the blind accountant should fire again. After all, perhaps nothing will happen, the old man with the black eyepatch had come up with an idea before they went, possibly better than the earlier ones, that these companions here should start to talk at the top of their voices, even to shout, besides they had every reason to do so, so that they might drown the inevitable noise of their comings and goings, and also whatever might happen in the meantime, God knows what. In a few minutes, the rescuers reached their destination, they knew it before even coming into contact with the bodies, the blood over which they were crawling was like a messenger come to tell them, I was life, behind me there is nothing,

My God, thought the doctor's wife, all this blood, and it was true, a thick pool, their hands and clothing stuck to the ground as if the floorboards and floor tiles were covered in glue. The doctor's wife raised herself on her elbows and continued to advance, the others had done the same. Stretching out their arms, they finally reached the corpses. Their companions back there continued to make as much noise as they could, and now sounded like professional mourners in a trance. The hands of the doctor's wife and of the old man with the black eyepatch grabbed the ankles of one of the casualties, in their turn the doctor and the other woman had grabbed an arm and leg of the other wounded man, now they were trying to drag them away out of the firing line. It was not easy, to achieve this they had to raise themselves up a little, to go on all fours, it was the only way of putting to good use the little strength they still possessed. The shot rang out, but this time did not hit anyone. The overwhelming terror did not make them flee, on the contrary, it helped them to summon that last ounce of energy that was needed. An instant later they were already out of danger, they got as close as they could to the wall on the side where the ward door was situated, only a stray bullet could possibly reach them, but it was doubtful that the blind accountant was skilled in ballistics, even elementary ones such as these. They tried to lift the bodies but gave up. Because of their weight they could only drag them, and with them, half congealed, trailed the blood already spilled as if spread by a roller, and the remaining blood, still fresh, that continued to flow from the wounds. Who are they, asked those who were waiting, How are we to know if we cannot see, said the old man with the black eyepatch, We can't stay here, said someone, if they decide to launch an attack we'll have more than two casualties, remarked another, Or corpses, said the doctor, at least I cannot feel their pulse. Like an army in retreat, they carried the corpses along the corridor, on reaching the hallway they came to a halt, and one would have said they had decided to camp there, but the truth of the matter was different, what had happened was that they were drained of all energy, I'm staying right here, I can't go any further. It is time to acknowledge that it must seem surprising that the blind hoodlums, previously so overbearing and aggressive, revelling in their own easy cruelty, now only defend themselves, raise barricades and fire from inside there at will, as if they were afraid to go out and fight in open territory, face to face, eye to eye. Like everything else in this life, this too, has its explanation, which is that after the tragic death of their first leader, all spirit of discipline or sense of obedience had gone in the ward, the serious error on the part of the blind accountant was to have thought that it was enough to take possession of the gun in order to usurp power, but the result was exactly the opposite, each time he fires, the shot backfires, in other words, with each shot fired, he loses a little more authority, so let's see what happens when he runs out of ammunition. Just as the habit does not make the monk, the sceptre does not make the king, this is a fact we should never forget, and if it is true that the royal sceptre is now held by the blind accountant, one is tempted to say that the king, although dead, although buried in his own ward, and badly, barely three feet under the ground, continues to be remembered, at least he makes his powerful presence felt by the stench. Meanwhile, the moon appeared. Through the door of the hallway that looks out on to the outer yard enters a diffused light that gradually becomes brighter, the bodies that are on the ground, two of them dead, the others still alive, slowly begin gaining volume, shape, characteristics, features, all the weight of a horror without a name, then the doctor's wife understood that there was no sense, if there ever had been any, in going on pretending to be blind, it is clear that here no one can be saved, blindness is also this, to live in a world where all hope is gone.

She could tell in the meantime who was dead, this is the pharmacist's assistant, this is the fellow who said the blind hoodlums would shoot at random, they were both right after a fashion, and don't bother asking me how I know who they are, the answer is simple, I can see. Some of those who were present already knew as much and had remained silent, others had been suspicious for some time and now saw their suspicions confirmed, the surprise of the others was unexpected, and yet, on reflection, perhaps we should not be surprised, at another time the revelation would have caused much consternation, uncontrolled excitement, how fortunate for you, how did you manage to escape this universal disaster, what is the name of the drops you put in your eyes, give me your doctor's address, help me to get out of this prison, by now it came to the same thing, in death, blindness is the same for all. What they could not do was to remain there, defenceless, even the metal bars from their beds had been left behind, their fists would serve for nothing. Guided by the doctor's wife, they dragged the corpses out on to the forecourt, and there they left them in the moonlight, under the planet's milky whiteness, white on the outside, black at last on the inside. Let's return to the wards, said the old man with the black eyepatch, we'll see later on what can be organised. This is what he said, and they were mad words that no one heeded. They did not divide up according to where they had come from, they met up and recognised each other on the way, some heading for the wing on the left, others for the wing on the right, the doctor's wife had been accompanied this far by that woman who had said, Wherever you go, I go, this was not the idea she now carried in her head, quite the contrary, but she did not want to discuss it, vows are not always fulfilled, sometimes out of weakness, at other times because of some superior force with which we had not reckoned.

An hour passed, the moon came up, hunger and terror hold

sleep at bay, in the wards everyone is awake. But these are not the only reasons. Whether because of the excitement of the recent battle, even though so disastrously lost, or because of something indefinable in the air, the blind internees are restless. No one dares go out into the corridors, but the interior of each ward is like a beehive inhabited by drones, buzzing insects, as everyone knows, little given to order and method, there is no evidence that they have ever done anything in their lives or preoccupied themselves in the slightest with the future, even though in the case of the blind, unhappy creatures, it would be unjust to accuse them of being exploiters and parasites, exploiters of what crumb, parasites of what refreshment, one has to be careful with comparisons, in case they should turn out to be frivolous. However, there is no rule without an exception, and this was not lacking here, in the person of a woman who entered the ward, the second one on the right-hand side, and at once began rummaging through her rags until she found a tiny object which she pressed in the palm of her hand, as if anxious to conceal it from the prying eyes of others, old habits die hard, even when that moment comes when we thought they were lost for ever. Here, where it ought to have been one for all and all for one, we witnessed how the strong cruelly took the bread from the mouths of the weak, and now this woman, remembering that she had brought a cigarette lighter in her hand-luggage, unless she had lost it in all the upheaval, searched for it anxiously and is now furtively hiding it, as if her survival depended on it, she does not think that perhaps one of these companions in misfortune might have one last cigarette on them, and cannot smoke it because they do not have that tiny essential flame. Nor would there be time now to ask for a light. The woman has gone out without saying a word, no farewell, no goodbye, she makes her way along the deserted corridor, passes right by the door of the first ward, no one inside there noticed her pass, she crosses the hallway, the descending moon traced and painted a vat of milk on the floor tiles, now the woman is in the other wing, once more a corridor, her destination lies at the far end, in a straight line, she cannot go wrong. Besides, she can hear voices summoning her, figuratively speaking, what she can hear is the rumpus being made by the hoodlums in the last ward, they are celebrating their victory, eating and drinking to their heart's content, ignore the deliberate exaggeration, let us not forget that everything is relative in life, they eat and drink simply what is to hand, and long may it last, how the others would love to partake of the feast, but they cannot, between them and the plate there is a barricade of eight beds and a loaded gun. The woman is on her knees at the entrance to the ward, right up against the beds, she slowly pulls the covers off, then gets to her feet, she does the same with the bed on top, then with the third one, her arm cannot reach the fourth, no matter, the fuses are ready, now it is only a question of setting them alight. She can still remember how to regulate the lighter in order to produce a long flame, she got it, a tiny dagger of light, as bright as the sharp point of a pair of scissors. She starts with the bed on top, the flame laboriously licks the filthy bedclothes, then it finally catches fire, now the bed in the middle, now the bed below, the woman caught the smell of her own singed hair, she must be careful, she is the one who has to set the pyre alight, not the one who must die, she can hear the cries of the hoodlums within, at that moment it suddenly occurred to her, Suppose they have water and manage to put out the flames, in desperation she got under the first bed, ran the lighter along the mattress, here, there, then suddenly the flames multiplied, transformed themselves into one great curtain of fire, a spurt of water passed through them, splashed on to the woman, but in vain, her own body was already feeding the bonfire. What is it like in there, no one can risk entering, but our imagination must serve for something, the fire quickly spreads from bed to bed, as if wanting to set all of them alight at the same time, and it succeeds, the hoodlums wasted indiscriminately and to no avail the little water they still had, now they are trying to reach the windows, unsteadily they climb on to the headrests of the beds which the fire has still not reached, but suddenly the fire is there, they slip, fall, with the intensity of the heat the window-panes begin to crack, to shatter, the fresh air comes whistling in and fans the flames, ah, yes, they are not forgotten, the cries of rage and fear, the howls of pain and agony, there they have been mentioned, note, in any case, that they will gradually die away, the woman with the cigarette lighter, for example, has been silent for some time.

By this time the other blind inmates are fleeing in terror towards the smoke-filled corridors, Fire, fire, they are shouting, and here we may observe in the flesh how badly planned and organised these human communities in orphanages, hospitals and mental asylums have been, note how each bed, in itself, with its framework of pointed metal bars, can be transformed into a lethal trap, look at the terrible consequences of having only one door to wards occupied by forty people, not counting those asleep on the floor, if the fire gets there first and blocks their exit, no one will escape. Fortunately, as human history has shown, it is not unusual for good to come of evil, less is said about the evil that can come out of good, such are the contradictions of this world of ours, some warrant more consideration than others, in this instance the good was precisely the fact that the wards have only one door, thanks to this factor, the fire that burnt the hoodlums tarried there for quite a while, if the confusion does not get any worse, perhaps we will not have to lament the loss of other lives. Obviously, many of these blind inmates are being trampled under foot, pushed, jostled, this is the effect of panic, a natural effect, you could say that animal nature is like this, plant life would behave in exactly the same way, too, if it did not have all those roots to hold it in the ground, and how nice it would be to see the trees of the forest fleeing the flames. The protection afforded by the inner part of the yard was fully exploited by the blind inmates who had the idea of opening the existing windows in the corridors looking on to it. They jumped, stumbled, fell, they weep and cry out, but for now they are safe, let us hope that once the fire causes the roof to cave in and launches a whirlwind of flames and burning embers into the sky and the wind, it will forget to spread to the tree tops. In the other wing the panic is much the same, a blind man only has to smell smoke to imagine at once that the flames are right by him, which does not happen to be true, soon the corridor was crammed with people, unless someone imposes some order here, the situation will be disastrous. At a certain point, someone remembers that the doctor's wife still has her eyesight, where is she, people ask, she can tell us what is happening, where we should go, where is she, I'm here, I've only just managed to get out of the ward, the boy with the squint was to blame because no one knew where he had got to, now he's here with me and I'm holding him firmly by the hand, they would have to pull off my arm before I'd let go of him, with my other hand I'm holding my husband's hand, and then comes the girl with dark glasses, and then the old man with the black eyepatch, where there is the one there is the other, and then the first blind man, and then his wife, all together, as compressed as a pine-cone, which, I very much hope, will not open even in this heat. Meanwhile, a number of blind inmates from here had followed the example of those in the other wing, they jumped into the inner yard, they cannot see that the greater part of the building on the other side is already one great bonfire, but they can feel on their faces and hands the blast of heat coming from there, for the moment the roof is still holding up, the leaves on the trees are slowly curling. Then someone shouted, What are we doing here, why don't we get out, the reply, coming from amidst this sea of heads, needed only four words, The soldiers are there, but the old man with the black eyepatch said, Better to be shot than burnt to death, it sounded like the voice of experience, therefore perhaps he was not really the person speaking, perhaps through his mouth the woman with the cigarette lighter had spoken, she who had not had the good fortune to be struck by the last bullet fired by the blind accountant. Then the doctor's wife said, Let me pass, I'll speak to the soldiers, they cannot leave us to die like this, soldiers too have feelings. Thanks to the hope that the soldiers might indeed have feelings, a narrow gap opened up, through which the doctor's wife advanced with considerable effort, taking her group with her. The smoke clouded her vision, soon she would be as blind as the others. It was almost impossible to enter the hallway. The doors opening on to the yard had been broken down, the blind inmates who had taken refuge there quickly realised the place was unsafe, they wanted to get out, pushed with all their might, but those on the other side resisted, held out as best they could, for the moment their greater fear was that the soldiers might suddenly appear, but as their strength gave out and the fire spread nearer, the old man with the black eyepatch was proved to be right, it would be preferable to die by a bullet. There was not long to wait, the doctor's wife had finally managed to get out on to the porch, she was practically half naked and with both her hands occupied she could scarcely fight off those who wanted to join her small group as it advanced, to catch, in a manner of speaking, the moving train, the soldiers would be goggle-eyed when they saw her appear before them with her breasts half exposed. It was no longer the moonlight that was illuminating the wide empty space that extended as far as the gate, but the harsh glare of the blaze. The doctor's wife shouted, Please, for your own peace of mind, let us out, do not shoot. No reply came from over there. The searchlight was still extinguished, nothing could be seen to move. Nervously, the doctor's wife went down two steps, What's going on, asked her husband, but she did not reply, could not believe her eyes. She descended the remaining steps, walked in the direction of the gate, still dragging behind her the boy with the squint, her husband and company, there was no doubt about it, the soldiers had gone, or been taken away, they too stricken by blindness, everyone finally blind.

Then, to simplify matters, everything happened at once, the doctor's wife announced in a loud voice that they were free, the roof of the right wing collapsed with a terrifying crash, sending out flames on all sides, the blind inmates rushed into the yard, shouting at the top of their voices, some did not make it, they remained inside, crushed against the walls, others were trampled under foot and transformed into a formless, bloody mass, the fire that has suddenly spread will soon reduce all of this to ashes. The gate is wide open, the madmen escape.

Say to a blind man, you're free, open the door that was separating him from the world, Go, you are free, we tell him once more, and he does not go, he has remained motionless there in the middle of the road, he and the others, they are terrified, they do not know where to go, the fact is that there is no comparison between living in a rational labyrinth, which is, by definition, a mental asylum and venturing forth, without a guiding hand or a dog-leash, into the demented labyrinth of the city, where memory will serve no purpose, for it will merely be able to recall the images of places but not the paths whereby we might get there. Standing in front of the building which is already ablaze from end to end, the blind inmates can feel the living waves of heat from the fire on their faces, they receive them as something which in a way protects them, just as the walls did before, prison and refuge at once. They stay together, pressed up against each other, like a flock, no one there wants to be the lost sheep, for they know that no shepherd will come looking for them. The fire gradually begins to die down, the moon casts its light once more, the blind inmates begin to feel uneasy, they cannot remain there, For all eternity, as one of them said. Someone asked if it was day or night, the reason for this incongruous curiosity soon became apparent, Who knows, they might bring us some food, perhaps there has been some confusion, some delay, it has happened before, But the soldiers are no longer here. That doesn't mean a thing, they might have gone away because they're no longer needed, I don't understand, For example, because there is no longer any danger of infection, Or because a cure has been found for our illness, That would be good, it really would, What are we going to do, I'm staying here until daybreak, And how will you know it is daybreak, By the sun, by the heat of the sun, And what if the sky is overcast, There is only a limited number of hours and then it must be day at some point. Exhausted, many of the blind had sat down on the ground, others, weaker still, simply collapsed into a heap, some had fainted, it is possible that the cool night air will restore consciousness, but we can be certain that when it is time to break camp, some of these unfortunates will not get up, they have resisted until now, they are like that marathon runner who dropped dead three metres from the finish line, when all is said and done, what is clear is that all lives end before their time. Also seated or stretched out on the ground were those blind inmates who are still awaiting the soldiers, or others instead of them, the Red Cross is one hypothesis, they might bring them food and the other basic comforts, for these people disenchantment will come a little later, that is the only difference. And if anyone here believed that a cure had been discovered for our blindness, this does not appear to have made him any more contented.

For other reasons, the doctor's wife thought that it would be better to wait until night was over, as she told her group, The most urgent thing right now is to find some food and in the dark this would not be easy. Have you any idea where we are, her husband asked, More or less, Far from home, Quite a distance. The others also wanted to know how far they were from their homes, they told her their addresses, and the doctor's wife did her best to explain, the boy with the squint cannot remember, and little wonder, he has not asked for his mother for quite some time. If they were to go from house to house, from the one that is closest to the one furthest away, the first house will be that of the girl with dark glasses, the second one that of the old man with the black eyepatch, then that of the doctor's wife, and finally the house of the first blind man. They will undoubtedly follow this itinerary because the girl with dark glasses has already asked that she should be taken to her home as soon as possible, I can't imagine what state my parents will be in, she said, this sincere preoccupation shows how groundless are the preconceived ideas of those who deny the possibility of the existence of deep feelings, including filial ones, in the, alas, abundant cases of irregular conduct, especially in matters of public morality. The night turned cool, there is not much left for the fire to burn, the heat still coming from the embers is not enough to warm the blind inmates, numb with cold, who find themselves farthest away from the asylum gate, as is the case of the doctor's wife and her group. They are seated in a huddle, the three women and the boy in the middle, the three men around them, anyone seeing them there would say that they had been born like that, it is true that they give the impression of being but one body, one breath and one hunger. One after the other, they eventually fell asleep, a light sleep from which they were roused several times because blind inmates, emerging from their own torpor, got up and stumbled drowsily over this human obstacle, one of them actually stayed behind, there was no difference between sleeping there or in some other place. When day dawned, only a few thin columns of smoke rose from the embers, but not even these lasted for long, for it soon began to rain, a fine drizzle, a mere mist, it is true, but nevertheless persistent, to begin with it did not even touch the scorched earth, but transformed itself at once into vapour, but, as it continued to fall, as everybody knows, a soft water eats away hard stone, let someone else make it rhyme. It is not only the eyes of some of these inmates that are blind, their understanding is also clouded, for there can be no other explanation for the tortuous reasoning that led them to conclude that the much desired food would not arrive in this rain. There was no way of convincing them that the premise was wrong and that, therefore, the conclusion, too, had to be wrong, they simply would not be told that it was still too early for breakfast, in despair, they threw themselves to the ground in floods of tears. It won't come, it's raining, it won't come, they repeated, if that lamentable ruin were still fit for even the most primitive habitation, it would go back to being the madhouse it once was.

The blind man who, after tripping, had stayed behind that night, could not get to his feet. Curled up, as if anxious to protect the last of the heat in his belly, he did not stir despite the rain, which had started to get heavier. He's dead, said the doctor's wife, and the rest of us had better get away from here while we still have some strength. They struggled to their feet, tottering and dizzy, holding on to each other, then they got into line, in front the woman with eyes that can see, then those who though they have eyes cannot see, the girl with dark glasses, the old man with the black eyepatch, the boy with the squint, the wife of the first blind man, her husband, and the doctor last of all. The route they have taken leads to the city centre, but this is not the intention of the doctor's wife, what she wants is to find a place as soon as possible where she can leave those following behind in safety and then go in search of food on her own. The streets are deserted, either because it is still early, or because of the rain that is becoming increasingly heavy. There is litter everywhere, some shops have their doors open, but most of them are closed, with no sign of life inside, nor any light. The doctor's wife thought that it would be a good idea to leave her companions in one of these shops, taking care to make a mental note of the name of the street and the number on the door just in case she should lose them on the way back. She paused, said to the girl with dark glasses, Wait for me here, don't move, she went to peer through the glass-panelled door of a pharmacy, thought she could see the shadowy forms of people lying on the ground, she tapped on the glass, one of the shadows stirred, she knocked again, other human forms slowly began moving, one person got up turning his head in the direction where the noise had come from, They are all blind, the doctor's wife thought, but she could not fathom how they came to be here, perhaps they were members of the pharmacist's family, but if this was the case, why were they not in their own home, with greater comfort than a hard floor, unless they were guarding the premises, against whom, and for what purpose, this merchandise being what it is, can cure and kill equally well. She moved away, a little further ahead she looked inside another shop, saw more people lying down, women, men, children, some appeared to be preparing to leave, one of them came right up to the door, put his arm outside and said, It's raining, Is it raining much, was the question from inside, Yes, we'll have to wait until it eases off, the man, it was a man, was two paces from the doctor's wife, he had not noticed her presence, and was therefore startled when he heard her say, Good-day, he had lost the habit of saying Good-day, not only because the days of the blind, strictly speaking are never likely to be good, but also because no one could be entirely sure whether it was afternoon or night, and if now, in apparent contradiction to what has just been explained, these people are waking up more or less at the same time as morning, that is because some of them only went blind a few days ago and still have not entirely lost their sense of the succession of days and nights, of sleep and wakefulness. The man said, It's raining, and then asked, Who are you, I'm not from here, Are you out searching for food, Yes, we haven't eaten for four days, And how do you know it is four days, That's what I reckon, Are you alone, I'm with my husband and some companions, How many of them are there, Seven altogether, If you're thinking of staying here with us, forget it, there are far too many of us already, We're only passing through, Where have you come from, We've been interned ever since this epidemic of blindness began, Ah, yes, the quarantine, it didn't do any good, Why do you say that, They allowed you to leave, There was a fire and, at that moment, we realised that the soldiers who were guarding us had disappeared, And you left, Yes, Your soldiers must have been amongst the last to go blind, everyone is blind, the whole city, the entire country, if anyone can still see, they say nothing, keep it to themselves, Why don't you live in your own house, Because I no longer know where it is, You don't know where it is, And what about you, do you know where your house is, Me, the doctor's wife was about to reply that that was precisely where she was heading with her husband and companions, all they needed was a quick bite to eat to recover their strength, but at that very moment she saw the situation quite clearly, somebody who was blind and had left their home would only manage to find it again by some miracle, it was not the same as before, when blind people could always count on the assistance of some passerby, whether to cross the street, or to get back on to the right path in the case of having inadvertently strayed from the usual route, All I know is that it is far from here, she said, But you'll never be able to get there, No, Now there you have it, it's the same with me, it's the same with everyone, those of you who have been in quarantine have a lot to learn, you don't know how easy it is to find yourself without a home, I don't understand, Those who go around in groups as we do, as most people do, when we have to look for food, we are obliged to go together, it's the only way of not losing each other, and since we all go, since no one stays behind to guard the house, assuming that we ever manage to find it again, the likelihood is that it will already be occupied by another group also unable to find their house, we're a kind of merry-go-round, at the outset there was some conflict, but we soon became aware that we, the blind, in a manner of speaking, have practically nothing we may call our own, except for what we are wearing, The solution would be to live in a shop selling food, at least so long as supplies lasted there would be no need to go out, Anyone who did that, the least that might happen to them would be never to have another moment's peace, I say the least, because I've heard of the case of some who tried, shut themselves away, bolted the door, but what they could not do was get rid of the smell of food, those who wanted to eat gathered outside, and since those inside refused to open the doors, the shop was set alight, it was a blessed remedy, I didn't see it myself, others told me, in any case it was a blessed remedy, and as far as I know no one else dared to do the same, And do people no longer live in houses and flats, Yes, they do, but it comes to the same thing, countless people must have passed through my house, who knows if I'll ever find it again, besides, in this situation, it's much more practical to sleep in the shops at ground level, in warehouses, it saves us having to go up and down stairs, It's stopped raining, said the doctor's wife, It's stopped raining, repeated the man to those inside. On hearing these words, those who were still stretched out got to their feet, gathered up their belongings, haversacks, hand-luggage, bags made out of cloth and plastic, as if they were setting off on an expedition, and it was true, they were off in pursuit of food, one by one they began emerging from the shop, the doctor's wife noticed that they were well wrapped up even if the colours of their clothing scarcely harmonised, their trousers either so short that they exposed their shins, or so long that the bottoms had to be turned up, but the cold would not get to this lot, some of the men wore a raincoat or an overcoat, two of the women wore long fur coats, not an umbrella to be seen, probably because they are so awkward to carry, and the spokes are always in danger of poking someone's eye out. The group, some fifteen people, moved off. Along the road, other groups appeared, as well as people on their own, up against the walls men were satisfying the urgent need felt each morning by their bladder, the women preferred the privacy of abandoned cars. Softened by the rain, the excrement, here and there, was spread all over the pavement.

The doctor's wife went back to her group, huddled together out of instinct under the awning of a cake-shop that gave off a smell of soured cream and other rancid products. Let's go, she said, I've found a refuge, and she led them to the shop the others had just left. The stock in the shop was intact, there was nothing amongst the merchandise that could be eaten or worn, there were fridges, washing-machines for both clothes and dishes, ordinary stoves as well as microwave ovens, food mixers, juicers, vacuum cleaners, the thousand and one electro-domestic inventions destined to make life easier. The atmosphere was charged with unpleasant odours, making the invariable whiteness of the objects absurd. Rest here, said the doctor's wife, I'm going to look for some food, I have no idea where I'll find it, nearby, far away, I cannot say, wait patiently, there are groups out there, if anyone tries to come in, tell them the place is occupied, that ought to be enough to send them away, that's the custom now, I'm coming with you, said her husband, No, it's best I should go alone, we must find out how people are surviving now, from what I've heard everyone must have gone blind, In that case, quipped the old man with the black eyepatch, it's just as if we were still in the mental asylum, There's no comparison, we can move about freely, and there must be a solution to the food problem, we won't die of hunger, I must also try to get some clothes, we're reduced to rags, she herself was in the greatest need, practically naked from the waist upwards. She kissed her husband, at that moment she felt something akin to a pain in her heart. Please, whatever happens, even if someone should try to come in, do not leave this place, and if you should be turned out, although I don't believe this will happen, but just to warn you of all the possibilities, stay together near the door until I arrive. She looked at them, her eyes filled with tears, there they were, as dependent on her as little children on their mother. If I should let them down—she thought. It did not occur to her that all around her the people were blind yet managed to live, she herself would also have to turn blind in order to understand that people get used to anything, especially if they have ceased to be people, and even if they have not quite reached that point, take the boy with the squint there, for example, who no longer even asks for his mother. She went out to the street, looked and made a mental note of the door number, the name of the shop, now she had to check out the name of the street on that corner, she had no idea where this search for food might take her, or what food, it might be only three doors away or three hundred, she could not afford to get lost, there would be no one from whom to ask the way, those who could see before were blind, and she, who could see, would not know where she was. The sun had broken through, it shone on the pools of water that had formed amidst the litter and it was easier to see the weeds that were sprouting up between the paving stones. There were more people outside. How do they find their way around, the doctor's wife asked herself. They did not find their way around, they kept very close to the buildings with their arms stretched out before them, they were constantly bumping into each other like ants on the trail, but when this happened no one protested, nor did they have to say anything, one of the families moved away from the wall, advanced along the wall opposite in the other direction, and thus they proceeded and carried on until the next encounter. Now and then they stopped, sniffed in the doorways of the shops in the hope of catching the smell of food, whatever it might be, then continued on their way, they turned a corner, disappeared from sight, soon another group turned up, they did not seem to have found what they were looking for. The doctor's wife could move with greater speed, she did not waste any time entering the shops to find out if there were any edible goods, but it soon became clear that it would not be easy to stock up in any quantity, the few grocers' shops she found seemed to have been devoured from inside and were like empty shells.

She had already travelled far from where she had left her husband and companions, crossing and re-crossing streets, avenues, squares, when she found herself in front of a supermarket. Inside it was no different, empty shelves, overturned displays, in the middle wandered the blind, most of them on all fours, sweeping up the filth on the floor with their hands, hoping to find something they might be able to use, a can of preserves that had withstood the pounding of those who had desperately tried to open it, some packet or other, whatever the contents, a potato, even if trampled, a crust of bread, even if as hard as stone. The doctor's wife thought, Despite everything, there must be something, the place is vast. A blind man got to his feet and complained that a bit of glass had got lodged in his knee, the blood was already trickling down one leg. The blind persons in the group gathered round him, What happened, what's the matter, and he told them, A glass splinter in my knee, Which one, The left one, one of the blind women crouched down. Take care, there might be other pieces of glass around, she probed and fumbled to distinguish one leg from the other, Here it is, she said, and it's still pricking in the flesh, one of the blind men started laughing, Well if it's pricking, make the most of it, and the others, both men and women, joined in the laughter. Bringing her thumb and forefinger together, a natural gesture that requires no training, the blind woman removed the piece of glass, then bandaged the knee with a rag she found in the bag over her shoulder, finally she cracked her own little joke to the amusement of all, Nothing to be done, no more pricking, everyone laughed, and the wounded man retorted, Whenever you feel the urge, we can have a go and find out what pricks most, there certainly are no married men and women in this group, since no one appeared to be shocked, they must all be people with lax morals who enter into casual relationships, unless the latter happen to be indeed husband and wife, hence the liberties they take with each other, but they really do not give that impression, and no married couple would say these things in public. The doctor's wife looked around her, whatever was still usable was being disputed amidst punches that nearly always missed and much jostling that made no distinction between friend and foe, and it sometimes happened that the object provoking the struggle escaped from their hands and ended up on the ground, waiting for someone to trip over it, Hell, I'll never get out of here, she thought, using an expression that formed no part of her usual vocabulary, once more showing that the force and nature of circumstances have considerable influence over language, remember that soldier who said shit when ordered to surrender, thereby absolving future expletives from the crime of bad manners in less dangerous situations. Hell, I'll never get out of here, she thought again, and just as she was preparing to leave, another thought came to her like a happy inspiration, In an establishment like this there must be a storeroom, not necessarily a large deposit, for that would be located elsewhere, probably some distance away, but back-up supplies of certain products in constant demand. Excited at the idea, she began looking for a closed door that might lead her to the cave of treasures, but they were all open, and there inside, she found the same devastation, the same blind people rummaging through the same litter. Finally, in a dark corridor, where the light of day scarcely penetrated, she saw what looked like a cargo lift. The metal doors were closed and at the side there was another door, smooth, of the kind that slide on a track, The basement, she thought, the blind people who got this far found their path impeded, they must have realised there was an elevator, but it didn't occur to anyone that it was also normal for there to be a staircase in the event of there being a power cut, for example, as was now the case. She pushed the sliding door and received, almost simultaneously, two overwhelming impressions, first, that of the total darkness she would have to penetrate in order to reach the basement, and then the unmistakable smell of food, even when stored in jars and containers we call sealed, the fact is that hunger has always had a keen sense of smell, the kind that penetrates through all barriers, just as dogs do. She quickly turned back to rescue from the litter the plastic bags she would need to transport the food, at the same time asking herself, Without light, how am I to know what to take, she shrugged her shoulders, what a stupid thing to worry about, her concern now, given the state of weakness in which she found herself, ought to be whether she would have the strength to carry the bags once they were full, retrace her steps back from where she had come, at that moment, she was gripped by the most awful fear, that of not being able to return to the spot where her husband was waiting for her, she knew the name of the street, this she had not forgotten, but she had taken so many turnings, despair paralysed her, then slowly, as if her arrested brain had finally started to move, she saw herself bent over a map of the city, searching with the tip of her finger for the shortest route, as if she had two sets of eyes, one set watching her consult the map, another perusing the map and working out the route. The corridor remained deserted, a stroke of luck, given her nervous state because of the discovery she had made, she had forgotten to close the door. She now closed it carefully behind her only to find herself plunged into total darkness, as sightless as those blind people out there, the only difference was in the colour, if black and white can, strictly speaking, be thought of as colours. Keeping close to the wall, she began to descend the stairs, if this place should turn out not to be a secret, after all, and someone were to rise from the depths, they would have to proceed as she had seen on the street, one of them would have to abandon the safety of having somewhere to lean against, brushing against the vague presence of the other, perhaps for an instant foolishly fearing that the wall did not continue on the other side, I'm going mad, she thought, and with good reason, making this descent into a dark pit, without light or any hope of seeing any, how far would it be, these underground stores are usually never very deep, first flight of steps, Now I know what it means to be blind, second flight of steps, I'm going to scream, I'm going to scream, third set of steps, the darkness is like a thick paste that sticks to her face, her eyes transformed into balls of pitch, What is this before me, and then another thought, even more terrifying, And how shall I find the stairs again, a sudden unsteadiness obliged her to crouch down in order to avoid simply falling over, almost fainting, she stammered, It's clean, she was referring to the floor, it seemed remarkable to her, a clean floor. Little by little she recovered her senses, she felt dull pains in her stomach, not that this was anything new, but at this moment it was as if there were no other living organ in her body, there had to be others, but they gave no sign of being there, her heart, yes, her heart was pounding like a great drum, for ever working blindly in the dark, from the first of all darknesses, the womb in which it was formed, to the last where it would cease. She was still clutching the plastic bags, she had not let go of them, now all she had to do was to fill them, calmly, a storeroom is not a place for ghosts and dragons, here there is nothing but darkness, and darkness neither bites nor offends, as for the stairway I'm bound to find it, even if it means walking all the way round this awful place. Her mind made up, she was about to get to her feet, but then remembered she was as blind as all the others, better to do as they did, to advance on all fours until she came across something, shelves laden with food, whatever it might be, so long as it can be eaten as it is, without having to be cooked or specially prepared, since there is no time for fancy cooking.

Her fear crept surreptitiously back, she had scarcely gone a few metres, perhaps she was mistaken, perhaps right there before her, invisible, a dragon was waiting for her with its mouth open. Or a ghost with outstretched hand, to carry her off to the dreadful world of the dead who never cease to die, because someone always comes to resuscitate them. Then, prosaically, with an infinite, resigned sadness, it occurred to her that the place where she found herself was not a store for food, but a garage, she actually thought she could smell the gasoline, the mind suffers delusions when it succumbs to the monsters it has itself created. Then her hand touched something, not the ghost's viscous fingers, not the fiery tongue and fangs of the dragon, what she felt was the contact of cold metal, a smooth vertical surface, she guessed, without knowing what it was called, that this was the upright of a set of shelves, She calculated there must be others just like this, standing parallel to this one, as was the custom, it was now a question of finding out where the food products were, not here, for this smell is unmistakable, it is the smell of detergent. Without giving another thought to the difficulties she would have in finding the stairs, she began investigating the shelves, groping, sniffing, shaking.

There were cardboard containers, glass and plastic bottles, jars of all sizes, tins that were probably preserves, various cartons, packets, bags, tubes. She filled one of the bags at random, Could all this be for eating, she thought to herself with some disquiet. The doctor's wife passed on to the next set of shelves, and the unexpected happened, her blind hand that could not see where it was going, came up against and knocked over some tiny boxes. The noise they made on hitting the floor almost made her heart stop beating, Matches, she thought. Trembling with excitement, she stooped down, ran her hand over the ground, found what she was looking for, this is a smell one never confuses with any other, and the noise of the little match-sticks when we shake the box, the sliding of the lid, the roughness of the sand-paper on the outside, which is where the phosphorus is, the scraping of the match-head, finally the sparking of the tiny flame, the surrounding space a diffuse sphere as luminous as a star glimmering through the mist, dear God, light exists and I have eyes to see, praised be light. From now on, the harvest would be easy. She began with the boxes of matches, and almost filled a bag. No need to take all of them, the voice of common sense told her, then the flickering flames of the matches lit up the shelves, over here, then over there, soon the bags were full, the first had to be emptied because it contained nothing useful, the others already held enough riches to buy the city, nor need we be surprised at this difference of values, we need only recall that there was once a king who wanted to exchange his kingdom for a horse, what would he not give were he dying of hunger and was tempted by these plastic bags full of food. The stairway is there, the way out to the right. But first, the doctor's wife sits on the ground, opens a packet of chorizo sausage, another with slices of black bread, a bottle of water, and, without remorse, starts eating. If she were not to eat now she would not have the strength to carry the provisions where they were needed, she being the provider. When she had finished, she slipped the bags over her arms, three on each side, and with her hands raised before her, she went on striking matches until she reached the stairs, then she climbed them with some effort, she still had not digested her food, which needs time to pass from the stomach to the muscles and nerves, and, in her case, to what had shown the greatest resistance, her head. The door slid noiselessly open, And what if there is someone in the corridor, thought the doctor's wife, what shall I do. There was no one, but she started asking herself again, What shall I do. When she reached the exit, she could turn round and shout inside, There is food at the end of the corridor, stairs lead to the store in the cellar, make the most of it, I have left the door open. She could have done it, but decided not to. Using her shoulder, she closed the door, she told herself that it was better to say nothing, just imagine what would happen, the blind inmates running all over the place like madmen, a repetition of what happened in the mental asylum when fire broke out, they would roll down the stairs, be trampled and crushed by those coming behind, who would also stumble and fall, it is not the same thing to put one's foot on a firm step as to put it on a slippery body. And when the food is finished, I shall be able to come back for more, she thought. She now gripped the bags with her hands, took a deep breath, and proceeded along the corridor. They would not be able to see her, but there was the smell of what she had eaten, The sausage, what a fool I was, it would be like a living trail. She gritted her teeth, clutched the bags with all her strength, I must run, she said. She remembered the blind man whose knee had been cut by a splinter of glass, If the same thing happens to me, if I don't look out and step on broken glass, we may have forgotten that this woman is wearing no shoes, she still has not had time to go to a shoeshop like blind people in the city, who despite being unfortunates without sight, can at least choose footwear by touch. She had to run, and she did. At first, she had tried to slip through the groups of blind people, trying not to touch them, but this obliged her to go slowly, to stop several times in order to ascertain the way, enough to give off the smell of food, for auras are not only perfumed and ethereal ones, in no time a blind man was shouting, Who's eating sausage around here, no sooner were those words spoken than the doctor's wife threw caution to the wind and broke into reckless flight, colliding, jostling, knocking people over, with a devil-may-care attitude that was wholly reprehensible, for this is not the way to treat blind people who have more than enough reasons to be unhappy.

When she reached the street, it was raining buckets, All the better, she thought, panting for breath, her legs shaking, in this rain the smell will be less noticeable. Someone had grabbed the last rag that had barely covered her from the waist up, she was now going around with her breasts exposed and glistening, a refined expression, with the water from heaven, this was not liberty leading the people, the bags, fortunately full, are too heavy for her to carry them aloft like a flag. This is somewhat inconvenient, since these tantalising odours are travelling at a height that brings dogs on the scent, of course without masters to look after them and feed them, there is virtually a pack of them following the doctor's wife, let's hope none of these hounds remembers to take a bite to test the resistance of the plastic. In a downpour like this, which is almost becoming a deluge, you would expect people to be taking shelter, waiting for the weather to improve. But this is not the case, there are blind people everywhere gaping up at the heavens, slaking their thirst, storing up water in every nook and cranny of their bodies, and others, who are somewhat more far-sighted, and above all sensible, hold up buckets, bowls and pans, and raise them to the generous sky, clearly God provides the cloud according to the thirst. The possibility had not occurred to the doctor's wife that not so much as a drop of the precious liquid was coming from the taps in the houses, this is the drawback of civilisation, we are so used to the convenience of piped water brought into our homes, and forget that for this to happen there have to be people to open and close distribution valves, water towers and pumps that require electrical energy, computers to regulate the deficits and administer the reserves, and all of these operations require the use of one's eyes. Eyes are also needed to see this picture, a woman laden with plastic bags, going along a rain-drenched street, amidst rotting litter and human and animal excrement, cars and trucks abandoned any old way, blocking the main thoroughfare, some of the vehicles with their tyres already surrounded by grass, and the blind, the blind, open-mouthed and staring up at the white sky, it seems incredible that rain should fall from such a sky. The doctor's wife reads the street signs as she goes along, she remembers some of them, others not at all, and there comes a moment when she realises that she has lost her way. There is no doubt, she is lost. She took a turning, then another, she no longer remembers the streets or their names, then in her distress, she sat down on the filthy ground, thick with black mud, and, drained of any strength, of all strength, she burst into tears. The dogs gathered round her, sniffed at the bags, but without much conviction, as if their hour for eating had passed, one of them licks her face, perhaps it had been used to drying tears ever since it was a puppy. The woman strokes its head, runs her hand down its drenched back, and she weeps the rest of her tears embracing the dog. When she finally raised her eyes, the god of crossroads be praised a thousand times, she saw a great map before her, of the kind that town councils set up throughout city centres, especially for the benefit and reassurance of visitors, who are just as anxious to say where they have been as to know precisely where they are. Now that everyone is blind, you might be tempted to think that the money has been ill-spent, but it is a question of being patient, of letting time take its course, we should have learnt this once and for all, that destiny has to make many turnings before arriving anywhere, destiny alone knows what it has cost to bring this map here in order to let this woman know where she is. She was not as far away as she thought, she had simply made a detour in the other direction, all you have to do is to follow this street until you come to the square, there you count two streets to the left, then you take the first street on the right, that is the one you are looking for, the number you have not forgotten. The dogs gradually left her, something distracted them on the way, or they are familiar with the district and are reluctant to stray too far, only the dog that has dried her tears accompanied the person who had wept them, probably this encounter of the woman and the map, so well prepared by destiny, included the dog as well. The fact is that they entered the shop together, the dog of tears was not surprised to see people lying on the ground, so still that they might have been dead, the dog was used to this, sometimes they let him sleep amongst them, and when it was time to get up, they were nearly always alive. Wake up, if you're asleep, I've brought food, said the doctor's wife, but first she had closed the door, in case anyone passing in the street should hear her. The boy with the squint was the first to raise his head, weakness prevented him from doing any more, the others took a little longer, they were dreaming they were stones, and we all know how deeply stones sleep, a simple stroll in the countryside shows it to be so, there they lie sleeping, half buried, awaiting who knows what awakening. The word food, however, has magic powers, especially when hunger is pressing, even the dog of tears, who knows no language, began wagging its tail, this instinctive movement reminded it that it still had not done what is expected of wet dogs, to shake themselves vigorously, splashing everything around, for them it is easy, they wear their pelt as if it were a coat. Holy water of the most efficacious variety, descended directly from heaven, the splashes helped the stones to transform themselves into persons, while the doctor's wife participated in this process of metamorphosis by opening the plastic bags one after the other. Not everything smelled of what it contained, but the aroma of a chunk of stale bread would be as good, speaking in exalted terms, as the essence of life itself. They are all awake at last, their hands are shaking, their faces anxious, it is then that the doctor, as had happened before to the dog of tears, remembers who he is, Careful, it's not a good idea to eat too much, it could be harmful, What's doing us harm is hunger, said the first blind man, Take heed of what the doctor is saying, his wife rebuked him, and her husband fell silent, thinking with faint resentment, He doesn't even know anything about eyes, unjust words these, especially if we take into account that the doctor is no less blind than the others, the proof being that he was unaware that his wife was naked from the waist up, it was she who asked him for his jacket to cover herself, the other blind inmates looked in her direction, but it was much too late, if only they had looked before.

As they were eating, the woman told them of her adventures, of everything that had happened to her and everything that she had done, without mentioning that she had left the door to the storeroom closed, she was not entirely sure of the humanitarian motives she had given to herself, to compensate she told them about the blind man who got a piece of glass stuck in his knee, they all laughed heartily, well, not all of them, the old man with the black eyepatch only reacted with a weary smile, and the boy with the squint had ears only for the noise he made as he chewed his food. The dog of tears received his share, which he quickly repaid by barking furiously when anyone outside shook the door hard. Whoever it was, they did not persist, there was talk of mad dogs going around, not knowing where I'm putting my feet makes me quite mad enough. Calm was restored, and it was then, when everyone's initial hunger had been assuaged, that the doctor's wife related the conversation she had had with the man who had come out of this same shop to see if it was raining. Then she concluded, If what he told me is true, we cannot be certain of finding our homes as we left them, we don't even know whether we shall be able to get into them, I'm speaking of those who forgot to take the keys when they left, or lost them, we, for example, do not have them, they disappeared in the fire, it would be impossible to find them now amongst the ashes, she uttered that word and it was as if she were seeing the flames devouring her scissors, first burning the congealed blood that remained on them, then licking at the edges the sharp points, blunting them, and gradually making them dull, pliable, soft, formless, no one would believe that this instrument could have perforated someone's throat, once the fire has done its work it will be impossible in this unified mass of molten metal, to distinguish which are the scissors and which the keys, I've got the keys, said the doctor, and awkwardly introducing three fingers into a small pocket near the waistband of his tattered trousers, he brought out a tiny ring with three keys, How do you happen to have them when I had put them in my handbag which got left behind, I removed them, I was afraid they might get lost, I felt they were safer if they were always with me, and it was also a way of convincing myself that one day we would go back home, It's a relief to have the keys, but we might find the house with the door smashed in, They may not even have tried. For some moments, they had forgotten the others, but now it was important to know, from all of them, what had happened to their keys, the first to speak was the girl with dark glasses, My parents remained at home when the ambulance came to fetch me, I don't know what became of them afterwards, then the old man with the black eyepatch spoke up, I was at home when I went blind, they knocked at the door, the owner of the house came to tell me there were some male nurses looking for me, it wasn't the moment to be thinking about keys, that left only the wife of the first blind man, but she said, I cannot say, I've forgotten, she knew and remembered, but what she did not wish to confess is that when she suddenly saw that she was blind, an absurd expression, but so deeply rooted in the language that we've been unable to avoid it, she had run from the house screaming, calling out to her neighbours, those who were still in the building thought twice about going to her assistance, and she, who had shown herself so steadfast and capable when her husband had been struck by this misfortune, now went to pieces, abandoning her home with the door wide open, it did not even occur to her to ask that they should allow her to turn back, just for a minute, the time to close the door and say I'll be right back. No one asked the boy with the squint about the key to his house, since he cannot even remember where he lives. Then the doctor's wife gently touched the hand of the girl with dark glasses, Let's start with your house which is nearest, but first we must find some clothes and shoes, we can't go around like this, unwashed and in rags. She started to get up, but noticed that the boy with the squint, consoled by now and his hunger satisfied, had gone back to sleep. She said, let's rest then, let's sleep a little, then later we can go and see what awaits us. She took off her drenched skirt, then, to find some warmth, she snuggled up to her husband, and the first blind man and his wife did the same. Is that you, he had asked, she remembered their home and it pained her, she did not say, Console me, but it was as if she had thought it, what we do not know is what feeling could have led the girl with dark glasses to put her arm round the shoulder of the old man with the black eyepatch, but there is no doubt that she did so, and there they remained, she sleeping, but not him. The dog went to lie down at the door, blocking the entrance, he is a gruff, ill-tempered animal when he does not have to dry someone's tears.

They dressed and put their shoes on, what they still had not solved was some way of washing themselves, but they already looked quite different from the other blind people, the colours of their clothes, notwithstanding the relative scarcity of the range on offer, for, as people often say, the fruit is hand-picked, go well with each other, that is the advantage of having someone on the spot to advise us, You wear this, it goes better with those trousers, the stripes don't clash with the spots, details like that, to the men, of course, these matters do not make a blind bit of difference, but both the girl with dark glasses and the wife of the first blind man insisted on knowing what colours and styles they were wearing, so that, with the help of their imaginations they have some idea of how they look. As for footwear, everyone agreed that comfort should come before beauty, no fancy lacing and high heels, no calf or patent leather, given the state of the roads such refinements would be absurd, what they want here are rubber boots, completely waterproof and coming halfway up the leg, easy to slip into and out of, there is nothing better for walking through mud. Unfortunately, boots of this kind could not be found for everyone, there were no boots to fit the boy with the squint, for example, the larger sizes were like boats on him, so he had to settle for a pair of sports shoes with no clearly defined purpose, What a coincidence, his mother would say, wherever she might be, when someone told her what had happened, those are exactly the shoes my son would have chosen had he been able to see. The old man with the black eyepatch, whose feet were on the large side, solved the problem by wearing basketball shoes, specially made for players six foot tall and with extremities to match. It is true that he looks somewhat comical, as if he were wearing white slippers, but he will look ridiculous only for a while, within ten minutes the shoes will be filthy, just like everything else in life, let time take its course and it will find a solution.

It has stopped raining, there are no blind people standing about gaping. They go around not knowing what to do, they wander through the streets, but never for very long, walking or standing still is all the same to them, they have no other objective than the search for food, the music has stopped, never has there been so much silence in the world, the cinemas and theatres are only frequented by the homeless who have given up searching, some theatres, the larger ones, had been used to keep the blind in quarantine when the Government, or the few survivors, still believed that the white sickness could be remedied with devices and certain strategies that had been so ineffectual in the past against yellow fever and other infectious plagues, but this came to an end, not even a fire was needed here. As for the museums, it is truly heart-breaking, all those people, and I do mean people, all those paintings, all those sculptures, without a single visitor standing before them. What are the blind in this city waiting for, who knows, they might be awaiting a cure if they still believed in it, but they lost that hope when it became public knowledge that the epidemic of blindness had spared no one, that not a single person had been left with the eyesight to look through the lens of a microscope, that the laboratories had been abandoned, where there was no other solution for the bacteria but to feed on each other if they hoped to survive. In the beginning, many of the blind, accompanied by relatives who so far had maintained some sense of family solidarity, still rushed to the hospitals, but there they found only blind doctors feeling the pulse of patients they could not see, listening to them back and front, this was all they could do, since they still had their hearing. Then, feeling the pangs of hunger, those patients who could still walk began to flee the hospitals, they ended up dying unprotected on the streets, their families, if they still had them, could be anywhere, and then, so that they might be buried, it was not enough for someone to trip over them accidentally, their corpses had to start to smell, and even then, only if they had died in some main thoroughfare. Little wonder that there are so many dogs, some of them already resemble hyenas, the spots on their pelt are like those of putrefaction, they run around with their hind quarters drawn in, as if afraid that the dead and devoured might come back to life in order to make them pay for the shame of biting those who could not defend themselves. What's the world like these days, the old man with the black eyepatch had asked, and the doctor's wife replied, There's no difference between inside and outside, between here and there, between the many and the few, between what we're living through and what we shall have to live through, And the people, how are they coping, asked the girl with dark glasses, They go around like ghosts, this must be what it means to be a ghost, being certain that life exists, because your four senses say so, and yet unable to see it, Are there lots of cars out there, asked the first blind man, who was unable to forget that his had been stolen, It's like a cemetery. Neither the doctor nor the wife of the first blind man asked any questions, what was the point, when the replies were such as these. As for the little boy with the squint, he has the satisfaction of wearing the shoes he had always dreamt of having and he is not even saddened by the fact that he cannot see them. This is probably the reason why he does not look like a ghost. And the dog of tears, who trails after the doctor's wife, would scarcely deserve to be called a hyena, he does not follow the scent of dead meat, he accompanies a pair of eyes that he knows are alive and well.

The home of the girl with dark glasses is not far away, but after being starved for a week, it is only now that the members of this group begin to recover their strength, that is why they walk so slowly, in order to rest they have no option but to sit on the ground, it had not been worthwhile taking so much trouble to choose colours and styles, when in such a short time their clothes are filthy. The street where the girl with dark glasses lives is not only short but narrow which explains why there are no cars to be seen here, they could pass in one direction only, but there was no place to park, it was prohibited. That there were also no people was not surprising, in streets like these there are many moments throughout the day when there is not a living soul to be seen, What's the number of your house, asked the doctor's wife, number seven, I live on the second floor in the flat on the left. One of the windows was open, at any other time that would be a sign that there was almost certainly someone at home, now everything was uncertain. The doctor's wife said, No need for all of us to go up, we two shall go on our own, the rest of you wait below. She realised the front door leading on to the street had been forced, the mortice lock was clearly twisted, a long splinter of wood had almost come away from the doorpost. The doctor's wife mentioned none of this. She let the girl go ahead since she knew the way, she did not mind the shadows into which the stairway was plunged. In her nervous haste, the girl with dark glasses stumbled twice, but laughed it off, Just imagine, stairs that I used to be able to go up and down with my eyes closed, clichés are like that, they are insensitive to the thousand subtleties of meaning, this one, for example, does not know the difference between closing one's eyes and being blind. On the landing of the second floor, the door they were looking for was closed. The girl with dark glasses ran her hand over the moulding until she found the bell, There's no light, the doctor's wife reminded her, and the girl received these four words that only repeated what everyone knew like a message bringing bad news. She knocked at the door, once, twice, three times, the third time loudly, using her fists and calling out, Mummy, daddy, and no one came to open, these terms of endearment did not affect the reality, no one came to say to her, Dearest daughter, you've come at last, we had given up hope of ever seeing you again, come in, come in, and let this lady who is your friend come in too, the house is a little untidy, pay no attention, the door remained closed. There is no one here, said the girl with dark glasses, and burst into tears leaning against the door, her head on her crossed forearms, as if with her whole body she were desperately imploring pity, if we did not have enough experience of how complicated the human spirit can be we would be surprised that she should be so fond of her parents as to indulge in these demonstrations of sorrow, a girl so free in her behaviour, but not far away is someone who has already affirmed that there does not exist nor ever has existed any contradiction between the one and the other. The doctor's wife tried to console her, but had little to say, it is well known that it is practically impossible for people to remain for a long time in their houses, We could ask the neighbours, she suggested, if there are any, Yes, let's go and ask, said the girl with dark glasses, but there was no hope in her voice. They began by knocking on the door on the other side of the landing, where once again no one replied. On the floor above the two doors were open. The flats had been ransacked, the wardrobes were empty, in the cupboards where food had been stored there was nothing to be found. There were signs that someone had been here recently, no doubt a group of vagrants, as they were all more or less by now, wandering from house to house, from absence to absence.

They went down to the first floor, the doctor's wife rapped on the nearest door, there was an expectant silence, then a gruff voice asked suspiciously, Who's there, the girl with dark glasses stepped forward, It's me, your upstairs neighbour, I'm looking for my parents, do you know where I can find them, what happened to them, she asked. They could hear shuffling footsteps, the door opened and a gaunt old woman appeared, nothing but skin and bone, emaciated, her long white hair dishevelled. A nauseating smell of mustiness and an indefinable putrefaction caused the two women to step back. The old woman opened her eyes wide, they were almost white, I know nothing about your parents, they came to fetch them the day after they took you away, at that time I could still see, Is there anyone else in the building, Now and then I can hear people climbing up or going down the stairs, but they are from outside and only come here to sleep, And what about my parents, I've already told you I know nothing about them, And what about your husband, your son and daughter-in-law, They took them away too, But left you behind, why, Because I was hiding, Where, Just imagine, in your flat, How did you manage to get in, Through the back and up the fire escape, I smashed a window-pane and opened the door from inside, the key was in the lock, And how have you managed since then to live all alone in your flat, asked the doctor's wife, Who else is here, asked the startled old woman turning her head, She's a friend of mine, she's with my group, the girl with dark glasses reassured her, And it's not just a question of being alone, what about food, how have you managed to get food during all this time, insisted the doctor's wife, The fact is that I'm no fool and I'm perfectly capable of looking after myself, If you'd rather not say, don't, I'm simply curious, Then I'll tell you, the first thing I did was to go round all the flats and gather up any food I could find, whatever might go bad I ate at once, the rest I kept, Do you still have some left, asked the girl with dark glasses, No, it's finished, replied the old woman with a sudden expression of mistrust in her sightless eyes, a way of speaking that is always used in similar situations, but it has no basis in fact, because the eyes, the eyes strictly speaking, have no expression, not even when they have been plucked out, they are two round objects that remain inert, it is the eyelids, the eyelashes and the eyebrows, that have to take on board the different visual eloquences and rhetorics, notwithstanding that this is normally attributed to the eyes, So what are you living on now, asked the doctor's wife, Death stalks the streets, but in the back gardens life goes on, the old woman said mysteriously, What do you mean, The back gardens have cabbages, rabbits, hens, they also have flowers, but they're not for eating, And how do you cope, It depends, sometimes I pick some cabbages, at other times I kill a rabbit or chicken, And eat them raw, At first I used to light a fire, then I got used to raw meat, and the stalks of the cabbages are sweet, don't you worry yourselves, my mother's daughter will not die of hunger. She stepped back two paces, almost disappeared into the darkness of the house, only her white eyes shone, and she said from within, If you want to go into your flat, go ahead, I won't stop you. The girl with dark glasses was about to say no, many thanks, it isn't worth it, to what purpose, if my parents aren't there, but suddenly she felt the desire to see her room, to see my room, how foolish, if I'm blind, at least to touch the walls, the bedcover, the pillow where I used to rest my crazy head, over the furniture, perhaps on the chest of drawers there might still be the flowers in the vase she remembered, unless the old woman had thrown them on the floor, annoyed that they could not be eaten. She said, Well, if you don't mind, I'll accept your offer, it's very kind of you, Come in, come in, but don't expect to find any food, what I have is barely enough for me, besides it would be no good to you unless you like raw meat, Don't worry, we have food, Ah, so you have food, in that case you can repay the favour and leave me some, We'll give you some food, don't worry, said the doctor's wife. They had already walked down the corridor, the stench had become unbearable. In the kitchen, dimly lit by the waning light outside, there were rabbit skins on the floor, chicken feathers, bones, and on the table, in a dirty plate covered in dried blood, unrecognisable pieces of meat, as if they had been chewed over and over again, And the rabbits and hens, what do they eat, asked the doctor's wife, Cabbages, weeds, any scraps left over, said the old woman, Don't tell us the hens and rabbits eat meat, The rabbits don't yet, but the hens love it, animals are like people, they get used to everything in the end. The old woman moved steadily, without tottering, she moved a chair out of the way as if she could see, then pointed to the door that led on to the emergency stairs, Through here, be careful not to slip, the handrail is not very secure. And what about the door, asked the girl with dark glasses, You only have to push the door, I have the key, it's somewhere around, It's mine, the girl was about to say, but at that same instant reflected that this key would be no good to her if her parents, or someone acting on their behalf, had taken away the others, the ones for the front door, she could not ask this neighbour to allow her to pass every time she wanted to come in or go out. She felt her heart contract slightly, probably because she was about to enter her own home and discover that her parents were not there, or for whatever reason.

The kitchen was clean and tidy, the dust on the furniture was not excessive, another advantage of this rainy weather, as well as having made the cabbages and greens grow, in fact, the back gardens, seen from above, had struck the doctor's wife as being jungles in miniature, Could the rabbits be running around freely, she asked herself, most unlikely, they would still be housed in the rabbit-hutches waiting for that blind hand to bring them cabbage leaves then grab them by the ears and pull them out kicking, while the other hand prepares the blind blow that will break the vertebrae near the skull. The memory of the girl with dark glasses had guided her into the flat, just as the old woman on the floor below neither tripped nor faltered, her parents' bed was unmade, they must have come to detain them in the early hours of morning, she sat down there and wept, the doctor's wife came to sit beside her, and told her, Don't cry, what else could she say, what meaning do tears have when the world has lost all meaning, In the girl's room on the chest of drawers stood the glass vase with the withered flowers, the water had evaporated, it was there that her blind hands directed themselves, her fingers brushed against the dead petals, how fragile life is when it is abandoned. The doctor's wife opened the window, she looked down into the street, there they all were, seated on the ground, patiently waiting, the dog of tears was the only creature to raise his head, alerted by his keen hearing. The sky, once more overcast, began to darken, night was approaching. She thought that today they would not need to go and search for some refuge where they might sleep, they would stay here. The old woman is not going to be at all pleased if everyone starts tramping through her house, she murmured. Just at that moment, the girl with dark glasses touched her on the shoulder, saying, The keys were in the lock, they did not take them. The problem, if there was one, was therefore resolved, they would not have to put up with the ill-humour of the old woman on the first floor, I'm going down to call them, it will soon be night, how good, at least today we shall be able to sleep in a proper home with a roof over our heads, said the doctor's wife, You and your husband can sleep in my parents' bed, We'll see about that later, I'm the one who gives the orders here, I'm in my own home, You're right, just as you wish, the doctor's wife embraced the girl, then went down to look for the others. Climbing the stairs, chattering with excitement, now and then tripping on the stairs despite having been told by their guide, There are ten steps to each flight, it was as if they had come on a visit. The dog of tears followed them quietly, as if this were an everyday occurrence. From the landing, the girl with dark glasses looked down, it is the custom when someone is coming up, whether it be to find out who it is, if the person is a stranger, or to greet someone with words of welcome if they are friends, in this case no eyes were needed to know who was arriving. Come in, come in, make yourselves comfortable. The old woman on the first floor had come to her door to pry, she thought this lot was one of those mobs who turned up to sleep, in this she was not wrong, she asked, Who's there, and the girl with dark glasses replied from above, It's my group, the old woman was puzzled, how had she been able to reach the landing, then it dawned on her and she was annoyed with herself for having forgotten to retrieve the keys from the front door, it was as if she were losing her proprietorial rights over this building in which she had been the sole occupant for many months. She could find no better way of compensating for her sudden frustration than to say, opening the door, Remember you said you'd give me some food, don't go forgetting your promise. And since neither the doctor's wife nor the girl with dark glasses, the one busy guiding those who were arriving, the other in receiving them, made any reply, she shouted hysterically, Did you hear me, a mistake on her part, because the dog of tears, who at that precise moment was passing her, leapt at her and started barking furiously, the entire stairway echoed with the uproar, it was perfect, the old woman shrieked in terror and rushed back into her flat, slamming the door behind her, Who is that witch, asked the old man with the black eyepatch, these are things we say when we do not know how to take a good look at ourselves, had he lived as she had lived, we should like to see how long his civilised ways would last.

There was no food apart from what they had brought in the bags, they had to be sparing with it down to the very last drop, and, as for lighting, they had been most fortunate to find two candles in the kitchen cupboard, kept there to be used whenever there happened to be a power cut and which the doctor's wife lit for her own benefit, the others did not need them, they already had a light inside their heads, so strong it had blinded them. Though meagre rations were all this little group had, yet it ended up as a family feast, one of those rare feasts where what belongs to one, belongs to everybody. Before seating themselves at the table, the girl with dark glasses and the doctor's wife went down to the floor below, they went to fulfill their promise, were it not more exact to say that they went to satisfy a demand, payment with food for their passage through that customs house. The old woman received them, whining and surly, that cursed dog that only by some miracle did not devour her, You must have a lot of food to be able to feed such a beast, she insinuated, as if expecting, by means of this accusing observation, to arouse in the two emissaries what we call remorse, what they were really saying to each other, it would be inhumane to leave a poor old woman to die of starvation while a dumb animal gorges itself on scraps. The two women did not turn back to get more food, what they were carrying was already a generous ration, if we take into account the difficult circumstances of life at present, and this strangely enough, was how the old lady on the floor below appraised the situation, when all is said and done, less mean-hearted than she seemed, and she went back inside to find the keys for the back door, saying to the girl with dark glasses, Take it, this key is yours, and, as if this were not enough, she was still muttering as she closed her door, Many thanks. Amazed, the two women returned upstairs, so the old witch had feelings after all, She was not a bad person, living all that time alone must have unhinged her, commented the girl with dark glasses without appearing to think what she was saying. The doctor's wife did not reply, she decided to keep any conversation for later, and once all the others were in bed, some of them asleep, and the two women were sitting in the kitchen like mother and daughter trying to gather strength for the other chores to be done around the house, the doctor's wife asked, And you, what are you going to do now, Nothing, I'll wait here until my parents return, Alone and blind, I've got used to being blind, And what about solitude, I'll have to accept it, the old woman below also lives alone, You don't want to become like her, feeding on cabbages and raw meat, while they last, in these buildings around here there appears to be no one else living, you would be two women hating each other for fear that the food might come to an end, each stalk you gathered would be like taking it from the other's mouth, you didn't see that poor woman, you only caught the stench coming from her flat, I can assure you that not even where we were living before were things so repugnant, Sooner or later, we shall all be like her, and then it will all be over, there will be no more life, Meanwhile, we're still alive, Listen, you know much more than I do, compared with you I'm simply an ignorant girl, but in my opinion we're already dead, we're blind because we're dead, or if you would prefer me to put it another way, we're dead because we're blind, it comes to the same thing, I can still see, Lucky for you, lucky for your husband, for me, for the others, but you don't know how long you will go on seeing, should you become blind you will be like the rest of us, we'll all end up like the neighbour below, Today is today, tomorrow will bring what tomorrow brings, today is my responsibility, not tomorrow if I should turn blind, What do you mean by responsibility, The responsibility of having my eyesight when others have lost theirs, You cannot hope to guide or provide food for all the blind people in this world, I ought to, But you cannot, I shall do whatever I can to help, Of course you will, had it not been for you I might not be alive today, And I don't want you to die now, I must stay, it's my duty, I want my parents to find me if they should return, If they should return, you yourself said it, and we have no way of knowing whether they will still be your parents, I don't understand, You said that the neighbour below was a good person at heart, Poor woman, Your poor parents, poor you, when you meet up, blind in eyes and blind in feelings, because the feelings with which we have lived and which allowed us to live as we were, depended on our having the eyes we were born with, without eyes feelings become something different, we do not know how, we do not know what, you say we're dead because we're blind, there you have it, Do you love your husband, Yes, as I love myself, but should I turn blind, if after turning blind I should no longer be the person I was, how would I then be able to go on loving him, and with what love, Before, when we could still see, there were also blind people, Few in comparison, the feelings in use were those of someone who could see, therefore blind people felt with the feelings of others, not as the blind people they were, now, certainly, what is emerging are the real feelings of the blind, and we're still only at the beginning, for the moment we still live on the memory of what we felt, you don't need eyes to know what life has become today, if anyone were to tell me that one day I should kill, I'd take it as an insult, and yet I've killed, What then would you have me do, Come with me, come to our house, And what about the others, The same goes for them, but it's you I most care about, Why, I ask myself that question, perhaps because you have become almost like a sister, perhaps because my husband slept with you, Forgive me, It's not a crime that calls for pardon, We would suck your blood and be like parasites, There were plenty of them when we could see, and as for blood, it has to serve some purpose besides sustaining the body that carries it, and now let's try to get some sleep for tomorrow is another day.

Another day, or the same one. When he woke up, the boy with the squint wanted to go to the lavatory, he had diarrhoea, something that had disagreed with him in his weak condition, but it soon became obvious that it was impossible to go in there, the old woman on the floor below had clearly taken advantage of all the lavatories in the building until they could no longer be used, only by some extraordinary stroke of luck none of the seven, before going to bed last night, had needed to satisfy the urge to relieve their bowels, otherwise they would already know just how disgusting those lavatories were. Now they all felt the need to relieve themselves, especially the poor boy who could not hold it in any longer, in fact, however reluctant we might be to admit it, these distasteful realities of life also have to be considered, when the bowels function normally, anyone can have ideas, debate, for example, whether there exists a direct relationship between the eyes and feelings, or whether the sense of responsibility is the natural consequence of clear vision, but when we are in great distress and plagued by pain and anguish that is when the animal side of our nature becomes most apparent. The garden, exclaimed the doctor's wife, and she was right, were it not so early, we would find the neighbour from the flat below already there, it's time we stopped calling her the old woman, as we have disrespectfully done so far, she would already be there, as we were saying, crouched down, surrounded by hens, because the person who might ask the question almost certainly does not know what hens are like. Clutching his belly, protected by the doctor's wife, the boy with the squint went down the stairs in agony, worse still, by the time he reached the last steps, his sphincter had given up trying to resist the internal pressure, so you can imagine the consequences. Meanwhile, the other five were making their way as best they could down the emergency stairs, a most suitable name, if they have any inhibitions left since the time they lived in quarantine, this was the moment to lose them. Scattered throughout the back garden, groaning with the effort, suffering whatever remained of futile shame, they did what had to be done, even the doctor's wife who wept as she looked at them, she wept for all of them, which they seemed no longer to be able to do, her own husband, the first blind man and his wife, the girl with dark glasses, the old man with the black eyepatch, the boy, she saw them squatting on the weeds, between the knotty cabbage stalks, with the hens watching, the dog of tears had also come down to make one more. They cleaned themselves as best they could, superficially and in haste, with some handfuls of grass or broken bits of brick, wherever the arm could reach, in some cases the attempt to tidy up only made matters worse. They went back up the emergency stairs in silence, the neighbour on the first floor did not appear to ask them who they were, where they had come from, where they were going, she must still be sleeping off her supper, and when they got into the flat, first they did not know what to say, then the girl with dark glasses pointed out that they could not remain in that state, it is true that there was no water with which to wash themselves, pity there was no torrential rain like that of yesterday, they would go out once more into the garden, but now naked and without shame, they would receive on their head and shoulders the generous water from the sky above, they would feel it running down their back and chest, down their legs, they could gather it in their hands, clean at last and in this cup offer it to someone to quench their thirst, no matter who, perhaps their lips would gently touch their skin before finding the water, and desperately thirsty as they were, they would eagerly gather the last drops from that shell, thus arousing, who knows, another thirst. What leads the girl with dark glasses astray, as we have seen on other occasions, is her imagination, what would she have to remember in a situation like this, tragic, grotesque, desperate as it was. Despite everything, she is not without some sense of the practical, the proof being that she went to open the wardrobe in her room, then that of her parents, where she gathered up sheets and towels, Let's clean ourselves up with these, she said, it's better than nothing, and there is no doubt that it was a good idea, when they sat down to eat they felt quite different.

It was at the table that the doctor's wife told them what was on her mind. The time has come to decide what we want to do, I'm convinced the entire population is blind, at least that is my impression from observing the behaviour of the people I have seen so far, there is no water, there is no electricity, there are no supplies of any kind, this must be what chaos is, this is what is really meant by chaos. There must be a government, said the first blind man, I'm not so sure, but if there is, it will be a government of the blind trying to rule the blind, that is to say, nothingness trying to organise nothingness, Then there is no future, said the old man with the black eyepatch, I cannot say whether there will be a future, what matters for the moment is to see how we can live in the present, Without a future, the present serves no purpose, it's as if it did not exist, Perhaps humanity will manage to live without eyes, but then it will cease to be humanity, the result is obvious, which of us think of ourselves as being as human as we believed ourselves to be before, I, for example, killed a man, You killed a man, asked the first blind man in alarm, Yes, the one who gave orders on the other side, I stabbed him in the throat with a pair of scissors, You killed him to avenge us, only a woman could avenge the women, said the girl with dark glasses, and revenge, being just, is something human, if the victim has no rights over the wrong-doer then there can be no justice, Nor humanity, added the wife of the first blind man, Let's get back to the matter we were discussing, said the doctor's wife, if we stay together we might manage to survive, if we separate we shall be swallowed up by the masses and destroyed, You mentioned that there are organised groups of blind people, observed the doctor, this means that new ways of living are being invented and there is no reason why we should finish up by being destroyed, as you predict, I don't know to what extent they are really organised, I only see them going around in search of food and somewhere to sleep, nothing more, We're going back to being primitive hordes, said the old man with the black eyepatch, with the difference that we are not a few thousand men and women in an immense, unspoiled nature, but thousands of millions in an uprooted, exhausted world, And blind, added the doctor's wife, When it starts to become difficult to find water and food, these groups will almost certainly disband, each person will think they have a better chance of surviving on their own, they will not have to share anything with others, whatever they can grab belongs to them and to no one else, The groups going around must have leaders, someone who gives orders and organises things, the first blind man reminded them, Perhaps, but in this case those who give the orders are just as blind as those who receive them, You're not blind, said the girl with dark glasses, that's why you were the obvious person to give orders and organise the rest of us, I don't give orders, I organise things as best I can, I am simply the eyes that the rest of you no longer possess, A kind of natural leader, a king with eyes in the land of the blind, said the old man with the black eyepatch, If this is so, then allow yourselves to be guided by my eyes so long as they last, therefore what I propose is that instead of dispersing, her in her house, you in yours, let us continue to live together, We can stay here, said the girl with dark glasses, Our house is bigger, Assuming it has not been occupied, the wife of the first blind man pointed out, When we get there we'll find out, and if it should be occupied we can come back here, or go and take a look at your house, or yours, she added, addressing the old man with the black eye-patch, and he replied, I have no home of my own, I lived alone in a room, Have you no family, asked the girl with dark glasses, No family whatsoever, Not even a wife, children, brothers and sisters, No one, Unless my parents turn up, I shall be alone just like you. I'll stay with you, said the boy with the squint, but did not add, Unless my mother turns up, he did not lay down this condition, strange behaviour, or perhaps not so strange, the young quickly adapt, they have their whole life before them. What do you think, asked the doctor's wife, I'm going with you, said the girl with dark glasses, all I ask is that you should bring me here once a week just in case my parents should happen to return, Will you leave the keys with the neighbour below, There's no alternative, she cannot take more than she has taken already, She might destroy things, Now that I've been here, perhaps not, We're coming with you too, said the first blind man, although we should like, as soon as possible, to pass by our home and find out what has happened, Of course, No point in passing by my house, I've already told you it was just a room. But you'll come with us, Yes, on one condition, at first sight it must seem scandalous for someone to lay down conditions when he is being done a favour, but some old people are like that, they make up in pride for the little time remaining to them, What condition is that, asked the doctor, When I start becoming an impossible burden, you must tell me, and if, out of friendship or pity, you should decide to say nothing, I hope I'll still have enough judgment to do the necessary, And what might that be, I'd like to know, asked the girl with dark glasses, Withdraw, take myself off, disappear, as elephants used to do, I've heard it said that recently things have been different, none of these animals reach old age, You're not exactly an elephant, Nor am I exactly a man, Especially if you start giving childish replies, retorted the girl with dark glasses, and the conversation went no further.

The plastic bags are now much lighter than when they were brought here, not surprisingly, the neighbour on the first floor also ate from them, she ate twice, first last night, and today they left her some more food when they asked her to take the keys and look after them until the rightful owners turned up, a question of keeping the old girl sweet, because as for her character we have learned more than enough, and the dog of tears also had to be fed, only a heart of stone would have been capable of feigning indifference before those pleading eyes, and while we are on the subject, where has the dog disappeared to, he is not in the flat, he did not go out the door, he can only be in the back garden, the doctor's wife went off to take a good look, and this was, in fact, where he was, the dog of tears was devouring a hen, the attack had been so quick that there was not even time to raise the alarm, but if the old woman on the first floor had eyes and kept a count on her hens, who can tell, out of anger, what fate might befall the keys, Between the awareness of having committed a crime and the perception that the human being whom he was protecting was going away, the dog of tears hesitated only for an instant, then began at once to scratch the soft earth, and before the old woman on the first floor appeared on the landing of the fire escape to sniff out the sounds that were coming into her flat, the hen's carcass was buried, the crime covered up, remorse reserved for some other occasion. The dog of tears sidled upstairs, brushed like a breath of air past the skirts of the old woman, who had no idea of the danger she had just faced, and went to settle beside the doctor's wife, where he announced to the heavens the feat he had just achieved. The old woman on the first floor, hearing him bark so ferociously, feared, but as we know all too late, for the safety of her larder, and, craning her neck upwards, called, This dog must be kept under control before he kills one of my hens, Don't worry, replied the doctor's wife, the dog isn't hungry, he has already eaten, and we're leaving right away, Right away, repeated the old woman, and there was a break in her voice as if of pain, as if she wanted to be understood in a quite different way, for example, You're going to leave me here all alone, but she did not utter another word, only that Right away which asked for no reply, the hard of heart also have their sorrows, this woman's heart was such that later she refused to open her door to bid farewell to these ingrates to whom she had given free access to her house. She heard them go downstairs, they were talking amongst themselves, saying, Watch you don't stumble, Put your hand on my shoulder, Hold on to the bannister, the usual words, but now much more common in this world of blind people, what did surprise her was to hear one of the women say, It's so dark in this place that I can't see a thing, that this woman's blindness should not be white was already surprising in itself, but that she could not see because it was so dark, what could this mean, She wanted to think, tried hard, but her weak head did not help, soon she was saying to herself, I must have misheard, whatever it was. In the street, the doctor's wife remembered what she had said, she must watch what she was saying, she could move like someone who has eyes, But my words must be those of a blind person, she thought.

Assembled on the pavement, she arranged her companions in two rows of three, in the first one she placed her husband

and the girl with dark glasses, with the boy with the squint in the middle, in the second row the old man with the black eye-patch and the first blind man, one on either side of the other woman. She wanted to keep all of them close to her, not in the usual fragile Indian file, which can be broken at any moment, they only needed to encounter a more numerous or more aggressive group, and it would be like a steamer at sea cutting in two a sailboat that happened to cross its path, we know the consequences of such accidents, shipwrecks, disasters, people drowned, futile cries for help in that vast expanse of water, the steamer already sailing on ahead, not even aware of the collision, this is what would happen to this group, a blind person here, another there, lost in the disordered currents of the other blind people, like the waves of the sea that never stop and do not know where they are going, and the doctor's wife, too, not knowing to whose assistance she should hasten first, placing her hand on her husband's arm, perhaps on that of the boy with the squint, but losing the girl with dark glasses, the other two, the old man with the black eyepatch, far away, heading for the elephants' graveyard. What she is doing now is to pass around herself and all the others a cord made from strips of cloth knotted together while the rest were asleep, Don't hold on to me, she said, but hold on to the rope with all your strength, do not let go under any circumstances, whatever may happen. They were careful not to walk too closely to avoid tripping each other, but they needed to feel the proximity of their neighbours, a direct contact if possible, only one of them did not have to worry himself with these new questions of overland tactics, this was the boy with the squint who walked in the middle, protected on all sides. None of our blind friends thought to ask how the other groups navigate, if they too are advancing tied to each other by this or other processes, but the reply should be easy from what we have been able to observe, groups in general, except in the case of a more cohesive group for good reasons unknown to us, gradually gain and lose adherents throughout the day, there is always one blind man who strays and is lost, another who was caught by the force of gravity and tags along, he might be accepted, he might be expelled, depending on what he is carrying with him. The old woman on the first floor slowly opened the window, she does not want anyone to know that she has this sentimental weakness, but no noise can be heard coming from the street, they have already gone, they have left this place where almost no one ever passes, the old woman ought to be pleased, in this way she will not have to share her hens and rabbits with the others, she should be pleased but is not, in her blind eyes appear two tears, for the first time she asked herself if she had some good reason for wanting to go on living. She could find no reply, replies do not always come when needed, and it often happens that the only possible reply is to wait for them.

Along the route they were taking they would pass two blocks away from the house where the old man with the black eyepatch had his bachelor room, but they had already decided that they would travel on, there was no food to be found there, clothing they do not need, books they cannot read. The streets are full of blind people out searching for food. They go in and out of shops, enter empty-handed and nearly always come out empty-handed, then they debate among themselves the need or advantage of leaving this district and going to forage elsewhere in the city, the big problem is that, things being as they are, without running water, the gas cylinders empty, as well as the danger of lighting fires inside the houses, no cooking can be done, assuming that we would know where to look for the salt, the oil and seasoning, were we to try and prepare a few dishes with some hint of the flavours from the past, if there were some greens, simply having them boiled would leave us satisfied, the same being true of meat, apart from the usual rabbits and hens, dogs and cats could be cooked if they could be caught, but since experience is truly the mistress of life, even these animals, previously domesticated, learned to mistrust caresses, they now hunt in packs and in packs they defend themselves from being hunted down, and since, thanks be to God, they still have eyes, they are better equipped to avoid danger, and to attack if necessary. All these circumstances and reasons have led us to conclude that the best food for humans is what is preserved in cans and jars, not only because it is often already cooked, ready to be eaten, but also because it is so much easier to transport and handy for immediate use. It is true that on all these cans, jars and different packets in which these products are sold there is a date beyond which it could be risky to consume them and even dangerous in certain cases, but popular wisdom was quick to put into circulation a saying to which in a sense there is no answer, symmetrical with another saying no longer much used, what the eyes do not see the heart does not grieve over, people would now often say, eyes that do not see have a cast-iron stomach, which explains why they eat so much rubbish. Heading the group, the doctor's wife makes a mental calculation of the food she still has in reserve, there will be enough, if that, for one meal, without counting the dog, but let him sort himself out with the means at his disposal, the same means that served him so well to grab the hen by the neck and cut off its voice and life. She will have at home, as you may remember, and provided that no one has broken in, a reasonable quantity of preserves, enough for a couple, but there are seven persons here who have to be fed, her reserves will not last long, even if she were to enforce strict rationing. Tomorrow, or within the next few days, she will have to return to the underground storeroom of the supermarket, she will have to decide whether to go alone or to ask her husband to accompany her, or the first blind man who is younger and more agile, the choice is between the possibility of carrying a larger quantity of food and acting speedily, without forgetting the conditions of the retreat. The rubbish on the streets, which appears to be twice as much since yesterday, the human excrement, that from before semi-liquified by the torrential downpour of rain, mushy or runny, the excrement being evacuated at this very minute by these men and women as we pass, fills the air with the most awful stench, like a dense mist through which it is only possible to advance with enormous effort. In a square surrounded by trees, with a statue in the middle, a pack of dogs is devouring a man's corpse. He must have died a short while ago, his limbs are not rigid, as can be seen when the dogs shake them to tear from the bone the flesh caught between their teeth. A crow hops around in search of an opening to get close to the feast. The doctor's wife averted her eyes, but it was too late, the vomit rising from her entrails was irresistible, twice, three times, as if her own still-living body were being shaken by other dogs, the pack of absolute despair, this is as far as I go, I want to die here. Her husband asked, What's the matter, the others bound together by the cord, drew closer, suddenly alarmed, What happened, Did the food upset you, Something that was off, I don't feel a thing, Nor me, All the better for them, all they could hear was the uproar from the dogs, the sudden and unexpected cawing of a crow, in the upheaval one of the dogs had bitten its wing in passing, quite unintentionally, then the doctor's wife said, I couldn't stop myself, forgive me, but some of the dogs here are eating another dog. Are they eating our dog, asked the boy with the squint, No, our dog as you call him, is alive, and prowling around them but he keeps his distance. After eating that hen, he can't be very hungry, said the first blind man. Are you feeling better, asked the doctor, Yes, let's be on our way, The dog isn't ours, it simply latched on to us, it will probably stay behind now with these other dogs, it may have stayed with them before, but it has refound its friends, I want to do a poo, Here, I've got stomachache, it hurts, complained the boy. He relieved himself on the spot as best he could, the doctor's wife vomited once more, but for other reasons. Then they crossed the vast square and when they reached the shade of the trees, the doctor's wife looked back. More dogs had appeared and they were already contesting what remained of the corpse. The dog of tears arrived with its snout touching the ground as if it were following some trail, a question of habit, for this time a simple glance was enough to find the woman he was looking for.

The march continued, the house of the old man with the black eyepatch was already some way behind them, now they are making their way along a broad avenue with tall imposing buildings on either side. The cars here are expensive, capacious and comfortable, which explains why so many blind people are to be seen sleeping in them, and from all appearances, an enormous limousine has actually been transformed into a permanent home, probably because it was much easier to return to a car than to a house, the occupants of this one must do what was done back there in quarantine to find their bed, groping their way along and counting the cars from the corner, twenty-seven, right-hand side, I'm back home. The building at whose door the limousine is parked is a bank. The car had brought the chairman of the board to the weekly plenary meeting, the first to be held since the epidemic of white sickness had been declared, and there had been no time to park it in the underground garage until the meeting was over. The driver went blind just as the chairman was about to enter the building by the main entrance as usual, he let out a cry, we are referring to the driver, but he, meaning the chairman, did not hear it. Moreover, attendance at the plenary board meeting would not be as complete as its designation suggested, for during the last few days some of the directors had gone blind. The chairman did not get round to opening the session, the agenda of which had provided for a discussion of measures to be taken in the event that all the directors and their deputies went blind, and he was not even able to enter the board-room for when the elevator was taking him up to the fifteenth floor, between the ninth and the tenth floors to be exact, the electric power was cut off, never to be restored. And since disasters never come singly, at that same moment the electricians went blind who were responsible for maintaining the internal power supply and consequently that also of the generator, an old model, not automatic, that had long been awaiting replacement, this resulted, as we said before, in the elevator coming to a halt between the ninth and tenth floors. The chairman saw the attendant who was accompanying him go blind, he himself lost his sight an hour later, and since the power did not come back and the cases of blindness inside the bank multiplied that day, in all probability the two are still there, dead, needless to say, shut up in a coffin of steel, and therefore happily safe from voracious dogs.

There being no witnesses, and if there were there is no evidence that they were summoned to the post-mortems to tell us what happened, it is understandable that someone should ask how it was possible to know that these things happened so and not in some other manner, the reply to be given is that all stories are like those about the creation of the universe, no one was there, no one witnessed anything, yet everyone knows what happened. The doctor's wife had asked, What will have happened to the banks, not that she was much concerned, despite having entrusted her savings to one of them, she raised the question out of simple curiosity, simply because she thought of it, nothing more, nor did she expect anyone to make a reply such as, for example, In the beginning, God created heaven and earth, the earth was without form and empty, and darkness was upon the face of the deep, and the spirit of God moved upon the face of the waters, instead of this what really happened was that the old man with the black eyepatch said as they were proceeding down the avenue, As far as I could judge when I still had an eye to see, at first, it was pandemonium, the people, afraid of ending up blind and unprovided for, raced to the banks to withdraw their money, feeling that they ought to safeguard their future, and this is understandable, if someone knows they will no longer be able to work, the only remedy, for as long as they might last, is to have recourse to the savings made in times of prosperity when long-term provisions were made, assuming in fact that the people were prudent enough to build up their savings little by little, the outcome of this precipitous run on the banks was that within twenty-four hours some of the main banks were facing ruin, the Government intervened to plead for calm and to appeal to the civic conscience of citizens, ending the proclamation with the solemn declaration that it would assume all the responsibilities and duties resulting from this public calamity they were facing, but this calming measure did not succeed in alleviating the crisis, not only because people continued to go blind but also because those who could still see were interested only in saving their precious money, in the end, it was inevitable, the banks, bankrupt or otherwise, closed their doors and sought police protection, it did them no good, between the noisy crowds that gathered in front of the banks there were also policemen in plain clothes who demanded what they had saved with so much effort, and some, in order to demonstrate at will, had even advised their command that they were blind and were therefore dismissed, and the others, still in uniform and on active service, their weapons trained on the dissatisfied masses, suddenly lost sight of their target, the latter, if they had money in the bank, lost all hope and, as if that were not enough, they were accused of having entered into a pact with the established authority, but there was worse to come when the banks found themselves attacked by furious hordes of whom some were blind and others not, but all of them desperate, here it was no longer a question of calmly handing in a cheque to be cashed at the counter and saying to the teller, I wish to withdraw my savings, but to lay hands on everything possible, on the cash in the till, whatever had been left in some drawer or other, in some safe-deposit box carelessly left open, in some old-fashioned money-bag as used by the grandparents of an older generation, you cannot imagine what it was like, the vast and sumptuous halls of the head office, the smaller branch offices in various districts witnessed truly terrifying scenes, nor should we forget the automatic tills, forced open and stripped of the very last note, on the screen of some of them appeared an enigmatic message of thanks for having chosen this bank. Machines are really very stupid, it might be more precise to say that these machines had betrayed their owners, in a word, the whole banking system collapsed, blown over like a house of cards, and not because the possession of money had ceased to be appreciated, the proof being that anyone who has it does not want to let go of it, the latter allege that no one can foresee what will happen tomorrow, this no doubt also being in the thoughts of the blind people who installed themselves in the vaults of the banks, where the strong-boxes are kept, waiting for some miracle to open wide those heavy metal doors that separate them from this wealth, they leave the place only to go in search of food and water or to satisfy the body's other needs, and then return to their post, they have passwords and hand signs so that no stranger may penetrate their stronghold, needless to say they live in total darkness, not that it matters, in this particular blindness everything is white. The old man with the black eyepatch related these tremendous happenings about banks and finance as they slowly crossed the city, with the odd stop so that the boy with the squint might pacify the unbearable turmoil in his intestines, and, despite the persuasive tone he gave to this impassioned description, it is logical to suspect that there was some exaggeration in his account, the story about the blind people who live in the bank vaults, for example, how could he have known if he does not know the password or the hand signal, in any case it was enough to give us some idea.

The light was fading when they finally arrived in the street where the doctor and his wife live. It is no different from the others, there is squalor everywhere, groups of blind people wandering aimlessly about, and, for the first time, but it was mere chance that they had not encountered them before, two huge rats, even the cats avoid them as they go on the prowl, for they are almost as big as they are and in all certainty much more ferocious. The dog of tears looked at both the rats and the cats with the indifference of someone who lives in another sphere of emotions, this we might say, were it not for the fact that the dog continues to be the dog that he is, an animal of the human type. At the sight of familiar places, the doctor's wife did not make the usual melancholy reflection, that consists in saying, How time passes, only the other day we were happy here, what shocked her was the disappointment, she had unwittingly believed that, being hers, she would find the street clean, swept, tidy, that her neighbours would be blind in their eyes, but not in their understanding, How stupid of me, she said aloud, Why, what is wrong, asked her husband, Nothing, daydreams, How time passes, what will the flat be like, he wondered, We'll soon find out. They did not have much strength, and so climbed the stairs very slowly, pausing for breath on each landing, It's on the fifth floor, the doctor's wife had said. They went up as best they could, each under his or her own steam, the dog of tears now in front, now behind, as if it had been born to guide a flock, under orders not to lose a single sheep. There were open doors, voices within, the usual foul odour wafting out, twice blind people appeared on the threshold and looked with vacant eyes, Who's there, they asked, the doctor's wife recognised one of the voices, the other voice was not that of someone who lived in the building. We used to live here, was all she said. A flicker of recognition also showed on her neighbour's face, but she did not ask, Are you the doctor's wife, perhaps she might say once back inside, The people from the fifth floor are back. On reaching the last flight of stairs, even before setting foot on the landing, the doctor's wife was already announcing, The door is locked. There were signs of an attempt at a forced entry but the door had withstood the assault. The doctor put his hand into the inside pocket of his new jacket and brought out the keys. He held them in mid-air, waiting, but his wife gently guided his hand towards the keyhole.

Leaving aside the household dust that takes advantage of a family's absence to leave a subtle film on the surface of the furniture, it may be stated in this connection that these are the only occasions the dust has to rest, without being disturbed by a duster or vacuum cleaner, without children running back and forth unleashing an atmospheric whirlwind as they pass, the flat was clean, any untidiness was only what might be expected when one leaves in a hurry. Even so, while on that day they were expecting a summons from the Ministry and the hospital, the doctor's wife with the kind of foresight that leads sensible people to settle their affairs while alive, so that after their death, the tiresome need for a frantic putting of things in order does not arise, washed the dishes, made the bed, tidied the bathroom, the result was not exactly perfect, but truly it would have been cruel to ask any more of her with those trembling hands and tear-filled eyes. It was nevertheless a kind of paradise that the seven pilgrims had reached and this impression was so overwhelming, with no great disrespect for the strict meaning of the term, we could call it transcendental, that they stopped in their tracks in the entrance as if paralysed by the unexpected smell in the flat and it was simply that of a flat in need of a good airing, at any other time we would have rushed to open all the windows, To air the place, we would say, today the best thing to do would be to have them sealed up so that the putrefaction outside would be unable to come in. The wife of the first blind man said, We're going to dirty the whole place, and she was right, if they were to come in with these shoes covered in mud and excrement, paradise would in a flash become hell, the latter being the second place, according to the competent authorities where the putrid, fetid, nauseating, pestilential stench is the worst thing condemned souls have to bear, not the burning tongs, the cauldrons of boiling pitch and other artefacts of the foundry and the kitchen. From time immemorial it has been the custom of housewives to say, Come in, come in, really, it doesn't matter, I can clean up any dirt later, but this one, like her guests, knows where they have come from, she knows that in the world she lives in what is dirty will get dirtier still, therefore she asks them if they would be so kind as to remove their shoes on the landing, it is true that their feet are not clean either, but there is no comparison, the towels and sheets of the girl with dark glasses had some effect, they've got rid of most of the muck. So they went in without their shoes, the doctor's wife searched for and found a large plastic bag into which she put all the shoes intent upon giving them a good scrub, she had no idea when or how, then she carried them out on to the balcony, the air outside would not get any worse on this account. The sky began to darken, there were heavy clouds, If only it would rain, she thought. With a clear idea of what had to be done, she returned to her companions. They were in the sitting-room, silent, on their feet, for, despite their exhaustion, they had not dared to find themselves a chair, only the doctor vaguely ran his hands over the furniture leaving marks on the surface, the first dusting was under way, some of this dust is already stuck to his fingertips. The doctor's wife said, Take your clothes off, we can't remain in this state, our clothes are almost as dirty as our shoes,

Take off our clothes, asked the first blind man, here, in front of each other, I don't think it's right, If you wish, I can put each of you in a different part of the flat, the doctor's wife replied ironically, then there will be no need to feel embarrassed, I'll take off my clothes right here, said the wife of the first blind man, only you can see me, and even were that not the case, I haven't forgotten that you have seen me worse than being naked, it's my husband who has the poor memory, I can't see what possible interest there can be in recalling disagreeable matters long since forgotten, muttered the first blind man, If you were a woman and had been where we have been, you would change your tune, said the girl with dark glasses, starting to undress the boy with the squint. The doctor and the old man with the black eyepatch were already naked from the waist up, now they were removing their trousers, the old man with the black eyepatch said to the doctor who was at his side, Let me lean on you while I get out of these trousers. They looked so ridiculous the poor fellows as they jumped about, it almost made you want to weep. The doctor lost his balance, dragged the old man with the black eyepatch with him as he fell, fortunately they both found the situation amusing, and it was pitiful to watch them, their bodies covered with every kind of filth imaginable, their private parts all besmeared, white hairs, black hairs, this was what the respectability of old age and a worthy profession had come to. The doctor's wife went to help them get to their feet, shortly there would be darkness all around and no one will have any cause to feel embarrassed, Are there any candles in the house, she wondered, the answer was that she recalled having seen two ancient lamps, an old oil lamp, with three nozzles, and an old paraffin lamp of the kind with a glass funnel, for the present, the oil lamp will be good enough, I have oil, a wick can be improvised, tomorrow I'll go in search of some paraffin in one of those stores, it will be much easier to find than a can of food,

Especially if I don't look for it in the grocer's, she thought, surprising herself that she was still capable of joking even in this situation. The girl with the dark glasses was slowly undressing, in a way that gave the impression that there would always be something more no matter how many clothes she removed, one last article of clothing to cover her nakedness, she cannot explain this sudden modesty, but had the doctor's wife been closer, she would have seen the girl blushing, even though her face was so dirty, let those who can, try to understand women, one of them suddenly assailed by shame after having gone around sleeping with men she scarcely knew, the other perfectly capable of whispering in her ear perfectly calmly, Don't be embarrassed, he cannot see you, she would be referring to her own husband, of course, for we must not forget how the shameless girl tempted him into bed, well, as everyone knows, with women it is always a case of buyer beware. Perhaps, in the meantime, the reason is something else, there are two other naked men here, and one of them has slept with her.

The doctor's wife gathered up the clothes lying scattered on the floor, trousers, shirts, a jacket, petticoats and blouses, some soiled underwear, the latter would take at least a month's soaking before she got them clean again, she bundled them up into an armload, Stay here, she told them, I'm coming straight back, She took the clothes out on to the balcony, as she had done with the shoes, there she in turn undressed, looking at the black city under the heavy sky. Not so much as a pale light in the windows, nor a waning reflection on the house fronts, what was there was not a city, it was a great mass of pitch which, on cooling, had hardened in the shape of buildings, rooftops, chimneys, all dead, all faded. The dog of tears appeared on the balcony, it was restless, but now there were no tears to lick up, the despair was all inside her, eyes were dry. The doctor's wife felt cold, she remembered the others, standing naked in the middle of the room, waiting for who knows what. She entered. They had turned into simple, sexless forms, vague shapes, shadows losing themselves in the half-light, But this does not affect them, she thought, they fade into the surrounding light, and it is the light which does not allow them to see. I'm going to put a light on, she said, At the moment I'm almost as blind as the rest of you, Has the electricity come back on, asked the boy with the squint, No, I'm going to light an oil lamp, What's that, the boy asked again, I'll show you later. She rummaged for a box of matches in one of the plastic bags, went to the kitchen, she knew where she had stored the oil, she did not need much, she tore a strip from a dish towel in order to make wicks, then returned to the room where the lamp stood, it was going to be useful for the first time since it was manufactured, at first this did not appear to be its destiny, but none of us, lamps, dogs or humans, knows at the outset, why we have come into this world. One after the other, over the nozzles of the lamp, three tiny almonds of light lit up, from time to time they flicker until they give the impression that the upper part of the flames is lost in mid-air, then they settle down again as if they were becoming dense, solid, tiny pebbles of light. The doctor's wife said, Now that I can see, I'm going to get clean clothes, But we're dirty, the girl with the dark glasses said. Both she and the wife of the first blind man were covering their breasts and their sex with their hands, This is not for my sake, the doctor's wife thought, but because the light of the lamp is looking at them. Then she said, It is better to have clean clothes on a dirty body, than to have dirty clothes on a clean body. She took the lamp and went to search in the drawers of the chest, in the wardrobe, after a few minutes she returned, she brought pyjamas, dressing-gowns, skirts, blouses, dresses, trousers, underwear, everything necessary for dressing seven people decently, it is true that the people were not all the same size, but in their gauntness they were like so many twins. The doctor's wife helped them to dress, the boy with the squint finished up with a pair of the doctor's trousers, the kind you wear to the beach or in the countryside, and which turn us all into children. Now we can sit down, sighed the wife of the first blind man, Please guide us, we do not know where to put ourselves.

The room is like all sitting-rooms, it has a low table in the middle, all around there are sofas that can accommodate everyone, on this one here sit the doctor and his wife along with the old man with the black eyepatch, on the other the first blind man and his wife. They are exhausted. The boy fell asleep at once, with his head on the lap of the girl with dark glasses, having forgotten all about the lamp. An hour passed, this was akin to happiness, under the softest of lights their grimy faces looked washed, the eyes of those who were not asleep shone, the first blind man reached out for his wife's hand and pressed it, from this gesture we can see how a rested body can contribute to the harmony of the mind. Then the doctor's wife said, Shortly we'll have something to eat, but first we should decide how we are going to live here, don't worry, I am not about to repeat the speech that came over the loudspeaker, there's enough room to accommodate everyone, we have two bedrooms that can be used by the couples, the others can sleep in this room, each on his own sofa, tomorrow I must go in search of some food, our supplies are running out, it would be helpful if one of you were to come with me to help me carry the food, but also so that you can start to learn the way home, to recognise the street corners, one of these days I might fall ill, or go blind, I am always waiting for it to happen, in which case I'll have to learn from you, on another matter, there will be a bucket on the balcony for our physical needs, I know that it is not pleasant to go out there, what with all the rain we've had and the cold, but it is, in any case, better than having the house smelling to high heaven, let us not forget that that was our life during the time when we were interned, we went down all the steps of indignity, all of them, until we reached total degradation, the same might happen here albeit in a different way, there we still had the excuse that the degradation belonged to someone else, not now, now we are all equal regarding good and evil, please, don't ask me what good and what evil are, we knew what it was each time we had to act when blindness was an exception, what is right and what is wrong are simply different ways of understanding our relationships with the others, not that which we have with ourselves, one should not trust the latter, forgive this moralising speech, you do not know, you cannot know, what it means to have eyes in a world in which everyone else is blind, I am not a queen, no, I am simply the one who was born to see this horror, you can feel it, I both feel and see it, and that's enough of this dissertation, Let's go and eat. No one asked any questions, the doctor simply said, If I ever regain my sight, I shall look carefully at the eyes of others, as if I were looking into their souls, Their souls, asked the old man with the eyepatch, Or their minds, the name does not matter, it was then that, surprisingly, if we consider that we are dealing with a person without much education, the girl with the dark glasses said, Inside us there is something that has no name, that something is what we are.

The doctor's wife had already put on the table some of the little food that was left over, then she helped them to sit down and said, Chew slowly, that helps to deceive your stomach. The dog of tears did not come to beg for food, it was used to fasting, moreover it must have thought that, after the banquet that morning, it had no right to take even a little food from the mouth of the woman who had wept, the others appeared not to interest him. In the middle of the table, the lamp with three flames was waiting for the doctor's wife to give the promised explanation, it finally happened after they had eaten, Give me your hands, she said to the boy with the squint, then guided his fingers slowly, saying, This is the base, round as you can see, and this the column that sustains the upper part with the oil container, here, watch you don't burn yourself, these are the nozzles, one, two, three, from these emerge twisted strips of material that suck up the oil from inside, a match is put to them and they start burning until the oil is finished, they give off a weak light but it's good enough to see each other, I can't see, One day you will see and on that day I'll give you the lamp as a present. What colour is it, Have you ever seen anything made of brass, I don't know, I don't remember, what is brass, Brass is yellow, Ah. The boy with the squint pondered for a moment, Now he is going to ask for his mother, thought the doctor's wife, but she was wrong, the boy simply said that he wanted water, that he was very thirsty, You will have to wait till tomorrow, we have no water in the house, at this very moment she remembered that there was water, some five litres or more of precious water, the whole contents of the toilet cistern, it could not be worse than what they had been drinking during the quarantine. Blind in the darkness, she went to the bathroom, feeling her way along, she raised the lid of the cistern, she really could not see if there was water, there was, her fingers told her, she searched for a glass, plunged it in with great care and filled it, civilisation had returned to the primitive sources of slime. When she entered the room everyone remained seated where they were. The lamp lit up their faces which turned towards her, it was as if she had said, I am back, as you can see, take advantage, remember this light won't last for ever. The doctor's wife brought the glass to the boy with the squint's lips and said, Here is your water, drink slowly, slowly, and savour it, a glass of water is a marvellous thing, she was not talking to him, she was not talking to anyone, simply communicating to the world what a marvellous thing a glass of water is. Where did you get it, is it rain water, asked the husband, No, it's from the cistern. Didn't we have a large bottle of water when we left this place, he asked again, the wife said, Of course, why didn't I think of it, a half-full bottle and another that had not even been started, what luck, don't drink, don't drink anymore, she said to the boy, we are all going to drink fresh water, I'll put our best glasses on the table and we are going to drink fresh water. This time she took the lamp and went to the kitchen, she returned with the bottle, the light shone through it, it made the treasure inside sparkle. She put it on the table, went to fetch the glasses, the best they had, of finest crystal, then, slowly, as if she were performing a rite, she filled them. At last, she said, Let's drink. The blind hands groped and found the glasses, they raised them trembling. Let's drink, the doctor's wife said again. In the middle of the table, the lamp was like a sun surrounded by shining stars. When they had put the glasses back on the table, the girl with the dark glasses and the old man with the eyepatch were crying.

It was a restless night. Vague in the beginning, and imprecise, the dreams went from sleeper to sleeper, they lingered here, they lingered there, they brought with them new memories, new secrets, new desires, that is why the sleepers sighed and murmured, This dream is not mine, they said, but the dream replied, You do not yet know your dreams, in this way the girl with the dark glasses came to find out who the old man with the black eyepatch was, lying there asleep two paces away, in this way he thought he knew who she was, he merely thought he did, it is not enough for dreams to be reciprocal in order to be the same. As dawn broke it began to rain. The wind beating fiercely against the windows sounded like the cracking of a thousand whiplashes. The doctor's wife woke up, opened her eyes and murmured, Listen to that rain, then she closed them again, in the room it was still black night, now she could sleep. She barely managed a minute, she woke abruptly with the idea that she had something to do, but without yet understanding what it might be, the rain was saying to her, Get up, what did the rain want, Slowly, so as not to disturb her husband, she left the bedroom, crossed the sitting-room, paused for an instant to make sure they were all sleeping on the sofas, then she proceeded along the corridor as far as the kitchen, it was over this part of the building that the rain fell with the greatest force, driven by the wind. With the sleeve of her dressing-gown she cleaned the steamed-up glass panel of the door and looked outside. The entire sky was one great cloud, the rain poured down in torrents. Piled up on the balcony-floor were the dirty clothes they had taken off, there was the plastic bag with the shoes waiting to be washed. Wash. The last veil of sleep was suddenly torn, this was what she had to do. She opened the door, took one step, immediately the rain drenched her from head to foot, as if she were beneath a waterfall. I must take advantage of this water, she thought. She went back into the kitchen and, making as little noise as possible, began gathering together bowls, pots and pans, anything in which she could collect some of the rain that was falling from heaven in sheets, harried about by the wind, sweeping over the roofs of the city like a large and noisy broom. She took them outside, arranged them along the balcony up against the railing, now there would be water to wash the dirty clothes and filthy shoes, Don't let it stop, she murmured as she searched in the kitchen for soap and detergents, scrubbing brushes, anything that might be used to clean a little, at least a little, of this unbearable filth of the soul. Of the body, she said, as if to correct this metaphysical thought, then she added, It's all the same. Then, as if this had to be the inevitable conclusion, the harmonious conciliation between what she had said and what she thought, she quickly took off her drenched dressing-gown, and, now, receiving on her body, sometimes a caress, sometimes the whiplash of the rain, she began to wash the clothes and herself at the same time. The sound of water that surrounded her prevented her from noticing right away that she was no longer alone. At the door to the balcony stood the girl with dark glasses and the wife of the first blind man, we cannot tell what presentiments, what intuition, what inner voices might have roused them, nor do we know how they found their way here, there is no point searching for explanations for the moment, conjectures are free. Help me, said the doctor's wife when she saw them, How, since we cannot see, asked the wife of the first blind man. Take off your clothes, the less we have to dry afterwards, the better, But we can't see, the wife of the first blind man repeated, It does not matter, said the girl with the dark glasses,We shall do what we can, And I shall finish off later, said the doctor's wife, I shall clean whatever is still dirty, and now to work, let's go, we are the only woman in the world with two eyes and six hands. Perhaps in the building opposite, behind those closed windows some blind people, men, women, roused by the noise of the constant beating of the rain, with their head pressed against the cold window-panes covering with their breath on the glass the dullness of the night, remember the time when, like now, they last saw rain falling from the sky. They cannot imagine that there are moreover three naked women out there, as naked as when they came into the world, they seem to be mad, they must be mad, people in their right mind do not start washing on a balcony exposed to the view of the neighbourhood, even less looking like that, what does it matter that we are all blind, these are things one must not do, my God, how the rain is pouring down on them, how it trickles between their breasts, how it lingers and disappears into the darkness of the pubis, how it finally drenches and flows over the thighs, perhaps we have judged them wrongly, or perhaps we are unable to see this the most beautiful and glorious thing that has happened in the history of the city, a sheet of foam flows from the floor of the balcony, if only I could go with it, falling interminably, clean, purified, naked. Only God sees us, said the wife of the first blind man, who, despite disappointments and setbacks, clings to the belief that God is not blind, to which the doctor's wife replies, Not even he, the sky is clouded over, Only I can see you, Am I ugly, asked the girl with the dark glasses, You are skinny and dirty, you will never be ugly, And I, asked the wife of the first blind man, You are dirty and skinny like her, not as pretty, but more than I, You are beautiful, said the girl with the dark glasses, How do you know, since you have never seen me, I have dreamt of you twice, When, The second time was last night, You were dreaming about the house because you felt safe and calm, it's only natural after all we've been through, in your dream I was the home, and in order to see me you needed a face, so you invented it, I too see you as beautiful, and I never dreamt of you, said the wife of the first blind man, Which only goes to show that blindness is the good fortune of the ugly, You are not ugly, No, as a matter of fact I am not, but at my age, How old are you, asked the girl with the dark glasses, Getting on for fifty, Like my mother, And her, Her, what, Is she still beautiful, She was more beautiful once, that's what happens to all of us, we were all more beautiful once, You were never more beautiful, said the wife of the first blind man. Words are like that, they deceive, they pile up, it seems they do not know where to go, and, suddenly, because of two or three or four that suddenly come out, simple in themselves, a personal pronoun, an adverb, a verb, an adjective, we have the excitement of seeing them coming irresistibly to the surface through the skin and the eyes and upsetting the composure of our feelings, sometimes the nerves that cannot bear it any longer, they put up with a great deal, they put up with everything, it was as if they were wearing armour, we might say. The doctor's wife has nerves of steel, and yet the doctor's wife is reduced to tears because of a personal pronoun, an adverb, a verb, an adjective, mere grammatical categories, mere labels, just like the two women, the others, indefinite pronouns, they too are crying, they embrace the woman of the whole sentence, three graces beneath the falling rain. These are moments that cannot last for ever, these women have been here for more than an hour, it is time they felt cold, I'm cold, said the girl with the dark glasses. We cannot do anything more with the clothes, the shoes are spick and span, now it is time for these women to wash themselves, they soak their hair and wash each other's backs and they laugh as only little girls laugh when they play blind man's buff in the garden before becoming blind. Day broke, the first rays of sun peered over the shoulder of the world before hiding once more behind the clouds. It continues to rain but with less force. The washerwomen went back to the kitchen, they dried themselves and rubbed themselves with the towels the doctor's wife had gone to fetch from the bathroom cupboard, their skins smell strongly of detergent, but such is life, if you haven't got a dog to hunt with use a cat, the soap disappeared in a twinkling of the eye, even though this house seems to have everything or is it just that they know how to make the best use of what they have got, at last, they covered themselves, paradise was out there, the dressing-gown of the doctor's wife is soaking wet, but she put on a flowered dress that she had not worn for years and which made her the prettiest of the three.

When they entered the sitting-room, the doctor's wife saw that the old man with the black eyepatch was sitting up on the sofa where he had slept. He held his head between his hands, his fingers plunged into the thatch of white hair which still grew from his forehead to the back of his neck, and he was calm, tense, as if he wanted to hold on to his thoughts, or, on the contrary, to stop them altogether. He heard them come in, he knew where they came from, and what they had been doing, that they had been naked, and if he knew all this it was not because he had suddenly regained his sight and, like the other old men, crept up to spy on not one Susanna in her bath, but on three, he was blind, he stayed blind, he had only got to the kitchen door from where he heard what they were saying on the balcony, the laughter, the noise of the rain and the beating of the water, he breathed in the smell of the soap, then he returned to the sofa, thinking that there was still life in this world, to ask whether there was still any part of it left for him. The doctor's wife said, The women have already washed, Now it is the men's turn, and the old man with the black eyepatch asked, Is it still raining, Yes, it is raining and there is water in the basins on the balcony, Then I prefer to wash in the bathroom, in the tub, he pronounced the word as if he were showing his birth certificate, as if he were explaining, I am of the generation in which people did not speak of baths but of tubs, and added, If you don't mind, of course, I do not want to dirty the house, I promise that I shall not spill any water on the floor, at least, I shall do my best, In that case I shall bring you some water into the bathroom, I'll help, I can manage on my own, I have to be of some use, I am not an invalid, Come, then. On the balcony, the doctor's wife pulled an almost full basin of water inside. Take a hold here, she said to the old man with the black eyepatch, guiding his hands, Now, they lifted the basin at one go. Just as well that you came to help me, I could not have managed alone, Do you know the saying, What saying, Old people cannot do much but their work is not to be despised, That's not the way it goes, All right, instead of old people, it should be children, and instead of despise, it should be disdain, but if sayings are to retain any meaning and to continue to be used they have to adapt to the times. You are a philosopher, What an idea, I am just an old man. They emptied the basin into the bath, then the doctor's wife opened a drawer, she remembered that she still had one new bar of soap.

She put it into the hand of the old man with the black eyepatch, You are going to smell nice, better than us, use it all, do not worry, there may not be any food, but there is bound to be soap in these supermarkets, Thank you, Watch you don't slip, if you want I'll call my husband to help you, Thanks, I prefer to wash by myself, As you like, and here, wait, give me your hand, there's a razor and a brush, if you want to shave off that beard, Thanks. The doctor's wife left. The old man with the eyepatch took off the pyjamas which had been allotted to him in the distribution of clothes, then, carefully, he got into the bath. The water was cold and there was little of it, less than a foot, how different is this sad puddle from receiving it in buckets from heaven as the three women had. He knelt on the bottom of the bath, took a deep breath, with both hands together he suddenly splashed water against his chest which almost took his breath away. He rapidly splashed water all over himself so as not to have time to shiver, then, step by step, systematically, he started to soap himself, to rub heavily starting from the shoulders, arms, chest and stomach, his groin, his penis, between his legs, I am worse than an animal, he thought, then the thin thighs down to the layer of grime that covered his feet. He made lather so that the cleaning process should be extended, he said, I have to wash my hair and moved his hands back to untie the eyepatch, You too need a bath, he loosened it and dropped it into the water, now he felt warm, he wet and soaped his hair, he was a man of foam, white in the middle of an immense white blindness where nobody could find him, if that was what he thought, he was deceiving himself, at that moment he felt hands touching his back, gathering the foam from his arms, and from his chest and spreading it over his back, slowly, as if, being unable to see what they were doing, they had to pay closer attention to the job. He wanted to ask, Who are you, but he couldn't speak, now he was shivering, not from the cold, the hands continued to wash him gently, the woman did not say, I am the doctor's wife, I am the wife of the first blind man, I am the girl with dark glasses, the hands finished their task, withdrew, in the silence one could hear the gentle noise of the bathroom door closing, the old man with the eyepatch was alone, kneeling in the bath as if imploring a favour from heaven, trembling, trembling, Who could it have been, he asked himself, his reason told him that it could only have been the doctor's wife, she is the one who can see, she is the one who has protected us, cared for us and fed us, it would not be surprising that she should have given me this discreet attention, it is what his reason told him, but he did not believe in reason. He continued to shiver, he did not know whether it was from excitement or from cold. He found the eyepatch at the bottom of the bath, rubbed it hard, wrung it dry and put it back, with it he felt less naked. When he entered the sitting-room, dry, perfumed, the doctor's wife said, We already have one man who is clean and shaven, and then, in the tone of voice of someone who has just remembered something that should have been done and was not, You had no one to wash your back, what a pity. The old man with the black eyepatch did not reply, he merely thought that he had been right not to believe in reason.

They gave what little food there was to the boy with the squint, the others would have to wait for fresh supplies. In the larder there were some jars of preserves, some dried fruit, sugar, some left-over biscuits, some dry toast, but they would use these reserves and others added to them only in case of extreme necessity, the food from day to day would have to be earned, just in case by some misfortune the expedition returned empty-handed, meanwhile two biscuits per person with a spoonful of jam, There is strawberry and peach, which do you prefer, three walnut halves, a glass of water, a luxury while it lasts. The wife of the first blind man said that she too wanted to look for food, three would not go amiss, even being blind, two of them could help to carry the food and besides, were it possible, bearing in mind that they were not that far away, she would like to go and see what state her home was in, if it had been occupied, if the people were known to her, for example neighbours from the building whose family had grown because some relatives from the provinces had arrived with the idea of saving themselves from the epidemic of blindness that had attacked their village, the city always enjoys better resources. Therefore the three of them left, dressed in what dry clothes they could find in the house, the others, those that have been washed, have to wait for better weather. The sky remained overcast but there was no threat of rain. Swept along by the water, especially in the steeper streets, the rubbish had piled up in small heaps leaving wide stretches of pavement clean. If only the rain would last, in this situation sunshine would be the worst that could happen to us, said the doctor's wife, we've got enough filth and bad smells already, We notice it more because we are washed, said the wife of the first blind man and her husband agreed, although he suspected that the cold bath had given him a cold. There were crowds of blind people in the streets, they took advantage of the break in the weather to search for food and to satisfy there and then their need to defecate which they still had despite the little food and drink they took in. Dogs sniffed everywhere, they scrabbled in the rubbish, the odd one carried a drowned rat in its mouth, a very rare occurrence that could only be explained by the extraordinary abundance of the recent downpours, the flood caught him in the wrong place, being a good swimmer was of no use to him. The dog of tears did not mix with his former companions in the pack and the hunt, his choice is made, but he does not wait to be fed, he is already chewing heaven knows what, these mountains of rubbish hide unimaginable treasures, it is all a matter of searching, scratching and finding. The blind man and his wife will also have to search and scratch in their memory when the occasion arises, now they had memorised the four corners, not of the house where they live, which has many more, but of their street, the four street corners which will serve them as cardinal points, the blind are not interested where east and west lie, or north or south, all they want is that their groping hands tell them that they are on the right road, formerly, when they were still few, they used to carry white sticks, the sound of the continuous taps on the ground and the walls was a sort of code which allowed them to identify and recognise their route, but today, since everybody is blind, a white stick, in the middle of the general clamour, is less than helpful, quite apart from the fact that, immersed in his own whiteness, the blind man may come to doubt whether he is actually carrying anything in his hand. Dogs, as everyone knows, have, in addition to what we call instinct, other means of orientation, it is certain that because of their shortsightedness they do not rely much on their sight, however, since their nose is well ahead of their eyes, they always get to where they want, in this case, just to be sure, the dog of tears lifted its leg to the four corners of the wind, the breeze will take on the task of guiding it home if it were to get lost one day. As they went along the doctor's wife looked up and down the streets in search of food shops where she could build up their much reduced larder. The looting had not been complete because in old-fashioned groceries there were still some beans or some chick peas in the storerooms, they are dried pulses which take a long time to cook, one thing is water, another thing is fuel, therefore they are not much appreciated these days. The doctor's wife was not particularly keen on the tendency of proverbs to preach, nevertheless something of this ancient lore must have remained in her memory, the proof being that she filled two of the bags they had brought with beans and chick peas, Keep what is of no use at the moment, and later you will find what you need, one of her grandmothers had told her, the water in which you soak them will also serve to cook them, and whatever remains from the cooking will cease to be water, but will have become broth. It is not only in nature that from time to time not everything is lost and something is gained.

Why they were loaded with bags of beans and peas and anything else they happened to pick up when they were still some distance away from the street where the first blind man and his wife lived, for that is where they are going, is a question that could only occur to someone who has never in his life suffered shortages. Take it home, even if it's a stone, that same grandmother had said, but she forgot to add, Even if you have to go around the earth, this was the feat they were now embarked upon, they were going home by the longest route. Where are we, the first blind man asked, he addressed the doctor's wife, that is what she had eyes for, and he said, This is where I went blind, on this corner with the traffic lights, Right here, on this corner, Precisely on this spot. I do not want to remember what happened, trapped in the car without being able to see, people shouting outside, and me shouting desperately that I was blind, until that man turned up and took me home, Poor man, the wife of the first blind man said, he will never steal a car again, We are so afraid of the idea of having to die, said the doctor's wife, that we always try to find excuses for the dead, as if we were asking beforehand to be excused when it is our turn, All this still seems like a dream, the wife of the first blind man said, it is as if I were dreaming that I am blind, When I was at home, waiting for you, I also thought so, said her husband. They had left the square where it had happened, now they climbed some narrow labyrinthine streets, the doctor's wife hardly knows these places but the first blind man does not get lost, he knows the way, she says the names of the streets and he says, Let's turn to the left, Let's turn to the right, finally he says, This is our street, the building is on the left-hand side, roughly in the middle, What is the number, asked the doctor's wife, he can't remember, Now then, it's not that I cannot remember, it's gone from my head, he said, that was a bad omen, if we do not even know where we live, if the dream has replaced our memory, where will that road take us, All right, this time it is not serious, it was lucky that the first blind man's wife had the idea of coming on the excursion, there we already have her saying the house number, this helped her to avoid having to have recourse to the first blind man, who was priding himself on the fact that he can recognise the door by the magic of touch, as if he were carrying a magic wand, one touch, metal, one touch, wood, with three or four more he would arrive at the full pattern, I'm sure it is this one. They entered, the doctor's wife first, What floor is it, she asked, The third, answered the first blind man, his memory was not as bad as had appeared, some things we forget, that's life, others we remember, for example, to remember when, already blind, he had entered this door, On what floor do you live, asked the man who had not yet stolen the car, Third, he replied, the difference being that this time they are not going up in the elevator, they walk up the invisible staircase which is at once dark and luminous, how people who are not blind miss electric light, or sunlight, or the light of a candle, now the doctor's wife has got used to the semi-darkness, halfway up they run into two blind women from the upper floors coming down, perhaps from the third, nobody asked, it is true the neighbours are not, in fact, the same.

The door was closed. What are we going to do, asked the doctor's wife, Leave it to me, said the first blind man. They knocked once, twice, three times. There's nobody in, one of them said at exactly the moment when the door opened, the delay was not surprising, a blind person at the back of the flat cannot come running to answer the door. Who is it, what do you want, asked the man who opened the door, he had a serious look on his face, he was polite, he must be someone we can talk to. The first blind man said, I used to live in this flat, Ah, the other replied, Is there anybody with you, My wife, and also a friend of ours, How can I be sure that this was your flat, That's easy, the wife of the first blind man said, I can tell you everything there is inside. The other man paused a few seconds, then he said, Come in. The doctor's wife went in last, here nobody needed a guide. The blind man said, I am alone, my family went to look for food, perhaps I should have said the women, but I do not think it would be proper, he paused and then added, Yet you may think that I should know, What do you mean, asked the doctor's wife, The women I referred to are my wife and my two daughters, and I should know when it is proper to use the expression "women." I am a writer, we are supposed to know such things. The first blind man felt flattered, imagine, a writer living in my flat, then a doubt rose in him, was it good manners to ask him his name, he might even have heard of his name, it was even possible that he had read him, he was still hesitating between curiosity and discretion, when his wife put the question directly, What is your name, Blind people do not need a name, I am my voice, nothing else matters, But you wrote books and those books carry your name, said the doctor's wife, Now nobody can read them, it is as if they did not exist. The first blind man felt that the conversation was moving too far from the topic which he was most interested in, And how do you come to be in my flat, he asked, Like many others who no longer live where they used to live, I found my house occupied by people who did not want to listen to reason, one might say that we were kicked down the stairs, Is your house far away, No, Did you try to get it back, asked the doctor's wife, it is now quite common for people to move from house to house, I have already tried twice, And are they still there, Yes. And what are you going to do now that you know that this is our flat, the first blind man wanted to know, are you going to throw us out as they did to you, No, I have neither the age nor the strength for that, and even if I did, I do not believe that I would be capable of such a speedy procedure, a writer manages to acquire in life the patience he needs to write. You will leave us the flat, though, Yes, if we cannot find another solution, I cannot see what other solution could be found. The doctor's wife had already guessed what the writer's reply would be, You and your wife, like the friend who is with you, live in a flat, I imagine, Yes, in her flat in fact, Is it far away, Not really, Then, if you'll permit me, I have a proposal to make, Go on, That we carry on as we are, at this moment we both have a place where we can live, I shall continue to keep a watchful eye on what is happening to mine, if one day I find it free, I shall move in immediately, you will do the same, Come here at regular intervals and when you find it empty, move in, I am not sure I like the idea, I didn't expect you to like it but I doubt whether you would prefer the only remaining alternative, What is that, For you to recover this flat which is yours, But, in that case, Precisely, in that case we shall have to find somewhere else to live, No, don't even think about it, intervened the wife of the first blind man, Let's leave things as they are, and see what happens, It occurred to me that there is another solution, said the writer, And what might that be, asked the first blind man, We shall live here as your guests, the flat is big enough for all of us, No, said the wife of the first blind man, We shall carry on as before, living with our friend, there is no need to ask if you agree, she added, addressing the doctor's wife, And there is no need for me to reply, I am obliged to all of you, said the writer, all this time I have been waiting for someone to reclaim the flat, To accept what one has is the most natural thing when one is blind, said the doctor's wife, How have you managed since the outbreak of the epidemic, We came out of internment only three days ago, Ah, you were in quarantine, Yes, Was it hard, Worse than that, How horrible, You are a writer, you have, as you said a moment ago, an obligation to know words, therefore you know that adjectives are of no use to us, if a person kills another, for example, it would be better to state this fact openly, directly, and to trust that the horror of the act, in itself, is so shocking that there is no need for us to say it was horrible, Do you mean that we have more words than we need, I mean that we have too few feelings, Or that we have them but have ceased to use the words they express, And so we lose them, I'd like you to tell me how you lived during quarantine, Why, I am a writer, You would have to have been there, A writer is just like anyone else, he cannot know everything, nor can he experience everything, he must ask and imagine, One day I may tell you what it was like, then you can write a book, Yes, I am writing it, How, if you are blind, The blind too can write, You mean that you had time to learn the braille alphabet, I do not know braille, How can you write, then, asked the first blind man, Let me show you. He got up from his chair, left the room and after a minute returned, he was holding a sheet of paper in his hand and a ball-point pen, this is the last complete page I have written, We cannot see it, said the wife of the first blind man, Nor I, said the writer, Then how can you write, asked the doctor's wife, looking at the sheet of paper where in the half-light of the room she could make out tightly compressed lines, occasionally superimposed, By touch, the writer answered smiling, it is easy, you place the sheet over a soft surface, for example some sheets of paper, then it's just a question of writing, But if you cannot see anything, said the first blind man, A ball-point pen is an excellent tool for blind writers, it does not permit them to read what they have written, but it tells them where they have written, they only have to follow with their fingers the impression left by the last written line, then you write as far as the edge of the paper, and calculating the distance to the next line is very easy, I notice that some lines overlap, said the doctor's wife, gently taking the sheet out of his hand, How do you know, I can see, You can see, have you recovered your sight, how, when, the writer asked excitedly, I suppose I am the only person who has never lost it, And why, what is the explanation for this, I have no explanation, there may not be one, That means that you saw everything that has happened, I saw what I saw, I had no option, How many people were in the quarantine, Nearly three hundred, From when, From the beginning, we only came out three days ago, as I said, I believe that I was the first person to go blind, said the first blind man, That must have been horrible, That word again, said the doctor's wife, Forgive me, suddenly everything I have been writing about since we turned blind, my family and I, strikes me as being ridiculous, About what, About what we suffered, about our life, Everyone has to speak of what they know, and what they do not know they should ask, That's why I ask you, And I will answer, I don't know when, some day. The doctor's wife brushed the writer's hand with the paper. Would you mind showing me where you work and what you are writing, Not at all, come with me, Can we come too, asked the wife of the first blind man, The flat is yours, said the writer, I am only passing through. In the bedroom there was a tiny table with an unlit lamp. The dim light entering through the window, allowed one to see to the left some blank sheets, others on the right-hand side had been written on, in the middle there was one half written. There were two new ball-point pens next to the lamp. Here it is, said the writer. The doctor's wife asked, May I? without waiting for a reply she picked up the written pages, there must have been about twenty, she passed her eye over the tiny handwriting, over the lines which went up and down, over the words inscribed on the whiteness of the page, recorded in blindness, I am only passing through, the writer had said, and these were the signs he had left in passing. The doctor's wife placed her hand on his shoulder, and with both hands he reached out for it and raised it slowly to his lips, Don't lose yourself, don't let yourself be lost, he said, and these were unexpected, enigmatic words that did not seem to fit the occasion.

When they returned home, carrying enough food for three days, the doctor's wife, interrupted by the excited interjections from the first blind man and his wife, told what had happened. And that night, as was only right, she read to all of them a few pages from a book she had gone to fetch from the study. The boy with the squint was not interested in the story, and after a little while he fell asleep with his head on the lap of the girl with the dark glasses and his feet resting on the legs of the old man with the eyepatch.

Two days later the doctor said, I'd like to know what has happened to the surgery, at this stage we are no use for anything, neither it nor I, but perhaps one day people will recover their sight, the instruments must still be there waiting, We can go whenever you want, said his wife, Right now, And we could take advantage of this walk to pass by my home, if you don't mind, said the girl with the dark glasses, Not that I believe that my parents have returned, it's only to ease my conscience, We can go to your house too, said the doctor's wife. Nobody else wanted to join this reconnoitre of homes, not the first blind man and his wife, for they already knew what they could count on, the old man with the black eyepatch also knew, but not for the same reasons, and the boy with the squint because he still could not remember the name of the street where he had lived. The weather was bright, it seemed that the rain had stopped and the sun, though pale, could already be felt on their skin, I don't know how we can continue to live if the heat gets any worse, said the doctor, all this rubbish rotting all over the place, the dead animals, perhaps even people, there must be dead people inside the houses, the worst thing is that we are not organised, there should be an organisation in each building, in each street, in each district, A government, said the wife, An organisation, the human body is also an organised system, it lives as long as it keeps organised, and death is only the effect of a disorganisation, And how can a society of blind people organise itself in order to survive, By organising itself, to organise oneself is, in a way, to begin to have eyes, Perhaps you're right, but the experience of this blindness has brought us only death and misery, my eyes, just like your surgery, were useless, Thanks to your eyes we are still alive, said the girl with the dark glasses, We would also be alive if I were blind as well, the world is full of blind people, I think we are all going to die, it's just a matter of time, Dying has always been a matter of time, said the doctor, But to die just because you're blind, there can be no worse way of dying, We die of illnesses, accidents, chance events, And now we shall also die of blindness, I mean, we shall die of blindness and cancer, of blindness and tuberculosis, of blindness and AIDS, of blindness and heart attacks, illnesses may differ from one person to another but what is really killing us now is blindness, We are not immortal, we cannot escape death, but at least we should not be blind, said the doctor's wife, How, if this blindness is concrete and real, said the doctor, I am not sure, said the wife, Nor I, said the girl with the dark glasses.

They did not have to force the door, it opened normally, the key was on the doctor's key ring which had remained in the house when they had been taken off for quarantine. This is the waiting-room, said the doctor's wife, The room I was in, said the girl with the dark glasses, the dream continues, but I don't know what dream it is, whether it is the dream of dreaming which I experienced that day when I dreamt that I was going blind, or the dream of always having been blind and coming, still dreaming, to the surgery in order to be cured of an inflammation of the eyes in which there was no danger of becoming blind, The quarantine was no dream, said the doctor's wife, Certainly not, nor was it a dream that we were raped, Nor that I stabbed a man, Take me to my office, I can get there on my own but you take me, said the doctor. The door was open. The doctor's wife said, The place has been turned upside down, papers on the floor, the drawers of the file cabinet have been taken, It must have been the people from the Ministry, not to waste time looking, Probably, And the instruments, At first sight, they seem to be in good order, That, at least, is something, said the doctor, he advanced alone with his arms outstretched, he touched the box with the lenses, his ophthalmoscope, the desk, then, addressing the girl with the dark glasses, he said, I know what you are trying to say, when you say that you are living a dream. He sat down at the desk, placed his hands on the dusty top, then with a sad, ironic smile, as if he were talking to someone sitting opposite him, he said, No, my dear doctor, I am very sorry, but your condition has no known cure, if you want me to give you one last piece of advice, cling to the old saying, they were right when they said that patience is good for the eyes. Don't make us suffer, said the woman, Forgive me, both of you, we are in the place where miracles used to be performed, now I don't even have the evidence of my magic powers, they have taken it all away, The only miracle we can perform is to go on living, said the woman, to preserve the fragility of life from day to day, as if it were blind and did not know where to go, and perhaps it is like that, perhaps it really does not know, it placed itself in our hands, after giving us intelligence, and this is what we have made of it, You speak as if you too were blind, said the girl with the dark glasses, In a way I am, I am blind with your blindness, perhaps I might be able to see better if there were more of us who could see, I am afraid you are like the witness in search of a court to which he has been summoned by who knows who, in order to make a statement about who knows what, said the doctor, Time is coming to an end, putrescence is spreading, diseases find the doors open, water is running out, food has become poison, that would be my first statement, said the doctor's wife, And the second, asked the girl with dark glasses, Let's open our eyes, We can't, we are blind, said the doctor, It is a great truth that says that the worst blind person was the one who did not want to see, But I do want to see, said the girl with dark glasses, That won't be the reason you will see, the only difference would be that you would no longer be the worst blind person, and now, let's go, there is nothing more to be seen here, the doctor said.

On their way to the home of the girl with dark glasses, they crossed a large square with groups of blind people who were listening to speeches from other blind people, at first sight, neither one nor the other group seemed blind, the speakers turned their heads excitedly towards their listeners, the listeners turned their heads attentively to the speakers. They were proclaiming the end of the world, redemption through penitence, the visions of the seventh day, the advent of the angel, cosmic collisions, the death of the sun, the tribal spirit, the sap of the mandrake, tiger ointment, the virtue of the sign, the discipline of the wind, the perfume of the moon, the revindication of darkness, the power of exorcism, the sign of the heel, the crucifixion of the rose, the purity of the lymph, the blood of the black cat, the sleep of the shadow, the rising of the seas, the logic of anthropophagy, painless castration, divine tattoos, voluntary blindness, convex thoughts, or concave, or horizontal or vertical, or sloping, or concentrated, or dispersed, or fleeting, the weakening of the vocal cords, the death of the word, Here nobody is speaking of organisation, said the doctor's wife, Perhaps organisation is in another square, he replied. They continued on their way. A bit further on, the doctor's wife said, There are more dead in the road than usual, Our resistance is reaching its end, time is running out, the water is running out, disease is on the increase, food is becoming poison, you said so before, the doctor reminded her, Who knows whether my parents are not among these dead, said the girl with dark glasses, and here, I am passing by without seeing them, It's a time-honoured custom to pass by the dead without seeing them, said the doctor's wife.

The street where the girl with dark glasses lived, seemed even more deserted than usual. At the door to the building there was the body of a woman. Dead, half devoured by stray animals, luckily the dog of tears had not wanted to come today, it would have been necessary to keep him from digging his teeth into this corpse. It is the neighbour from the first floor, said the doctor's wife, Who, where, asked her husband, Right here, the first-floor neighbour, you can smell her, Poor woman, said the girl with dark glasses, why did she have to go out into the street, she never went out, Perhaps she felt that her death was near, perhaps she could not stand the idea of staying alone in the flat to rot, said the doctor. And now we can't go in, I don't have the keys, Perhaps your parents have returned and are inside waiting for you, said the doctor, I don't believe it, You are right not to believe it, said the doctor's wife, here are the keys. In the palm of the dead woman's half-open hand resting on the ground there was a set of keys, shining, sparkling. Perhaps they are hers, said the girl with dark glasses, I don't think so, she had no reason to bring her keys to where she was thinking of dying, But being blind, I would not be able to see them, if she thought of bringing them down so that I would be able to get into the flat, We don't know what she was thinking of when she decided to take the keys, perhaps she thought that you would regain your eyesight, perhaps she suspected that there was something unnatural, too easy, about the way we moved around when we were here, perhaps she heard me say that the stair was dark, that I could barely see, or perhaps it was none of that, delirium, dementia, as if, having lost her mind, she had got it into her head to give you the keys, the only thing we know is that her life ended when she set foot outside the door. The doctor's wife picked up the keys, handed them to the girl with dark glasses and then asked, And now, what do we do, are we going to leave her here, We cannot bury her in the street, we have no tools to lift the stones, said the doctor, There is the garden in the back, In that case we'll have to take her up to the second floor and then down by the emergency stairs, That's the only way, Do we have enough strength for this task, asked the girl with dark glasses, The question is not whether we have enough strength, the question is whether we can allow ourselves to leave this woman here, Certainly not, said the doctor, Then the strength must be found. They did manage, but it was hard work dragging the body upstairs, not because of what it weighed, little enough, and less still since the cats and dogs had been at it, but because the body was rigid, stiff, they had trouble turning the corners of the narrow staircase, during the short climb they had to rest four times. Neither the noise, nor the voices, nor the smell of putrefaction brought any other of the inhabitants of the building on to the landings, Just as I thought, my parents are not here, said the girl with dark glasses. When they finally got to the door they were exhausted and they still had to cross to the back of the building and go down the emergency stairs, but there with the help of the saints, they get down the stairs, the burden is lighter, the bends easier to manoeuvre because the stairs were out in the open, one only had to be careful not to let the poor creature's body slip from one's hands, a tumble would leave it beyond repair, not to mention the pain which, after death, is worse.

The garden was like an unexplored jungle, the recent rains had caused the grass and the weeds carried on the wind to grow in abundance, there would be no lack of fresh food for the rabbits which jumped about, and chickens manage even in hard times. They were sitting on the ground, panting, the effort had exhausted them, by their side the corpse rested like them, guarded by the doctor's wife who chased off the hens and rabbits, the rabbits only curious, their noses twitching, the chickens with their beaks like bayonets, ready for anything. The doctor's wife said, Before leaving, she remembered to open the doors of the rabbit hutches, she did not want the rabbits to die of hunger, The difficult thing isn't living with other people, it's understanding them, said the doctor. The girl with dark glasses cleaned her dirty hands on a clump of grass that she had pulled up, it was her own fault, she had grasped the corpse where she should not have, that's what happens when you're blind. The doctor said, What we need is a spade or a shovel, here one can see that the true eternal return is that of words, which now return, spoken for the same reasons, first for the man who stole the car, now for the old woman who returned the keys, once buried nobody will know the difference, unless somebody remembers them. The doctor's wife had gone up to the flat of the girl with dark glasses in order to find a clean sheet, she had to choose the least dirty of them, when she came down the hens were at it, the rabbits were merely chewing the fresh grass. Having covered and wrapped the body, the wife went in search of a spade or shovel. She found both in a garden shed along with other tools. I'll deal with this, she said, the ground is damp, it is easy to dig, you take a rest. She chose a spot where there were no roots of the type that have to be cut with an axe, and don't imagine that this is an easy job, roots have their own little ways, they know how to take advantage of the softness of the soil in order to avoid the blow and weaken the deadly effect of the guillotine. Neither the doctor's wife nor her husband nor the girl with dark glasses, the former because she was digging, the latter two because their eyes were of no use to them, noticed the appearance of blind people on the surrounding balconies, not many, not on all of them, they must have been attracted by the noise of the digging, even in soft soil there is noise, not forgetting that there is always some hidden stone that responds loudly to the blow. There were men and women who appeared as fluid as ghosts, they could have been ghosts attending a burial out of curiosity, merely to recall how it had been when they were buried. The doctor's wife finally saw them when she had finished digging the grave, she straightened her aching back and raised her arm to her forehead to wipe away the sweat. Then, carried away by an irresistible impulse, without thinking, she called out to those blind people and to all the blind of this world, She will rise again, note that she did not say She will live again, the matter was not quite that important, although the dictionary is there to confirm, reassure or suggest that we are dealing with complete and absolute synonyms. The blind people took fright and went back inside their flats, they could not understand why such words had been said, besides they could not have been prepared for such a revelation, it was clear that they did not go to the square where the magic utterances were made, in respect of which all that was needed to complete the picture was the addition of the head of the praying mantis and the suicide of the scorpion. The doctor said, Why did you say she will rise again, to whom were you talking, To a few blind people who appeared on the balconies, I was startled and I must have frightened them, And why those words rather than any others, I don't know, they came into my head and I said them, The next we know you'll be preaching in the square we passed along the way, Yes, a sermon about the rabbit's tooth and the hen's beak, come and help me now, over here, that's right, take her by the feet, I'll raise her from this end, careful, don't slip into the grave, that's it, just so, lower her slowly, more, more, I made the grave a little deeper because of the hens, once they start scratching, you never know where they'll finish up, that's it. She used the shovel to fill the grave, stamped the earth firmly down, made the little mound that always remains of the earth that is returned to the earth, as if she had never done anything else in her life. Finally, she picked a branch from a rosebush growing in the corner of the yard and planted it at the head of the grave. Will she rise again, asked the girl with the dark glasses, Not her, no, replied the doctor's wife, those who are still alive have a greater need to rise again by themselves and they don't, We are already half dead, said the doctor, We are still half alive too, answered his wife. She put the shovel and the spade back in the shed, took a good look around the yard to check that everything was in order, What order, she asked herself and provided her own answer, The order that wants the dead where they should be among the dead, and the living among the living, while the hens and rabbits feed some and feed off others, I'd like to leave a small sign for my parents, said the girl with dark glasses, just to let them know that I am alive, I don't want to destroy your hopes, said the doctor, but first they would have to find the house and that is most unlikely. Just remember that we wouldn't have got there without someone to guide us, You're right, and I don't even know if they are still alive, but unless I leave them some sign, anything, I shall feel as if I had abandoned them. What's it to be then, asked the doctor's wife, Something they might recognise by touch, said the girl with the dark glasses, the sad thing is that I no longer have anything on me from the old days. The doctor's wife looked at her, she was sitting on the first step of the emergency stairs, with her hands limp on her knees, her lovely face anguished, her hair spread over her shoulders, I know what sign you can leave them, she said. She went rapidly up the stairs, back into the house and returned with a pair of scissors and a piece of string, What are you thinking of, asked the girl with dark glasses, worried when she heard the snipping of the scissors cutting off her hair, If your parents were to return, they would find hanging from the door handle a lock of hair, who else could it possibly belong to but their daughter, asked the doctor's wife, You make me want to weep, said the girl with the dark glasses, and she had no sooner said it, than she lowered her head over the folded arms on her knees and gave in to her sorrows, her sadness, to the emotions aroused by the suggestion made by the doctor's wife, then she noticed, without knowing by what emotional route she had arrived there, that she was also crying for the old woman on the first floor, the eater of raw meat, the horrible witch, who with her dead hand had restored to her the keys to the flat. And then the doctor's wife said, What times we live in, we find the order of things inverted, a symbol that nearly always signified death has become a sign of life, There are hands capable of these and greater wonders, said the doctor, Necessity is a powerful weapon, my dear, said the woman, and now that's enough of philosophy and witchcraft, let's hold hands and get on with life. It was the girl with dark glasses herself who tied the lock of hair to the door handle, Do you think my parents will notice it, she asked, The door handle is like the outstretched hand of a house, said the doctor's wife, and with this commonplace expression, as one might say, they concluded the visit.

That night once again they had a reading, there was no other way of distracting themselves, what a pity, the doctor was not, for example, an amateur violinist, what sweet serenades might otherwise be heard on this fifth floor, their envious neighbours would say, Either they are doing very well or else they are completely irresponsible and think they can escape misery by laughing at the misery of others. Now there is no music other than that of words, and these, especially those in books, are discreet, and even if curiosity should bring someone from the building to listen at the door, they would hear only a solitary murmur, that long thread of sound that can last into infinity, because the books of this world, all together, are, as they say the universe is, infinite. When the reading ended, late that night, the old man with the eyepatch said, That's what we have come to, listening to someone reading, I'm not complaining, I could stay here for ever, said the girl with dark glasses, I am not complaining either, I only mean that this is all we are good for, listening to someone reading us the story of a human mankind that existed before us, let's be glad of our good fortune at still having a pair of seeing eyes with us here, the last pair left, if they are extinguished one day, I don't even want to think about it, then the thread which links us to that human mankind would be broken, it will be as if we were to separate from each other in space, for ever, all equally blind, As long as I can, the girl with dark glasses said, I'll keep on hoping, hoping to find my parents, hoping the boy's mother will turn up, You forgot to speak of the hope we all have, What's that, Regaining our sight, It's mad to cling to such hopes, Well, I can tell you, without such hopes I would already have given up, Give me an example, Being able to see again, We've already had that one, give me another, I won't, Why, You wouldn't be interested, And how do you know that I wouldn't, what do you think you know about me that you can by yourself decide what interests me and what doesn't, Don't get angry, I didn't mean to hurt you, Men are all the same, they think because they came out of the belly of a woman they know all there is to know about women, I know very little about women, and about you I know nothing, as for men, in my opinion, by modern criteria I am now an old man and one-eyed as well as being blind, Have you nothing else to say against yourself, A lot more, you can't imagine how the list of self-recriminations grows with advancing age, I am young and have my fair share already, You haven't done anything really bad yet, How do you know, if you've never lived with me, You're right, I have never lived with you, Why do you repeat my words in that tone of voice, What tone of voice, That one, All I said was that I have never lived with you, Come on, come on, don't pretend that you don't understand, Don't insist, I beg you, I do insist, I want to know, Let's return to hopes, All right, The other example of hope which I refused to give was this, What, The last self-accusation on my list, Please, explain yourself, I never understand riddles, The monstrous wish of never regaining our sight, Why, So that we can go on living as we are, Do you mean all together, or just you and me, Don't make me answer, If you were only a man you could avoid answering, like all others, but you yourself said that you are an old man, and old men, if longevity has any sense at all, should not avert their face from the truth, answer me, With you, And why do you want to live with me, Do you want me to tell in front of everybody, We have done the dirtiest, ugliest, most repulsive things together, what you can tell me cannot possibly be worse, All right, if you insist, let it be, because the man I still am loves the woman you are, Was it so very difficult to make a declaration of love, At my age, people fear ridicule, You were not ridiculous, Let's forget it, please, I have no intention of forgetting it or of letting you forget it either, It's nonsense, you forced it out of me and now, And now it's my turn, Don't say anything you may regret later, remember the black list, If I'm sincere today, what does it matter if I regret it tomorrow, Please stop, You want to live with me and I want to live with you, You are mad, We'll start living together here, like a couple, and we shall continue living together if we have to separate from our friends, two blind people must be able to see more than one, It's madness, you don't love me, What's this about loving, I never loved anyone, I just went to bed with men. So you agree with me then, Not really, You spoke of sincerity, tell me then if it's true that you really love me, I love you enough to want to be with you, and that is the first time I've ever said that to anyone, You would not have said it to me either if you had met me somewhere before, an elderly man, half bald with white hair, with a patch over one eye and a cataract in the other, The woman I was then wouldn't have said it, I agree, the person who said it was the woman I am today, Let's see then what the woman you will be tomorrow will have to say, Are you testing me, What an idea, who am I to put you to the test, it's life that decides these things, It's already made one decision.

They had this conversation facing each other, blind eyes staring into blind eyes, their faces flushed and impassioned and when, because one of them had said it and because both of them wanted it, they agreed that life had decided that they should live together, the girl with dark glasses held out her hands, simply to give them, not in order to know where she was going, she touched the hands of the old man with the eyepatch, who gently pulled her towards him, and so they remained sitting side by side, it was not the first time, obviously, but now the words of engagement had been spoken. None of the others said anything, nobody congratulated them, nobody expressed wishes of eternal happiness, to tell the truth these are not the times for festivities and hopes, and when the decisions are so serious as these seem to have been, it is not even surprising that someone might think that one would have to be blind to behave in this way, silence is the best applause. What the doctor's wife did, however, was to put some sofa cushions out in the hallway, enough to make a comfortable bed, then she led the boy with the squint there and told him, From today you will sleep here. As to what happened in the living-room, there is every reason to believe that on that first night it finally became clear whose was the mysterious hand that washed the back of the old man with the black eyepatch on that morning when there was such an abundance of water, all of it purifying.

The next day, while still in bed, the doctor's wife said to her husband, We have little food left, we'll have to go out again, I thought that today I would go back to the underground food store at the supermarket, the one I went to on the first day, if nobody else has found it, we can get supplies for a week or two, I'm coming with you and we'll ask one or two of the others to come along as well, I'd rather go with you alone, it's easier, and there is less danger of getting lost, How long will you be able to carry the burden of six helpless people, I'll manage as long as I can, but you are quite right, I'm beginning to get exhausted, sometimes I even wish I were blind as well, to be the same as the others, to have no more obligations than they have, We've got used to depending on you, If you weren't there, it would be like being struck with a second blindness, thanks to your eyes we are a little less blind, I'll carry on as long as I can, I can't promise you more than that, One day, when we realise that we can no longer do anything good and useful we ought to have the courage simply to leave this world, as he said, Who said that, The fortunate man we met yesterday, I am sure that he wouldn't say that today, there is nothing like real hope to change one's opinions, He has that all right, long may it last, In your voice there is a tone which makes me think you are upset,

Upset, why, As if something had been taken away from you, Are you referring to what happened to the girl when we were at that terrible place, Yes, Remember, it was she who wanted to have sex with me, Memory is deceiving you, you wanted her, Are you sure, I was not blind, Well, I would have sworn that, You would only perjure yourself, Strange how memory can deceive us, In this case it is easy to see, something that is offered to us is more ours than something we had to conquer, But she didn't ever approach me again, and I never approached her, If you wanted to, you could find each other's memories, that's what memory is for, You are jealous, No, I'm not jealous, I was not even jealous on that occasion, I felt sorry for her and for you, and also for myself because I could not help you, How are we fixed for water, Badly. After the extremely frugal breakfast, lightened by some discrete, smiling hints at the events of the previous night, the words appropriately veiled out of consideration for the presence of a minor, an odd precaution if we remember the terrible scenes that he witnessed during the quarantine, the doctor's wife and her husband set off, accompanied this time only by the dog of tears, who did not want to stay at home.

The state of the streets got worse with every passing hour. The rubbish seemed to increase during the hours of darkness, it was as if from the outside, from some unknown country where there was still a normal life, they were coming in the night to empty their trash cans, if we were not in the land of the blind we would see through the middle of this white darkness phantom carts and trucks loaded with refuse, debris, rubble, chemical waste, ashes, burnt oil, bones, bottles, offal, flat batteries, plastic bags, mountains of paper, what they don't bring is leftover food, not even bits of fruit peel with which we might be able to allay our hunger, while waiting for those better days that are always just around the corner. It is still early in the morning but the heat is already oppressive. The stench rises from the enormous refuse pile like a cloud of toxic gas, It won't be long before we have outbreaks of epidemics, said the doctor again, nobody will escape, we have no defences left, If it's not raining, it's blowing gales, said the woman, Not even that, the rain would at least quench our thirst, and the wind would blow away some of this stench. The dog of tears sniffs around restlessly, stops to investigate a particular heap of rubbish, perhaps there was a rare delicacy hidden underneath which it can no longer find, if it were alone it would not move an inch from this spot, but the woman who wept has already walked on, and it is his duty to follow her, one never knows when one might have to dry more tears. Walking is difficult, in some streets, especially the steep ones, the heavy rainwater, transformed into torrents, had thrown cars against other cars or against buildings, knocking down doors, smashing shop windows, the ground is covered with thick pieces of broken glass. Wedged in between two cars the body of a man is rotting away. The doctor's wife averts her eyes. The dog of tears moves closer, but death frightens it, it still takes two steps forward, suddenly its fur stands on end, a piercing howl escapes from its throat, the trouble with this dog is that it has grown too close to human beings, it will suffer as they do. They crossed a square where groups of blind people entertained themselves by listening to speeches from other blind people, at first sight neither group seemed to be blind, the speakers turned their heads excitedly towards the listeners and the listeners turned their heads attentively to the speakers. They were extolling the virtues of the fundamental principles of the great organised systems, private property, a free currency market, the market economy, the stock exchange, taxation, interest, expropriation and appropriation, production, distribution, consumption, supply and demand, poverty and wealth, communication, repression and delinquency, lotteries, prisons, the penal code, the civil code, the highway code, dictionaries, the telephone directory, networks of prostitution, armaments factories, the armed forces, cemeteries, the police, smuggling, drugs, permitted illegal traffic, pharmaceutical research, gambling, the price of priests and funerals, justice, borrowing, political parties, elections, parliaments, governments, convex, concave, horizontal, vertical, slanted, concentrated, diffuse, fleeting thoughts, the fraying of the vocal cords, the death of the word. Here they are talking about organisation, said the doctor's wife to her husband, I noticed, he answered, and said no more. They continued walking, the doctor's wife went to consult a street plan on a street corner, like an old roadside cross pointing the way. We are very close to the supermarket, around here she had broken down and wept the day that she had got lost, grotesquely weighed down by the plastic bags which luckily were full to the brim, in her confusion and anguish she had to depend on a dog to console her, the same dog who is here snarling at the packs of other dogs who are coming too close, as if it were telling them, You don't fool me, keep away from here. A street to the left, another to the right and there is the entrance to the supermarket. Only the door, that's it, there is the door, there is the whole building, but what cannot be seen are people going in and coming out, that ant-heap of people which we find at all hours in these shops that live on the comings and goings of vast crowds. The doctor's wife feared the worst and said to her husband, We have arrived too late, there won't be a crumb left in there, Why do you say that, I don't see anybody going in or coming out, Perhaps they have not yet discovered the basement storeroom, That's what I am hoping for. They were standing on the pavement opposite the supermarket when they spoke these words. Beside them, as if they were waiting for the traffic lights to turn green, there were three blind people. The doctor's wife did not notice the expression on their faces, which was of puzzled surprise, a kind of confused fear, she did not see that one of them opened his mouth to speak and then closed it again, she did not notice the sudden shrug of shoulders, You'll find out, we assume the blind man was thinking. As they were crossing the middle of the road, the doctor's wife and her husband were unable to hear the comment of the second blind person, Why did she say that she did not see, that she did not see anybody going in or coming out, and the third blind person answered, It's just a manner of speaking, a moment ago, when I stumbled you told me to watch where I was putting my feet, it's the same thing, we still haven't lost the habit of seeing, Oh God, how many times have I heard that before, exclaimed the first blind man.

The daylight illuminated the whole of the wide hall of the supermarket. Almost all the shelves were overturned, there was nothing but refuse, broken glass, empty wrappers, It is strange, said the doctor's wife, even if there is no food here, I don't understand why there is nobody around. The doctor said, You are right, it does not seem normal. The dog of tears whimpered softly. Its hair was standing on end again. The doctor's wife said to her husband, There is a bad smell in here, There's a bad smell everywhere, said the husband, It's not that, it's another smell, of rotting, There must be a dead body somewhere, I don't see anything, In which case you must be imagining it. The dog began to whine. What's the matter with the dog, asked the doctor, He's nervous, What are we going to do, Let's see, if there is a corpse we just give it a wide berth, at this stage the dead no longer frighten us, For me it's easier, I can't see them. They crossed the hall of the supermarket until they reached the door which opened on to the corridor leading to the basement store. The dog of tears followed them, but it stopped from time to time, howled to them, then duty obliged it to continue. When the doctor's wife opened the door, the stench grew stronger, It smells terrible, said her husband, You stay here, I'll be right back. She went down the corridor, it became darker with every step and the dog of tears followed her as if it were being dragged along. Filled with the stench of putrefaction, the air seemed thick. Halfway down, the woman vomited, What can have happened here, she thought between retchings and then she murmured these same words over and over again until she got to the metal door which went down into the basement. Confused by her nausea, she had not noticed before that there was a tenuous shimmer of light down there. Now she knew what it was. Small flames flickered around the edges of the two doors, that of the staircase and that of the goods lift. A new attack of vomiting gripped her stomach, it was so violent that it attracted the attention of the dog. The dog of tears gave a very long howl, it let out a wail that seemed never-ending, a lament which resounded through the corridor like the last voice of the dead down in the basement. The doctor heard the vomiting, the convulsions, the coughing, he ran as well as he could, he stumbled and fell, he got up and fell again, at last he held his wife in his arms, What happened, he asked, with a trembling voice she replied, Get me out of here, please, get me out of here, for the first time since the onset of blindness, it was the doctor who guided his wife, he guided her without knowing where, anywhere away from those doors, those flames that he could not see. When they had got out of the corridor, her nerves suddenly went to pieces, her sobbing became convulsive, there is no drying tears like these, only time and exhaustion can stop them, therefore the dog did not approach, it just looked for a hand to lick. What happened, the doctor asked again, what did you see, They are dead, she managed to say between sobs, Who is dead, They are, and she could not go on. Calm yourself, tell me when you can. A few minutes later she said, They are dead, Did you see anything, did you open the door, asked her husband, No, I only saw will-o'-the-wisps around the doors, they clung there and danced around and did not let go, I think it must have been phosphorised hydrogen as a result of the decomposition of the bodies, What could have happened, They must have found the basement, rushed down the stairs looking for food, I remember how easy it was to slip and fall on those steps, and if one fell, they would all fall, they probably never reached where they wanted to go, or if they did they could not return because of the obstruction on the staircase, But you said that the door was closed, Most likely other blind people closed it, converting the basement into an enormous tomb and I am to blame for what happened, when I came running out of there with my bags, they must have suspected that it was food and went in search of it, In a way, everything we eat has been stolen from the mouths of others and if we rob them of too much we are responsible for their death, one way or another we are all murderers, A small consolation, I don't want you to start burdening yourself with imaginary guilt, when you already have a hard enough time shouldering the responsibility for six real and useless mouths, How could I live without your useless mouth, You would live in order to support the other five who are there, The question is, for how long. It won't be for much longer, when everything is finished we shall have to roam the fields in search of food, we'll pick all the fruit from the trees, we'll kill all the animals we can lay our hands on, if in the meantime dogs and cats do not start devouring us. The dog of tears did not react, this matter did not concern it, its recent transformation into a dog of tears had not been in vain.

The doctor's wife could hardly drag herself along. The shock had robbed her of all her strength. When they left the supermarket, she fainting, he blind, neither would be able to say who was assisting the other. Perhaps the intensity of the light had made her dizzy, she thought that she was losing her eyesight, but she was not afraid, it was only a fainting fit. She did not fall, nor even lose consciousness. She needed to lie down, close her eyes, breathe steadily, if she could just rest for a few minutes she was sure that she would regain her strength, she had to, her plastic bags were still empty. She did not want to lie down on the filth in the street, or return to the supermarket, not even dead. She looked around. On the other side of the street, a bit further on, was a church. There would be people inside, as everywhere, but it would be a good place to rest, at least it always had been. She said to her husband, I need to recover my strength, take me over there, There, where, I'm sorry, bear with me, and I'll tell you, What is it, A church, if I could only lie down for a while, I'd feel like new, Let's go. Six steps led up to the church, six steps, which the doctor's wife climbed with great difficulty, especially since she also had to guide her husband. The doors were wide open, which was a great help, a revolving door, even of the simplest type, would on this occasion have been a difficult obstacle to overcome. The dog of tears hesitated on the threshold. Despite the freedom of movement enjoyed by dogs in recent months, all of them had genetically programmed into their brains the prohibition which once, long ago, fell on the species, that on entering churches, probably because of that other genetic code which obliges them to mark their territory wherever they go. The good and faithful services rendered by the forebears of this dog of tears, when they licked the festering sores of saints before they were recognised and approved as such, nevertheless acts of compassion of the most selfless kind, because, as we well know, not just any beggar can become a saint, no matter how many wounds he may have on his body, and in his soul too where the tongues of dogs cannot reach. The dog now had the courage to enter the sacred space, the door was open, there was no doorkeeper, and the strongest reason of all, the woman who had wept had already gone in, I do not know how she manages to drag herself along, she murmurs but a single word to her husband, Hold me, the church is full, it is almost impossible to find even a foot of floor unoccupied, one might literally say that there is no stone upon which to rest one's head, again the dog of tears proved its usefulness, with two growls and a couple of charges, all without malice, it opened up a space where the doctor's wife let herself fall, giving in to the faint, at last fully closing her eyes. Her husband took her pulse, it is firm and regular, only a little faint, then he tried to lift her up, she's not in a good position, it is important to get the blood back into the brain quickly, to increase the cerebral irrigation, the best thing would be to sit her up, put her head between her knees and trust to nature and the force of gravity. At last, after some failed attempts, he managed to lift her up. A few minutes later, the doctor's wife gave a deep sigh, moved almost imperceptibly, and started to regain consciousness. Don't get up just yet, her husband told her, keep your head down for a while longer, but she felt fine, there was no sign of vertigo, her eyes could already distinguish the tiles on the floor which the dog of tears had left reasonably clean thanks to his energetic scrabbling before lying down himself. She raised her head to the slender pillars, to the high vaults, to confirm the security and stability of her blood circulation, then she said, I am feeling fine, but at that very moment she thought she had gone mad or that the lifting of the vertigo had given her hallucinations, it could not be true what her eyes revealed, that man nailed to the cross with a white bandage covering his eyes, and next to him a woman, her heart pierced by seven swords and her eyes also covered with a white bandage, and it was not only that man and that woman who were in that condition, all the images in the church had their eyes covered, statues with a white cloth tied around the head, paintings with a thick brushstroke of white paint, and there was a woman teaching her daughter how to read and both had their eyes covered, and a man with an open book on which a little child was sitting, and both had their eyes covered, and another man, his body spiked with arrows, and he had his eyes covered, and a woman with a lit lamp, and she had her eyes covered, and a man with wounds on his hands and feet and his chest, and he had his eyes covered, and another man with a lion, and both had their eyes covered, and another man with a lamb, and both had their eyes covered, and another man with an eagle, and both had their eyes covered, and another man with a spear standing over a fallen man with horns and cloven feet, and both had their eyes covered, and another man carrying a set of scales, and he had his eyes covered, and an old bald man holding a white lily, and he had his eyes covered, and another old man leaning on an unsheathed sword, and he had his eyes covered, and a woman with a dove, and both had their eyes covered, and a man with two ravens, and all three had their eyes covered, there was only one woman who did not have her eyes covered, because she carried her gouged-out eyes on a silver tray. The doctor's wife said to her husband, You won't believe me if I tell you what I have in front of my eyes, all the images in this church have their eyes covered, How strange, I wonder why, How should I know, perhaps it was the work of someone whose faith was badly shaken when he realised that he would be blind like the others, maybe it was even the local priest, perhaps he thought that when the blind people could no longer see the images, the images should not be able to see the blind either, Images don't see, You're wrong, images see with the eyes of those who see them, only that now blindness is the lot of everyone, You can still see, I'll see less and less all the time, even though I may not lose my eyesight I shall become more and more blind because I shall have no one to see me, If the priest covered the eyes of the images, That's just my idea, It's the only hypothesis that makes any sense, it's the only one that can lend some dignity to our suffering, I imagine that man coming in here from the world of the blind, where he would have to return only to go blind himself, I imagine the closed doors, the deserted church, the silence, I imagine the statues, the paintings, I see him going from one to the other, climbing up to the altars and tying the bandages with a double knot so that they do not come undone and slip off, applying two coats of paint to the pictures in order to make the white night into which they are plunged still thicker, that priest must have committed the worst sacrilege of all times and all religions, the fairest and most radically human, coming here to declare that, ultimately, God does not deserve to see. The doctor's wife did not have a chance to reply, somebody beside her spoke first, What sort of talk is that, who are you, Blind like you, she said, But I heard you say that you could see, That's just a manner of speaking which is hard to give up, how many more times will I say it, And what's this about the images having their eyes covered, It's true, And how do you know when you are blind, You would know too if you did what I did, go and touch them with your hands, the hands are the eyes of the blind, And why did you do it, I thought that in order to have got to where we are someone else must have been blind, And that story about the parish priest covering the eyes of the images, I knew him very well, he would be incapable of doing such a thing, You never know beforehand what people are capable of, you have to wait, give it time, it's time that rules, time is our gambling partner on the other side of the table and it holds all the cards of the deck in its hand, we have to guess the winning cards of life, our lives, Speaking of gambling in a church is a sin, Get up, use your hands if you doubt my words, Do you swear it is true that the images have their eyes covered, What do you want me to swear on, Swear on your eyes, I swear twice on the eyes, on yours and mine. Is it true, It's true. The conversation was overheard by the blind people in their immediate vicinity, and it goes without saying that there was no need to wait for the confirmation by oath before the news started to circulate, to pass from mouth to mouth, in a murmur which shortly changed its tone, first incredulous, then alarmed, again incredulous, it was unfortunate that there were several superstitious and imaginative people in the congregation, the idea that the sacred images were blind, that their compassionate or pitying eyes only stared out at their own blindness, became all of a sudden unbearable, it was tantamount to having told them that they were surrounded by the living dead, one scream was enough, then another and another, then fear made all the people rise up, panic drove them to the doors, here the inevitable repeated itself, since panic is much faster than the legs which carry it, the feet of the fugitive trip up in their flight, even more so when one is blind, and there he lies on the ground, panic tells him, Get up, run, they are going to kill you, if only he could get up, but others have already run and fallen too, you have to be strong-minded not to burst out laughing at this grotesque entanglement of bodies looking for arms to free themselves and for feet to get away. Those six steps outside will be like a precipice, but finally, the fall will not be very serious, the habit of falling hardens the body, reaching the ground is, in itself, a relief, I'm staying where I am is the first thought, and sometimes the last, in fatal cases. What does not change either is that some take advantage of the misfortune of others, as is well known, since the beginning of the world, the heirs and the heirs of the heirs. The desperate flight of these people made them leave their belongings behind, and when necessity conquers fear, they come back for them, then the difficult problem will be to settle in a satisfactory manner what is mine and what is yours, we shall see that some of the little food we had has vanished, probably this was a cynical ruse on the part of the woman who said that the images had their eyes covered, the depths some people will stoop to, they invent such tall tales merely to rob poor people of the few crumbs remaining to them. Now, the fault was the dog's, seeing the square empty it went foraging around, it rewarded itself for its efforts, as was only fair and natural, and it showed, in a manner of speaking, the entrance to the mine which meant that the doctor's wife and her husband left the church without remorse over the theft, with their bags half full. If they can use half of what they grabbed they can be content, regarding the other half they will say, I don't know how people can eat this, even when misfortune is common to all, there are always some who have a worse time than others.

The report of these events, each one of its kind, left the other members of the group aghast and confused, it has to be noted that the doctor's wife, perhaps because words failed her, did not even manage to convey to them the feelings of utter horror she experienced at the basement door, that rectangle of pale flickering lights at the top of the staircase which led to the other world. The description of the bandaged eyes of the images left a strong enough impression on their imaginations, though in quite different ways, the first blind man and his wife, for example, were rather uneasy, for them it was mainly an unpardonable lack of respect. The fact that all human beings were blind was a calamity for which they were not responsible, these are misfortunes nobody can avoid, and for that reason alone covering the eyes of the holy images struck them as an unpardonable offence, and if the parish priest had done it, even worse. The reaction of the old man with the black eyepatch was quite different, I can imagine the shock you must have had, I imagine a museum in which all the sculptures have their eyes covered, not because the sculptor did not want to carve the stone until he reached the eyes, but covered, as you say, with bandages, as if a single blindness were not enough, it's strange that a patch like mine does not create the same effect, sometimes it even gives people a romantic air, and he laughed at what he had said and at himself. As to the girl with the dark glasses, she said that she only hoped she would not have to see this cursed gallery in her dreams, she had enough nightmares already. They ate the rancid food at their disposal, it was the best they had, the doctor's wife said that it was becoming ever more difficult to find food, perhaps they should leave the city and go to live in the country, there at least the food they gathered would be healthier, And there must be goats and cows on the loose, we can milk them, we'll have milk, and there is water from the wells, we can cook what we want, the question is to find a good site, then everybody gave his opinion, some more enthusiastic than others, but for all of them it was obvious that the decision was pressing and urgent, the boy with the squint expressed his approval without any reservations, possibly because he retained pleasant memories from his holidays. After they had eaten, they stretched out to sleep, they always did, even during the quarantine, when experience taught them that a body in repose can put up with a lot of hunger. That evening they did not eat, only the boy with the squint got something to assuage his complaints and to allay his hunger, the others sat down to hear the reading, at least their minds would not be able to complain of lack of nourishment, the trouble is that the weakness of the body sometimes leads to a lack of attention of the mind, and it was not for lack of intellectual interest, no, what happened was that the brain slipped into a half sleep, like an animal settling down for hibernation, goodbye world, therefore it was not uncommon that the listeners gently lowered their eyelids, forced themselves to follow with the eyes of the soul the vicissitudes of the plot until a more energetic passage shook them from their torpor, it was not simply the noise of the book snapping shut, the doctor's wife had these subtle touches, she did not want to let on that she knew that the dreamer was drifting off to sleep.

The first blind man appeared to have entered into this soft state, but this was not the case. True, his eyes were closed, and he paid only scant attention to the reading, but the idea that they would all go to live in the country kept him from falling asleep, it seemed to him a serious error to go so far from his home, however kind the writer was, it would be useful to keep an eye on it, turn up from time to time. The first blind man was therefore wide awake, if any other proof were needed it would be the dazzling whiteness before his eyes, which probably only sleep would darken, but one could not even be sure of that, since nobody can be asleep and awake at the same time. The first blind man thought that he had finally cleared up this doubt when suddenly the inside of his eyelids turned dark, I've fallen asleep, he thought, but no, he had not fallen asleep, he continued hearing the voice of the doctor's wife, the boy with the squint coughed, then a great fear entered his soul, he thought he had passed from one blindness to another, that having lived in the blindness of light, he would now pass into a blindness of darkness, the fear made him tremble, What's the matter, his wife asked, and he replied stupidly, without opening his eyes, I am blind, as if that were news, she tenderly held him in her arms, Don't worry, we're all blind, there's nothing we can do about it, I saw everything dark, I thought I had gone to sleep, but I hadn't, I am awake, That's what you should do, sleep, don't think about it. He was annoyed by this advice, here was a man in great distress, and his wife could say nothing other than that he should sleep. He was irritated and, about to utter a harsh reply, he opened his eyes and saw. He saw and shouted, I can see. His first shout was still one of incredulity, but with the second and the third and many more the evidence grew stronger, I can see, I can see, he madly embraced his wife, then he ran to the doctor's wife and embraced her too, it was the first time he had seen her, but he knew who she was, and the doctor, and the girl with dark glasses and the old man with the black eyepatch, there was no mistaking him, and the boy with the squint, his wife came behind him, she did not want to let him go, and he interrupted his embraces to embrace her again, then he turned to the doctor, I can see, I can see, doctor, he addressed him by his title, something they had not done for a long time, and the doctor asked, Can you see clearly, as before, are there no traces of whiteness, Nothing at all, I even think that I can see better than before, and that's no small thing, I've never worn glasses. Then the doctor said what all of them were thinking without daring to say it, It is possible that we have come to the end of this blindness, it is possible that we will all recover our eyesight, hearing those words, the doctor's wife began to cry, she should have been happy yet she was crying, what strange reactions people have, of course she was happy, my God, it is easy to understand, she cried because all her mental resistance had suddenly drained away, she was like a new-born baby and this cry was her first and still-unconscious sound. The dog of tears went up to her, it always knows when it is needed, that's why the doctor's wife clung to him, it is not that she no longer loved her husband, it is not that she did not wish them all well, but at that moment her feeling of loneliness was so intense, so unbearable, that it seemed to her that it could be overcome only by the strange thirst with which the dog drank her tears.

The general joy turned into nervousness, And now, what are we going to do, asked the girl with dark glasses, after all that has happened I won't be able to sleep, Nobody will, I believe we should stay here, said the old man with the black eyepatch, he broke off as if he still had some doubts, then he concluded, Waiting. They waited. The three flames of the lamp lit up the circle of faces. At first, they had talked animatedly, they wanted to know exactly what had happened, if the change had taken place only in the eyes or whether he had also felt something in his brain, then, little by little, their words grew despondent, at a certain moment it occurred to the first blind man to say to his wife that they would be going home the next day, But I am still blind, she replied, It doesn't matter, I'll guide you, only those present who heard it with their own ears could grasp how such simple words could contain such different feelings as protection, pride and authority. The second person to regain his eyesight, already late into the night, when the lamp, running out of oil, was flickering, was the girl with dark glasses. She had kept her eyes open as if sight had to enter through them rather than be rekindled from within, suddenly she said, I think I can see, it was best to be prudent, not all cases are the same, it even used to be said there is no such thing as blindness, only blind people, when the experience of time has taught us nothing other than that there are no blind people, but only blindness. Here we already have three who can see, one more and they would form a majority, but even though in the happiness of seeing again we might ignore the others, their lives will be very much easier, not the agony it was until today, look at the state of that woman, she is like a rope that has broken, like a spring that could no longer support the pressure it was constantly subjected to. Perhaps it was for this reason that the girl with dark glasses embraced her first, and the dog of tears did not know whose tears it should attend to first, both of them wept so much. Her second embrace was for the old man with the black eyepatch, now we shall know what words are really worth, the other day we were so moved by the dialogue which led to the splendid commitment by these two to live together, but the situation has changed, the girl with dark glasses has before her an old man whom she can now see in the flesh, the emotional idealisations, the false harmonies on the desert island are over, wrinkles are wrinkles, baldness is baldness, there is no difference between a black eyepatch and a blind eye, that is what, in other words, he is going to say to her. Look at me, I am the man you said you were going to live with, and she replied, I know you, you're the man I am living with, in the end these are words that are worth even more than those that wanted to surface, and this embrace as much as the words. The third one to regain his sight the next day at dawn was the doctor, now there could no longer be any doubt, it was only a question of time before the others would recover theirs. Leaving aside the natural and foreseeable expansive comments of which there has already been sufficient mention above, there is now no need for repetition, even concerning the chief characters of this narrative, the doctor asked the question which hung in the air, What is happening out there, the reply came from the very building in which they lived, on the floor below someone came out on the landing shouting, I can see, I can see, it looks like the sun will rise over a city in celebration.

The next morning's meal turned into a banquet. What was on the table, besides being very little, would repel any normal appetite, as happens at all moments of elation, the strength of feelings took the place of hunger and their happiness was the best nourishment, nobody complained, even those who were still blind laughed as if the eyes which could already see were theirs. When they had finished, the girl with dark glasses had an idea, What if I now went to the door of my own flat with a piece of paper saying that I'm here, my parents would know where to find me if they return, Let me come with you, I want to know what is happening out there, said the old man with the black eyepatch, And we will go out too, said he who had been the first blind man to his wife, Perhaps the writer can already see and is thinking about returning to his own place, on the way I shall try to find something to eat. I'll do the same, said the girl with dark glasses. Minutes later, alone now, the doctor sat down beside his wife, the boy with the squint was dozing in a corner of the sofa, the dog of tears, stretched out with his muzzle on its forepaws, opened and closed its eyes from time to time to show that it was still watchful, through the open window, despite the fact that they were so high up, the noise of excited voices could be heard, the streets must be full of people, the crowd shouting just three words, I can see, said those who had already recovered their eyesight and those who were just starting to see, I can see, I can see, the story in which people said, I am blind, truly appears to belong to another world. The boy with the squint murmured, he must be in the middle of a dream, perhaps he saw his mother and was asking her, Can you see me, can you see me, The doctor's wife asked, And the others, and the doctor answered, He will probably be cured by the time he wakes, it will be the same with the others, most likely they are already regaining their sight at this very moment, our man with the black eyepatch is in for a shock, Why, Because of the cataract, after all the time since I last examined him it must have deteriorated, Is he going to stay blind, No, when life gets back to normal, and everything is working again, I shall operate, it is a matter of weeks, Why did we become blind, I don't know, perhaps one day we'll find out, Do you want me to tell you what I think, Yes, do, I don't think we did go blind, I think we are blind, Blind but seeing, Blind people who can see, but do not see.

The doctor's wife got up and went to the window. She looked down at the street full of refuse, at the shouting, singing people. Then she lifted her head up to the sky and saw everything white, It is my turn, she thought. Fear made her quickly lower her eyes. The city was still there.

PUBLISHERS' NOTE

The translator died before completing his revision of this translation. The Publishers acknowledge the help of Margaret Jull Costa in fulfilling this task.

Turn the page for an excerpt

from José Saramago's

new novel

SEEING

In a secluded spot, rather like a village forgotten in the middle of the city, there was a slightly neglected park, with large shady trees, sandy walks and flower beds, rustic, green-painted benches, and, in the middle, a lake in which a statue, representing a female figure, bent over the water with her empty water jar. The doctor's wife sat down, opened the bag she had brought with her and took out a book. Until she had opened the book and started reading, the dog would not move from there. She looked up from the page and said, Off you go, and he ran off to do, as people used to say in more euphemistic days, what no one else could do for him. The superintendent watched from a distance and remembered his question to himself after breakfast, And what shall I do. For about five minutes he lurked behind the bushes, it was lucky the dog hadn't come this way, he might have recognized him and this time done more than just growl at him. The doctor's wife wasn't waiting for anyone, she had, as so many other people do, simply taken her dog for a walk. The superintendent went straight over to her, making the sand crunch underfoot, and stopped a few feet away. Slowly, as if she found it hard to tear herself away from her reading, the doctor's wife raised her head and looked at him. She did not appear to recognize him at first, probably because she wasn't expecting to see him there, then she said, We were waiting for you, but when you didn't come and the dog was getting impatient for his walk, I decided to bring him here, but my husband's at home, he'll look after you until I get back, unless, of course, you're in a hurry, No, I'm not in a hurry, You go ahead, then, I'll be right there, once the dog has had a bit of a run, after all, it's not his fault people decided to cast blank ballot papers, If you don't mind, and since chance seems to have arranged it this way, I'd prefer to talk to you here, without witnesses, And I assumed that this interrogation, to continue calling it by that name, would take place with my husband present, like the first one, It wouldn't be an interrogation, my notebook won't leave my pocket, and I haven't got a tape-recorder concealed about my person either, besides, I have to say that my memory isn't what it was, it forgets easily, especially when I don't tell it to record what it hears, Oh, I had no idea the memory could hear, It's our second set of ears, those on the outside only serve to carry the sound inside, What do you want then, Like I said, I want to talk to you, About what, About what's happening in this city, Superintendent, I'm very grateful to you for coming to my house yesterday evening and for telling us, and my friends too, that there are people in the government interested in the strange phenomenon of the doctor's wife who failed to go blind four years ago and who now, it seems, is the organizer of a conspiracy against the state, but, to be perfectly frank, unless you have something more to say to me on the subject, I really don't think there's much point in our talking about anything else, The interior minister made me hand over the group photograph of you, your husband and your friends, this very morning I went to a military post on the frontier to do so, So you did have something to tell me, but there really wasn't any need for you to follow me, you could have gone straight to my house, you know the way, But I didn't follow you, I wasn't hiding behind a tree or pretending to read a newspaper while I waited for you to leave your house so that I could follow you, as the inspector and the sergeant engaged with me on this investigation will be doing with your friends right now, although the only reason I ordered them to do so was to keep them occupied, that's all, Do you mean to tell me you're here by chance, Yes, I happened to be walking down the street and I saw you leaving your house, It's hard to believe that it was pure chance that brought you to the street where I live, Call it what you like, But it was, at any rate, a happy coincidence, if you prefer to call it that, without it I wouldn't have found out that the photograph is now in the hands of your minister, Oh, that I would have told you on another occasion, And what, may I ask, does he want with it, I've no idea, he didn't tell me, but I'm sure it won't be for any good purpose, So you didn't come to submit me to a second interrogation, said the doctor's wife, No, not today, not tomorrow, never, as far as I'm concerned, I know all I need to know about this story, You'll have to explain yourself better, sit down, don't just stand there like that woman with the empty water jar. The dog suddenly appeared and came bounding out from behind some bushes heading straight for the superintendent, who instinctively drew back, Don't be frightened, said the doctor's wife, grabbing the dog by the collar, he won't bite you, How did you know I was afraid of dogs, Oh, I'm no witch, I just observed you when you were in our apartment, Is it that obvious, It is rather, steady, this last word was addressed to the dog, who had stopped barking and was instead producing a low, continuous noise in its throat, far more intimidating than a growl, the sound of an organ the bass notes of which have been badly tuned. You'd better sit down, that way he'll know you mean me no harm. The superintendent gingerly sat down, keeping his distance, Is his name Steady, No, it's Constant, but for us and for my friends he's the dog of tears, we called him Constant for short, Why the dog of tears, Because four years ago I was crying and this creature came and licked my face, During the time of the white blindness, Yes, during the time of the white blindness, this dog is the second marvel from those wretched days, first the woman who did not go blind when it seems it was her duty to do so, then this compassionate dog who came and drank her tears, Did that really happen, or was I dreaming, What we dream also happens, superintendent, Hopefully not everything, Do you have some reason for saying that, No, not really, I was just talking for the sake of it. The superintendent was lying, the sentence he had refused to allow his mouth to utter would have been quite different, Hopefully the albatross will not come and poke out your eyes. The dog had come closer and was almost touching the superintendent's knees with its nose. It was looking at him and its eyes were saying, I won't hurt you, don't be afraid, she wasn't when I found her on that other day. Then the superintendent slowly reached out his hand and touched the dog's head. He felt like crying and letting the tears course down his face, perhaps the marvel would be repeated. The doctor's wife put her book away in her bag and said, Let's go, Where, asked the superintendent, You'll have lunch with us, won't you, if you've nothing more important to do, Are you sure, About what, That you want to have me sitting at your table, Yes, I'm sure, And you're not afraid I might be tricking you, Not with those tears in your eyes, no.

978-0-15-600624-8 * $14.00

978-0-15-600520-3 * $14.00

978-0-15-600401-5 * $14.00

978-0-15-600141-0 * $15.00

978-0-15-699693-8 * $15.00

Prices are higher in Canada.
Reading group guides to *Blindness*, *The Double*, and *All the Names* are available online at www.HarcourtBooks.com.